P9-DBK-671

THE EXTRAORDINARY LIFE OF SAM HELL

Center Point
Large Print

Also by Robert Dugoni and available from
Center Point Large Print:

Close to Home
A Steep Price
The Eighth Sister
A Cold Trail
The Last Agent
In Her Tracks

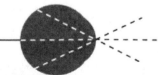

**This Large Print Book carries the
Seal of Approval of N.A.V.H.**

THE EXTRAORDINARY LIFE OF SAM HELL

ROBERT DUGONI

CENTER POINT LARGE PRINT
THORNDIKE, MAINE

This Center Point Large Print edition
is published in the year 2023 by arrangement with
Amazon Publishing, www.apub.com.

Copyright © 2018 by LaMesa Fiction LLC.

All rights reserved.

Originally published in the United States
by Amazon Publishing, 2018.

This is a work of fiction. Names, characters,
organizations, places, events, and incidents are either
products of the author's imagination or are used
fictitiously. Any resemblance to actual persons, living
or dead, or actual events is purely coincidental.

The text of this Large Print edition is unabridged.
In other aspects, this book may vary
from the original edition.
Printed in the United States of America
on permanent paper sourced using
environmentally responsible foresting methods.
Set in 16-point Times New Roman type.

ISBN: 978-1-63808-690-1

The Library of Congress has cataloged this record
under Library of Congress Control Number: 2022951682

For my mother, Patty Branick Dugoni, who gave me my love of reading and my passion for writing. None of this would have been possible without your unconditional love, support, and faith. I could not have asked for a better childhood or better parents. Thank you for making my life extraordinary.

There comes a day in every man's life when he stops looking forward and starts looking back.

—*Maxwell Hill*

FOREWORD

My mother called it "God's will." At those moments in my life when things did not go as I had hoped or planned, and there were many, she would say, "It's God's will, Samuel." This was hardly comforting to a six-year-old boy, even one "blessed" with a healthier dose of perspective than most children at that age.

For one, I never understood how my mother *knew* God's will. When I would ask her that very question, she would answer with another of her stock refrains—"Have faith, Samuel." I realize now that this was circular reasoning impregnable to debate. My mother might just as well have responded with that other impenetrable parental reply, "Because I said so."

Now, as an adult with that healthy dose of perspective we call experience, I realize my mother was right, as she was so often when it came to my life. We think we have control over our lives, especially when we're young and seemingly invulnerable. We're told we can do anything we set our minds to, that the world is our oyster, that all we have to do is shuck the hard shell and pluck the rich, nourishing meat inside. I realize now, however, that the shell is a lot harder than I appreciated, and that I never could have controlled or even predicted the things that would happen in my life. We believe we choose the paths we take when we come to those forks in our lives—the friends we make, the careers we undertake, the spouses we marry.

But we don't.

Life is either a collision of random events, like billiard balls during a break careening off and into one another, or if you are so inclined to believe, our predetermined fate—what my mother took such great comfort in calling God's will.

I desperately wanted to believe my mother was right.

I wanted to believe God had a plan for me when David Bateman hit me in the face with a rubber ball on the schoolyard playground and placed us on a cataclysmic course ultimately leading to his death. I wanted to believe God sent Ernie Cantwell from Detroit, Michigan, the only African American child in my class, to be the friend I so desperately needed. I wanted to believe it had been God's design that Mickie Kennedy would storm into my life in the sixth grade like a Midwest tornado, uprooting every precept I'd been taught about the roles of boys and girls and toppling the Catholic ideology my mother and the nuns at Our Lady of Mercy spoon-fed us as a remedy for every personal and societal ailment. Mostly, I wanted to believe that I was fated to live the extraordinary life my mother so ardently believed I was destined for, the life she dutifully prayed for each night as she sat on our floral couch in our wood-paneled family room, kneading the beads of her rosary.

Was it God's will that I should buy this house just two blocks from the shingled home in which I was raised and live in a town I had once sought desperately to escape? I thought I purchased my home because it was a sound investment, a plot of land in an up-and-coming real estate market. My parents had not been so practical. My mother's only real estate criteria had been that our home be within walking distance of a Catholic church and school. The end result, however, has been the same. Except for a decade when I fled, I have lived my entire life close enough to hear the bells ringing in the steeple of Our Lady of Mercy Catholic Church. And yet, despite my proximity, I can only recall hearing those bells on a hand-ful of occasions. Today was one of those times, and for some unknown reason—fate, destiny, or perhaps "God's will"—the toll of those bells has compelled me to sit at this keyboard and write of my mother and father, and of David Bateman, of Daniela and Trina Crouch, and, of course, of Ernie and Mickie. The sound of those bells has even provided me with a logical place to start this story, my story—a memory of another day when I heard those same bells—or thought I did.

PART ONE

A Stain on the Carpet

1

The bells sounded so clear they caused me to sit up, though intuitively I knew I could not have heard them in that sterile, cramped doctor's office.

"Everything okay?" Dr. Kenji Fukomara peered at me over his glasses, an inquisitive gaze.

It was an interesting question given my circumstances. I sat on a narrow examination table, one sheet of thin paper crinkling beneath me and a second sheet draped over my naked lower half. That morning I'd shaved my groin in anticipation of my vasectomy, a task in which I had taken great care. During an earlier consult, Dr. Fukomara told me a story of how a particularly hairy patient caught fire during the cauterization, and the doctor immediately commenced to beat at the flames. Urban myth, probably, but the image of Dr. Fukomara pounding my groin with his fists had caused me to be precise.

So instead of asking if he, too, had heard the church bells, I said, "Can we wait a minute?"

"It's perfectly natural to be nervous," Dr. Fukomara said. He stood at a stainless-steel sink

13

scrubbing his hands with disinfectant soap and rinsing them beneath a stream of hot water.

"I just need a moment." I sat up farther, the paper beneath me protesting.

The bells had sounded exactly like those that rang in the steeple of Our Lady of Mercy, the Catholic church just blocks from my boyhood home, which made me think of my mother, whom I always considered more infallible than the pope when it came to Catholic ideology. Though I was no longer a practicing Catholic, the remnants of her steadfast tutelage, like those bells, still occasionally rang loud and clear. Catholic guilt, they call it; my mother would have chastised my decision to get a vasectomy as a violation of a church tenet.

"Is there something in particular, some concern?" Dr. Fukomara asked, drying his hands with a coarse brown paper towel.

"I wish there was," I said. "Something particular, I mean."

"You won't have any change in sexual function." He'd given me the same assurance in our consult. "And you'll still be able to pee like a racehorse"—as well as the same joke. Dr. Fukomara smiled easily. Humor was his technique to put his patients at ease, a necessity when your specialty involved cutting other men's scrotums. The week before, when he walked into that same room for my fifteen-minute consult, he'd held a machete and had donned Coke bottle–thick, magic-store glasses. "This won't hurt a bit," he'd deadpanned.

"Is it your wife?" he asked. "Is she having second thoughts?"

"Oh no, she's very sure," I said, though Eva was not my wife. Eva and I lived together in the house I'd bought two blocks from the church I no longer attended with the steeple bells I no longer heard except at odd moments, like that one.

Eva moving in with me had seemed like a good idea at the time, but as the months had passed, our living arrangement had started to feel like it was more for convenience than love, which, ironically, was how I had pitched her the idea. "You won't have to pay rent," I'd rationalized. "And we'll save on utilities and groceries and other incidentals." It was all very practical.

"What about your mother?" had been Eva's reply.

From my mother's perspective, Eva and I were living in sin. She'd never used those words, but she'd also not set foot in my house from the moment Eva did, and on those rare occasions when the three of us got together, usually for dinner at a restaurant, my mother was cordial but never asked about the details of Eva's and my relationship. Neither did I. Eva and I had *discussed* marriage, but always in vague terms that also usually provoked a reference to my mother.

15

"I won't get married just to appease her," Eva had said. "And when I do, it won't be in a Catholic church, either."

Eva's use of the pronoun *I* as opposed to *we* was not lost on me. Nor was the fact that Eva always seemed to refer to my mother when the subject of marriage came up and never to us.

Dr. Fukomara smiled and walked closer to the table. "And you?"

"What's that?" I asked, having missed his question.

"Are you having second thoughts?"

"Do you have kids?" I asked.

"Three boys," he said. "We sent our last off to college in September. We're officially empty nesters. We can run around the house naked and have sex in any room."

"Do you?" I asked.

His smile waned. "How old are your children?"

"I don't have any," I said, which seemed to give him pause. He fixed me again with that inquisitive look. I was just thirty-two. Eva was three years older, a pilot for Alaska Airlines committed to her career and uncertain she wanted children, though apparently very certain she did not want mine—hence, my shaved groin and decision to end my chance to be a father.

"And you think you still might want to?"

"I don't know." I didn't think I did. I'd told myself as much for most of my adult life, but

16

now at the moment of decision, I was no longer so certain.

Dr. Fukomara nodded. "Listen, I schedule these at the end of my day. I have another patient in the room next door. Think it over. I'll be back in forty-five minutes."

But even after Dr. Fukomara had left the room, I could not think it over, not with my past continuing to invade my present. The first recollection started as a trickle that, as soon as I attempted to block it, found another path to weep through, the way water will always bleed through concrete, no matter how many times you patch it. I was recalling a particular moment on an unusually hot summer day when I'd sat beside my father in the shade of a two-hundred-year-old oak tree. It had become our routine to sit in the shade provided by those gnarled branches and broad leaves, my father listing in his wheelchair. I don't remember much else about that day or even the topic of conversation, but I do remember his words.

"There comes a time in every man's life," he'd said in the halting, ghostly voice his stroke had left him, "when he stops looking forward and starts looking back."

I recall thinking my father too young to be imparting such wisdom, despite his infirmity, and I too young to be receiving it. Now, sitting in Dr. Fukomara's office, I wondered if I had already reached that time in my life. The thought frightened me, because I had done very little to leave a mark on this world. My death would be noted with nothing more than a headstone bearing the dates of my birth and my death to let the world know I had been here.

I am the only son of an only son. My father's lineage will end with me.

And as that thought weighed on me, I decided, for no rational reason, that I hated that room with its mustard-yellow walls and poorly disguised cheap pressboard cabinets. I slid off the table and paced the orange linoleum, imagining what Eva might say when she arrived home from her East Coast flight to find I had changed my mind.

"We talked about this," she'd say. "We agreed."

But saying "we agreed" was akin to saying the French and British agreed to give Germany most of Czechoslovakia at the Munich Conference. I had grown weary of Eva's complaints about how condoms numbed the pleasure for her and how a vasectomy was the least intrusive and most effective form of birth control—for her, certainly. But she was not the one facing the blade, or worse, a possible fire and Dr. Fukomara's beating fists.

My eyes wandered to the stainless-steel metal stand and the gleaming forceps, tweezers, and scalpels. The two mountains of gauze seemed far more than necessary given the small task to be performed. And I again thought of my father, who had never had to make this decision. I knew what he would have said if I had ever confided in him about this trip to the doctor. My father would have said what he always said when my actions dumbfounded him, the same four words he uttered the very first moment he'd laid eyes on me and unwittingly bestowed upon me my name.

"What the Sam Hell?"

2

Burlingame, California

I'd heard the story of my birth so often I could recount it as if I actually recalled the event. For some unknown reason, my mother always chose to begin with the weather.

"March 15, 1957, was a cold and clear winter day of little or no consequence until," she'd say, leaning forward on the couch and pressing the palms of her hands together, the college actress performing, "I felt a kick."

This had apparently occurred shortly after my father sat in his favorite recliner to read the newspaper and nurse his evening indulgence, a single Manhattan.

"What did you do?" I'd ask from my spot on the carpet at her feet.

"I ignored you," my mother would say, feigning indifference with a dramatic pause and a wave of her hand. "After all, we weren't expecting you for another five weeks." She would then reenact how she had rearranged the two decorative pillows at the small of her back while sitting in her customary spot on the sofa kneading the beads of her rosary. "And when the pain returned, I offered it up for some poor soul trapped in purgatory."

I learned at a very young age that purgatory was the nebulous place between heaven and earth where the dead must be purified of sin through the prayers of others before Saint Peter allows entrance through heaven's pearly gates. "Give it up for some poor soul in purgatory" would be my mother's mantra in response to any suffering I would endure throughout my childhood, though I don't recall a single instance in which it proved particularly effective. It certainly didn't rid her of the pain I was to inflict that evening and most of the following day. That my mother had been praying the rosary, however, came as no surprise. My mother was always in the midst of a novena to the Blessed Mother for one thing or another, including the time the water heater quit and we couldn't afford a new one. I never asked if she believed the Blessed Mother would drop a new Jetglas from the heavens—my mother would have admonished me for being sacrilegious—but such was the depth of her faith and her devotion. Much later, after my mother's death, I found her tiny blue novena book in the drawer of her nightstand with an incalculable number of lead pencil marks to record each of her fifty-four-day novenas.

"And don't forget how you groaned," my father would chime in from behind his newspaper.

"I didn't groan," my mother would say. "You make me sound like a barnyard cow."

With that, my father would peek at me from behind his newspaper and smile.

My mother prided herself as a descendant of the toughest of Irish stock, but somewhere in the middle of the third decade of the joyful mysteries, her water broke, and I could no longer be ignored.

"Even before your birth, you left a stain on the carpet," she'd say. The stain, an amoeba-shaped discoloration that no cleaner known to man could remove, served for years as a reminder of my untimely arrival.

Had my mother's water not broken, my father might never have moved from his beloved recliner positioned near the fireplace we used once a year to burn the Christmas wrapping paper.

"Your father catapulted from his chair like it ejected him," my mother would say.

"That's a bit of an exaggeration," my father would respond, still hidden behind his sports page.

"Samuel, your father sprinted up those stairs," she'd say, gesturing over her shoulder to our staircase, "stuffed my clothes in a suitcase, and rushed out the front door." She'd dramatize the latter by flinging her arm as if slamming the door. I loved it. "It was only after he threw my suitcase in the trunk and jumped behind the wheel that he realized he'd left me still struggling to get up from the couch."

"Yes," my father would say, lowering the paper, "and by the time I got back to the house, your mother had already managed to not only get her coat and handbag from the closet; she'd also had the presence of mind to unplug every appliance in the house!"

This would send me into raucous laughter. Every trip, no matter how far from home, started with my mother worrying that she'd forgotten to unplug some appliance and lamenting the catastrophic fire she was certain it would cause.

"The drive to Mercy Medical Center takes eight minutes, Samuel. I made it in five minutes flat," my father would say with noticeable pride.

"That's because you drove like a bat out of hell," my mother would say.

My father would wink at me. "I'd mapped the route through the back streets."

"You rolled through every stop sign. You're lucky you didn't get a ticket."

"With a pregnant woman in the car? I would have received a police escort."

It turned out the rush was much ado about nothing. As my mother liked to say, "You were early, but you took your sweet time."

Her labor lasted thirty-two hours, a number she would remind me of whenever I acted up. Still, the wait turned out to be nothing compared to the stir my arrival caused. "You emerged with your eyes shut tight," my mother would say, speaking in a hushed whisper that mesmerized me. In hindsight, I wondered if my entering this world with my eyes shut tight was a genetically predisposed instinct.

My father, who'd chosen to remain down the hall in the hospital's waiting room, would at this point resume his narrative, explaining how the young doctor entered the room looking more perplexed than tired. "He said, 'It's a boy,' " but the doctor's rote proclamation did not temper my father's paternal instinct that something was amiss. "I sprinted down the tile linoleum into that room," he'd say. "And when I entered, I found a crowd of nurses and hospital staff hovering around your mother's bed like she was Marilyn Monroe."

But my mother was not the object of their interest. It seemed that when the doctor had placed me upon my mother's stomach to cut the umbilical cord, I'd finally opened my eyes. And that's when the euphoria became bewilderment. The doctor froze, slack jawed. The attending nurse let out a yip, which she belatedly tried to cover by placing her hand over her mouth.

"Give me my son," my mother had said amid the silent stares, whereupon the nurse had swaddled me in a blanket and handed me to her.

This was how my father found us when he waded through the crowd for a closer inspection and looked me in the eyes for the first time.

"What the Sam Hell?" he whispered.

3

My father turned quickly to the obstetrician, who had entered the room and retaken his position at the foot of my mother's bed. "His eyes are red. Why are his eyes red?"

"I don't know," the doctor said.

"Will they stay that color?"

But back then the doctor didn't know, and he had little ability to research the question. He could only shrug. Another silence ensued, those present holding their collective breath, uncertain what to say or what to think of me. That's when my mother again took over. "Out," she'd ordered. "I would like everyone to please leave."

"That was our first private moment together as a family," she'd say when recounting the story. "Just you, me, and your father."

Finally alone, my father started to ask the pertinent question. "Why are—"

But my mother was not interested in why my eyes were red, and she put up a hand to stop him. "I don't care why," she'd said.

Several more minutes passed before my father, ever pragmatic, said, "Well then, what shall we call him? We don't have a name."

Because of my premature arrival, they'd failed to reach a consensus. My mother suggested

Maxwell, but my father had never cared for his name. He'd lobbied for William.

"But we do have a name," my mother said. "A beautiful name. A name his father has given him. Samuel. We'll call him Samuel."

And so, my father being Maxwell James Hill, I became Samuel James Hill.

Sam Hill. Or, as I would soon become known, Sam Hell.

4

My mother wasted no time doting on me and recording every detail of my life, as evidenced by the dozens of scrapbooks and photo albums she filled and kept on the mahogany bookshelves in our living room. When it came to my life, my mother acted as if she were preserving the legacy of a future president for his presidential library. Even before cameras digitally recorded the date on individual photographs, she would write the day, month, and year on the white borders to note such momentous occasions as my first bath, my first meal in a high chair, and the obligatory first potty-training session. I also possess the hospital beanie and ankle bracelet I wore home from the hospital, as well as every report card I earned and every high school newspaper article I wrote. Whether my mother's diligence was intended to document the extraordinary life she was convinced I was destined to lead or simply the result of her having too much time on her hands, I cannot say, but this meticulous recording of my life, along with the extended hours I would later spend with my father under the shade of that retirement center oak tree, allowed me to piece together much of these first years of my life.

My mother, of course, deemed my red eyes

to be "God's will." And so, when some hospital administration types advised that hospital policy dictated I be examined by a specialist before I could be discharged, she turned them down cold. She suspected the hospital was more concerned with their potential legal liability than my health. "I'll sign a waiver," she'd said. "And we'll be out of your hair."

My mother's suspicion was only partially accurate. It seems word of the child with red eyes traveled quickly through the hospital corridors and surrounding medical community, and there was no shortage of doctors eager to examine me. My mother brushed them aside as "charlatans." "They were only interested in being published in the *New England Journal of Medicine*," she'd told me.

My father, not a man to rock the boat, had suggested a compromise. "Perhaps we can allow one doctor to examine Samuel, just to be certain."

My mother reluctantly consented, and both sides agreed upon Dr. Charles Pridemore, an ophthalmologist at the Stanford University Medical Center in Palo Alto.

I don't know to what extent Dr. Pridemore educated my parents that day or on subsequent visits, but I soon became well versed in my "condition," the only word my mother would ever use to describe my eyes. A soft-spoken, bearded man of quiet dignity, Dr. Pridemore would become a lifelong mentor and friend. What I recall about him from my youth, however, was that he always had the appearance and demeanor of a slightly distracted science professor—plaid shirts and wrinkled corduroys, an unkempt beard, wisps of curly hair protruding at odd angles, and glasses mottled with dust and fingerprints.

"Ocular albinism," he'd later explained to me on one of my frequent visits, "is best understood with a rudimentary explanation of the components of the eye." He used a diagram hanging on the wall to show me the two layers of pigment in the iris. "There is the front, which we see, and the back, which we don't see, but which blocks light transmission. The iris without pigment is white," he explained, chewing hard on his ever-present stick of spearmint gum. "And the presence or absence of melanin in the iris accounts for the color of our eyes. A lot of melanin at the front results in brown eyes. No melanin in front, blue eyes. Some melanin and the eyes can appear green, hazel, and every shade in between, depending on the amount and distribution."

"And what about red?" I had asked.

"Technically, there is no such thing as red pigment."

"But my eyes *are* red," I said. And they were, though let me clarify. I am not talking about fire-engine, glow-in-the-dark red, or even the red of a ripe apple. The color was more subtle, bordering on pink. But I'm also not an albino. Though I was born a towhead, my hair gradually darkened to its current nondescript light brown. And though I burn if I don't use sunblock, my skin pigmentation is otherwise normal. And that is how my mother considered me from the moment of my birth. Normal. In the hospital room, when Dr. Pridemore came to conduct his examination, she asked the only question that mattered to her. "Will it affect his vision?"

But Dr. Pridemore did not know that answer in 1957, there being scant literature on the topic. "All I can say is that Samuel's eyes are very rare."

"Not rare, Doctor," my mother corrected. "Extraordinary."

5

My father dutifully called the few relatives I had with the news of my birth. My father had been an only child, born and raised in Chicago. He had lost his father to cancer two years before I was born. His German mother, whom I referred to as Oma Hill, made an annual sojourn to Burlingame for the Christmas holidays. Either my birth did not rate a separate visit, or my father politely steered her away from coming. I presume my father thought it best to spare everyone Oma Hill's lamentations about all the pitfalls that awaited a child born with red eyes.

Grandma O'Malley, on the other hand, rode the first bus from San Francisco to Burlingame, suitcase in hand. Also a widow, Grandma O'Malley had never possessed a driver's license and saw little need of obtaining one. She raised my mother and my auntie Bonnie in a San Francisco Victorian in the Mission District, where bus lines were plentiful, specialty shops abundant, and she could walk to Saint James Catholic Church for morning Mass. Unlike Oma Hill, Grandma O'Malley did not acknowledge afflictions, neuroses, diseases, or maladies, a trait I have since attributed to her Irish heritage. She apparently marched into my parents' bedroom, unswaddled me from my cocoon in the bassinet, and proclaimed, "Two eyes, two ears, ten fingers, ten toes, and a nose. Perfect."

And that was her final word on the subject.

6

Sunday, three days after we arrived home from the hospital, my mother dressed me for my first visit to Our Lady of Mercy. It would take something far more severe than giving birth to keep my mother from attending Sunday Mass. My parents arrived early and marched down the long aisle to the third pew on the left, what would become our unwavering spot. My mother later would say this was so that God could note our presence, though a skeptic might believe it was to ensure a less divine being would take notice— our pastor, Father Brogan. Parishioners' regular attendance at Mass, and their offerings in the weekly envelopes, went a long way when it came time to enroll their children in OLM's crowded Catholic grammar school.

Before slipping into the pew that first Sunday, my mother took me to the alcove just to the right of the altar to present me to the Blessed Mother of Jesus Christ. Mary stood atop a globe, dressed in a blue-and-white shawl, rosary beads in hand and a snake crushed beneath her bare feet. It was the first of what would be many visits I would make to that alcove.

That my parents' first encounter with intolerance would occur in church is less a commentary on Catholic hypocrisy than it is a testament to the frequency of their attendance. They were regular Sunday churchgoers, not "Christmas Catholics," as my father dubbed those who attended Mass only on Christmas and Easter. Had my parents been as fervent about baseball, I'm sure the first inappropriate comment about the color of my eyes would have come from a child wearing a baseball cap and eating a hot dog. As it was, the offender was a young boy in blue knickers sitting in the pew behind us.

"Mom," he'd apparently exclaimed, "what's wrong with that baby's eyes?"

"What did you do?" I would ask when my mother recounted this story.

"Why, I turned around and gave him a closer look," she'd say. "Then I told him, 'There's nothing wrong with his eyes. God made them that color. They're extraordinary.' "

Following Mass, my mother also did not hesitate to present me to Father Brogan. A petite man with a white beard and thick Irish brogue, Father Brogan hid his shock—it was not possible that he did not notice. According to my father, the priest scooped me into his arms, lifted me overhead, and pronounced me to be "a fine lad indeed."

7

In my thirteenth month, I took my first step, or so I was told. I found no snapshot to document this momentous occasion in the photo album labeled *1958*. I do know that I took this step at home during a weekday, prompting my mother to stage a reenactment when my father arrived home from work so he could capture it on camera. Some months after my mother died, I found a cardboard box containing canisters of film in her attic. In the grainy, silent film documenting that day, I'm standing in a diaper with wobbly legs and clutching the corner of our living room coffee table. My mother is also in the film, clapping her hands and silently coaxing me to let go, without success. It seems that I had become distracted by my mother's rosary, alternately slapping the beads on the table or shoving them in my mouth and drooling. My mother, sensing an opportunity, took the rosary from me and dangled the silver cross just out of my reach.

"Walk for Mary," she mouthed on the film. "Walk for Mary, Samuel."

And that was when I responded, though not with my first step. In those black-and-white frames, my mother suddenly stopped clapping.

Her eyes shifted from me to the camera a fraction of a second before my father dropped it. By the time he had recovered, I was in mid-walk, reaching for the dangling crucifix, a feat completely overshadowed by what had been my first uttered word.

"Mary," I'd said.

To my mother, of course, this was solid evidence to support her conviction that God had a divine plan for me and my red eyes. If someone had told her that someday white smoke would rise above the Vatican before the proclamation of my name as pope, she would not so much have batted an eye. She immediately went to work to ensure that when that momentous occasion did occur, I would not embarrass her, as I did each time she took me to buy a new pair of shoes and I revealed holes in my socks. By age five I could recite the Lord's Prayer, the Hail Mary, and the Glory Be, which meant I could recite the rosary. This tutelage often occurred at night, with me holding my own rosary and mimicking her devotion, and just as frequently on trips to kneel before that statue of the Blessed Mother in the alcove of the church.

"Prayers are like coins deposited in a piggy bank, Samuel," my mother assured me. "Save them until you need them for something important."

And so I would silently recite the rosary and

deposit my prayers in my prayer piggy bank, comforted by the knowledge that they would be there when the need presented itself, which would be much sooner than I anticipated.

8

While I do not specifically recollect my enrollment at OLM, like my birth it is a story I heard often enough to tell with authority of fact. A newspaper article in the scrapbook marked *1963* also helped fill in the blanks, and what I cannot document I can deduce from a profound understanding of my mother and her steadfast and unyielding insistence that her son would receive a Catholic education. And God help anyone who got in her way.

The envelope from OLM's admissions office arrived in our mailbox the week before the start of the school year. Both that envelope and the letter it contained became keepsakes in my mother's scrapbook. Though the paper has yellowed and the typewritten font has faded, I remember the envelope my mother pulled from our mailbox as having been a bright white. Almost as bright as my mother's smile that afternoon.

"Isn't this exciting, Samuel?"

Her smile quickly faded upon reading the letter.

"We are sorry to advise that your application for enrollment in the first grade at Our Lady of Mercy has been denied." Unfortunately, Our Lady of Mercy did not have enough spots for every applicant.

That evening, after we'd finished dinner, my mother handed my father the letter along with a cup of coffee. Upon reading it, my father placed the letter facedown on the kitchen table, momentarily stumped. "The public school is very good," he'd eventually said with some degree of caution. "Given Samuel's . . . condition, perhaps it's better not to draw attention to the situation. He can attend CCD, and of course there is no better religion teacher than you."

My mother added two lumps of sugar to his coffee and poured the cream in his lap. To his credit my father hardly flinched. He simply excused himself to change his pants. The son of Madeline Hill, whose first uttered word had been the name of the Blessed Mother of Jesus Christ, would not attend public school. Of this my mother was quite certain.

9

The following sun-drenched Monday morning, my mother dressed me in the school uniform she had purchased in anticipation of this big day—a short-sleeved white shirt, navy-blue pants, and a red sweater. We drove first to the church, where we knelt in the alcove before the Blessed Mother.

"You might want to consider opening your prayer bank," my mother suggested, but after years of saving I couldn't bear to do it. Instead I mentally pulled the rubber stopper on the bottom and shook out just one or two.

"What do I pray for?" I whispered.

My mother did not raise her head or open her eyes. "Righteousness," she whispered.

After our visit to the church, my mother parked on Cortez Avenue and marched me up the steep red steps to the wrought iron–gated entrance to the OLM school quad. Built in 1932, this older section of OLM, like the homes nearby, had been influenced by Spanish architecture and consisted of salmon-colored stucco walls with rounded archways and red-tile roofs. Eight mahogany doors faced an inner courtyard of red concrete slabs with an elevated white statue of the Blessed Mother at the epicenter. I felt the eyes of every student watching our assault as we marched up those stairs, through that quad, and across the asphalt playground. Our destination was the admissions office in the modern portion of the school. I would subsequently learn that the admissions office was readily accessed from the adjacent block, Cabrillo Avenue, but that would have been far too subtle an entrance for my mother. She wasn't interested in just rocking this boat. She intended to capsize it.

Sister Beatrice, OLM's principal, met us in an austere lobby. She wore her solid-black habit, which fell in folds from her throat to her shins, cinched at the waist by a woven wool girdle from which hung a black rosary and ebony cross. Add to this a black wimple, thick black-framed glasses, a prominent nose, and two equally prominent front incisors, and I was certain I was staring at the Wicked Witch of the West. I was terrified.

"How can I help you, Mrs. Hill?" Sister Beatrice asked, pleasantly enough.

"I'm here to enroll my son, Samuel, in the first grade," my mother replied.

"Did you receive my letter?" Sister Beatrice asked.

My mother held up the envelope. "I did indeed."

"Then you understand why that is not going to occur today."

"To the contrary," my mother said, "that is

exactly why I am here, to see that it does occur today. I don't want Samuel to fall behind a single day."

Sister Beatrice's lips puckered, making the wisps of black hair adorning her upper lip twitch. "I am the principal of this school, Mrs. Hill. As the principal it is my obligation to make decisions that are in the best interests of the child."

"To which child are you referring?" my mother asked, both women still cordial at this point.

Sister Beatrice frowned. "Why, yours, of course."

"Really? You're going to make a decision in the best interest of Samuel? Before you do, tell me, Sister, if you would be so kind, all of the things that you know about Samuel . . ."

"Excuse me?"

"With the exception of the color of his eyes, of which I am quite certain you are fully aware."

Until that moment, Sister Beatrice had never once considered me. When her gaze shifted to my face, I felt an instant lump in my throat. She folded her arms, and her hands disappeared in the wide sleeves of her habit. "I beg your pardon?"

"I asked that you tell me everything you can about Samuel, Sister."

"I've never met the boy."

"Precisely. So I fail to see how you are in a position to be making a decision that is in Samuel's best interests."

At this proclamation, I noticed several of the office women seated behind the wood laminate counter raise their heads and put aside any pretense of being engaged in work. Apparently Sister Beatrice was rarely, if ever, challenged.

"Perhaps we should continue this conversation inside my office?"

"Perhaps we should," my mother agreed.

Sister Beatrice spun, a swirl of black cloth, and marched into her office. She turned and raised a hand to stop me from proceeding. "The boy will wait in the lobby."

"Samuel will not wait in the lobby. As this is a matter that involves him directly, he will need to be present. I believe it will be an insightful lesson for him on Catholic compassion and empathy."

Lips pursed, Sister Beatrice gestured to two cloth chairs across from a metal desk. I followed my mother inside and sat. If the lobby was austere, Sister Beatrice's office was downright spartan. Photographs of Pope Paul VI and our pastor, Father Brogan, hung side by side on one wall. On her otherwise spotless desk sat a six-inch cactus that looked in desperate need of water.

Sister Beatrice's posture was impeccable, back straight and hands folded on her desk blotter. My mother's spine likewise never touched the back of her chair, and yet she still managed to cross her legs. I didn't dare slouch.

"This is a private school, Mrs. Hill. Father Brogan has seen fit to make *me* its principal. As such I have the authority to decline admittance to any child. This school is not subject to the admissions requirements that govern public institutions."

"In other words, you have the right to discriminate in the name of God."

Sister Beatrice's face flushed. "It is not discrimination. It is . . . careful analysis."

My mother smiled, and I could not help but think her beautiful in her black-and-white-checked wool skirt and matching jacket, a simple strand of pearls adorning her neck. With blonde hair and blue eyes, my mother always had a youthful appearance, and I would learn—to my horror—an hourglass figure that would generate catcalls well into her forties. My father called her "a looker," which in my day equated to "a total babe."

"Tell me, Sister. Would you have denied enrollment to Samuel had he been black?"

Sister Beatrice bristled. "Of course not."

"Chinese?"

"No."

"Russian?"

She hesitated, it being the Cold War. "No."

"My son is of German-Irish descent. He was baptized Catholic in the church at the end of this school's playground. My husband and I have been faithful and generous parishioners. Samuel can recite the Our Father, the Hail Mary, and the Act of Contrition. He can make the sign of the cross and knows how to say the rosary. So explain to me, if you will, on what basis you have chosen to deny him admission."

"It is my belief that because of certain attributes, your son's presence in the classroom could be detrimental to the learning environment of the other children."

"You denied Samuel admission because he was born with red eyes, a condition over which he has no control."

"I believe it will be difficult for your son to fit in, to make friends." My mother started to speak, and Sister Beatrice added, "The children refer to him as 'Sam Hell.' "

"Jesus, Mary, and Joseph, what does that have to do with—"

"They call him 'the devil boy.' "

My mother flinched. So did I, having been well versed in the concept of the devil.

"As such, I think your son could be a disruption to the classroom—a distinct likelihood to which we all must be sensitive," Sister Beatrice finished.

"But not to Samuel," my mother said, quickly recovering.

"Excuse me?"

"You think it right to be sensitive to the

possibility that other children will be insensitive, un-Christian, un-Catholic, un-Christ-like," she said, "but not to be sensitive to a six-year-old boy whom *God* created and whom *God* gave red eyes?"

"Nevertheless, I have twenty-three other students in the first grade to consider."

"Then perhaps you should consider that Samuel's presence might very well be a perfect opportunity to put into practice some of the principles to which this school, and this parish, give lip service—to love one another and to display compassion to those who are different."

"I can assure you, Mrs. Hill, this school very much enforces Christian ideals." These being the days of wooden rulers and bullet-tipped pointers, Sister Beatrice's use of the word *enforce* had surely been intended.

"At the moment, I think you can appreciate that your words ring rather hollow, Sister. Now, since there is no justifiable reason *not* to enroll Samuel, kindly advise me to whom I should write a check to cover his tuition, and into which classroom he will be placed."

The two women locked eyes. There ensued a sickening moment of silence. Sister Beatrice broke the deadlock. "As I said, that is not going to happen, Mrs. Hill. I've made my decision."

My mother stood. "Then I will have to make mine. Samuel."

Taking that as my cue, and grateful for it, I stood to leave. My mother opened the office door, and though she turned to face Sister Beatrice, she kept her voice loud enough for all in the outer office to hear. "I will pray for you, Sister." With that pronouncement, she left.

I trudged out behind her, stumbling into her legs when she stopped to address the two women behind the counter. "Prepare yourselves, ladies. It's about to get very busy."

10

"Don't listen to a word that woman uttered," my mother said as she shuffled me back across the courtyard, this time without an audience; the students were already in their classrooms. "A woman like that shames the habit she is wearing."

Without further word, we climbed into the convertible Falcon and drove off, though not in the direction of our home. I can recall thinking my mother was driving straight to my father's store, but we passed Broadway Avenue without slowing.

"Where are we going?" I asked.

"To see a college friend," she said.

We continued south on the El Camino Real to a nondescript high-rise building and parked in a lot beside multiple white vans with the number four stenciled on the sides. Inside the building, my mother sat me in a chair in a reception area while she went to address a woman behind the counter. A minute later a man in a shirt and tie with perfect teeth and hair that looked like it could withstand fifty-mile-an-hour wind gusts greeted her with a hug and, to my astonishment, a kiss on the cheek.

My mother beckoned me forward. "Samuel, this is Dan, an old college friend."

Dan bent down to shake my hand. "Hi there, Sam. How would you like something to drink and a morning snack?"

I looked to my mom, who nodded her consent.

"Emily," Dan said to the woman behind the counter, "can you take Sam to the lunchroom and get him a juice and snack?"

I wasn't sure about leaving my mother with a man who so easily kissed her, but I was also hungry, having not been able to stomach much for breakfast that morning.

"No problem," Emily said, coming out from behind the counter. She stopped suddenly, staring at me.

"And get Sam some paper and colored markers to pass the time," Dan said, but Emily must not have heard him. "Emily?"

"What's that?" she asked, breaking off eye contact with me.

"I said, get Sam some paper and colored markers."

Emily looked to my mother, whose eyebrows arched. "Right. Markers. Sure, not a problem."

I remember thinking it must have been everyone's break time, because a considerable number of people came into the lunchroom while I was drawing and eating my snack. By the time my mother and Dan finally returned, I had filled three sheets of blank paper with multiple drawings.

Dan was now wearing a checked sports coat.

"Don't you worry," he said, giving my mother another hug, though thankfully not another kiss. "We'll take care of it."

11

That evening I was in my room feeling a certain dread, though I'm equally certain I could not have fully understood what was transpiring. When my mother called me down to dinner, I closed the book I was supposed to be reading and walked to the bathroom across the hall. I rinsed my hands under the tap and dried them on my pants, sprinkling water on the soap in the dish in case my mother checked. Standing at the sink, I looked into the mirror and stared at the two red circles gazing back at me. It is my first recollection of looking upon my reflection and wondering why I was different.

"Devil Boy," I said, despite my mother's admonition not to listen to a word Sister Beatrice had said. How could I not? I'd been standing right there when she'd said it.

"Devil Boy," I said again, leaning closer to my reflection. "Devil Boy."

"Samuel, I am not going to call you again!"

I turned off the bathroom light and hurried downstairs. My father, seated in his recliner, motioned me over as I jumped down the final two steps. "I hear you had quite the day," he whispered. "You know, Jefferson Elementary"—where I had attended kindergarten—"is a very good school. I spoke to the principal, and they'd be delighted to have you continue there."

"I don't know," I said.

My father winked. "These things have a way of working themselves out, Sam. No use rocking the boat—you only take on more water."

At that, my mother pronounced dinner served, and my father and I proceeded to the kitchen.

My mother sanctified our dinner ritual as much as our attendance at Mass. Our evening meal began promptly after my father finished his Manhattan. As in church, we each had our assigned places at the table. We did not begin passing food until after we had joined hands and said grace. Upon uttering "Amen," I was to take my napkin and place it in my lap while my mother commenced serving. I was not allowed to slouch or put my elbows on the table, and I was expected to liberally use the words *please* and *thank you. Can I* was forbidden. "May I," my mother would correct. Dinner conversation also had a set of rules. We were expected to discuss our days, though not anything "unsettling."

"It will disrupt your digestion," my mother would say.

Despite these regulations, I recall our dinners together fondly. I enjoyed hearing my father discuss the comings and goings at the pharmacy, and I wanted very much to someday follow in his footsteps.

When we entered the kitchen this evening, however, my father came to a sudden stop, staring at our black-and-white portable television with rabbit-ear antennae on the Formica counter. I had last seen it the day my father placed it in the hall closet, replacing it with the RCA Victor in the living room. I would have found it less unusual had a bear walked in at that moment and sat at the table. So, apparently, would have my father.

"We're eating dinner with the TV on?" my father asked.

"I want to watch the news." My mother set a bowl of green beans on the table without further explanation for this serious breach in dinner protocol. "Samuel, did you wash your hands?"

"Yes."

"With soap?"

I looked to my father, but he remained dumb-struck by the television.

"Go into the bathroom and use soap," my mother said.

I used the bathroom just beneath the staircase and again considered my eyes in the mirror. They looked the same as they had that morning, but I didn't feel the same. All of this breach in protocol was upsetting my stomach.

My father had taken his customary seat, but my mother continued to break tradition, sitting where I normally sat to better view the television.

She pointed to her usual chair. "You sit there tonight, Samuel."

She reached across the table and grabbed my hand, and I took my father's to complete the circle. After saying grace, my mother passed me a plate of fried chicken. I took a leg while sneaking a glance over my shoulder at the television. "Put your napkin in your lap," she said.

"Is there something in particular you're interested in watching?" my father asked.

My mother passed him the green beans as a washed-out image of Walter Cronkite looked into the camera and signed off. "And that's the way it is, September 4, 1963."

I assume the channel went to commercial, because I recall asking, "Can I have the potatoes?"

"Please pass the potatoes," my mother corrected.

"Please pass the potatoes," I said.

My father got as far as picking up the bowl when the local newscast began.

"Today in Burlingame a Catholic school denied admittance to a young boy because he was born with a rare genetic condition that causes the irises of his eyes to be red."

My father dropped the bowl. My mother appeared on the grainy television, standing beside Dan, a microphone under her chin and Sister Beatrice's letter in her hand.

"It seems that when it comes to Catholic

54

values, Our Lady of Mercy is good at preaching them but not at practicing them," my mother said to Dan. "My son is no different from any other child, save for the color of his eyes, over which he has no control."

Our Lady of Mercy's school grounds appeared on the television, the shot angling up at the quad from the lower parking lot. It then switched to a close-up of the salmon-colored door of the administration office. The blinds had been drawn to cover the thin sidelights. Dan peered into the camera. "Attempts to contact the school principal, Sister Beatrice, were not successful," he said, tone grave.

The camera shot returned to my mother standing beside Dan in the parking lot. "She said the decision was hers alone to make, so I can only assume she speaks for the entire parish."

"But that appears not to be the case," the newscaster said, and I recognized the sudden appearance of our pastor, Father Brogan, dressed in his mud-brown Franciscan frock.

"This is clearly a misunderstanding," Father Brogan said to Dan. He looked uncomfortable. "Here at OLM we do far more than preach Catholic ideals. I can assure you they are very much put into practice."

Dan asked, "So is there any truth to the assertion that the boy was denied admittance because of the color of his eyes?"

Father Brogan looked pale, even on the washed-out screen. "We had more applicants than space," he managed. "We certainly do not discriminate at OLM."

With that pronouncement, my mother returned to the screen beside Dan. This time she sounded more conciliatory. "We're hopeful that this misunderstanding will be quickly rectified."

The newscast moved on to the next story. My father and I sat as if frozen.

"Samuel, turn off the television," my mother said, piercing a green bean with her fork and bringing it to her mouth.

The click of the knob was the last sound I recall until the telephone down the hall rang. My mother casually transferred her napkin from her lap to the table, and left to answer it. "Hill residence. This is Mrs. Hill." Pause. "It's nice of you to call, Father Brogan." Another pause. "No. As a matter of fact, we were just finishing up." Longer pause. "I understand. Of course. These things do happen. Samuel is very much looking forward to it."

I looked to my father. He sat rigid, his face red.

My mother continued to speak into the phone. "We'd like to have you to dinner one evening, Father. Yes, we'll have to do that."

I heard her replace the receiver in its cradle. A moment later she reseated herself and draped her napkin in her lap. "You'll need to get a good night's sleep tonight, Samuel. You start first grade in the morning at Our Lady of Mercy."

12

We spent the rest of the evening in a chilly silence. I pretended to watch television until my bedtime at seven thirty. The minute hand had no sooner struck the six when my mother and father spoke nearly simultaneously—"Time for bed, Samuel." I needed no further encouragement this night.

I hurried upstairs, brushed my teeth, washed my face, and pulled on my pajamas. Then I slid beneath my bed and inched close to the floor vent. Ordinarily I had to press my ear to hear my parents' conversations in the room below, but this evening I could hear them both just fine.

"Why on God's green earth would you do that, Madeline?"

"I won't have him discriminated against."

"You drew more attention to him than if you stood on the church steps and blew a bugle."

"Don't be melodramatic. I stood up for my son; if that makes me a bad mother—"

"And don't pull the martyr act. This isn't about you, Maddy. This is about Sam. He is the one who has to walk into that school tomorrow and confront the bed you have made for him."

"He will be stronger for it."

"He's six years old!"

"And what? You think it will get easier for him as he gets older?"

"Precisely my point—the cruelty will begin soon enough."

Cruelty? What kind of school was OLM? Jefferson Elementary was looking better and better.

"The cruelty has already been inflicted by a Dominican nun who had the temerity to call my son, our son—"

"Who will be his principal—"

"The 'devil boy.' "

"Good God!" my dad shouted. "And you want to send him there?"

"She won't be his principal for long, not if I have anything to do with it."

"Please. Are you going to get every teacher who is unkind to Samuel fired? What about every child who mistreats him—are you going to have them expelled?"

Unkind? Mistreatment? What had I gotten myself into?

"Don't be ridiculous, Maxwell." My mother rarely called my father Maxwell.

"Me being ridiculous? I'm not the one who made a spectacle of myself on local television."

"I certainly didn't make a spectacle of myself."

"You indicted the entire community. Our community." There was a lull in the battle. Then my father said, "Sam is different. There's nothing that can be done about that."

"He certainly is."

"Then why draw more attention to him? Why make him stand out any more than he already does? Why not let him just . . ." My father did not finish.

"What? Blend in?"

"Yes, to whatever extent he can."

"Because he can't blend in, and the sooner Samuel learns that is the case, the sooner he can learn to deal with it."

There was another silence. Then I heard my father say, "Devil Boy?"

Later, I lay in bed listening to the rhythmic flow of my mother's prayers. The cadence of her Our Fathers and Hail Marys ordinarily helped me drift to sleep. Not this night. I contemplated breaking that piggy bank and using my stored prayers for a good case of the flu, but I knew the flu would not last, and, eventually, I would be forced to attend OLM and face the *cruelty* and the *mistreatment,* whatever that meant.

While lying in bed, I heard my mother's footsteps ascending the stairs. Though I pretended to be asleep, I was a poor actor, and as she tucked me in, she asked, "Have you been crying?"

"Why am I different?" I asked.

She sat on the edge of my bed. "You're not different."

"No one else has red eyes. No one."

"And who gave you those eyes?"

I swallowed hard. "God," I said.

"God gave you extraordinary eyes, Samuel, because he intends for you to lead an extraordinary life."

"What if I don't want to? What if I just want to be like other kids?"

She brushed my hair from my forehead. Then she touched her finger to my chest. "You are every bit as normal as any other boy, in here, where it counts. Our skin, our hair, and our eyes are simply the shell that surrounds our soul, and our soul is who we are. What counts is on the inside."

"People don't make fun of what's on the inside," I said.

She sighed. "People make fun of things they don't understand."

"I don't even know them. Why would they call me that?"

"They'll like you when they get to know you."

"She doesn't. Sister Beatrice. She hates me."

"She doesn't hate you."

"She called me Devil Boy."

"We don't always know God's will, Sam."

"Is it his will for her to hate me?"

My mother seemed to give this further consideration. Her answer surprised me. "It might be," she said. "No one knows."

"Then how do you know?"

She stood. "Have faith, Samuel. Can you do that for me?"

I wasn't sure I could. I wasn't too happy with God at that moment. I'd spent prayers from my prayer bank, and that hadn't worked out too well. "I guess so," I said.

"Now close your beautiful eyes and go to sleep. You have a big day tomorrow." She bent and kissed my forehead.

But I did not fall asleep, not right away. I lay awake wondering what kind of cruelty awaited me, the devil boy. I got an idea, closed my eyes, and in my mind I smashed the piggy bank and emptied out all my prayers.

13

That night I dreamed of a black crow with a sharp beak pecking at my eyes. It would be a recurring nightmare throughout my youth. When I awoke I was so tired, my stomach so upset, that for a brief moment I thought maybe God had answered my prayers and I did indeed have the flu. No such luck. Looking back, I now know that my mother had taken a stand. She'd drawn a line in the sand. Though I'm certain I didn't completely understand it then, I sensed even at that tender young age that attending school that day was about far more than beginning my Catholic education. It was about what my mother had whispered in my ear when we had knelt before the Blessed Mother the prior morning.

Righteousness.

I'm not sure exactly what I expected, but when I looked in the bathroom mirror that morning, I saw the same two red orbs. Even though I'd used all my prayers, the Blessed Mother had not changed the color of my eyes. It was the first—but not the last—time I would empty my bank for that request and be disappointed.

My mother and father stood at the bottom of the stairs, my father documenting the occasion in black-and-white film with the camera. My worry and concern are etched in deep grooves on my forehead. And, watching the movie as an adult, it dawned on me that my mother had not recorded the prior morning—clear evidence she never expected OLM to accept me that day.

"First day. Big day," my father said from behind the camera.

"Smile, Samuel," my mother said. "This is the start of a new adventure."

"I am smiling," I recall saying. But in that film I do not look like a child about to embark on an exciting new adventure. I look like a child about to be sick.

My father lowered the camera. "What do you say we celebrate and have dinner at Santoro's tonight?"

"I pulled out a pot roast from the freezer," my mother said.

"We'll eat it tomorrow night. Samuel, what do you say?"

Ordinarily the anticipation of eating Santoro's pizza would have sent my spirits soaring, but this morning the thought of liquefied cheese and greasy pepperoni only made me queasier. "I don't care," I said, considering it the safest response.

"Well, I know I care," my father said. "Santoro's it is."

I pushed Cheerios around a bowl until it was time for my father to leave for work. He embraced me in a long hug. "I love you, son," he said and quickly turned to leave, though not before I saw a tear run down his cheek.

My mother did her best to calm me with details, explaining that OLM had two first-grade classrooms, 1A and 1B, each with twenty-three students, though I now would make twenty-four in class 1B. "An even two dozen," she said. "That has to be lucky."

I failed to see why.

"Father Brogan said you'll be in 1B. That's Sister Kathleen's classroom. I hear she is a very good teacher. Finish up, Sam. We don't want to be late your first day."

14

As my mother drove down Cortez Avenue and parked on the street below the red steps leading up to the gated entrance, I noticed mothers and schoolchildren in their uniforms standing on the sidewalk. I didn't know if this was usual or not, this being my first day. Then I noticed Dan standing alongside them and another man holding a large camera on his shoulder. A third man held a notebook and pen. I had the sense this was definitely not normal.

"Let's go, Samuel," my mother said, opening her car door. "Punctuality is a sign of respect for your teacher."

When I stepped from the car, I felt the eyes of every mother and every kid staring at me. Mothers held their children's hands as if to prevent them from venturing too close to a stray dog. The man with the camera was pointing it in my direction, and Dan looked to be directing him where to film. I was grateful when the kids began to climb the stairs until I looked up and saw Sister Beatrice in her black habit unlocking and opening the gate. My mother walked me up the steps with the other students, and that was the picture I would later find in her scrapbook, cut from the front page of the local newspaper, along with a short article on my admittance. Whether my ascent up those steps also aired on the evening news, I do not know, though I assume there was some follow-up story. We never again watched television in the kitchen.

Sister Beatrice stood inside the gates, as rigid as the white stone statue of the Blessed Mother in the courtyard behind her.

My mother nodded. "Sister."

Sister Beatrice set her gaze upon me. "Samuel, welcome to Our Lady of Mercy," she said. "You will be in Sister Kathleen's classroom." She pointed to her right. When my mother attempted to step forward, Sister Beatrice slid into her path. "I'm sorry, Mrs. Hill. No adults are allowed past these gates without first obtaining a visitor's pass from the office. It's procedure . . . to protect the children. I'm sure you understand."

My mother smiled in that way I'd seen before, closed lips, no visible teeth. Then she bent and arranged my shirt collar. "You have a good first day, Samuel, and mind Sister Kathleen. I'll be here at three o'clock sharp to pick you up." She straightened, and the two women again locked gazes. "I'm certain you will have the best first day of any child who has ever attended this school."

I watched my mother descend the steps just as an ear-piercing bell clattered in the courtyard. The students scattered and disappeared into their classrooms. Sister Beatrice walked off. When she looked back, I took that as my cue to follow. Sister Beatrice never broke stride, and she did not otherwise acknowledge me, but I heard her loud and clear above the fading din of the bell. "Arrogance is a sin, Mr. Hill. God punishes the arrogant. Humility will be taught, and it will be a hard lesson learned."

15

I spent much of that first day in dread of the cruelty and mistreatment that was to come, but not a single student even approached me. I caught just about every kid in my class staring at me at one point or another throughout the day, but not one said a word to me. Since I did not raise my hand to answer a question, I also did not speak. Sister Kathleen seemed content to leave me be.

At recess and at lunch I ate while sitting alone on the bloodred bleachers that separated the upper playground from the lower playground, which was where the older students played. Mothers called "lunch ladies" dutifully watched over us to prevent any "horseplay." They also would not allow us to leave those bleachers until they had inspected our lunch boxes to ensure we did not waste food that could otherwise feed the starving children in Africa. I would have been content to remain on my bleacher the entire lunch period, but there was apparently a rule against sitting, because a lunch lady instructed me to "go get some exercise."

I wandered the playground aimlessly. When I did muster the courage to approach my classmates playing kickball or wall ball, they either treated me as if I were invisible or took the ball and ran to another area of the playground. Once or twice I heard a whisper behind me. "Devil Boy."

The entire week went pretty much the same as that first day, which was problematic, because each night at dinner I was expected to provide my parents a detailed accounting of my day—something, I could tell, they awaited with great anticipation. Not wanting to disappoint, I did what any six-year-old would have done. I lied.

"I made another friend," I said Friday evening when my father asked how the day had gone.

"Another one?" My father lowered his fork. "My word, but you're popular."

"They all want me to be on their kickball team," I said. "They had a big fight about it."

"I hope not a fistfight," my mother said, passing a bowl of peas.

"No, just some yelling."

"I don't doubt it, with all those home runs you've been kicking. Maddy, we might have ourselves a soccer star."

"I don't know," I said, concerned I'd possibly overdone it.

I convinced myself these were not real lies—not the kind that caused a person to burn in hell, anyway. These fit squarely in the category of lies my mother had once explained were okay if they were intended to avoid hurting a person's feelings. I knew how badly my mother and father wanted me to fit in, and the smiles that lit up their faces while sitting at that table were worth the daily pain of my isolation. I thought it the perfect plan.

"You'll have to invite some of your friends over after school to play," my mother said, which nearly caused me to choke on a piece of steak.

"But my word, where will we fit them all?" my father asked. "We've created a regular Bobby Kennedy. Do they have student government? Maybe you could run for class president."

"I don't know," I said. "I think you have to be older before they let you do that stuff."

"Any problems?" my mother would ask.

"No," I'd quickly say.

My father's concern that others would be cruel seemed as far from reality as the world I created each night at our dinner table.

All of that would soon change, however.

16

The following Monday, I took what had become my customary spot on a bleacher near a cinderblock wall that provided a wedge of shade in which I tried to hide from the lunch ladies. I had no trouble getting this spot. As I ascended the bleachers, the other students would either move to another bleacher or slide away. The void expanded as each student quickly ate, eager to depart for their all-important exercise.

Not me. In just five days, I had mastered the art of eating so slowly I could take up an entire thirty-minute lunch period, much to the annoyance of the lunch ladies—who, I'd come to learn, some of the older kids called lunch Nazis. The longer I took to eat, the longer I could remain on the bleachers. I doubt that I fully understood my predicament at six years of age, but I had a strong sense that I was different, and not in the extraordinary way my mother wanted me to believe.

I started by eating the crust of my Wonder Bread sandwich in a circular fashion. I worked my way inward to the cheese and mayonnaise while periodically sipping milk from the small carton we purchased for five cents a day. After eating my sandwich, I moved on to the apple slices, eating the skin first before crunching the remainder. When the apples were consumed, I opened the plastic wrap to my Hostess Twinkie and commenced to eat the sponge-like golden cake as one would eat the kernels from an ear of corn, left to right and back again. My goal was to leave the tube of vanilla cream for last.

The beginning of the second week, as I proceeded with this delicate operation, I noticed a dark-skinned boy sitting two bleachers below staring up at me with a furrowed brow. Though school had started a week earlier, I recognized immediately that this was his first day. He was the only black kid in the entire school. Sister Kathleen had introduced him that morning as Ernie Cantwell, though he was placed in Sister Reagan's class to even out the number of students in each class.

I had never seen a black person, except on television, and to my knowledge he was not just the only black child in OLM school; he was the only black child in Burlingame, though that was likely an observation based on the limited breadth of my world at that age. Ernie had finished his lunch and sat holding his brown paper sack by the neck. When I glanced at him, he blew into the bag and smashed it with a loud *pop!* Fortunately, the lunch ladies were engaged in conversation and didn't stop to admonish him or to notice me.

Ernie climbed the bleachers and sat on my row. "Do you always eat it that way?"

I nodded.

He slid closer. "Why?"

I shrugged.

He sat beside me, focused on the Twinkie. "I peel the chocolate from the top of my cupcake," he said. "But I eat the cake with the cream."

I didn't answer, hoping he would leave.

"What's the matter with your eyes?" he asked. I turned my head. He came around the other side. "They're red."

"No duh."

"I've never seen anyone with red eyes before."

"So, I've never seen anyone with black skin before."

He shrugged. "Most of the kids where I come from have black skin . . . and brown eyes."

I had nearly finished removing the cake exterior. "Where do you come from?"

"Detroit. It's really far away, like another country. My father made cars there, but now he mostly works in the garage."

"We had to take our car to a garage when it broke."

"No. He works in *our* garage. He's building something."

"My dad gives people drugs," I said.

"We had a lot of those in Detroit; that's why we moved. I'm Ernie."

"I'm Sam."

"You sure take a long time to eat a Twinkie. You want to go play?"

The invitation shocked me. Eager to accept, I turned the vanilla tube, about to shove it in my mouth, when a red orb entered my peripheral vision and hit me flush in the face. The vanilla tube exploded. The force of the blow knocked me backward, and my head smacked the bleacher behind me with a sickening, dull thud. When I managed to sit up, dazed, the side of my face felt as though it had burst into flames.

"Look! Devil Boy has a red face to go with his red eyes."

"Hey, it's Sam *Hell!*"

Of the three boys climbing the bleachers, the one in the middle was by far the biggest. I did not know David Bateman, but I knew *of* him. I'd heard a couple of students say he'd been held back. Bateman stood a good head taller than the two boys accompanying him, and each towered over me.

"Devil Boy and Black Boy," Bateman said. "What are you doing with my ball, darkie? Give it here."

That's when I realized Ernie held a soccer-size rubber ball. Ernie would later recount how the ball had ricocheted off my face, hit the bench one level below, and bounced straight up. He plucked it from the air, a real feat given that the splatter of cream had also hit him.

"What, are you deaf or just stupid?"

Ernie's eyes narrowed. He did not look the least bit scared.

"I don't think this boy had enough to eat for lunch," Bateman said. "I think he wants a knuckle sandwich." He balled his fist. "You want a knuckle sandwich, darkie?"

Ernie looked to me.

"Last chance. Give it here."

Ernie held up the ball. "You want this ball?"

"No, the other ball, stupid."

"You threw it away."

"I threw it at Devil Boy. It's mine. Give it back."

Ernie shook his head. My heart pounded.

"Count of three . . . nigger."

Ernie stared.

"One . . . two . . ."

Ernie quickly leaped off the bleachers to the asphalt playground, leaving David Bateman and his two friends flat-footed. "Get him," Bateman yelled, but that would be easier said than done. Ernie moved with the fluidity of a bird in a flock, never in the same direction long. When one boy approached, he swerved; when another appeared, he dodged, ducked, or dived, each time with a burst of speed. Initially he managed to do this while deftly avoiding other students playing foursquare and hopscotch, but soon the entire playground had stopped playing and taken notice.

"Get on the other side," Bateman yelled. "Corner him."

They came close to catching Ernie once or twice, but then he would twist and weave and be gone, leaving all three bent over and gasping for air. When they had seemingly given up, Ernie jumped onto the top bleacher, tossed the ball in the air, and kicked it higher and farther than I had ever seen anyone kick a ball.

The students gasped.

"Told you they didn't want it," Ernie said, smiling down at me.

"Look out!" I yelled, but my warning came too late. David Bateman had come up behind Ernie like a raging bull. He struck Ernie in the kidneys with a fist, causing him to double over in pain. Bateman's face was a mask of anger and fury as he pulled back his fist a second time, about to deliver a lethal uppercut I was sure would remove Ernie's head. That's when something inside me snapped. I leaped from the top bleacher onto Bateman's back, causing him to stumble off balance, though he ultimately remained upright. Almost immediately I realized both the insanity of my decision and my shortsightedness; there was seemingly no way to get off without encountering a raging bull. Terrified, I gripped Bateman about the neck, holding on for dear life as he twisted and turned, arms flailing to get at me. Students circled us, chanting, "Fight! Fight! Fight!"

It wasn't much of a fight, and it was my intent to keep it that way. David Bateman sank to his knees and pitched forward. I heard him gagging and wheezing but still did not comprehend that I was strangling him. Just as quickly as the chanting had started, it stopped, and the students scattered as if having heard a silent bell.

Sister Beatrice peered down at me with the same black-eyed, menacing glare of the crow in my nightmare just before its sharp beak pecked at me.

17

Sister Beatrice pinched my ear in a vise grip, and I instantly released my choke hold on David Bateman. She maintained pressure as she dragged me across the playground to her office, so focused on her retribution she did not even bother to check David Bateman's condition. The last I saw of him, he lay rolling on the ground, gasping.

Sister Beatrice dropped me in a chair outside her office and spoke to one of the women behind the counter. "I believe you know Mrs. Hill's telephone number. See to it she is here immediately."

My mother did not work outside the home (I don't recall any of my fellow students' mothers having jobs, except Ernie's mom). So my mother was at home to receive the phone call about my "escapade." It seemed like I sat for hours in that chair, my ear red and throbbing, the side of my face on fire, and my head aching where I'd smacked it against the bench. Finally, my mother entered the office. She was beet red in the face and, for her, unkempt in blue jeans and a blouse. She hadn't fixed her hair or put on makeup.

"What is all over your face and hair?" she asked upon seeing me.

I had forgotten about the exploding Hostess. I reached up and pulled a slightly hardened glob of cream from a strand of hair. "Twinkie," I said.

She grabbed me by the chin and turned my head. "Your face is swollen and red, and your ear looks like someone lit it on fire."

One of the women behind the counter spoke. "Mrs. Hill? Sister Beatrice would like to see you and Samuel now."

My mother spun and proceeded to the closed door, neither knocking nor waiting for an invitation to enter. I reluctantly followed. Sister Beatrice nodded to the two familiar chairs across from her desk. My mother's posture was even more erect. She sat on the edge of her seat cushion, legs crossed and folded beneath her chair.

"This is exactly the type of thing I was concerned about," Sister Beatrice said.

"What exactly happened?" my mother asked, sounding calm.

"Your son," Sister Beatrice said, "nearly strangled another student. He's being treated in the health room this very moment."

My mother looked down at me. "Samuel, is this true?"

I nodded.

"What in heaven possessed you?" she asked.

But before I could speak, Sister Beatrice answered. "I don't believe heaven had anything to do with this, Mrs. Hill."

My mother shot her a look. "What does that mean?"

"It means your son is suspended, Mrs. Hill. It means I intend to take this matter up with Father Brogan and the parish board." Her crooked finger took aim at me. "It means that my judgment about this situation was correct."

"Did you even bother to ask Samuel what happened?"

"I saw what happened," she said. "Your son assaulted another student. I watched it with my own eyes."

"He has Twinkie in his hair and the side of his face has a red welt on it." She gripped my chin and snapped my head to the side. "How did that happen?"

"Irrelevant to the issue at hand—fighting is grounds for expulsion."

"I would like to give Samuel a chance to defend himself."

"You can do that at home; I have a school to run and four hundred other children to consider."

"You're going to suspend him without any investigation?"

"As I mentioned during our introduction, Mrs. Hill, I alone have the authority to run this school, and I alone have the authority to decide upon the appropriate punishment. And let me assure you, should there be any inquiries from your friends in the press, this time I will not hesitate to explain, in detail, what occurred here."

"How long is his suspension?"

"That remains to be determined. It is my opinion that you never should have enrolled him in the first place."

"You're expelling him?"

A voice emanated from a black box on the corner of the desk. "Sister Beatrice, Mrs. Bateman is—"

If the woman finished her sentence I did not hear her. A shrill squawk burst through the intercom, though none of us had any trouble hearing the voice through the closed door. "I demand to see her!"

When I turned, the woman filled the door frame, wearing a sleeveless navy-blue shirt that revealed flabby biceps as big around as one of my mother's legs. Wide-eyed and bristling, she dragged David Bateman by the wrist into the office and commenced to stutter and cluck like the giant rooster from the Bugs Bunny cartoons I watched on Saturday mornings, Foghorn Leghorn. "Look . . . look . . . look at my son's throat." She yanked David's head back by his hair to show Sister Beatrice a red scratch. Then, spotting me behind my mother, she said, "Is that the little troublemaker who attacked my David?"

My mother, who had stood from her chair, seemed to grow two inches, but she didn't even reach Mrs. Bateman's chin. "Don't you dare call my son a troublemaker."

"Look at my son's throat." She yanked David forward like a rag doll. "He has scratches."

My mother, not to be outdone, pulled me out from behind her. "And look at my son's face." She turned my head to display the red welt. "Look at his hair and clothes."

"Your son choked my son."

"Yes, he did," Sister Beatrice said. "I saw it."

David Bateman's mother said, "Fighting is grounds for expulsion."

"My son has not had a chance to defend himself," my mother countered.

"I expect that it be enforced," Bateman's mother said. "And I'm sure my fellow members of the parish board will agree. You will recall that I was dead set against this . . . this boy being allowed admittance. And I think we need no further evidence that my intuition was one hundred percent accurate."

"I intend to take the matter up with Father Brogan and the board," Sister Beatrice said. "I can assure you, Mrs. Bateman, violence will not be tolerated."

"You haven't even given Samuel the chance to defend himself," my mother repeated. "Do you think he did this to himself?"

"That will be a matter for the board to decide. Your son admitted choking another student."

"But you never asked him why."

"Why is irrelevant. Good day, Mrs. Hill."

"This is not like him."

"I said good day, Mrs. Hill."

As my mother turned to retrieve her handbag, a knock drew our attention. Sister Kathleen stood at the office door.

"Why are you not in class, Sister Kathleen?" Sister Beatrice asked.

"I've asked Sister Reagan to watch my class for the moment."

"Sister Reagan has her own class and students to care for."

"Yes, Sister, but I thought it important you hear what happened on the playground."

"I don't need to hear what happened, Sister. I saw it with my own two eyes."

"Begging your pardon, Sister, but I don't think you saw *everything* that happened."

"I saw enough, Sister."

"I believe there are extenuating circumstances," Sister Kathleen persisted.

"I am not about to get into a debate between two first-grade boys about who started what. I have no doubt Mr. Hill would have quite the story to tell, were I to allow him to do so."

"You're implying my son would lie?" my mother asked. "Samuel does not lie."

"Nor does he fight or cause disturbances, I presume?" Mrs. Bateman said.

"He does not," Sister Kathleen said, regaining everyone's attention.

Sister Beatrice said, "The circumstances would suggest otherwise."

"Sam has been a model student in my classroom; he keeps to himself and does not bother any of the other students. In fact, he rarely speaks."

This revelation caused my mother to glance down at me.

"Be that as it may," Sister Beatrice said with a smoldering glare, "we're not talking about your classroom."

"We're certainly not," Mrs. Bateman said.

"We're talking about the playground. Were you on the playground, Sister Kathleen?" Sister Beatrice asked.

"Not at the time, Sister."

Mrs. Bateman waved a hand in the air. "So, she couldn't possibly have seen what happened."

"I did not."

Mrs. Bateman looked to Sister Beatrice. "I think that just about—"

"But there is someone who was on the playground and did see what happened."

Without prompting, Sister Kathleen motioned to whoever waited in the hall. I was astonished to see Ernie Cantwell step forward, his hair still splattered with bits of white Twinkie cream. "This is Ernie Cantwell," Sister Kathleen said.

"I saw the whole thing," Ernie said. He pointed at Bateman. "That kid started it. Sam was trying to keep him from killing me."

Mrs. Bateman bristled. "Not likely. These boys are clearly friends and are ganging up on my David."

Sister Kathleen's voice remained even. "Also not likely. This is Ernie's first day at school. He arrived late from Detroit. He and Sam have never met before today."

"I think we should end this discussion now," Sister Beatrice said.

"I think we should hear what Ernie has to say," my mother said. "Ernie, can you tell us how this started?"

"Sam was eating his Twinkie, and that kid threw the ball and hit him in the face."

"Clearly an accident," Mrs. Bateman said.

"No, it wasn't," Ernie said. "He said he did it on purpose. He said he did it so 'the devil boy could have a red face to go with his red eyes.'"

Ernie recounted every detail of the confrontation—the red ball smacking the side of my face and exploding the Twinkie, David Bateman's less than brilliant admission that it had been no accident, the kidney punch that dropped Ernie from the bleachers, and the second punch Bateman had been prepared to throw had I not hurled myself onto his back. Sister Beatrice stood throughout the recounting with the pinched face of someone who had just detected an awful smell. The smell was about to get a whole lot worse.

"He called me a darkie," Ernie said.

Sister Beatrice flinched. A palpable silence filled the room and Ernie seemed to use it for dramatic effect.

"And then he called me a nigger."

Sister Beatrice's eyes widened. Mrs. Bateman's head began to swivel. "I . . . I . . . I . . . I have no . . . no . . . no idea where he could have heard such a word. We would never use such a word in our house. Never. It's the television. They hear it on the television." She yanked David forward by his wrist. "Did you call that boy a nigger?"

"No," he wailed.

She shook him, the flab of her arm jiggling. "Did you call that boy a nigger?"

Each time she said the word, it cut through the room like a hot knife. She said it with such ease, there was little doubt where David had heard it.

"You're hurting me."

"What have I told you about using that word?"

"Dad says it," Bateman cried.

Mrs. Bateman flushed. "Never," she said to the rest of us. Then, "What have I told you about lying?" And with that Mrs. Bateman swatted David across the back of the head. The force certainly would have caused him to pitch over had she not also maintained her grip on his wrist.

"I didn't," he shouted, his face beet red, tears

streaming down his cheeks. "Don't hit me again."

Mrs. Bateman raised her hand. "Did you call that boy a nigger?"

"Yes. Okay. Okay. I threw the ball and I called him the devil boy."

His mother shook him again, flab jiggling. "And . . ."

"And—and I called him a nigger."

Mrs. Bateman spun, tugging her son from the office by his arm. Sister Kathleen and Ernie barely had time to remove themselves from her path through the doorway. We heard David Bateman's wails even after the outer door to the administration office shut. The aftermath felt like the passing of a storm, the room silent and still. Sister Beatrice's eyes focused on the top of her desk.

Sister Kathleen's gentle voice broke the silence. "Sam, please show Ernie to the lavatory, and the two of you get cleaned up and return to class, straight away."

I looked to my mother, who silently nodded her permission. Sister Beatrice cleared her throat as if about to speak, but my mother gave her the same withering look she directed at me if I "acted up" in church. Whatever words Sister Beatrice had been prepared to speak, my mother's look forced her to swallow them.

18

I stood on my toes to wash my hands at the white porcelain sink. Ernie stood at the sink beside me. The left side of my face remained ruby red. I tugged at tufts of hair stiff with dried Twinkie cream and used water and a brown paper towel to try to scrub the cream out, but I was only partially successful. Pointed strands of hair stuck out from my head. Just what the devil boy needed, horns.

"How'd you learn to run like that?" I asked.

Ernie shrugged. "Where'd you learn to wrestle like that?"

His question left me momentarily confused, not having equated my clinging to David Bateman's back to wrestling. "I don't know," I said.

As we made our way from the bathroom down the corridor toward our classrooms, Ernie asked, "Do you want to be friends?"

I almost didn't respond, too surprised at the invitation. Quickly recovering I said, "Sure." I watched Ernie run down the corridor to his classroom. When Ernie pulled open the door, a loud cheer erupted and then just as quickly silenced. I could only imagine that Sister Reagan had squelched the applause. As I approached my classroom, I initially hoped for the same reception. I was, after all, the kid who had beaten up

David Bateman. But as I reached the mahogany door, I became filled with a sense of dread—if the other kids had been afraid of me because of the color of my eyes, what were they now to think of me, the whirling dervish who had attacked not just another student but the monster himself? I was certain they would be downright terrified of me, considering me some sort of crazed lunatic or wild animal. I expected them to shriek in horror and recoil at the sight of me. But when I opened the door, no sound greeted me as I stepped through. My days of anonymity might have been over, but not my isolation.

19

My parents did not discuss the incident at dinner, the topic being one my mother would consider "unsettling" to our digestion. Instead they discussed my father's workday and how business at the pharmacy continued to pick up. As dinner wore on, without discussion of my "escapade," my feeling of being seated on a live grenade slowly gave way, and I sensed my parents had already spoken of the incident and didn't care to discuss it again in front of me. While this was much easier on my digestive tract, it did little to assuage my curiosity.

After dinner, we retired to the living room, where my mother began her rosary, my father snapped open his newspaper, and I diligently pretended to be reading the sixth book in the Hardy Boys series, *The Shore Road Mystery*. When it again became apparent that my parents were not about to discuss the subject of the schoolyard fight in my presence, I announced that I was tired and even faked a yawn. Then I quickly trudged up the stairs and slid beneath my bed to listen through the grate.

"She was going to expel him?" My father's voice sounded flat and disbelieving. "Looks like you made an enemy for you and for Samuel.

She's looking for any excuse to get even with you for going to that television news reporter."

"If it wasn't for that Ernie boy standing up for Samuel, she would have succeeded. Sister Kathleen said they moved from Detroit. The father worked at one of the car factories."

"Well, he arrived just in time." I heard the newspaper ruffle. "What about Sam's other friends? Why didn't any of them stick up for him?"

My mother softened her tone enough that I had to press my ear closer to the grate. "I didn't get the chance to tell you this afternoon. I spoke to Sister Kathleen about something she said in the meeting, that Sam had never spoken in class."

"Not spoken? I was under the impression he never shut up."

"Not a word," she said. "And he doesn't have any friends, except for maybe this Ernie boy."

"What about all the friends he talks about at dinner, Dillon and Barry?"

"There is no Dillon or Barry in his class."

"He made them up?"

"And all of his accolades on the playground, apparently."

"He made them up," my father said.

My mother's next words caught in her throat. "Sister Kathleen said he sits alone on the bleachers at recess and lunch until the bell rings."

"What was her take on the situation?" my father asked.

"Well, she's certainly sympathetic, but . . ."

"But what?"

"Well, doesn't it seem odd that she would bring Ernie with her to the office to clear up what happened on the playground?"

"Odd? How?"

"I don't know. There's something more to this, Max. I felt as though Sister Kathleen wanted to tell me something to explain the situation, but couldn't. She seemed to know more than she was letting on."

"What about this boy who started the fight?"

"David Bateman. He's twice as big as the other boys. But I doubt he'll be expelled. His mother sits on the parish board. And she is quite the piece of work."

"Perhaps I should give his father a call."

"If he's anything like the mother, I wouldn't bother."

My father hesitated. "Do you think this boy is capable of more violence? Is Sam in any danger?"

Up until that moment, I hadn't considered that possibility, but now that I did, David Bateman did not strike me as the kind of kid to let bygones be bygones, and I wasn't likely to surprise him a second time. In a fair fight, he would surely pummel me. I felt sick to my stomach and started to slide out from under the bed.

"Sister Kathleen said she initially thought Sam might be slow."

"Slow?" my father asked.

I stopped my retreat. I'd heard my mother use that word once to describe a retarded boy.

"Well, what else would she think if he hadn't said a word in class for a week?"

"Samuel is not slow," my father said.

"Of course not," my mother said. "I have something else to show you, something Sister Kathleen gave to me."

Another extended pause followed. I heard my mother's footsteps grow faint, then become more pronounced, indicating she had left the room to retrieve something and returned.

"What's this?" my father asked.

"They gave each student a test at the beginning of the year to get a sense of where the students are in each subject."

I remembered the test. I'd finished it early, and Sister Kathleen told me to put my head on the desk and take a nap while the other students completed it.

"So, what do these numbers mean? Ninety-six, ninety-eight, ninety-seven."

"Samuel tested off the charts in every subject," my mother said. "Sam is not slow, Max. He's gifted."

20

The next morning, my mother drove me to school with the top down on the Falcon. She pulled to the curb and started to get out, but I stopped her. "I can walk in by myself," I said, having noticed that my classmates' mothers did not walk them up the steps after the first day.

"Are you still capable of kissing your mother goodbye?" she asked.

I pecked her cheek and shouted my goodbye as I slid from the seat.

"Samuel," my mother said. I turned back. My mother smiled, but it had a sad quality to it. Then she brightened. "Have a good day, son," she said.

At that precise moment Ernie Cantwell shut the door to an old Volkswagen Beetle and ran down the block toward me.

"Cool car," Ernie said.

"My dad built it," I said, though that was not entirely accurate.

The Falcon was a used car. When my father brought it home, my mother said it looked "worse for the wear" with rust stains on the hood and bumpers. She wasn't thrilled to have it sitting in the driveway for the neighbors to see, though she definitely liked that it was a convertible and metallic blue—her favorite color. She called it "a muscle car." My sense was my father hadn't really bought the car for my mother, but he'd said so hoping she would decline it in favor of the Plymouth station wagon. His mistake was taking us out for a drive with the top down. I knew from my mother's beaming smile that she had made her choice. My dad drove the Plymouth to work, though my mother allowed him to drive the Falcon on Saturdays.

The bell sounded as Ernie and I raced up the steps, lunch boxes jiggling. I said goodbye to Ernie in the courtyard and pivoted toward my classroom, only to hit what felt like the stucco wall. The jolt knocked my lunch box from my hand, the top sprang open, and my lunch scattered on the ground. David Bateman towered above me, smacking a fist against his palm. Then he lifted his foot and stepped on my peanut butter and jelly sandwich before walking away.

PART TWO

The Bike Accident

1

1989
Burlingame, California

Dr. Fukomara's eyes widened at the sight of me sitting on the examination table fully dressed and clearly having decided against the vasectomy.

"I know this is an inconvenience, and I'm happy to pay for a clinical visit," I said. As an ophthalmologist, I knew I had taken a spot he could have filled with another patient. Money from his pocket.

"Absolutely not," he said. "Professional courtesy."

"I'm sorry I—"

He waved off my apology. "You have nothing to be sorry for; you've made the right decision."

"I have?"

"This is *your* decision, which means it is absolutely the right decision. There's no rush. Think it over." He raised his two fingers, imitating a pair of scissors. "Dr. Snip It will still be here." He laughed and patted my shoulder as he departed.

It had been my decision. Eva remained somewhere high above the United States, headed to Boston, I believe. As an airplane pilot, Eva was usually high above someplace. When we first started dating, I kept a closer tab on her schedule, but as time passed I'd paid less attention. The cockpit was her office; it just happened to be an office that could be in one location in the morning and three thousand miles across the United States in the afternoon. In our first few months together, I would fly to meet her for a weekend in Boston or New York, or she would surprise me at my home late at night, sliding beneath the covers and pressing up against me, but the frequency of those getaways and late-night surprises had, with time, diminished. The demands of my own practice had also increased. When Eva arrived home late, she usually stayed in the guest bedroom so she wouldn't disturb me.

As I drove north on the El Camino Real, I wondered if Eva would be as understanding as Dr. Snip It. She expected to come home to a man no longer able to fertilize her eggs, at least not after shooting off the cannon another twenty-five times—the number of ejaculations Dr. Fukomara said would be necessary to expunge the billion or so sperm still actively on the hunt.

"Still locked and loaded. That's the good part," he'd said during the consult. "Lots of sex."

When Eva and I first started dating, we could have knocked out that number in a month. I had joked before I dropped her at the airport the other morning that it might take us six months to clear the chamber. She didn't laugh. She kissed me lightly and got out of the car.

"I'll call you if I don't get in too late," she'd said.

I parked in one of three reserved parking spaces at the back of my building on Broadway Avenue and took the rear staircase to my offices on the second floor. When my father had his stroke, my mother refused to sell his pharmacy practice or the building he had purchased with it. Money was never a factor in my mother's decisions, and it had not been her reason to keep both the practice and the building.

"Your father put his blood, sweat, and tears into that pharmacy," she'd said.

So, years later, when my business partner and best friend, Mickie, and I were looking to open an ophthalmology practice together, I purchased the building and kept Broadway Pharmacy as the ground-floor tenant. My mother had wanted to give me the building as an early inheritance, but I had refused her generosity.

"You're going to get it when I die anyway," she'd said when we broached the subject one Sunday night over dinner, something I tried to do every week, usually on a night when Eva was traveling.

"Yes, but that won't be for decades, and you might need the money to pay for your own retirement care," I'd said. "Otherwise I'll have to put you out on the street with a 'For Sale' sign around your neck."

"Decades? I hope not. I'll throw myself in front of a bus before I allow myself to see ninety."

"I might push you in front of that bus if you remain this cantankerous."

"Don't be insolent, Samuel." She cleared my plate, signaling that I had finished eating. "Fine. Make me a fair offer."

"I'll call Jerry Conman in the morning," I'd said, referring to my high school classmate who had, despite his unfortunate last name, carved a pretty good career in commercial real estate. Conman and I met for beers the following week at Behrman's Irish Pub on Broadway, and he told me over a Guinness what I had already suspected. "Your father's pharmacy has very little goodwill as an ongoing business. It's losing customers to the chain drugstores. You'd be better off selling it."

My father had run a successful practice for nearly two decades on the strength of his personality. He had an uncanny ability—a gift, really—to remember everyone's first name and something about their lives. Going to Broadway Pharmacy was not so much an errand as an occasion. Frank, the pharmacist I had hired after my father's stroke, lacked the same charisma. Allegiance had its price, and the more the chain drugstores discounted their prices, the higher the number of regulars who defected.

"At best," Conman told me, "Frank could sell the store's files and stock to one of the chain drugstores, and you could rent the space to a more lucrative concern, like a hair salon. Otherwise it will be a slow, expensive death."

Honoring my mother's wishes, I came up with an alternative plan, which was to open my ophthalmology practice in the five rooms above the store that had served as an apartment. Taking out a small business loan to remodel and open my own business was a risky financial venture, and I could have existed just fine paying my dues in an established practice, but Mickie, who would become my business partner, did not have the temperament to be anyone's minion, and I could not bear the thought of my mother having to sell something so dear to her. We paid a hefty price, all financed through a bank loan at an outrageous interest rate. I was my own boss and poorer for it. Go figure.

After I opened Burlingame Ophthalmology and Vision Center, Broadway Pharmacy's prescriptions doubled in a month, and it sold more reading glasses and eye-care products than any drugstore in the area, once again proving that old real estate adage—location, location, location.

"Dr. Hill? I wasn't expecting you back until Monday," my receptionist, Kathy, said as I entered the clinic. I had told my staff I was spending the weekend at Lake Tahoe, where I owned a small cabin.

"Change of plans," I said. "The cabin is rented for the weekend."

"That's too bad."

I noticed a tall, heavyset woman and a young girl sitting in the lobby and smiled at them before continuing down the hall, barely avoiding Mickie, who motored from her office in the direction of one of the treatment rooms.

"Whoa! What are you doing here?" She did not sound happy to see me. Mickie had been in a funk, which was unlike her.

"Couldn't get the cabin. The rental agency rented it out this weekend."

She grunted in disgust. "Couldn't the Con Man have told you that before you made the plans?"

Jerry Conman also managed my cabin in Tahoe. I'd made the mistake of setting him up with Mickie. When he squeezed her thigh under the table at a five-star restaurant in San Francisco, she'd nearly broken his finger. I told him to consider himself fortunate she hadn't stabbed him in the eye with her fork.

"My fault," I said. "I told Jerry to rent the cabin as much as possible."

She crossed her arms. "How is that asshole?"

"He still loves you and wants you to bear his children."

"I'd rather pull my uterus out through my nostrils with a coat hanger."

"Nice, Mick."

I had not intended on being in the office, so I had not scheduled consults for the afternoon, but since Eva would be in Boston for the evening, I offered my services. "How many patients do you have left?"

"Two, but one is an emergency consult. The mother, Trina Crouch, asked for you, actually, but since we thought you were gone, I scheduled her."

"What's the emergency?"

Mickie handed me one of the two files. "Seven-year-old girl is going blind in one eye." I flipped the pages. "She began having trouble reading the blackboard in school three weeks ago after a bike accident," Mickie said. "The mother had her eyes checked. She's lost a significant portion of vision in her left eye. No neurological deficit noted. The visual acuity was light perception with poor light projection on both eyes. No other neurological deficits resulting from a head trauma."

I read another note in the file. The girl had been with her father at the time of the accident. "Divorced?"

"Who isn't? The mother and daughter are in the lobby."

"I'll take it."

"You're a god. I can make my five-thirty yoga

class." Mickie's slim and toned figure reflected the metabolism of a rabbit and her twice-a-day workout regimen—she swam laps in the morning and did hot yoga at night.

"I'm glad I can help keep you in top physical condition."

"Not as glad as my date is going to be."

"The golf pro?"

"Please, he was so last week."

"I thought you liked him."

"I did, until he brought his short game to bed with him."

"No driver?"

"No irons at all."

"Well, thank goodness you'll always have hot yoga to burn off energy."

"Laugh all you want, but you won't get a better workout, especially if you keep dating your roommate."

"Subtle," I said.

In our eighteen-year friendship, I'd never known Mickie to have a steady boyfriend, which she said was too much bother. She kept three pit bulls for companionship and maintained a stable of male admirers and wannabe boyfriends whom I assumed she called on to satisfy her inner urges. In her spare time she criticized my love life.

Mickie looked about to say something more—Mickie always had something more to say—but I think making her hot yoga class took precedence.

She shrugged and departed. She'd never liked Eva, but she had refrained from ever telling me why. Instead she resorted to snide comments, such as referring to Eva as my roommate, as in, "So, where's the roommate this weekend?" or "So, when's the last time you and the roommate did it?"

Since my nurse had left for the day, I greeted Trina Crouch in the lobby. From her red and swollen eyes, she looked to have been crying, or she had terrible allergies. When she stood she nearly matched me in height, perhaps a shade over six feet. She was sturdy, which my mother had taught me was the polite word to describe someone overweight. Dirty-blonde hair pulled back in a tight ponytail accentuated a broad forehead.

"They said you wouldn't be here," she said.

"I had some personal plans change this afternoon." I looked to the little girl and extended my hand. She didn't accept it. I crouched. "And you must be Daniela. Daniela, I'm Dr. Sam." I'd worn brown contacts for years. Red eyes had a way of upsetting the children. "We're going to have a look at your eyes today. Is that okay with you?"

She was tall like her mother, with the same color hair and worried expression, but she was thin—too thin, it seemed—and skittish. She also looked familiar, but I could not place her or her mother. "Have we met?" I asked her mother.

"I don't think so," Trina Crouch said.

In my consult room, I asked Daniela to sit up on the table. Her mother stood beside her. I sat on a swivel chair and continued to review the file and to ask questions.

"It started about three weeks ago," Trina Crouch said. "She hit her head."

"How bad was the bike accident?"

"Her father didn't see it; he came out and found her lying on the sidewalk. He lives at the bottom of a pretty steep hill. He thinks she rode to the top and lost control coming down, that she went over the handlebars and hit her forehead."

"How long was she in the hospital?"

"Just a couple of hours for observation."

I reviewed the emergency room and attending physicians' reports and was surprised at the lack of other significant injuries save for a skinned knee. I also discovered that Daniela did not share her mother's last name. I realized where I had seen that round face and those blunt features. Daniela had her father's last name, one with which I was quite familiar, though I had not spoken it in many years.

Bateman.

2

Despite his threat of a knuckle sandwich, David Bateman either had the good sense, or had been forewarned, to leave me alone, at least in appearance. During the day Bateman was in the other classroom, and on the playground I had the nuns and lunch ladies close by. But whenever I grew comfortable, or started to believe Bateman had forgotten our encounter and his promise of retribution, he'd surface with a swift reminder, a balled fist silently smacking the palm of his hand to indicate a knuckle sandwich, a menacing sneer, or a sharp elbow as we passed in the corridor. Every day felt as though I was swimming in shark-infested waters, and it was only a matter of time before Bateman struck.

On the playground, I was included in kickball and wall ball only because I was either Ernie's partner or Ernie would not play unless I was also picked for a team. But Ernie's influence only went so far. Throughout the year I would hear my classmates inviting one another to each other's homes after school, having sleepovers, or arranging playtime on the weekend. Invitations were never extended to me. When students had birthdays, they brought invitations and passed them out at recess, a heartless process in which students would assemble expectantly, like soldiers during the war gathering to receive mail from loved ones. Inevitably, several of us would depart empty-handed. It stung at first, but I quickly learned not to get my hopes up, and I avoided the process by playing in the yard with Ernie, who, despite his prowess on the playground—and for reasons I did not yet understand—was also frequently excluded.

Given my classmates' proclivity to exclude me, I anticipated Valentine's Day with such dread that when my mother asked me if I wanted to bring valentine cards to school, I told her the teachers didn't allow us to pass out cards. In truth, I didn't want to feel the rejection of handing out a card and having it torn up or thrown away. Sister Kathleen had explained the day before that we were to pass out cards in an allotted time just before recess so that we weren't distracted the remainder of the day. The following day, when Sister Kathleen announced that we had ten minutes to engage in the Hallmark holiday, I stayed seated while my classmates ran to the cloakroom to retrieve their bundles and proceeded to hand them out. It felt like the longest ten minutes of my life. I sat watching the clock, about to bolt out the door when Valerie

Johnson appeared at my desk and handed me a white envelope.

"Happy Valentine's Day, Sam," she said and quickly ran off.

This was an unexpected development. Valerie Johnson had already established herself as the most popular girl in our class. I heard other girls constantly talk about her large house and swimming pool. She'd apparently thrown the best birthday party. As my classmates piled their valentines and the candy inside the envelopes on their desks, I sat up with my emotions soaring and opened my lone card.

Inside I did not find a card. When I turned the envelope upside down, a dead fly fell onto my desk, which caused a chorus of snickering and laughter as Valerie Johnson and her entourage rushed out the door onto the playground.

3

I spent the lunch hour playing a game of kickball. When the first bell rang, a five-minute warning to get to class, I realized I'd neglected a basic necessity. "I have to pee," I said to Ernie as we approached the steep stairway leading from our play area up to the quad.

"You're going to be late," Ernie said.

But I didn't just have to pee, I *really* had to pee. So as Ernie and the other students shuffled up the steps, the din of their voices reverberating off the stucco walls, I ducked into the bathroom, fumbling with the button that always felt a size too large for the hole. Stepping to the urinal, I unzipped my fly and prepared to relieve myself when I heard a loud, obnoxious, and all too familiar voice in the corridor, followed by an equally familiar cackle. I froze. David Bateman and his two brutes were, by the sound of it, about to enter. Panicked, I scurried to a toilet stall, managing to get the stall door shut just as I glimpsed the bathroom door fling open and bang hard against the wall.

Since the old-fashioned porcelain toilet had no lid, I balanced a shoe on each side of the rim and rested my bottom on the bowl mounted to the wall. Perched atop the toilet, I took full advantage of my mother's religious tutelage. "Hail Mary, full of grace, the Lord is with thee . . . please don't let them find me . . . please don't let them find me . . . blessed art thou among women and blessed is the fruit of thy womb, Jesus . . . please don't let them find me . . ."

I peeked out the gap between the stall door and jamb and saw the backsides of the three thugs standing shoulder to shoulder at the urinal trough. I had come to learn that Bateman's henchmen were second graders, Patrick O'Reilly and Tommy Leftkowitz. Bateman pushed O'Reilly's shoulder, trying to knock his stream off the mark. Then Bateman spun, rotating like a sprinkler, and peed all over the bathroom, much to his goons' delight.

"My dad says Batman is a fag; that's why he wears tights," Bateman said, zipping himself up.

"What's a fag?" Leftkowitz asked.

"They're sissies," O'Reilly said. "At least that's what my dad said it meant."

"What about Superman? He wears tights," Leftkowitz said.

"My dad says he's okay because he likes Lois Lane."

Bateman cranked out what seemed like an excessively long sheet of paper towel from the dispenser, crumpled it in the sink under a stream of water, and mashed it into a giant dark-brown spitball, like the ones I'd seen stuck to the bathroom ceiling. As I watched through the crack, I realized that in my hurry to hide, I had failed to slide the latch to lock the door. I reached for it at the precise moment Bateman wheeled and hurled the wet mass directly at my stall, causing the unlatched door to spring open.

Bateman's eyes widened, then the corners of his mouth slanted upward. "Well, well. What do we have here, Devil Boy?" He approached. "You taking a shit with your pants on?"

"No," O'Reilly said. "I think maybe the devil boy pees sitting down, like a girl."

In my haste, I had not only forgotten to latch the door; I had forgotten to tuck myself back into my trousers, and now the head of my penis protruded out my unzipped fly.

"Yeah, maybe we should call him Devil *Girl*," Bateman said. He slapped Leftkowitz's shoulder. "Watch the door. I think Devil Girl needs a drink of water."

My fear at that moment caused every limb of my body to grow instantly rigid. If my pants had not remained unzipped, I would have been forced to endure a different form of humiliation the remainder of the day. Instead, given my position atop the seat, the height was such that my inadvertent stream hit Bateman directly in the face.

Bateman screamed, wiping at his eyes and face as if squirted with acid. "It's burning my eyes. It's burning my eyes."

O'Reilly quickly tried to retreat, but his shoes slipped in the puddle of urine Bateman had shot on the floor. He skated unsteadily for a moment, then reached out and grabbed hold of Bateman's shoulder, but Bateman's feet were also dancing, as if on a sheet of ice. The two looked for a moment as if they might regain their balance, but O'Reilly's feet came out from beneath him, and he toppled them both, Bateman cursing a blue streak and shouting threats when they hit the ground. "I'm going to kill you. You're dead!"

The second bell rang.

Leftkowitz, who'd been standing guard, pushed open the door and yelled what I presume to have been "Bell!" though now I recall it as a silent scream. I shot from the stall, felt a hand grip my ankle, but shook it free and continued running past a surprised Tommy Leftkowitz, knocking him into one of the trash cans. I fully expected Bateman and O'Reilly to tackle me from behind as I scaled the steep steps, but I reached the summit untouched and raced across the quad to where Sister Kathleen stood sentry outside her classroom door waiting for us to line up in single file. Only when we were sufficiently "calm and orderly" would she allow us the privilege of reentering her classroom. Someone, I don't know who, had broken that rule, giving me a reprieve. But I could not be bothered with the formality of a line, not with David Bateman threatening to kill me. I raced by my stunned fellow students, a serious breach in line protocol and etiquette, and did not stop until I had reached the front of the line.

"Samuel Hill!" Sister Kathleen said. "You know there is no running in the corridor."

"Sorry, Sister. I didn't want to be late, Sister."

"Well, I admire your determination to be punctual, but perhaps you can give yourself more time to get to class?"

"Yes, Sister. Sorry, Sister." What I wanted to shout was, "Open the door, Sister—there's a monster loose!"

"Now go to the back of the line," she said. When my feet did not immediately comply, she said, "Samuel, did you not hear me? I said walk to the back of the line."

I trudged to the final spot behind Mary Beth Potts and looked across the courtyard. Ernie and his well-behaved classmates had nearly completed their orderly procession inside Sister Reagan's classroom when David Bateman raced around the corner. Red in the face, Bateman came to an abrupt stop when he met Sister Reagan's outstretched palm.

"No tardy students are allowed in my classroom without a tardy slip," she said.

"But—"

"No buts. Please proceed to the principal's office and explain why you were unable to make it from the playground to class in the time allotted."

The last thing I saw before I stepped inside the sanctity of Sister Kathleen's classroom was Bateman's menacing glare, and one balled fist smacking an open palm.

4

When the bell rang to signal the end of the school day, I made sure I was first in line, imploring my classmates to line up quickly and quietly. Sister Kathleen opened the door, and I raced out. On the other side of the red steps, the door to Sister Reagan's classroom opened, and I was just as certain David Bateman would be first in his line, ready to deliver on his threat to kill me. As my feet shuffled down the steps, I spotted my salvation. My mother sat in the blue Falcon with the top down. She smiled up at the sight of me from behind large, round sunglasses, a white scarf tied beneath her chin to protect her hair. She looked like a Hollywood movie star.

I pulled open the passenger door, slid in, and buckled my seat belt without being reminded. "Hi, Mom. Ready to go."

"How was school?"

"It was good. Can we go?"

"Did you finish your lunch?" She unsnapped my lunch box and flipped open the lid. I looked to my right but did not see David Bateman descending the stairs. "You didn't eat your apple slices again."

I leaned over and glanced inside. "I must have forgot." I quickly turned to the school and saw

David Bateman on the top step, searching for me.

"You must have forgotten," my mother corrected. "You have to eat your fruit and vegetables or I won't put in any more Hostess."

"I will, Mom."

She reached into her purse, giving me another opportunity to consider Bateman. This time we made eye contact. God knows now what possessed me, but safe within the Falcon, my mother seated close beside me, I lost my mind and stuck out my tongue.

"Sam, I need you to take this form up to Sister Kathleen." My mother had pulled a slip of paper from her purse. "I forgot to put it in your lunch box this morning. It's the permission slip for your field trip to the zoo next week. Sam?"

I stared at the permission slip, signed at the bottom in my mother's flowing handwriting. "I can't," I said.

"Why not?"

"I . . . I think I'm sick."

"Sick?"

It wasn't an outright lie. At that moment, I very much felt as though I could vomit. "I haven't felt good since lunch. I think I might puke."

"We don't say 'puke,' Samuel. We say 'vomit.' "

"I think I might vomit," I quickly said.

"Is that why you didn't eat your apples?"

"Yes, that's it."

"Why didn't you say so?"

"I, uh, I forgot."

My mother put her hand to my forehead. "You do feel a bit warm." Her hand slid to the glands beneath my jaw and to the back of my neck. "And your neck is clammy."

"I can turn it in next week. Let's go home."

My mother sighed. "I better do it before I forget again." She turned, reaching for the door handle.

"No!"

She looked back to me. "It will only take a minute."

"I think I might vomit."

"That bad?"

I threw my head back against the seat and moaned.

"But if I don't get it in today, you won't be able to go to the zoo."

Now this was a dilemma. I very much wanted to go to the zoo, but I also very much did not want David Bateman to kill me. I looked back to the stairs. Bateman had vanished. I searched up and down the street but saw no sign of him. "I'm better now," I said. "I think I'm okay."

Her brow furrowed. She removed her sunglasses. "You're sure?"

"I think maybe it was just gas." I belched, loud and long, which I could do on cue if I sucked in enough air.

"Samuel Hill," my mother said.

"Sorry, Mom, but I feel a lot better."

"Just don't make a habit of it." She slid out the driver's side and jogged around the back of the car. I didn't take my eyes off her until she'd ascended the stairs and disappeared into the quad. When I turned back, David Bateman had his face pressed against my window. I screamed and tried to retreat across the seat, but the seat belt, tight across my lap, prevented me from moving. The best I could do was lie flat, with Bateman reaching over the top of the window and grabbing at air.

"I'm going to kill you, Devil Boy," he said. "I'm going to flush your head down the toilet. Then I'm going to kill you." He glanced up at the top steps, backing away with a sneer, and disappeared around the corner of the building.

My mother slipped back behind the wheel and did a double take, her sunglasses still atop her scarfed head. "Are you sure you're feeling better? You're pale as a ghost."

"I feel sick again," I said.

She grimaced. "I was hoping to take the car to Eddy's for an oil change. I'm five hundred miles overdue, and your father's been after me."

Eddy's? I immediately perked up. "I'm fine," I said and let out another belch. "Sorry, Mom."

5

Other than my father's pharmacy, Fast Eddy's Chevron station at the end of Broadway Avenue was my favorite place to visit. Eddy let me in the service area to watch the mechanics raise and lower the cars on the hydraulic lifts, and he would point out the various parts of the engine. He said I was a quick learner and hoped someday I would work for him. What I really liked, though, was at the end of every visit, Eddy allowed me to pull a Tootsie Pop from the jar on the counter. My mother made me save the treat until after dinner, but that just made it all the more special.

Eddy greeted us in his grease-stained blue coveralls. "What will it be this time, Mrs. H?"

"I'm overdue for an oil change, Eddy. Max's been after me for two weeks. I was hoping you might squeeze me in."

"I can always fit you in, Mrs. H—you know that. You're one of my best customers." He turned and surveyed his garage. "Put it in the second bay, and I'll have Ron get started on it."

My mother pulled the car into the second bay as instructed, and we walked to the office to wait. "I have to go to the bathroom," I said.

My mom wrinkled her brow.

I looked at Fast Eddy, which was what everyone, except my mom, called him. She said it was impolite. "May I use your lavatory, Eddy?"

Eddy handed me the foot-long stick to which he'd tied the key to the bathroom. "You let me know if it needs any servicing while you're in there, okay, sport?"

I butted the stick against my shoulder, shooting at invisible Nazis as I made my way around the corner of the building to the door marked **MEN**. Inside I surveyed the mosaic-tiled floor and walls as if doing so for an inspection. I'd seen them cleaner but declared them sufficient to pass. After using the urinal, I washed my hands—my mother would ask if I had—and made my way back to the office. Fast Eddy was not behind the counter, and my mother was not seated on the red bench seat. I walked to the loading bays and found Eddy talking with another mechanic, Gary. They had their backs to me and were looking at the Falcon raised on the lift.

"Best pair of headlights in Burlingame," Fast Eddy said.

"And the bumper ain't bad, either." Gary laughed.

I felt myself swell with pride.

"I'd like the chance to bend her over the bumper and check her oil with my dipstick," Eddy said. "I'd give her the lube job of a lifetime."

I didn't know exactly what they meant, but I did sense they were not talking about the Falcon.

When they separated, I saw what they were talking about. My mother stood in her white sweater next to Ron, one of the technicians. He was pointing to something on the underside of the Falcon, and my mother was leaning forward to get a better look.

The stick in my hand hit the asphalt with a clatter.

Eddy turned. "Hey there, sport; everything shipshape in there?"

I picked up the stick and handed it to him without comment.

"Looks like the Falcon's in need of a new radiator hose," he said. "Take a few more minutes. Can you put the stick back on the wall for me?"

Gary rubbed my hair as I walked past him and entered the office. "Hey, there, Sammy boy."

I hooked the leather strap on the nail. Moments later my mother joined me in the waiting area. She sat, flipping through the pages of a magazine. When she crossed her legs, her skirt inched above her knee. I looked up at Gary, who was now behind the counter. He wasn't looking, but I slid forward to block his view, just in case.

Thirty minutes later, Eddy backed the Falcon out of the garage, wiped the door handle with his red rag, and held the door open for my mom. "You bring her in any time, Mrs. H. The boys and me look forward to working on the Falcon."

Eddy grinned down at me. "Hey, Sam, you forgot to get your Tootsie Pop." He shouted over his shoulder. "Hey, Gary, get Sam a Tootsie Pop."

"Forget it," I said. "I don't want one."

"Samuel!" my mother snapped. "That's not polite. How about, 'No, thank you.' "

Eddy was no longer smiling. His eyes narrowed, considering me. Gary jogged over, carrying a purple Tootsie Pop, and held it over the top of the window. "Favorite color, right, kid?"

I just wanted to leave. "Samuel?" my mother said. "Do you have something to say?"

"Thanks," I said and took the candy.

6

When I got home, I professed to not feeling well. Again, it was not a complete lie. I went upstairs to my room, but not before throwing the Tootsie Pop in the garbage pail in the kitchen. Minutes later my mother was in my room, shaking the thermometer. As she sat on my bed watching the second hand of her watch and holding the end of the thermometer under my tongue, I began to realize my mother was something special to look at. I believe kids have an innate sense about this but choose not to think about it.

My mother pulled the thermometer from under my tongue. "You don't have a fever," she said. She pressed the back of her hand to my forehead and my cheeks to confirm this. "Everything okay at school today?"

"Fine." I rolled onto my side and shut my eyes.

After she'd left the room, I lay atop the covers, staring at the model airplane my father and I had built the past weekend and hung from the ceiling with fishing wire. I thought of the newsman smiling and kissing my mom and the times my mother and I would drive with the top down and cars would pull alongside us and the men would rev their engines. I'd thought they were admiring the Falcon.

"Ignore them, Samuel," my mother would say, but I would sneak a peek anyway, and the men would smile and wink and otherwise try to get my mother's attention.

"I think he knows you," I said the first couple of times this happened.

"I'm most certain he does not," my mother would say.

"Then why is he waving to you?"

"He wants to race," she'd say.

"Can we?" I'd blurt out.

"Absolutely not. Racing is against the law and dangerous. A car is not a toy, Samuel."

But I also couldn't help noticing that when the light changed, the Falcon would usually surge through the intersection.

I thought about Fast Eddy and Gary and about what they'd said. I'm sure I didn't understand the dipstick part, but I understood enough to know what they'd said was wrong. With all the problems I already had with David Bateman and Sister Beatrice, I didn't need people complicating things by making nasty comments about my mother. And I never wanted her to go back to Fast Eddy's again.

When my father came home, I heard my parents talking but didn't bother to get off the bed to listen through the floor vent. I deduced enough to know my mother was telling my father I was upstairs and didn't feel well. No, she didn't think I was sick. And yes, she'd taken the car in for its oil change, but it had cost more because they had to replace a radiator hose. My father wasn't happy about this, lamenting that he could have done it himself and saved the labor cost.

Minutes later, I heard his heavy footsteps bounding up the stairs. The door to my room crept open, and my father stepped into the striped shadows from the fading light through the wood shutters covering the window above my head-board. He touched my forehead. "Your mother says you don't feel well."

"I'm okay."

"I hope so. I need my partner for *Bonanza* tonight."

"I think I'll be okay."

"Something happen at school today? Something you want to talk about?"

"No, nothing."

"Well, if I were a betting man, I'd bet something was bothering you." He held up the Tootsie Pop, still wrapped.

I sat up. "Dad, what does it mean when some-one says they'd like to bend someone over a bumper and use their dipstick to check the oil?"

My father straightened. "Where on earth did

you hear . . . ?" Then before I could answer, he reconsidered the Tootsie Pop. "Oh."

"What does it mean?"

My father pursed his lips. "It means it's time to find another mechanic," he said.

7

David Bateman now lurked everywhere, hiding behind a pillar, circling the playground as I ate my lunch. The last thing I did each morning before leaving my house and the first thing I did upon getting home was go to the bathroom; I was not about to take the chance of being caught alone in the school bathroom. Fridays were the only day I enjoyed going to school. I knew when the afternoon bell rang I had a solid two and a half days before I had to reenter Bateman-infested waters. It was on one of those Friday afternoons, while hurrying down the school steps, that I saw my mother talking to a tall, black-skinned woman.

"Samuel," my mother said. "This is Mrs. Cantwell, Ernie's mom."

Mrs. Cantwell's hair sat atop her head like a halo. I extended my hand as I had been taught. "How do you do," I said.

"My, what a polite young man," she said. "Ernie has told me all about you, Sam. He doesn't stop talking about you. Sam this and Sam that."

"He does?" I said.

"He certainly does," she said. "And I wanted to thank you for being such a good friend to Ernie."

"You're welcome," I replied, though her comment confused me. Being Ernie's friend had been the easiest thing about school, and, if anything, I should have been thanking him. Without him, I'd have still been on the bleachers.

Ernie ran down the sidewalk to meet us. "Did you ask? What did she say?"

Mrs. Cantwell's penciled eyebrows arched. "Excuse me?"

"Excuse me," Ernie said. "Did you ask?"

"We were just discussing it," Mrs. Cantwell said.

My mother put her hand on my shoulder, smiling. "You've been invited to Ernie's house tomorrow afternoon."

"Ernie's been asking all week," his mother said.

I was stunned. I'd never been invited to anyone's home before. "Can I, Mom, please?"

My mother's smile widened. "Of course you can."

"Why don't you drop him off just before lunch," Mrs. Cantwell said.

"Can we ride bikes?" Ernie asked.

"Does Samuel have a bike?" Ernie's mom asked.

"He does," my mom said.

"Then we'll see you tomorrow," Mrs. Cantwell said.

Ernie turned around several times as he walked up the sidewalk to their Volkswagen Beetle, but my enthusiasm had quickly dissipated. My bike

131

was the one I'd learned to ride as a baby, with training wheels. I was convinced Ernie would take one look at it, burst out laughing, and that would be the last time he invited me over.

8

My father had been out Friday night at a pharmacy meeting, preventing me from talking to him about the bike situation. In hindsight, I'm not sure why I didn't ask my mom, but she tended to push aside my concerns about things like bikes. I didn't realize it then, but money was tight. My father's business was doing all right, but he had loans he was repaying to buy the business and the building. So a bike was an extravagance we couldn't afford.

The following morning, I got up early on my own. When my dad saw me sitting at the kitchen table, fully dressed and wearing my coat, he laughed.

"You're a bit anxious, don't you think?"

"I'm going to Ernie's house," I said.

"I heard. No cartoons this morning?" I had completely forgotten about Saturday-morning cartoons. "I think you have some time," my father said. "How about I pour us both a bowl of cereal?"

As we slurped and crunched our Cap'n Crunch cereal, I eased, as subtle as a buffalo, into the subject. "Ernie wants to ride bikes," I said.

My father's spoon stopped halfway to his mouth. "Bikes, huh?"

I raised my eyebrows in case my father hadn't

caught my subtlety. He looked up at the clock on the wall, picked up his bowl, and put it in the sink. "Your mother's in the shower," he said. "Tell her I had to leave early." And before I could question him further about the bike problem, he was out the door.

Several minutes later, my mother entered the kitchen with a towel turban on her head. "Where's your father?"

"He said to tell you he left early."

She looked up at the clock. "He did, did he?"

At eleven thirty, my mother's designated time to walk to Ernie's, I wheeled my bike from the garage. I contemplated letting it roll into the street to get run over by a car but didn't want to risk my mother thinking it irresponsible and have her change her mind about my going to Ernie's. The bike was so small I could stand over it. When I sat on the seat, my knees bent so severely it was difficult to pedal. Resigned to my humiliation, I hoped my mom at least knew how to take off the training wheels.

She came out the front door in a pair of shorts and a T-shirt, sunglasses embedded in her hair.

"I wonder why your father didn't take the Falcon?" she said.

In my misery, I hadn't noticed. Though it was Saturday, the Falcon remained parked in the driveway, an empty space in the garage reserved for our Plymouth station wagon.

"Mom, do you think you could take off the training wheels?"

At that moment I heard a familiar honk and turned to see the station wagon driving up the tree-lined street and turning into our driveway. My dad jumped out wearing his white pharmacy smock. My mother looked at him like he'd gone mad. "What are you doing home? Who's watching the store?"

"I had to run a quick errand this morning."

"Why didn't you tell me? I could have done it for you."

My father was lowering the tailgate. "This errand was for Samuel," he said, and he slid out the most glorious, fire-engine-red Schwinn bicycle I had ever seen. He pushed it toward me, lowered the kickstand, and stepped back.

I circled the bike, unsure it was really mine. It had mudguards over both wheels, reflectors on the spokes, and, best of all, no training wheels.

"Look at the license plate," my father said. I walked to the back. Hanging below the seat was my name engraved in red on a tiny white plate. **SAM**. "And look at this. It has a light on the handlebars that turns on automatically when you pedal. Well, do you like it?"

I nodded, speechless. Then I ran to where my father stood and buried my head in his stomach. "Thanks, Dad."

"Don't forget to thank your mom, too," he said.

I hugged her. "Thanks, Mom."

"It can be an early birthday present," she said.

"One more thing Santa won't have to put together," my father said.

I didn't care. I didn't care if I ever got another birthday present for the rest of my life.

"Can you ride it?" my dad asked.

I climbed on board, kicked up the stand, and rode in a circle around our driveway. The lack of training wheels was no impediment.

"Seat too high?"

"It's fine," I said.

"Try the brakes," he instructed. I did, and the bike dutifully stopped. "Not too jerky?"

"No," I said. "What's this?" I pushed a lever, causing a bell to ring. "Cool."

"Well, you better get back to work," my mother said. "So we can afford that new bike."

My father kissed her goodbye and rubbed my hair. "Have fun at Ernie's," he said. "I want to hear all about your big day when I get home."

My mother walked and jogged beside me as I rode the bike on the sidewalk. She didn't want me to ride it in the street. The only tricky part of our journey was crossing the El Camino Real, which divided west Burlingame from east Burlingame. The El Camino was a four-lane roller coaster of bumps and dips caused by the roots of eucalyptus trees that lined each side of the street. I had never crossed the El Camino on bike or on foot. There had never been a reason. We waited at the corner until the traffic light changed, then crossed. Nothing to it.

Several turns and a few blocks later, I saw Ernie riding his bike up and down a short driveway and making U-turns in a cul-de-sac. When he saw me coming, he dropped the bike in the street and ran to greet me. His mother chased after him. "Ernie, how many times have I told you not to leave your bike in the street?"

"Cool bike," Ernie said, reaching us. I swelled with pride.

My mom stayed for a few minutes talking to Mrs. Cantwell, but when Mrs. Cantwell asked if she'd like to have lunch, I looked at her with alarm. This was my day with Ernie. I didn't want my mom there.

"I have a few errands to run," she said. "Why don't you just call when it's time for Sam to come home?"

Ernie's mom made us boiled hot dogs, potato chips, and grape juice, which we ate at a picnic table in his backyard. At one point Ernie made me laugh so hard the juice shot out my nose, staining my shirt, but I didn't care. After lunch, he wanted to play baseball. I'd played a few times with my dad, but I wasn't very good at catching or throwing.

"I didn't bring my glove," I said.

"I have two," Ernie said. And before I could come up with another excuse, he had run into his garage and emerged with two well-used mitts, a bat, a ball, and two black-and-orange Giants baseball caps, shoving one on my head. I looked around the small patch of lawn beside the concrete patio.

"We might break a window," I said.

"We'll go to the park," he said. "It's just down the street."

With that he ran to the front yard, where we'd left our bikes.

"Should we tell your mom?"

"It's okay. I know the way."

Following Ernie's lead, I hung the mitt by the strap on my handlebars. "How far is it?" I asked.

"It's close," he said and pedaled off down the street.

Village Park wasn't far, but getting there involved several turns on winding streets. When we arrived, Ernie dropped his bike on the lawn just inside a gap in a chain-link fence. I carefully lowered the kickstand, not wanting to scratch the paint of my new bike. Except for a man chasing his dog and a couple lying on a blanket reading books, we had the park to ourselves. We set up in a corner facing the south fence, which towered nearly as high as the two-story house behind it. Ernie said he'd watched other boys set up so that when they hit the ball it would bounce off that fence.

"I'll go first," he said.

I was relieved. I had no idea what he meant to do. I stood at the base of the fence as Ernie walked perhaps forty feet and dropped his mitt. "Okay?" he yelled.

"Okay," I shouted back, having no idea why.

Ernie tossed the ball into the air and, as it descended, swung. The ball shot straight up from his bat. I stood there, admiring its arc and watching it drop just a few feet from where I stood.

"You're supposed to catch it," Ernie yelled.

Thinking quickly, I shouted back, "I thought that was a practice one."

"Throw it in."

I picked up the ball and threw it as my dad had taught me. It bounced well short and to the right of Ernie. He chased it down and repeated the process. This time I put my glove up and raced in, only to have the ball soar over my head and roll to the fence. I could feel my face burning with embarrassment, but Ernie just smiled and hollered encouragement—"Good try."

After hitting me another dozen, none of which I caught, Ernie took pity on me. "Let's switch." I was terrified of looking even more incompetent. I set down my mitt and picked up the bat and ball, mimicking each of Ernie's moves, but when

I swung, the bat generated only a rush of air. The ball fell at my feet.

I picked up the ball and tried again. This time I made contact, but the ball skittered across the lawn, stopping ten feet in front of me. "I'll get it," I shouted, running forward.

"Just hit it from there," Ernie said. We were now no more than twenty feet apart. "Throw it higher."

I did as instructed and realized that by tossing the ball higher I had more time to swing. This time everything clicked. I swung as hard as I could. The bat hit the ball with a loud crack, and I watched in shock and amazement as the ball soared high into the sky, much higher than any of the balls Ernie had hit. It also did not descend as it neared the fence, continuing on an upward plane. It cleared the top of the fence, followed by the unmistakable sound of a window shattering.

Ernie ran.

I stood paralyzed, still in awe of my majestic shot, not immediately realizing that everything had taken a sudden turn for the worse. When I finally turned, Ernie had already raced across the field to his bike, jumped onto the seat, and started pedaling. I couldn't cross the patch of lawn nearly as fast as Ernie, especially carrying my mitt and the bat. By the time I reached my bike, Ernie was already halfway down the street. I couldn't get the glove on the handlebar. Then I couldn't get the kickstand up. Once on my bike, my feet slipped off the pedal, and I stumbled and nearly toppled over. I pushed the bike, did a sort of kick jump onto the pedal, and swung my other leg over the bar. When I felt balanced, I put the bat across the handlebars. I had no idea how to get back to Ernie's house and realized I'd made a wrong turn only when I'd reached the El Camino, though not at the location my mother and I had crossed earlier. This corner had no stoplight.

I knew Balboa, my street, was somewhere across this great divide, and if I could make it across, I could find my way home. I got off the seat and waited for a break in traffic. I started across, realized I had to also judge the cars in the two lanes on the opposite side, and pulled back to the corner. A moment later I saw a gap in the traffic and again pushed away from the curb. My head swiveled left to right. Halfway across, a car neared. I picked up my pace, but the mitt slid from the handlebars and hit the pavement. To retrieve it, I'd have to put the kickstand down or lay the bike down. Meanwhile the car closed distance. I couldn't leave Ernie's mitt to get run over, but I also couldn't sacrifice my bike. A thought came to me. I kicked the glove as I continued to push the bike. With the car nearly upon me, I kicked the mitt again. A third kick carried it all the way to the gutter strewn with eucalyptus leaves and shredded bark. Hearing the blare of the car

141

horn, I shoved the bike forward and bounced the tires over the curb onto the sidewalk.

I'd made it. I'd crossed the El Camino on my own. After a moment to consider my achievement and to catch my breath, I repositioned Ernie's glove on the handlebars and rode up the street. I recognized the familiar green backstop and baseball fields of Ray Park and realized, thankfully, I was just two blocks from my house. Surely whatever rules I had broken would be tempered by the fact that I had been responsible enough to make it home. Everything would be fine, I thought, breathing easier. Then I heard that voice.

"Hey, it's the devil boy!"

9

David Bateman and his two bullies had been kneeling in the third-base dugout at the ball field. I would later come to learn they had been using a magnifying glass to burn ants and beetles and ignite small piles of dry leaves. I had the bad luck to pass just as Tommy Leftkowitz, the designated lookout, raised his head. At Leftkowitz's pronouncement, the three of them saw an opportunity for infinitely more fun than burning insects, and they raced for their bikes.

My instinct for survival kicked into high gear. I pedaled as fast as I could, my pursuers speeding along the grass outfield on the opposite side of the cyclone fence. I had the advantage, riding on concrete, and probably would have made it safely to my driveway, but I lost focus when I looked back at them, no doubt a survival instinct, and my foot slipped from the pedal. The toe of my Keds struck the ground, acting like an unintended brake, and it sent me careening onto gravel. As I struggled to untangle myself from the bike, Bateman came to a skidding stop, back tire fishtailing and spitting rocks at me.

He dropped his bike and grabbed me by my shirt collar, shoving me into the park while Leftkowitz grabbed my bike and the baseball bat. Bateman pushed me toward the cinder-block bathroom building. I was certain he intended to make good on his promise to drown me in one of the toilets. Instead he pushed me around to the back of the building, out of sight from the playground equipment and whatever parents were there that afternoon.

"Hold him."

O'Reilly and Leftkowitz each grabbed an arm while Bateman walked to where Leftkowitz had dropped my stricken bike. He picked up the baseball bat.

"Nice bike, Devil Boy."

The first blow smashed the light attached to the handlebar. The second removed the license plate. O'Reilly and Leftkowitz laughed as Bateman raised and lowered the bat again and again, knocking off the chain and cracking the reflectors and spokes. He saved the final blow for the bell. It died with a sorrowful clang.

Breathing heavily, Bateman dropped the bat. Sweat beaded on his forehead. He looked like some deranged, sneering dog. And yet, at that moment, I also recall an odd sense of calm. Perhaps this was acceptance of my fate, resignation to the fact that I was about to be pummeled and there was nothing I could do about it. Or maybe it was an acknowledgment that I had it coming for peeing in David Bateman's face, then sticking out my tongue at him. Or it could have

144

been that I was so distraught over what Bateman had done to my new bike that I didn't care what he did to me. My sudden lack of fear could have been due to any of those reasons, or a product of all three, but I no longer believe that to be the case. I remember thinking this was what I deserved, the devil boy with the red eyes. This was what I had coming to me for being different. It was only a matter of time before, as my father had predicted, I would encounter the cruelty the world held for me. David Bateman was just the person who would deliver the first blow.

His punch to my stomach knocked the air out of me and buckled my knees. I would have dropped had O'Reilly and Leftkowitz not held me upright. Yet the pain was almost a relief. Almost. In truth, it hurt like hell. I couldn't breathe, couldn't catch my breath, and David Bateman didn't wait until I could. He clenched both his fists and systematically smashed me about the face and stomach, just as he had smashed my bike.

10

I don't know how long the beating continued, when it stopped, or why. I suppose that Bateman tired, or it could have been O'Reilly and Leftkowitz lost their courage. Initially riled, I recall the smiles on their faces fading to uncertain grimaces over the course of Bateman's attack. Smashing a bike was one thing. Smashing another kid repeatedly required a completely different genetic disposition—emotionally primitive, impulsive, lacking any remorse, sense of guilt, or human compassion.

"I think he's had enough," one of them said.

"Hold him up or I'll hit you," Bateman said.

"He's bleeding. You're getting blood on your shirt."

And that might have been the reason Bateman stopped. Maybe even then, just a boy, Bateman had already developed a criminal's instinct to avoid incriminating evidence.

I slumped to the ground, unable to raise my head, and listened to the sound of their shoes in the gravel as they ran to their bikes and made their escape. Hidden in the shade behind the cinder-block bathroom, I felt my left eye swelling shut. The metallic taste of warm blood filled my mouth, and my lower lip was going numb. When

I ran my tongue over it, I felt a small cut and a sharp, stinging pain. At some point, I managed to get to my feet and hobble to my stricken bike. I don't recall how I lifted it or got it to roll. What I do remember, very clearly, were the mothers in the nearby playground pushing their children on swings and sitting on benches. I remember a man and a woman who had been sunbathing on towels sitting up and watching me make my way back to the fence. I remember a man walking his dog on a leash continuing past me.

My mother and father could call my red eyes a "condition," but I realized it was more than that. I *was* different. I could not hide my eyes.

My bike and I wobbled down the sidewalk together, and though it was only two blocks to my home, I remember thinking the trek to be an arduous journey I would never survive. Leaving the park and halfway down the block, I saw the blue Falcon inching toward me. My mother looked to be standing behind the wheel, her head hovering just above the windshield, swiveling left and right. Mrs. Cantwell knelt on the passenger seat, eyes also searching. I could see the top of Ernie's head in the back seat.

When my mother saw me, it was as if time momentarily stopped. She seemed paralyzed at the sight of me. I recall her looking at me, brow furrowed as if she did not recognize me. I remember her eyes shutting for what seemed like seconds but was likely only a fraction of a moment. Then the car door flung open, and she was running between the parked cars, hand covering her mouth, tears streaming down her face. I recall her lips moving, her hands touching me. "What happened? My God, what happened?"

I could have told her, but I sensed, somehow, that was not the intent of her questions. My mother could see what had happened. She wasn't even really directing her questions to me; she was crying out to the God in whom she put so much trust and faith. In her grief and pain, my mother simply wanted to know why. "Dear God, why?"

But that was a question for which I did not have an answer.

11

I don't know who loaded my bike into the trunk of the Falcon. I assume it was Mrs. Cantwell, because my mother did not let go of me until she got me to the car and put me in the back seat. Ernie had slid to the opposite side, pressed against the armrest. He kept his chin down, but I recall tears streaking his cheeks. I found out later that he did not have permission to ride his bike alone to Village Park. I'd suspected as much when he suggested and proffered the lie, but I didn't question it, swept up in the adventure and thrilled with the idea I was a normal kid doing normal things with my friend.

At some point during the car ride, I felt his fingertips on my shoulder, a tentative touch I ignored. His fingers retreated. I was not mad at Ernie for leaving me. Nor did I consider him responsible for what had happened. My refusal to look at Ernie came from my abject embarrassment, my humiliation to have a friend, my only friend, see me so weak and helpless.

My mother drove straight to the emergency room at Our Lady of Mercy Hospital. She did not park or turn off the engine. She jumped from the car and pulled her seat forward. "Come on, Sam," she whispered, lifting me into her arms and carrying me through the sliding glass doors as she called out, "My son's been hurt. He's hurt."

A nurse helped my mother place me on a gurney, and together they wheeled me down a fluorescent-lit hall into a curtained room. "Can you tell me what happened?" the nurse asked.

"I don't know," my mother said. "I think he fell off his bike. Maybe a car hit him. He was at a friend's house. He hasn't said anything. My baby. Look at my baby."

"What's his name?" the nurse asked, helping me onto the bed behind the curtain.

"Sam. Samuel."

When the nurse looked down at me, I saw the familiar squint before she quickly looked away. "How old are you, Samuel?"

"Six," I said, my lip numb and the word difficult to pronounce.

"Where do you go to school?"

"OLM," I slurred.

"Where does it hurt, Sam? Can you tell me where it hurts?"

Where didn't it hurt would have been an easier question to answer, but I dutifully pointed out each area as the nurse enunciated them. "Your eye. And your lip. Your stomach. Your elbow. And your knee. Both knees? How did you get hurt, Sam?"

I did not answer.

"Sam?" the nurse asked, voice gentle. "How did you get hurt?"

My mother stared, face scrunched in worry. I wish I could say that my response was a heroic act to spare her more pain, but that would be a lie. My answer came from my cowardice, born from a desire for self-preservation that in turn was the product of another cold, harsh realization that came to me at the hands of David Bateman. My mother and father could not always be there to protect me. No matter the depth of my mother's love or how fierce her embrace, she could not protect me from the evil in the world, nor, it seemed, could all her novenas. Even then I began to question my faith and my mother's belief in God's will. What kind of God would allow this to happen to a child?

"I fell off my bike," I said.

12

The nurse cut away what remained of my shirt and shorts and washed and disinfected the cuts and scrapes, which stung, but not nearly to the degree of the blows administered by Bateman's fists. When the doctor, a man with silver-framed glasses and matching hair, arrived, he placed his chilled stethoscope against my skin.

"Take a deep breath," he repeated as he moved the metal sphere across my chest and over my back. Then he manipulated my arms and legs and asked me to wiggle my fingers and toes. He prodded around my abdomen, which remained sore, and pressed against my rib cage.

"Does that hurt?" he asked. "Is it a sharp pain?"

"Just kind of sore," I said.

He pressed a Popsicle stick against my tongue, flashed a light in my eyes, and asked me to follow his finger as he moved it about. "Well," he said, "I don't think anything's broken. We'll get a couple of X-rays, but I think it's mostly scrapes and bruises. Does your head hurt? Do you have a headache?"

"Sort of," I said.

He turned to my mother. "I don't think he has a concussion, but if he has any nausea, vomiting, bring him back in. Wake him during the night and ask him a few questions." Then he looked back at me. "You're a tough kid, Sam. That must have been a nasty spill."

I nodded.

"Did you run into anything?"

"I don't think so," I said. "I think I swerved."

"You swerved?"

"I think there was a branch and I swerved. I lost my balance."

"But you didn't hit anything?"

At this point I suspected the doctor had doubts about my bike accident. My mother had once told me a priest was sworn to keep confidences, even if you told them you'd done something really bad, but I didn't know if the rule applied to doctors.

"I don't think so," I said.

"Okay, do you think you could handle a sucker?" He pulled a red one from his pocket.

"I think I could," I said. My mother didn't even make me save it until after dinner.

The doctor suggested to my mother that they talk in the hall. When they'd departed, the nurse dressed my wounds. She wrapped bandages around my knees, my elbows, and my head, the latter to cover the cut above my left eye. "That must have been some nasty bike accident," she said.

"Pretty bad," I said.

"You must have hit your mouth on the handle-bars."

"I don't remember," I said.

"Sit up," she instructed.

I could see my reflection in a mirror and thought I very much looked like the wounded soldier I had imagined myself to be. Since my bloody shirt had been cut up and tossed in the trash, the nurse gave me a baggy blue shirt she called a "scrub" and said it was the kind the doctors wore. As she helped me slip it over my head, she leaned close, close enough to whisper. "Never be afraid to tell the truth, Sam. Not to the people who love you."

"All set?" the doctor asked, reentering the room with my mom.

The nurse winked at me. "All set. You're a brave little soldier, Sam."

My mom asked if I felt up to walking or wanted to ride in the wheelchair. Beginning to relish the attention, I chose the wheelchair.

Neither Ernie nor Mrs. Cantwell spoke on the drive home. When we stopped at their house, Mrs. Cantwell began to apologize. "Ernie knows better," she said. "We never let him ride his bike alone in the street. I'm so sorry. I just . . ."

My mother was gracious. "These things happen," she said, but she did not get out of the car to say goodbye. Ernie and I also departed without saying anything to each other. As we drove off, I looked back and saw Ernie and Mrs. Cantwell standing in the street, watching us leave. Ernie lifted his right hand and gave me a tentative wave, but because of my dressings, I did not return it.

13

My mother helped me straight upstairs and into my pajama bottoms; I wanted to continue to wear the blue doctor's shirt. After I climbed into bed, she surprised me with a bowl of Neapolitan ice cream, telling me it would probably be easier on my lip and tongue. Who was I to refute such logic? She sat on the edge of the bed looking forlorn, caressing the top of my head as I spooned the ice cream into my mouth. "Can you tell me a little more about the accident, Sam, how it happened?"

I allowed the spoon to linger in my mouth, stalling. "I'm not really sure I remember."

"The doctor seems to think that maybe there was more than a bike accident."

Now I was certain doctors were not like priests.

"Did someone do this to you, Sam? Did someone hit you?" I allowed the ice cream to melt and slide down my throat. "Sam, it's okay to tell me. I'm not going to let anyone hurt you again."

Oh, how I wanted to believe her; how I wanted to believe all her novenas could protect me and that David Bateman's reign of terror had ended, that I would be safe, but I knew at some point I was going to have to go back to school and David Bateman would still be there.

"It was an accident," I said.

My mother patted my arm and went downstairs, leaving the door open. She told me if I needed anything I could just holler, which ordinarily I wasn't allowed to do.

I picked up *The Count of Monte Cristo* from my nightstand. Reading it had been tough going, the words harder to pronounce than those in my schoolbooks, but I had gotten the hang of it about halfway through. I set aside my ice cream, thinking about Edmond Dantès and the sufferings he'd endured, as well as his revenge. I very much wished I could be like him, find a treasure, and come back with a new identity, rich and powerful enough to get even with David Bateman and his two goons. Then a more sobering thought replaced the fantasy: I could never disguise my identity; my eyes would betray me.

I thought again of my prayer bank. Though I had my doubts, I decided to give it one last try. "Please God," I prayed, mentally pulling the plug and shaking out the few prayers inside. "Please let me have brown eyes like everyone else."

As I prayed, I heard a faint, muffled gasp through the floor vent and sat up. I heard it again. I got out of bed and made my way to the stair-case, stopping when I heard the sound a third time. Slowly, carefully, I stepped down two steps and peered through the spoke railing with my un-swollen eye. I'd done this several times when

I wanted to watch television after being sent to bed. But this time the television was not on. My mother sat on the couch, her back to me. She was rocking, as if fighting a stomach pain. "Hail Mary, full of grace," I heard my mother pray in between her stifled sobs.

At some point the sound of the station wagon engine—a funny idle that caused it to tick and sputter—drew my attention. My father was home, and I thought of something I had not yet considered. *My bike.* I had told everyone that I crashed. What would my father say? I got up slowly, the sting in my knees making movement painful, and went as fast as my injuries allowed back to my room. I climbed onto my bed and knelt at the headboard to look out the shuttered window, watching as my father got out of the station wagon and dropped the laundry sack he brought home each Saturday filled with his white smocks. He stared at the wreckage of what, just that morning, had been a new and—I suspected from my mother's comments—expensive bike. In one swift motion, he picked up the bike and hurled it over my mother's flower bed onto the front lawn. Red in the face and teeth clenched, he shook his fists. I'd never seen him that angry, and I'd never been so scared.

As he started up the walk to our covered porch, I dropped from the window and slid beneath the covers, pulling the bedspread to my chin before

158

remembering the melting remnants of ice cream in the bowl on the nightstand. The last thing my dad needed to see was that my mother had rewarded me for ruining the bike. I threw off the covers, briefly contemplated making a dash for the bathroom across the hall, then hid the bowl under my bed.

The front door slammed with such force it rattled the window over my bed. "Did you see his bike?" my father yelled.

"Of course I saw it." My mother sounded calm.

"It's ruined. Completely destroyed."

"I called a bike shop. I'll take it in to see how much it will cost to fix."

"That's not good enough, Madeline. Not this time. That was a new bike."

"This isn't about the bike."

"You're damn right it isn't about the bike; it's about responsibility."

"Do not swear. Samuel will hear you."

"Somebody is going to pay for this."

I quickly tried to calculate how much money I had in my piggy bank—not my prayer piggy bank but the real one on my dresser—and deduced it would not be nearly enough.

"Is he upstairs? Have you checked on him?"

"I just brought him up some ice cream," my mom said. I grimaced and retrieved the bowl, placing it on the nightstand. "The doctor said he's going to be fine."

"But the doctor said he has a concussion?"

"He said he *might* have a concussion. He wants us to monitor him throughout the night. Why don't you go up and see him?"

No. That was a terrible idea. What was my mother thinking? My father should stay downstairs and have his Manhattan, read the paper, eat dinner—fried chicken, his favorite. By then I would be fast asleep.

Asleep. That was it. The last ruse of any child hoping to avoid getting in trouble.

As my father climbed the stairs, I shut my eyes and tried to control my breathing. I heard him stop outside my door, then sensed he'd entered and stood at the side of my bed. I kept my eyes shut tight.

"Sam? Sam!" He shook me, but I was determined and kept my eyelids closed. When I didn't immediately open my eyes, my dad started shouting. "Maddy! Maddy! Something's wrong!"

I sat up quickly and saw that he'd rushed to the doorway, shouting down the stairs. "Maddy, get up here. Call the hospital."

"No. I'm okay. Dad! I'm okay."

My mother hurried up the stairs as my father reentered the room, gasped a great sigh of relief, and collapsed on the edge of the bed.

"What is it? What's wrong?" My mother raced into the room and cradled my head as she rattled off a series of questions. "How old are you, Sam?

What school do you go to? Who am I? Do you recognize me? Dear God, he has brain damage!"

"No, Mom, I'm fine. I'm fine. I'm six. I go to OLM."

My mother turned and slapped my father's shoulder. "Jesus, Mary, and Joseph. What's wrong with you?"

My father rubbed his eyes with the heels of his hands. "He had his eyes closed. He wasn't responding." Turning to me, he said, "Sam, why didn't you respond?"

I started to cry, and this time the tears were real. "I didn't want you to yell at me."

He stood and came around the bed to where my mother stood. "Yell at you? Why would I yell at you?"

"Because I ruined my bike."

"Oh, Sam," my mom and father said in unison.

"Sam, I don't care about the bike," my father said, sitting. "We can buy a new bike. I care about you. There's only one Sam. We can't go to the store to replace you."

"But I saw you throw the bike on the lawn, and your face was all red. And downstairs you swore."

My mother crossed her arms and arched her eyebrows at my father.

"I'm not mad at you, Sam. I'm mad . . . at the situation. I'm just mad at the situation."

"Being mad is no excuse for swearing," my mother said.

"No, it's not," my father agreed.

My mother breathed a sigh of relief. "I'm going to go finish getting dinner ready."

My father sat with his elbows on his thighs, his gaze on the hardwood floor. "You know, Sam, I saw this karate store in the plaza. There were kids your age, even younger. Maybe we should go and check it out, see if you might like it." He looked to me. "Would you like that?"

I shrugged. "Maybe," I said.

"And I used to box in college; did you know that?"

I shook my head. My father and I watched the Friday-night fights together, but he had never mentioned being a boxer. I was impressed. "Were you any good?"

"I held my own," he said. "I could show you a few things, like how to block a punch and how to throw one."

Taking a punch was the last thing I wanted to try, but I could sense the answer my father wanted to hear. "Okay, sure."

The telephone rang. My mother yelled up the stairs, "I'm getting the lasagna out of the oven. Can you answer that?"

My spirits soared. My mother's lasagna was her specialty, a rare treat on the weekends. I ran my tongue around the inside of my mouth to determine whether I might be able to chew without too much pain. My father patted my leg beneath the covers and left to answer the extension in the hallway.

"Hello," he said, then listened for a moment. "Thank you for calling, Father Brogan."

I sat up. OLM's pastor.

"Yes, that's accurate." My father paused. "He's doing better now. Thank you for asking. How did you find out, Father?" Another pause. "I see. Tonight? Yes, we can be there. Samuel?" My father looked from the hall into my bedroom. "Yes, I think he's up to it, and I think it would be good if Samuel was present."

And just like that, I lost my appetite, even for my mother's lasagna.

14

My mother mostly pushed the lasagna around her plate with bored detachment. She didn't correct my posture or tell me to get my elbows off the table, nor did she tell me not to chew with my mouth open, which I had to do because my lip was swollen. We did not discuss my day or my father's day. The silence was unnerving, and I almost asked why we were going to talk to Father Brogan, but I decided against it. When it was apparent that none of us was going to eat much, my mother silently gathered our plates and left them in the sink, not bothering to rinse them.

"Do you want to get Sam dressed?" my mother asked. My father stared at me. "Max?" she asked, turning from the sink.

"No," he said. "I think Sam looks fine just the way he is."

Fine? I looked like that guy from the American Revolution carrying the flag and limping along with a bandage on my head. This was not how one presented himself to the parish pastor. But I sensed when my mother did not argue that I should not, either.

We parked the Falcon in front of the rectory, and I shuffled up the brick walk in my blue scrub top with my too-long pajama bottoms dragging on the ground over my slippers. A woman invited us in and led us down a hall with stained-glass windows and burgundy carpet that smelled like our basement and had the same dim lighting. Halfway down the hall, she pivoted and directed us to enter an open door.

I froze.

On the far side of a long table sat David Bateman. He was dressed like a choirboy in a white collared shirt and red sweater-vest. Bateman's eyes narrowed in what I took to be a warning. Beside him sat his mother, the plump woman with the arm flab I had had the unpleasant experience of meeting in Sister Beatrice's office. On the other side of Bateman sat a man with the biggest, squarest head I'd ever seen. It looked like a block of cement with bristles of hair and thick, black-framed glasses. His eyes widened at the sight of me. Father Brogan sat at the head of the table. To his left, looking ghostly pale, sat Sister Beatrice.

Father Brogan stood and greeted us in his Franciscan robe, the knotted white rope and rosary beads dangling from his waist. His eyebrows, silver and black, looked like inverted *V*s. He thanked my parents for coming and turned his attention to me.

"And Samuel," he said. "Thank you, Samuel, for being here. You're feeling up to it, are you?" he asked, his Irish brogue thick as syrup. I said I was, and he touched the top of my head. "Good man."

Returning to his place at the head of the table, Father Brogan invited us to sit. My mother looked to Sister Beatrice. "Good evening, Sister."

Sister Beatrice looked startled to be addressed, her eyes glassy. "Good evening," she said softly.

My father didn't bother greeting Sister Beatrice, and taking that as a cue, I pulled out one of the high-back chairs.

"Samuel," my mother said. "Please be a gentleman and greet Sister Beatrice."

What I wanted to say was, "Dad didn't." Instead I walked behind Father Brogan's chair and extended my hand. I smelled something pungent and thought Father Brogan was wearing an awful lot of cologne, though I hadn't smelled it when he first greeted me.

"Hello, Sister Beatrice."

Sister Beatrice took my hand and gave me a curt nod. "Good evening, Samuel."

The instant Father Brogan sat, Mrs. Bateman squawked, "I'm not sure what lies this boy has spread about my David, but I can assure you he is not responsible for that boy's injuries. I've spoken to my David, and he has no idea what this is about."

Father Brogan stroked a soot-colored patch of hair on his chin and waited for me to take my seat. The big chair dwarfed me.

"Samuel, do you know why I asked you to come down here tonight?"

"No, Father."

"Your parents have said nothing to you?"

"No, Father."

"You look as though you've hurt yourself quite badly."

"Yes, Father."

"And I'd like to ask you, Samuel. How is it that you sustained your injuries?"

I could not help it. My gaze shifted to David Bateman. He had his eyes pinched nearly shut in a subtle warning. I tried to swallow, but the lump caught in my throat.

"You may speak freely, Samuel. I assure you no harm will come to you here," Father Brogan said.

Bateman's eyebrows furrowed.

"I . . . I fell off my bike," I said.

Sister Beatrice and Mrs. Bateman appeared to exhale in unison, but Father Brogan grimaced as if pained.

"Are you sure about that, Samuel?"

Now I was really in a dilemma. I knew it was wrong to tell a lie and could only imagine that to tell one to a priest was a one-way ticket to hell. I didn't want to take another pummeling from David Bateman, but I also didn't want to burn for all eternity. I fretted a moment before seeing a glimmer of light at the end of the tunnel. I *had* fallen from my bike and cut my hands and knees, and that was all that Father Brogan had really asked.

"I had a bike accident," I said.

"Well, we're all very sorry about that," Mrs. Bateman said, though she didn't sound very sorry.

"Silence yourself, woman," Father Brogan said.

Mrs. Bateman flinched. It was as if the temperature in the room had suddenly dropped twenty degrees.

"David," Father Brogan said, looking to Bateman, "now I'm going to ask you. And I want you to think very carefully about the answer you are about to give. Are you prepared?"

Bateman nodded.

"Did you have anything to do with Samuel's injuries today?"

That was an entirely different question, one I was glad I did not have to answer. I leaned forward, as did my mother, who had folded her hands in her lap, her knuckles white. The air between the two sides of the table seemed to crackle.

David Bateman never paused. "No."

Whatever happened at this point, I felt satisfied that Bateman was going straight to the fires of hell.

Father Brogan's lips pinched together. Then he asked, "Are you absolutely certain of your answer?"

"I didn't touch him. It's not my fault he can't ride a bike."

Father Brogan considered an eight-and-a-half-by-eleven-inch piece of paper on the table, smoothing it with his hands. When he looked up, he found my eyes. "I grew up in Dublin in a very large family. My mother could not be there for all of us. Not all the time. And my father worked every day, it seemed, very hard. I remember quite clearly the day when I first understood that. I'd been out playing with my brother Favian when three boys attacked us. We didn't have much of a chance, Favian and I. We weren't cowards, mind you, but they were sufficiently bigger and stronger to make easy work of us. When we got home, our mother grew angry because we'd ripped our school pants in the knees, and we didn't have the money for new ones. When we explained the situation to her, she told us we should have come home and changed our pants before going out to play, as she had told us many, many times before. Then she demanded our trousers and went in search of the needle and thread without so much as a word about the condition of our faces, which looked very much like yours, Samuel."

Looking back now, I had a sense of where Father Brogan was going with his story, and I remember listening intently.

Father Brogan sighed. "I felt as if my mother had abandoned me and my brother. I know now that was not the case. But that night I went to bed hurt and angry at her and at my father. With age and maturity, I came to realize she had no choice in the matter; she had eleven of us to raise. As it was, she ate every meal with a child over her knees and another in the bassinet. She couldn't run out and fight our battles for us. We had to fend for ourselves, even the battles we knew we couldn't win. So, you see, I can tolerate much, and I know how boys behave. It takes a big man to stand up to a bully and an even bigger man to take it."

I felt both proud and anxious. I knew Father Brogan was paying me a compliment of some sort, but that also meant he knew I was lying, and I could feel the fires of hell tickling the soles of my feet.

"Any man can raise his fists and fight. But it takes a special kind of man to take his beating without complaint, to not rat out another to save himself." Father Brogan turned his attention to David Bateman. "What I can't stand is a liar."

"I can assure you, Father Brogan—" Mrs. Bateman began.

"And I can assure you, Mrs. Bateman, that your son *is* a liar." Father Brogan had grown red in the face. His eyes blazed. I couldn't imagine any boy capable of beating him up, and I was certain Father Brogan put up one heck of a fight in defeat.

Mrs. Bateman bristled. "He's nothing of the sort."

This time Mr. Bateman joined her, mumbling, "Outrageous."

"Outrageous?" Father Brogan slapped the table with the palm of his hand. "I'll tell you what is outrageous, sir. What is outrageous is for three boys, each twice the size of another, to beat him until he can stand no more. You are a coward, David Bateman. A coward. And the only thing I can stomach less than a liar is a coward."

"See here, Father," Mr. Bateman said.

"I am president of the parish board," Mrs. Bateman shrieked.

"Not any longer, woman. As of this moment, you are relieved of your duties. And as of this moment, David Bateman, you are expelled from Our Lady of Mercy Grammar School."

The words struck like a dagger. Mrs. Bateman placed her hand over her heart, and Mr. Bateman nearly jumped in his seat. David, however, did not so much as flinch.

"Expelled?" Mrs. Bateman said. She pointed her finger across the table at me, the flab of her arm shaking. "But he said he fell off his bike, that my David had nothing to do with this."

"He is not your son's accuser. I received telephone calls earlier this evening from Mrs. O'Reilly and from Mrs. Leftkowitz. It seems their sons participated in the beating of this poor

171

child, holding him while your son punched with such ferocity they feared that maybe he had killed Samuel. And, unlike your son, they had enough of a conscience to tell their parents."

"They're lying," Mrs. Bateman said.

Father Brogan put his hands flat on the table and stood up. "I spoke to the two children myself in this very room not two hours ago." He held up two sheets of paper. "They both gave me a descriptive account of the beating your son administered and signed their names to it. I can assure you, the only liar in this room is the one sitting between the two of you."

This got Mr. Bateman out of his chair, and it was a scary sight. He towered over Father Brogan and was as big around as a barrel. Father Brogan did not back down an inch. "Your son is expelled, and all I can say is that you should thank your lucky stars that is all that may happen to him. If Samuel were my son, I'd be reporting this to the authorities, and David might very well not find himself at the local public school come Monday, but at juvenile hall."

Mrs. Bateman gathered a large handbag. "I am not going to sit here and allow you to insult my son."

David got up from his chair to follow his mother, but he got just one step before his father grabbed him by the back of the collar with a hand as big as a baseball mitt. "Is this true?" He shook

David like a rag doll. "I want to know. Did you lie to your mother and me? Did you beat up this boy?"

Tears poured down Bateman's reddened cheeks. "No," he cried. "No. Dad. I swear. Don't hit me. Please don't hit me. He's lying. He's a liar."

But Mr. Bateman hit David anyway, a slap across the face that sounded like the crack of a whip. "Don't you lie to me," he said, shaking David, finger in his face.

Bateman bawled. "You're hurting me, Dad. You're hurting me again."

His father lifted David by the collar so that his toes barely touched the carpet. He looked like a man carrying a wild animal by the scruff of the neck. "You wait till I get you home. You'll get the belt for this. You've embarrassed your mother and me."

I heard David Bateman's fearful wails from down the rectory hall and then even after the front door had slammed shut. When I looked back to those seated around the table, my mother had her head down, crying. That's when it hit me. I would never have to see David Bateman at school again, never have to live in fear that he lurked around every corner, that the next ball to come my way would smack me in the side of the head. I should have been leaping for joy, shouting to the heavens in grateful thanks for my newfound freedom. Instead I felt sad—a little, anyway. David Bateman's father would give him the whipping of a lifetime, though I had no doubt it would do little to change David's ways. I'd just watched him sit and lie to a priest's face not once, but twice. If that hadn't scared him to tell the truth, a whipping surely wasn't going to.

"Mr. and Mrs. Hill," Father Brogan said after the wailing had dissipated. His face remained flushed. "I want to apologize to you, and especially to you, Samuel. We failed you. Mr. O'Reilly and Mr. Leftkowitz advised me not just of the beating but of the bullying you have been forced to endure each and every day. It is an environment no child should have to accept, especially not here at a Catholic school. I can assure you that it will not happen again, not while I'm pastor." He turned to Sister Beatrice, and I thought for a moment he might actually expel her. She sat mute, looking pale, and I got the impression Father Brogan had already administered a different type of lashing.

When we stood to leave, Father Brogan reached into the pocket of his robe—the kangaroo pouch, we called it. He pulled out a card with a picture of a man dressed in green, wearing a tall white hat. He turned it over and showed me the back. "I'm going to give you this Irish blessing now, Samuel, man-to-man. You keep it with you, and it will bring you strength." He put the palm of his hand atop my head and said the words written on the back of the card as I read them.

"Dearest father in heaven, bless this child and bless this day of new beginnings. Smile upon this child and surround this child, Lord, with the soft mantle of your love. Teach this child to follow in your footsteps, and to live life in the ways of love, faith, hope, and charity."

I felt his fingers make the sign of the cross through my hair.

I would slide the card with the Irish blessing into the frame of the mirror above my dresser, and there it would remain until I moved out for good. I took it with me and slid it between the frame and the mirror in the bedroom of my home.

As we departed the room in the rectory that evening, my father draped an arm around my shoulder. I stopped and looked up at my parents. "I have to ask Father Brogan something," I said.

"What is it?" my mother asked.

"Just something."

"Okay, let's go back."

"No," I said. "I can do this on my own."

I needed to find out if my white lie had been okay. I didn't want to go to hell, especially now that I was certain David Bateman had been damned to eternal torment. I made my way back to the conference room, but Father Brogan had departed. Sister Beatrice stood with her back to the door. I watched as she pulled a small metal flask from the pouch at the front of her habit, twisted off the top, and took a long drink. Then, as if sensing my presence, she turned and looked at me. If she were embarrassed, or even the slightest bit self-conscious about what I had witnessed, she did not show it. She did not flinch in surprise or call out or try to hide the flask and make some excuse like she was drinking water or she had a cold and this was medicine. She raised the flask and took another, almost defiant, sip. When she lowered it, her eyes narrowed, as David Bateman's eyes had narrowed. It was a warning, and I realized that while David Bateman would no longer haunt my school days, Sister Beatrice very much would.

PART THREE

The Mick

1

Trina Crouch stood rigid in my treatment room, her daughter seated on the table, clinging close to her side. Crouch had blanched and stiffened when I mentioned the name of her ex-husband, David Bateman. I saw more than just surprise in her reaction. I saw fear.

"How do you know him?" she asked.

"We went to grammar school together for a while."

Crouch squinted, considering me. "You're not the kid. No."

"I am," I said and felt a twinge of fear that Crouch would know my history with her husband. If Crouch knew, Bateman had clearly not forgotten.

She shook her head. "You couldn't be."

"I'm the kid with the red eyes. I wear brown contact lenses."

I began wearing brown contact lenses not long after my father's stroke. That was also the day I vowed to never again set foot in a church or to pray. I no longer believed in God's will. I had stomached the refrain throughout my youth as an

179

explanation for the bullying and general lack of compassion I had endured, because I wanted to believe that my mother's ardent faith that I was destined to lead an extraordinary life had some glimmer of truth. But if believing in God's will also meant believing my father's stroke had a purpose, that something good would come from striking down a good man at so young an age, well, that was a proposition I could not accept. To strike my father down in his prime was simply cruel, and all the doctors' rationalizations of bad genetics didn't change that assessment.

"Was Daniela with her father when she fell off her bike?" I asked.

Trina Crouch looked away.

Daniela nuzzled against her mother's side, timid as a mouse. Long blonde strands of hair partially covered her face. "Daniela, would you mind if your mom and I stepped into the hall to talk for a minute?"

Daniela's wide-eyed look conveyed that she didn't want her mother out of her sight, not for a moment. I rolled my chair across the room to a glass jar with assorted candies—everything except Tootsie Pops—and held it out for Daniela to choose. She looked from the jar to her mother, who nodded her consent. Daniela reached her delicate hand inside and chose a red sucker. I wondered if it was prophetic.

"Red," I said. "My favorite color is purple."

Daniela lowered her eyes.

I joined Trina Crouch in the hall and had no sooner shut the door when she said, "I don't have much time."

"I won't keep you. Has Daniela had any other accidents while she's been at her father's house?"

Crouch folded her arms and raised her chin. "Why would you ask me that?"

What was I to say? That I had once sustained a beating administered by her former husband and I, too, had lied and said I'd had a bike accident? Or was I to say that I suspected her husband was beaten as a child and medical literature suggests a link between abused children and adults who abuse children? "The emergency room report . . . your daughter's injuries from the bike accident seem rather mild."

Crouch looked to a print on the wall. "What are you saying?"

"I'm not saying anything, Mrs. Crouch. It's just that, well, I guess I would have expected her injuries to be more severe, given the description of the accident and the force of the blow to the head required to cause this type of injury."

Crouch looked up and down the hall. Then she locked on me with a burning gaze. "What kind of mother do you think I am?"

"I'm sure you're a very good mother, Mrs. Crouch."

"Then what?"

"Your daughter is losing her vision. I might be able to save it, but if she sustains any more accidents, any more blows to the head—"

She uncrossed her arms. Her eyes had filled with tears. "She fell off her bike." Her voice cracked. "I told you she fell off her bike. That's what the police report says, doesn't it?"

"Yes, that's what the police report says."

"Then that's the end of it."

I nodded. "I just want you to know that if you suspect that your daughter is having too many accidents when she is in your husband's care—"

"You have no idea what you're talking about. She fell off her bike. It was an accident. I came here because I was told you could help Daniela."

"I hope I can."

She stepped past me into the examination room. When she reemerged, she held Daniela by the wrist. She pulled the candy from her little girl's mouth by the stick and slapped it in my palm as they left.

2

I retreated to my office, shut the door, and sat staring at the framed photograph of the Three Stooges hanging on the wall. Moe stood in the middle. He held a clump of Larry's hair with one hand and had two fingers of his other hand stuck up Curly's nostrils. Since I wasn't invited to birthday parties or to other children's homes, except for Ernie's, I spent much of my youth watching the Three Stooges, and they had brought me endless hours of laughter. Ernie had found the poster in a novelty shop and gave it to me, framed, as a gift when Mickie and I opened our practice.

My desk faced east, with a window that allowed me to consider the rooftops of the other businesses on Broadway. The view reminded me of one of those re-created Old West towns in the tourist theme parks with false fronts hiding flat, tar, and gravel roofs, except these roofs were cluttered with crisscrossing pipes and equipment to heat and cool the buildings. I looked to the picture of Eva framed on my desk. She lay on her side, elbow bent, head propped on her hand, hair cascading nearly to the floor. Her green eyes beckoned to me, as did the flesh of her exposed shoulder from which her white knit sweater had slipped. The sweater also revealed a flat, toned stomach that Eva worked hard to maintain and was proud to show off.

I checked my watch, but it was unlikely she was at her Boston hotel yet. The flight crew usually had dinner together and a few cocktails. Besides, Eva would not want to discuss my work problems. I thought of Mickie, the most fearless person I'd ever met, but she was stretching through hot yoga. Faced with the same circumstances, Mickie would not have hesitated to call Child Protective Services and tell them what I suspected, that Daniela was being abused by her father. Unfortunately, Trina Crouch was correct. I had no real evidence to prove it. The police report indicated the little girl had a bike accident. What I had in rebuttal was an emergency room doctor's report intimating Daniela's other injuries did not comport with a bike accident, as well as my personal experience of being pummeled by David Bateman. Without Trina and Daniela's cooperation, it was unlikely I could help them, and I could end up making the abuse worse.

I decided to call the emergency room doctor, Pat LeBaron. Given the hour of the day, I intended to leave a message with his call service. On the third ring, I was surprised that Dr. LeBaron answered and that he was actually a she.

I introduced myself and said I was the ophthalmologist to whom she had referred Trina

Crouch and that I had seen Daniela that after-noon.

"Nice kid," LeBaron said, "but awfully shy. She didn't say two words. The mother did all the talking."

"I read your report," I said. "I wanted to ask if, well, Daniela had much in the way of other injuries?" Maybe I should have just hit LeBaron over the head with a hammer like the Three Stooges used to do.

"You mean other injuries such as scrapes and bruises consistent with a fall from a bike that would result in the type of head trauma reported?" Dr. LeBaron was not as dense as the Stooges. She exhaled a long breath through the phone. "No, I didn't find such injuries."

"I sensed from your report that you might have considered that odd?"

She picked her words carefully. "It seemed . . . unusual to me."

"I asked the mother—"

"Yeah? How'd that go?"

"I suspect about as well as it went for you."

"She denied anything happened. I asked her point-blank if she suspected her ex-husband had struck her daughter. She gave me a song and dance about 'how dare I,' and 'the police issued a report,' 'what gave me the right,' and 'what kind of mother did I think she was.'"

"I got a candy slapped in my palm."

185

"Huh?"

"I got the same song. So I assume you didn't report it to CPS?"

"Report what? She denies it, and the police report says it was a bike accident. I got nothing to say it wasn't. Do you have something more?"

"No, nothing," I said, except a history with the husband.

"Do you think you can help the girl?" LeBaron asked.

"I'm going to need to run a series of tests," I said, "if they come back to see me. I think Daniela has a detached retina."

"I hope you can," she said, ending our conversation.

I stared out the window. In the near distance, rising above the eucalyptus trees along the El Camino Real, stood the steeple to the OLM church. Not wanting to go straight home to an empty house, I made another call. Ernie Cantwell answered his direct line, a number that only I, his wife, and his parents possessed.

"I'll be home in half an hour," he said.

"I hope you don't expect a big sloppy kiss," I said.

"Hell."

Throughout high school my classmates had bastardized my last name and called me Hell. Every so often Ernie fell back into that habit.

"What up, Hell?"

"Wondering if you wanted to catch a beer at Moon's and watch the Forty-Niners game, but it doesn't sound like you can get a hall pass, you pussy-whipped candy ass."

"Insult me all you want, you red-eyed son of the devil," Ernie roared in a very good imitation of Muhammad Ali. "We both know who wears the pants in my house, *if* I choose to wear pants at all. I have committed to nothing, and I am the king of my castle!"

"You want to call me back after you call and get permission?"

"You know it, brother."

3

Moon McShane's drew a lot of Burlingame regulars and Forty-Niners faithful, making parking on Broadway scarce.

Most of the tables inside had already filled by the time I arrived. I took a seat on a stool at the bar, ordered a beer, and immediately drank half the glass. The thought of David Bateman, even after so many years, had unnerved me. The belief that he could be abusing his child made me sick.

Ernie entered ten minutes after I'd taken a seat. It felt like another ten minutes before he reached the bar stool I'd saved for him. People were drawn to the great Ernie Cantwell like magnets to metal. It had always been that way—at OLM, at Saint Joe's High School, and at Stanford, where I followed a year behind him. Ernie had played wide receiver and studied computer science. The Pittsburgh Steelers drafted him in the third round, and he played in the NFL just long enough to bankroll his hefty salary and retire in the prime of his career. It had been Ernie's intention since childhood to join the computer company his father had started in the garage of their Burlingame home. Cantwell Computers had grown significantly, and Ernie said the company had only scratched the surface of its potential, that someday every desk in every office and home in the world would have a personal computer. I had my doubts. It seemed more *Star Trek* than reality, but I hoped he was right, because I had a vested interest—Ernie had strong-armed me into investing some of my early inheritance in Cantwell Computers.

Ernie shook my hand and told the bartender to pour whatever I was drinking. I ordered my second. Ernie held up his glass. "Cheers," he said, then got that look of disgust. "You still wearing those dumb-ass contact lenses?"

"How many times are you going to say that?"

"Until you take them out."

"I don't want to scare my patients."

"If that's the reason, you ought to wear a mask." He considered the overhead television. "I was listening on the radio. Sounds like the Niners are kicking some butt."

I didn't know the score. "How long is the hall pass?"

"I told her I'd leave at halftime." Ernie and his wife met and married in Pittsburgh before moving back to California. They owned a house just south of Burlingame and had two young boys who called me Uncle Sam. "I didn't push it. I'm holding out for something bigger."

"Bigger than the Niners on Monday Night Football? Blasphemy," I said.

Ernie reached inside his suit coat and produced

two tickets. I knew immediately what they were. Every sports fan in the Bay Area knew what they were. "You're shitting me! You scored a World Series ticket?"

"Two, my friend. So, I was going to ask . . ."

"This is unbelievable."

"Would you mind watching the boys while Michelle and I go to the game?" Ernie laughed so hard I was surprised beer didn't shoot from his nose the way grape juice did when we were kids. Michelle hated to watch sporting events on television or in person. How the two of them met and married was a mystery.

"You asshole," I said.

"Be nice or I won't take you."

"How'd you get them?"

With the San Francisco Giants playing the Oakland Athletics in what the media had dubbed the Battle of the Bay, finding a ticket had been next to impossible. "My dad's client can't make it, so he offered them to me. I was going to take someone else because I thought you were going to Tahoe. What happened?" he said.

I hadn't told Ernie about the vasectomy and didn't intend to. He would have chastised me about it until my ears were as red as my eyes.

"Turns out Conman rented it for the weekend, so change of plans. I had a consult today," I said. "A mother and her daughter—the daughter is losing her vision because of a head trauma."

"Sad." Ernie alternately glanced at me and watched the television.

"The mother's name is Trina Crouch."

Ernie shook his head to indicate he'd never heard of her and resumed watching the game.

"The mother and father are divorced. The daughter's name is Daniela Bateman."

Ernie lowered his beer.

I nodded. "No shit."

"His daughter?"

"His daughter."

We both drank in silence. After Bateman's expulsion from OLM, he became more myth than real. We'd heard he went to the local public school but got expelled when he punched one of his teachers. Rumor was his parents had sent him to a military school back east and that, upon graduation, he'd enlisted in the marines.

"He's back?"

"Apparently. The blow to his daughter's head was supposedly the result of a bike accident." Ernie stared at me, and I knew where his mind had gone. My "bike accident" remained firmly entrenched in both our memories. "The police report concludes a bike accident, but the emergency room doctor's report is not consistent. The injuries—a scrape to the knee and one elbow—aren't severe enough given the kind of accident needed to cause the vision problems."

"Could it be the mother?"

I shook my head. "Daniela was with him at the time of the injury. I spoke to the emergency room doctor. She has the same suspicions."

"What are you going to do?"

"I don't know. I don't have anything to substantiate it unless the mother will support the emergency room doctor's findings."

Ernie looked to the television but only for a moment. "Look, Sam, your job is to fix this little girl's eyesight."

"And what if I get a call in the middle of the night that the little girl is dead?"

Ernie dropped his gaze to the bar. "My dad is tight with the DA. Let me talk to him tomorrow and find out if there's anything that can be done. I won't use any names."

I nodded. "Thanks."

Ernie looked at his watch, then at the screen. "I better get home." He'd lost interest in the game. I never really had any after meeting Trina Crouch. "I'll pick you up for the game at three. I want to get there early for batting practice."

After Ernie left I contemplated ordering a Moon burger and fries, but with the size of the crowd I knew the game would likely be over before I got my food. So I drank my dinner—three more beers, more than I had drunk in a long time. When I got my bill, Ernie's beer was not on it, as usual.

4

Outside, it remained warm. A late Indian summer had caused the temperature to soar during the day into the upper eighties, and it had not cooled much. I wasn't complaining. October baseball in short sleeves? What could be better? I contemplated calling a cab, but I didn't have far to drive, just a couple of miles down the El Camino.

I was playing with the radio dial to find the station that carried the Forty-Niners postgame show when I heard the blast of a siren and looked up to see spinning lights in my rearview mirror.

"Damn," I said. The police car had come out of nowhere. I checked my speed, certain I had not been speeding, and equally certain I had not swerved or run a stoplight. I mentally counted the beers and the time span over which I had consumed them. Having not eaten since breakfast, I would be in trouble if given any type of sobriety test, but that was unlikely. Police officers do not like to give tickets to doctors, and for that reason I kept my medical ID card in my wallet directly across from my license. As far as the officer knew, I could be the emergency room surgeon who would someday save his life.

I lowered the window and sucked in fresh air as I turned off the El Camino and made a right into the parking lot of the Presbyterian church, parking behind a tall hedge. The police car pulled behind me, the lights still flashing blue and red. A bright spotlight illuminated the inside of my car. I adjusted the rearview mirror to cut the glare. The officer remained inside his car, no doubt radioing in my license plate and waiting to find out if I had any outstanding warrants. I flipped open the glove box for the registration and pulled my wallet from my back pocket as I glanced again at the side-view mirror. It seemed to take an inordinate amount of time before the driver's side door of the patrol car pushed open and the officer emerged. He fit a cap on his head and adjusted the utility belt at his waist, pushing a billy club into its holster as he approached, still backlit by the bright light. I held up my wallet so my driver's license and medical ID were obvious, but the officer did not immediately take it. When I looked up, he'd bent down so that his face was even with the window. I felt the blood drain from my face.

The round face had changed, but the eyes had not.

"Well, well," David Bateman said. "If it isn't the devil boy himself."

5

July 1969
Burlingame, California

Ernie and I would later refer to the years after David Bateman's expulsion as "AB," for "After Bateman." Our bully seemingly fell off the face of the earth, as far away as Neil Armstrong had been that dramatic day, July 20, 1969, when he took that last step down the ladder and uttered those never to be forgotten words, "One small step for a man, one giant leap for mankind." We used to joke that maybe Armstrong had left David Bateman on the moon. I did not see Bateman at the park; he no longer played Little League baseball, and his parents left the OLM parish. Rumors of a Bateman sighting occasionally surfaced, but I didn't meet anyone who would swear to having seen him. In time, he faded from our thoughts.

Patrick O'Reilly and Tommy Leftkowitz steered clear of me in school after that. My guess is that Father Brogan put the fear of Jesus in them and in their parents. Sister Beatrice also, for the most part, let me be, though I would catch her watching me on the playground, and I took those glances as a subtle warning never to reveal the little secret of the silver flask she kept in the front pouch of her habit.

I never did.

6

Ernie's mother worked while his father continued doing what he was doing in the garage, so on weekends and in the summer, my mother took Ernie and me to San Francisco's museums, to watch the children's theater, or to listen to concerts in Stern Grove. She also frequently took us to the Easton library to pick out books. It seemed my mother handed me a new book every week: *Huckleberry Finn, The Black Stallion, Old Yeller, The Mousewife, The Jungle Book.* Saturday afternoons before dinner, she would send me upstairs for quiet reading time. It was on one of those Saturdays after we'd started school, as I lay on my bed reading *The Adventures of Tom Sawyer,* that I heard a car pull into our driveway. I put the book down to look out my shuttered bedroom window and saw the Cantwells' Volkswagen Beetle. I thundered down the stairs shouting, "Ernie's here! Ernie's here!"

"Samuel!" my mother said as she came around the corner from the kitchen. "You sound like a herd of buffalo."

"Ernie's here."

"I heard."

A second later the doorbell chimed. When I

pulled open the door, Mrs. Cantwell stood alone, a balled-up Kleenex in her hand.

"Sam, go back upstairs," my mother said.

"Is Ernie here?" I asked.

"No, hon," Mrs. Cantwell said, wiping her nose.

"Sam," my mother said, this time giving me *the look*. "Go upstairs."

I rushed upstairs, hurled myself to the floor, and shimmied my way to the grate. My mother made tea. I knew this from the familiar sounds in the kitchen—the ping of the blue kettle when my mother removed the top, the sound of the tap water filling the kettle, and another ping when she replaced the top and placed the kettle on the stove. She and Mrs. Cantwell sat at the kitchen table—a deduction from the sound the chairs made scraping the linoleum. Mrs. Cantwell kept her voice so soft I had trouble picking up all the words, but it had something to do with coming from a doctor's office. Something about Ernie.

We'd had a girl in our class leave school because she got sick, and when she came back she was bald and thin with dark circles under her eyes. My mother said she had something wrong with her blood. So when I heard Mrs. Cantwell say, "The doctor says Ernie has trouble reading, that his brain causes letters to switch places and he gets mixed up," I felt a huge relief. But then Mrs. Cantwell said, "He suggested we take Ernie out of OLM and send him to the public school. They have specialists who can give Ernie more personal attention."

This was bad. Ernie remained my only friend. I would be lost without Ernie. Then another thought came to me. To send Ernie to the public school was to send him to where the monster now lurked—David Bateman.

"Samuel has been such a good friend to Ernie," Mrs. Cantwell said. "Being the only black child in school has been very difficult for Ernie. Sam was the only child to welcome him. You've all always made us feel so welcome."

This was news to me. I'd always thought of Ernie as the kid who had saved me. I was, after all, the devil boy. Next to that, having black skin never seemed like such a big deal to me, but then I'd never thought of Ernie as black. He was just my best friend. Now his mother was in my kitchen saying Ernie needed me.

The blue kettle whistled.

I crawled out from under my bed and lay atop the covers, staring at the assortment of model airplanes hanging from the ceiling by fishing wire.

I considered the problem all afternoon. When my father came home, I didn't rush downstairs to greet him. He stopped at my bedroom door to check in with me. "Hey, son, everything okay?"

"Just reading."

My dad picked up the copy of *Tom Sawyer* from my nightstand. "Mark Twain," he said. "My favorite American author. Did you know his real name was Samuel? Samuel Clemens."

Under other circumstances I might have been interested, but I was preoccupied. "Dad, can I ask you something?"

He set the book down on my bed. "You know you can."

I couldn't very well tell my dad I had been spying on my mom and Mrs. Cantwell, so I decided to keep things anonymous. "What if you had this friend and he wasn't doing so good . . . like in school. And you wanted to help him, but you didn't want him to know you were helping him."

"Would this friend be anyone I know?"

"No," I said. "I'm just supposing it."

"Well, just supposing, why wouldn't this friend want help?"

I recalled how Ernie had always stuffed his tests in his desk when our teachers returned them and never told me his scores. "Maybe because he's embarrassed about it, you know, maybe because he doesn't want people to think he's stupid or something."

My dad put his hands to his chin as if in prayer, rubbing the palms together. "I can see why you wouldn't want him to feel stupid." He pondered the question a bit longer, then smiled and picked up *Tom Sawyer*, flipping the pages. "You've read the part in the story where Tom has to whitewash the fence?"

"You mean the part where he tricks Ben Rogers into doing it for him?"

"Exactly. You see, what Tom did was take advantage of Ben Rogers's disposition."

"His what?"

"Tom knew what type of boy Ben was. He knew Ben would tease him because he had to work while Ben was going swimming. Before Ben could tease him, Tom made his work look like more fun than swimming. And that made Ben want to paint the fence. Do you follow?"

"Not really."

"What you need to do is find out this friend's disposition. Do you know him pretty well?"

"Pretty well," I said.

"Then you need to figure out how to get this friend to accept your help without him knowing you're doing it."

"You mean trick him like Tom Sawyer tricked Ben Rogers."

"As long as this trick isn't mean-spirited, yes."

I thought about that a bit longer. "Thanks, Dad." My father started for the door. "And Dad, can we not tell Mom about this friend?"

My father looked at me. "You know your mother and I don't keep secrets from each other,

Sam. But maybe I just won't bring it up." He winked and left.

I lay on my bed, considering Ernie's disposition. The one thing I knew about Ernie was that he hated to lose, at anything. His parents had had to rush him to the emergency room one time after he bet his cousin he could stuff more peanuts up his nose. I had to be like Tom Sawyer. I had to get Ernie to want to whitewash the fence.

7

The following Monday I set my plan in motion. During our scheduled free time in school, I met Ernie at the reading shelf. Most of my classmates were one packet behind me, reading from the red section, but Ernie had still not completed the yellow packet.

"I'll bet you can't finish the yellow packet before I finish the purple packet," I said.

Ernie's eyes narrowed. "That's not fair. You're a better reader than me."

"So? You're better than me at kickball and basketball, and I still play."

"That's different," he said.

"How?"

"It just is." I shrugged and returned to my seat. Ernie followed me. "You're already almost finished with purple, and I'm just starting yellow."

Sister Joan looked up from her desk. "Ernie, are we having trouble finding our seat?"

"No, Sister."

"Then I suggest you find it and read in silence."

Ernie took his seat in the row next to me. I opened my book and acted like I was reading quickly, turning the pages. "It's dumb," he whispered.

I turned the pages faster. Sister Joan walked

out to the quad. She kept the door open when the weather was nice. A draft rattled the window blinds, making a noise like baseball cards in the spokes of a bike wheel. I turned to Ernie. "It's not dumb when it's kickball or three flies up, when you *know* you're going to win." I checked the door out of the corner of my eye but saw no sign of Sister Joan. "But when I'm good at something, you're chicken."

Several people in the class heard this challenge and uttered, "Ooh."

"Fine," Ernie said, "but you have to finish purple and all of blue."

"I'll be done by Friday," I said.

Ernie finished the yellow packet Thursday.

One afternoon later that year, Mrs. Cantwell stopped by to pick up Ernie on her way home from work and delivered a chocolate cake she'd baked. I heard her talking to my mother about Ernie's dramatic improvement in his reading. After Mrs. Cantwell and Ernie had left for home, my mother called me down to the kitchen. Though it was nearing dinner, she cut me an enormous slice of cake and poured a tall glass of milk. I thought it was a test of some kind, but my mother handed me a fork and brushed her hand through my hair. "I'd say Ernie is lucky to have a friend like you."

8

I would remember middle school for the arrival of a new student at OLM who would have a profound impact on my life.

Michaela Kennedy started school shortly after the Christmas holidays, when we returned to start the second semester of the sixth grade. I overheard a couple of the girls talking about Michaela, who went by Mickie. Rumor had it Mickie got in some type of trouble at the public school, and her parents enrolled her at OLM hoping the nuns could "straighten her out." I sensed Mickie was different from other girls the very first day. She did not wear her hair long or pulled back in a ponytail or twisted in braids with bows and ribbons. She cut it so short it barely touched her ears, which were not pierced. The school required that skirts extend to one inch above the knee, but to me it seemed Mickie's skirt inched higher each day. I heard one of the lunch ladies admonish Mickie for "showing too much leg."

Mickie retorted, "I wouldn't be showing any leg if they'd let us wear pants like the boys."

That comment got her a detention picking up trash for the remainder of the lunch period.

Mickie gravitated to the boys and forsook the

girls entirely, not interested in practicing cheers or jumping rope. Mickie played kickball and basketball, though it didn't start out that way. Boys in the class denied her admittance into our exclusive domain, but we learned quickly that Mickie was not to be denied.

"What, are you afraid a girl might beat you?" she'd say, dropping the challenge that no self-respecting boy could walk away from. Then she would proceed to not just beat them but humiliate them. Only Ernie was willing to readily accept Mickie, and his doing so had nothing to do with any understanding of discrimination. Ernie liked to win, and he quickly recognized Mickie's proficiency at sports. This resulted in my being demoted from Ernie's partner, and I resented Mickie for it. For a month, I silently seethed as I watched her and Ernie beat the stuffing out of all challengers in foursquare and wall ball, ignoring their accomplishments as if I couldn't have cared less. But I would soon learn Mickie was also not a person one could easily ignore.

9

The end of January marked another all-school Mass, and our class was responsible for the presentation. This was not an insignificant affair. Not just the entire school attended the Mass but parents and members of the general congregation as well. My mother never missed one. As the responsible grade, we were to choose and present the readings, prayers of the faithful, serve as the altar boys, sing in the choir, and bring up the gifts. To be chosen as the lector, however, was universally considered the highest honor. The position offered the greatest exposure, and therefore the greatest risk. This wasn't to discount the off chance an altar boy could catch his robe on fire on a candle, or that a student carrying the gifts up the aisle might stumble and toss the wafers into the crowd, but I'd never seen that happen. I *had* seen a lector screw up a reading at an all-school Mass. We all had.

The prior year, Anna Louise Gretsky had walked up the steps to the lectern, looked out over the crowd, and failed to utter a single word. We all thought Gretsky was employing a dramatic pause, until Father Killian, our new pastor, looked up from his throne, anxious to get going. We quickly realized that Anna Louise

Gretsky had frozen as solid as a block of ice. After another tense minute, one of the nuns climbed the steps and escorted a dazed and still-silent Gretsky back to her seat. That had not been the end of her humiliation, however. She endured taunts and gibes for the better part of the remainder of the year.

Monday, as our class began the task of dividing up the assignments, the frozen image of Anna Louise Gretsky remained a vivid reminder that being lector was not for the faint of heart. Students could volunteer for any position, but you had to be nominated to be lector. Since the vote was by a show of hands, the winner was usually the most popular student in the class, like Ernie, or maybe Valerie Johnson, the head cheerleader.

"Let's start with the gift bearers," Sister Mary Williams said. The students had nicknamed the elderly nun Sister Muffin because her face looked squished and wrinkled beneath her coif. She also wore Coke bottle–thick, black-framed glasses that magnified her eyes to look like two blue marbles under water. Sister Mary Williams wrote the names of the first four volunteers on the chalkboard in her flowing cursive style. The slots for the ushers and greeters also quickly filled.

"Who would like to be an altar boy?" Sister asked.

I was about to raise my hand when Ernie said,

"I'll do it," taking himself out of contention for lector. I knew Ernie's decision had to do with his uneasiness about reading in public, and as I sat contemplating his decisions, two of my other classmates quickly raised their hands to join him. I had been shut out. The only thing left for those of us not chosen for any other tasks was the choir, which was like being a stagehand at a play—all the work without any of the glory.

Sister Mary Williams moved to the final position on the board and, without fanfare, said, "All right, I'll take nominations for lector."

The clock above the cloakroom buzzed as the big hand struck ten. With Ernie out of the running, Valerie Johnson, the girl who'd given me an envelope with a dead fly in it on Valentine's Day in the first grade, was a shoo-in. Taking nominations was a waste of time.

"I nominate Sam Hill."

I think every head in the class turned as if they'd heard a foreign language being spoken. The nomination had come from Mary Beth Potts, a cheerleader and Valerie Johnson's best friend. Potts had never said more than a few sentences to me. I had no idea why she'd nominated me. Even Sister Mary Williams hesitated before turning to scrawl my name on the blackboard. A loud murmur ensued, along with a lot of whispers and giggles. I heard Ernie urgently whispering my name.

"Sam. Sam!"

Ernie sat in the row to my right and two seats behind me. When I turned his face was grave, and he was shaking his head. "Say no," he said. "No!"

No? Was he crazy? Nothing short of my announcing that I intended to become a Catholic priest would make my mother prouder than to see me standing at the lectern in front of the entire school. As for me, this was my chance to show not only my classmates but all their parents that I was just a normal kid. As I contemplated this, with Ernie continuing to try to get my attention, I saw another hand go up.

Mickie Kennedy. My anger swelled. It would be just like this newcomer to tank my candidacy. She'd stolen Ernie. Now she intended to steal my chance at glory.

But to my surprise, Mickie said, "I second the nomination."

This was a clear breach of the election protocol, there being no need to second the nomination. Then Mickie blurted even louder, "And I say we vote."

Valerie Johnson quickly raised her hand, and the hands of the others in her entourage followed. The boys also raised their hands, Ernie being the last to do so and looking reluctant.

"Congratulations, Sam," Sister Mary Williams said.

It might have been the happiest moment of my short life, next to the day my father drove up the driveway with the red Schwinn bicycle. I only hoped for a better ending.

10

At recess Ernie quickly chased me down. "Sam. Sam!"

"What's wrong?" I said. "Why didn't you want to vote for me?"

Ernie hesitated. "They want you to fail, Sam. I saw Valerie Johnson whispering to Mary Beth to nominate you. I think they want you to freeze like Anna Louise Gretsky so they can make fun of you."

"What? How do you know that? Did you hear her?"

Ernie shook his head. "But it's Valerie Johnson," he said. "Why would she nominate *you?*"

"She didn't. It was Mary Beth—"

"Valerie told her to nominate you, Sam."

I ignored this well-reasoned rationale because I wanted the position. "So why shouldn't I be lector? I'm the best student in the class."

"You should turn it down, Sam. Just tell Sister you can't do it."

"No," I said emphatically.

"What if something happens?"

"Like what?"

"I don't know. They do something to embarrass you, and you screw up."

"I'm not going to screw up," I said.

As recess was coming to an end, I found myself walking back to class beside Mickie. With Ernie's admonition fresh on my mind, I asked her, "Why'd you nominate me?"

"Don't get a swollen head, Hill," she said. "You're a brain; you should be the lector. Better you than that airhead Valerie Johnson or one of her stupid friends." Then Mickie punched me on the arm and ran off to the classroom at the sound of the bell.

11

After school I raced home, dropped my bike on the lawn, and rushed through the front door. "Mom? Mom!"

"Samuel Hill." My mother emerged from the kitchen, wiping her hands on a dish towel. "What have I told you about bellowing my name like a banshee?"

"I got it," I said. "A girl in my class nominated me and Mickie seconded it and the vote was unanimous, every kid."

"Slow down," my mother said. "Start over. You got what?"

"Lector. At the all-school Mass on Friday. I got it."

My mother did not, however, whoop for joy or immediately embrace me as I had expected. "They elected you?"

"Yeah. It was unanimous."

"Samuel," my mother said, still somewhat solemn.

"What's the matter?" I said. "I thought you'd be happy."

"I am," my mother said, forcing a smile. Then she hugged me. "Oh, Samuel, I am happy and I'm proud of you. That is a great honor. Won't your father be proud."

"I have two readings and the responsorial psalm," I said, pulling back from her. "That's when you raise your hand, like this." I raised my hand. "Then everyone knows it's their turn. I have to get started right away."

"Well, I can certainly help," my mother said. "You know I did theater in college."

"Really?" The thought of my mother doing anything except being a mother seemed highly unlikely, but theater came as a real surprise. I would have thought she'd consider acting a display of vanity.

"I'll have you know I played Elizabeth in *Pride and Prejudice*."

I had no idea if that was a big deal, but from the grin on my mother's face, I could tell it meant something to her. "That's great, Mom. Can you help me?"

12

We studied and worked on the readings each day after school, my mother helping me with the pronunciations of the difficult words and then with my posture and presentation.

"Hold your head high," she said. "Make eye contact with the audience before you speak. Slow down—you're rushing."

After posture and presentation, she moved to voice inflection, which words to emphasize. This resulted in a few disagreements between my parents.

"No, no. Emphasize *not*. Don't emphasize *road*," my father would say.

"Emphasize *road*," my mother would correct.

My mother made a makeshift lectern by having me stand on several volumes of the *Encyclopedia Britannica*, and I would perform the readings after dinner. My parents surely must have tired of these performances, but if they did, they never complained.

"We have a regular showman," my father said one evening as we sat down for meat loaf and mashed potatoes with gravy.

"He gets it from me," my mother said. "You know I played Elizabeth in *Pride and Prejudice* in college."

"How could I forget," my father said, taking a piece of meat loaf and holding the plate for me. "You kissed Bill Mahler right there onstage before God and man."

I nearly dropped the meat loaf on the floor. "You kissed another man?" I asked. "I hope you socked him one, Dad."

"I did not kiss anyone," my mother said. "I was in character. That was Elizabeth."

My father rolled his eyes. "Well, Bill Mahler found it convincing. He asked you out for two years after that one kiss. And I would have socked him, Sam, but he was also captain of the basketball team."

My mother smiled. "I will have you know, Samuel Hill, that I have always only had eyes for one man, and he's sitting right here at this table."

I grinned and wedged a green bean between my tongue and the roof of my mouth.

"I wish I could be there in person to hear you, but I'll be there in spirit," my father said.

My father continued to work six days a week, leaving the house early and working so late sometimes that he'd even miss dinner. The table felt empty without him.

"We have to tighten our belts," my mother said during one of our meals without him. "A chain pharmacy just opened on Burlingame

Avenue, and your father's prescription count has dropped."

I was disappointed my father would miss my performance, but I understood how hard he was working.

13

Friday morning, I was nervous, mainly because throughout the week Ernie had continued to stew over all the things that could go wrong and suggested that I feign an illness, or laryngitis. I continued to focus on just one thought. I knew my classmates and their parents still considered me the devil boy. This was surely God's way for me to prove I was a normal kid, maybe even extraordinary, as my mother frequently professed. Who was I to argue with a woman who'd had the lead in *Pride and Prejudice*?

Arriving at school, I slid the front wheel of my bike into the bike stand and snapped the lock through the tire. Ernie skidded to a stop beside me. "Are you ready?"

"I guess so," I said.

We walked up the covered breezeway together, and I was certain the eyes of the entire student body were watching me, and that this would be the best day of my life. Then I opened the door to our classroom and froze. The face that wheeled to greet us had not the soft and comforting features of Sister Mary Williams but the laser-precise glare of Sister Beatrice.

14

Ernie stumbled into me, not seeing Sister Beatrice. "What the hell, Sam."

Our principal's eyes threw daggers at Ernie. "Detention, Mr. Cantwell. I will not tolerate profanity."

Ernie's shoulders sagged, and he stepped past me and found his seat.

"Do you not know where your seat is, Mr. Hill?"

"Yes, Sister. I mean, no, Sister."

"Then I suggest you find it."

I took my seat along with my equally depressed classmates.

"Sister Mary Williams is under the weather. I will serve as your substitute. When the bell rings, you will assemble in an orderly fashion and proceed to the church."

Ernie raised his hand. "Sister, the altar boys need to be at the church early to get set up—"

"Does Sister Mary Williams allow you to speak without permission, Mr. Cantwell?"

"No, Sister."

"Then I suggest you wait until called upon."
Ernie sat back.

"Was there something you wanted to ask, Mr. Cantwell?"

"No, Sister."

"Something about the altar boys having to leave early for church?"

Ernie still did not answer.

"Well, Mr. Cantwell?"

"Whatever . . ."

If the room had not already been deathly silent, this would have been one of those moments when you truly could have heard a pin drop.

"You just earned a second detention, Mr. Cantwell, and I shall be sending a note home to your mother to discuss your insolence."

"You're diabetic?" Peter Hammonds asked.

It was an innocent question, I'm sure. Hammonds wasn't the sharpest tool in the shed, and his vocabulary skills were less than stellar, but Sister Beatrice saw it as a further attack on her authority. "And you will be serving detention with Mr. Cantwell, Mr. Hammonds. Anyone else wish to test my patience?"

No one did.

"Now, who are the altar boys?" Ernie, Matty Montoya, and Billy Fealey raised their hands. Their arms looked like limp noodles. "The altar boys are excused."

Valerie Johnson then raised her hand and, when called upon, said, "Sister, the altar preparers also need to leave early to set up the church."

Sister Beatrice dismissed them. As they departed Sister Beatrice turned her attention to me. "I suppose you believe you should be allowed to leave ahead of your classmates as well, Mr. Hill."

"No, Sister, just the altar boys and the altar preparers."

"Vanity is a sin," she said, but it sounded like *thin.* "Can anyone in the class tell me what vanity is?" This time not even Peter Hammonds would venture a guess. "No one? Vanity is the excessive belief in one's own abilities or attractiveness. Do you believe you are better than your classmates, Mr. Hill?" Her words hissed at me like a rattler disturbed from sleep. I noticed her eyes were glassy.

I shook my head. "No, Sister."

"Smarter? More important?"

"No, Sister."

"Good, then you shall demonstrate your humility by being last in line entering the church."

When the bell mercifully rang, my classmates and I solemnly lined up against the wall. Sister Beatrice didn't have to worry about us talking. We marched down the playground to the church like prisoners on a forced death march. Not even the crisp winter air could raise our spirits.

Outside the grand cathedral doors, we waited for the younger grades to parade down the aisle and take their seats. When our line moved forward, Sister Beatrice reached out and put an arm across my path the way my mother did when she had to stop the car suddenly. Her eyes bored into mine, and I could smell the alcohol on her breath.

"Your classmates chose you because they want to see you fail," she said.

15

As we marched into the church, I became keenly aware of the parents and the rest of the congregation assembled in the pews behind the students in their school uniforms. Valerie Johnson and her cohorts had hung white **RESERVED** signs on the pews for the students. As we waited for the nuns to ensure the usual boy-girl-boy-girl seating, I saw my mother standing beside Mrs. Cantwell. They smiled at me, but my mother's smile quickly faded when her eyes shifted to Sister Beatrice. She bowed her head, and her chest heaved. She also must have uttered something audible, because Ernie's mom turned with a look of alarm and touched my mother's arm, like people do when they think someone is sick. My mother just closed her eyes and shook her head.

We filed into our designated pews. As I was last, the girl to my left, sitting at the end of the pew nearest the center aisle, was Sister Beatrice. I felt nauseated, and only partly from the smell of alcohol emanating from her. We stood at the first song. Moments later Ernie led the procession up the aisle, carrying the crucifix. Father Killian shuffled forward in his white-and-gold cassock, singing loudly, and ascended to his throne. When the song concluded, he gathered us in

Christ's name and welcomed our parents and the members of the congregation. After leading us in the profession of faith, he sat.

That was my cue.

I stood to exit the pew and noticed that Valerie Johnson and her cadre of friends had all turned their heads to stare at me and giggle. I chastised myself for not having listened to Ernie, for allowing my hopes to get raised. Clearly my classmates were waiting for me to fail. So, too, I was certain, was Sister Beatrice.

I was supposed to genuflect before climbing the steps to the altar, but I was wondering what would happen to our well-rehearsed choreography if I vomited right in the middle of the center aisle. I wanted to be anywhere but in that church. God's will, it seemed, was to humiliate me.

I caught sight of Ernie kneeling at the side of the altar, but he was looking past me, and when I followed his gaze, I saw Valerie Johnson leaning forward to whisper to one of the girls seated in the pew in front of her. I bent to a knee to genuflect, made the sign of the cross, and proceeded to the lectern, climbing the steps. Once at the podium, I adjusted the microphone as rehearsed. Then I reached for my readings, which the altar preparers were to place on the shelf in the lectern, but when I pulled out the pages I realized, to my horror, that Valerie Johnson had replaced my readings with pages that, at a quick glance, contained old Hebrew words I didn't have a clue how to pronounce. As my anxiety built, I felt myself becoming red in the face, more and more nauseated, and burning up as if I had a fever. I didn't know what to do.

And then I heard the bells.

At first I didn't know what was happening. No one did. I turned to the altar and saw that Ernie had grabbed the gold fingerhold and was ringing the four altar bells with more vigor and enthusiasm than I had ever heard before or since in that church. Father Killian's head swiveled, his facial expression a mixture of confusion and annoyance. He swung his arm at Ernie as if swatting at an annoying bee. Unfortunately, Father Killian swatted exactly where the altar servers had set his glass of water on a side table, sending it sailing.

I don't know who was first to laugh, but from my vantage point, perched above the congregation, I saw students with hands clasped over their mouths, fighting desperately to keep from breaking into hysterics, most without success. After what seemed a full minute, Ernie set the bells down, cutting off the chimes. He looked like someone who had just committed a totally innocent mistake, but I knew better. I knew Ernie had rung those bells on purpose, even before he admitted it when we got home that afternoon. He said he knew Valerie and her friends had done something and deduced from my facial expression that they had switched the readings. Ernie had screwed up on purpose. Only Ernie Cantwell had the self-confidence to absorb the impending ridicule he had to know would result, not to mention Sister Beatrice's inevitable punishment.

But his act worked. When I turned back to the lectern, I was no longer nervous, realizing that no matter how many words I fumbled or skipped, no one would be talking about anything except how Ernie had messed up on such a grand scale. I also realized something else. I didn't need the readings. I'd performed the actual readings so often I had darn near memorized every word, and I could see them now, on the pages, with all my mother's little pencil marks.

I paused as my mother and I had rehearsed and looked out over the red sweaters filling the front half of the church pews and then to the parents. My mother's face beamed up at me, but now Ernie's mother looked as downcast as she had that day she'd come to our home to inform us that Ernie had a learning disability. Her dejection made me realize the extent of Ernie's sacrifice. When my eyes shifted to Sister Beatrice, she was scowling, her eyes blazing with fury. There would be hell to pay for Ernie.

I looked last to Valerie Johnson and gave her a subtle burning gaze that wiped the smile from her face and caused her to sit back in genuine fear.

"A reading from the book of Daniel," I began. Valerie Johnson's eyes widened, and she looked to Mary Beth Potts, who seemed equally perplexed.

My classmates had chosen the readings, and they all were expecting the classic story of Daniel in the lions' den. I know this as fact because my mother kept the readings in a scrapbook, complete with her handwritten notes and pencil marks to cue my pronunciations, as we had practiced. As I recited the story of the king throwing Daniel into the pit of lions, and how God rewarded Daniel's faith and devotion by sending an angel to protect him, I realized Ernie was *my* guardian angel and had been since that first day on the playground.

I completed the reading certain I hadn't hit every word, but I had gotten close enough that no one noticed. Then I moved to the responsorial psalm. Again I paused, closing my eyes and seeing the reading in my mind's eye. My eyes shifted over the crowd. Sister Beatrice's face remained an angry mask.

"God is my shepherd, I shall not want." I raised my palm, the gesture for the congregation to repeat the phrase, which they did in unison.

"God is my shepherd, I shall not want. Though I walk in the valley of the shadow of death, I will fear no evil: for thou art with me; thy rod and thy staff, they comfort me."

As I neared the end of the psalm, I knew I could not allow Ernie to walk into that valley of darkness alone. I was determined to walk beside him, whatever the consequences.

The second reading was a short letter from Paul to the Corinthians.

"Brothers and sisters," I began. "Paul was called to be an apostle by the will of God . . ."

I had also memorized this reading. The rest of the sentence read, *to tell you the good news of Jesus Christ, of his virginal birth, death on the cross, and resurrection from the dead.*

"To tell you the good news of Jesus Christ," I proclaimed in a loud voice that reverberated from the speakers. Then I said, "Of his vaginal birth . . ."

If I had done the reading at an ordinary Sunday Mass, no one would have cared, but this was not a Sunday Mass made up of an adult congregation. The congregation was grade-school kids who still thought the funniest things in the world were the names given to the male and female sex organs. To say it in church was a mistake on a scale that trumped even ringing the bells at the wrong moment.

The congregation sucked in and held its collective breath, but, like Ernie, I had no intention of allowing this mistake to go unnoticed.

"Sorry." I cleared my throat and started over as the snickering began. "To tell you the good news of Jesus Christ," I repeated. "Of his vaginal . . ." I shook my head. "His *virginal* birth . . ."

That did it. There is nothing more contagious than a suppressed snicker in a church, and Ernie had already warmed up the crowd. Once the giggling started, it spread like a wave and soon became outright laughter. I watched, transfixed, as David Butterfield, a seventh grader sitting at the end of a pew, doubled over in laughter, lost his balance, and tumbled into the center aisle. If saying the word *vagina* in church was funny, watching a student roll out of a pew was downright hysterical. The nuns popped up from their seats, marching like penguins from one pew to the next, unsuccessfully trying to restore order.

I looked at my mother. I didn't want to, but I was drawn to her. We had worked so hard for this moment, and she had been so proud. I expected to see abject disappointment and sorrow, but my mother did not look disappointed or even sad— not in the least. She was smiling, a hand covering her mouth to suppress her own laugh.

16

My classmates and I marched in silence from the church narthex into the schoolyard. The nuns remained furious. Sister Beatrice waited until the door to our classroom had slammed shut before she unleashed her verbal assault, and it was a doozy. "Ernie Cantwell, you are a buffoon. And Sam Hill, you are a disgrace to your class, to your school, and to this community. Do not think for a minute I don't know what happened in there this morning. Do not think for one minute I believe either of you is innocent in any of this. Do you think the church is a stage for your comedic routines? Do you think this was funny?"

"I do."

For a second, no one reacted. As with the bells in the church, the comment was so foreign I think everyone was trying to decide if they'd heard it. I hadn't said it, and I knew it wasn't Ernie. The voice was higher pitched, a girl's voice. We all turned in unison. Mickie Kennedy sat in the last desk of the first row. "I think it was hilarious, and I say we take a vote," she said, thrusting her hand into the air. Mickie's defiance was so brazen, so outrageous, I think most of my classmates forgot the gravity of the situation, because just as suddenly half of them raised their hands.

"Put your hands down!" Sister Beatrice screamed. She wheeled on Mickie but, unable to find words, stood there with her face growing darker shades of red, like a child holding her breath. For one brief moment, I thought her head might explode. "How dare you!" she finally bellowed. "How dare you . . . you . . . you . . ." She looked like one of those robots stuck in a corner that can do nothing but turn and pivot, turn and pivot. Finally, she grabbed the seating chart from Sister Mary Williams's desk. "How dare you, Miss, Miss, Miss . . ."

"Kennedy," Mickie said. "Like the president, but we're not related."

"Michaela Kennedy!" Sister blurted.

"My name is . . . Mickie," she corrected. "What are you so mad about? At least Mass wasn't the same old boring stuff."

The color drained from Sister Beatrice's face. She looked as though she might faint. She hurried down the aisle, hovering over Mickie like the witch over Dorothy, apparently unsure where to begin. For some bizarre reason, she chose to say, "We do not use nicknames in this school."

"Then why does everyone call you Sister Beaver?"

It was Sister Beatrice's nickname, though I'm not certain when exactly I first heard it. Because of her two prominent front incisors, the older students had dubbed Sister Beatrice Beaver, or Beave for short.

Sister Beatrice yanked Mickie from her seat by the arm, half dragging her out of the room. When the door slammed shut, Ernie and I looked knowingly at each other. Having just acted to save each other, we suspected Mickie, too, had choreographed her actions, though she had taken it a step or two further, something that would become a common occurrence throughout our lifelong friendship. What we didn't understand was *why* Mickie had done it. She didn't owe us anything. In fact, I had largely ignored her, still miffed that she'd taken my place as Ernie's playground sidekick.

Five minutes after Sister Beatrice departed, one of the laywomen from the office came into our classroom looking harried and confused. "You are to take out your reading books and begin reading in silence," she said. "If anyone speaks, I am to send you to the principal's office."

No one did.

Mickie did not show up on the playground at lunch, nor did she return to the classroom that afternoon. Neither did Sister Beatrice. She'd perhaps forgotten about Ernie's and my detentions. Mary Beth Potts and Valerie Johnson sat like statues, paralyzed by their fear that I would tell on them. I never did. After school, Ernie and

I ran out with our classmates like prisoners on a jailbreak, and we rode as fast as we could until we reached my front yard. When I walked in the front door, I detected an aroma familiar to every child—chocolate-chip cookies. My mother had just taken a tray out of the oven. She placed a plate on the table along with two glasses of milk. The right side of her mouth inched into a grin as she looked from Ernie to me.

"You have inherited your mother's acting skills, Samuel Hill."

17

Mickie returned to class the following Monday. So did Sister Mary Williams. None of us ever spoke of the travesty that was the all-school Mass. Late in the morning, Sister instructed us to take out our math books, then called my name and asked me to accompany her outside the classroom. I thought for certain this conversation would be about me paying the piper.

We sat on the red lunch bleachers, the masonry wall hiding us from the rest of my classmates, who were no doubt peering out the window.

"I heard about what happened," Sister said.

"I'm sorry, Sister."

Her watery eyes held a kindness and warmth. "I think we both know what you and Ernie did, Sam."

I didn't respond.

She sighed. "Sister Beatrice has . . . some problems," she said. "She doesn't mean the things she says and does. Do you understand?"

I knew it had to do with the silver flask. "I think so," I said.

"You're a good boy, Sam. God gave you a cross to bear, just as he gave me one."

"You, Sister?" I asked.

She removed her thick glasses, which had

already turned a dark shade since we had ventured outdoors, and I noticed that her eyes, without them, were rather small, beady.

"I'm legally blind, Sam. These glasses only partially correct my vision. As I get older, I will go completely blind."

"When, Sister?"

"Only God knows."

I felt myself becoming angry. How could God take the eyesight of such a warm, loving person and leave such a rotten person as Sister Beatrice with twenty-twenty vision?

"Everything happens for a reason," Sister Mary Williams said, sounding very much like my mother. "I might not have become a nun, or a teacher, had it not been for my eyes. I am so sensitive to light I have always had to wear sunglasses, even as a young girl. The other children called me Bat Girl, because I was as blind as one. The only place I found comfort, outside my home, was in church. I could take off my glasses and feel normal. Everything God does is for a reason, Sam; every cross we bear is an opportunity. Do you understand?"

"I think so," I said, though I was becoming less sure I wanted to understand.

She slipped her glasses back on. "You and Ernie will remain fifteen minutes after school to clean the chalkboards and the erasers."

"Yes, Sister."

When we stood from the bleachers, I felt a compulsion too strong to ignore. It surprised me, and it surprised Sister Mary Williams. I reached out and hugged her. After a moment, I felt the warmth of her hand atop my head.

"I'm glad you became a teacher," I said.

At recess Ernie and I found Mickie waiting in line for her chance to kick the ball.

"Did you get in trouble?" I asked.

"My parents grounded me for a month. I can't watch TV."

"Sorry about that," I said.

"I didn't do it because I like you or anything," she said.

"I didn't mean that. I just—"

"Forget it, Hill." Mickie raced forward and booted the ball high over everyone's heads, then took off running away from me, something that would become a habit for Mickie Kennedy.

18

Two years later, 1971, my parents dropped me off at school in my graduation cap and gown, which, as luck would have it, were red and only served to further bring out the color of my eyes. The class was buzzing with excitement for our big night. We would graduate in the church, then walk through the playground to the gymnasium for our first dance.

Ernie greeted me when I walked in the door of the classroom. "We made it, Hill. We are escaping this prison. I can't wait to get out of here."

I smiled, but I wasn't sure I shared the same sentiment. My years at OLM had been anything but smooth, though they'd improved after David Bateman was banished, and got better still when, at the end of summer following sixth grade, we came back to school to find an interim principal—Sister Mary Francis. No one said what had happened to Sister Beatrice. Like David Bateman, she'd simply vanished, like a ghost. This meant my seventh- and eighth-grade years were relatively pain-free. While I couldn't look back on grammar school with fond memories, I was more apprehensive about the thought of starting over again at Saint Joseph's, the all-boys Catholic high school Ernie and I would attend, and trying to win over a bunch of kids who would once again not know a thing about me except that I had red eyes.

I took my seat at my desk as our first lay teacher, Ms. Trimball, went over the graduation ceremony one final time. Despite my screwup at the all-school Mass, I had been chosen by Ms. Trimball as one of three students to give a "reflection." The written pages were supposed to be at the lectern, but I'd kept a copy on me, just in case. When I opened my desk to retrieve the pages, I found a gift-wrapped package. I pulled it out thinking a similar package was in each student's desk, but no one else was holding one. I looked to Valerie Johnson, certain I would open the package and a snake would pop out, or a stink bomb, but Valerie was not paying any attention to me. She and her friends were engrossed in talk about their dresses, makeup, and the dance. I unwrapped the package. Inside I found a Bible. Perplexed, I flipped it open. It had been inscribed in flowing cursive handwriting.

Samuel,
May God bless you and watch over you
on your new adventure in high school.
Sister Beatrice

I shut the book as if to trap a rattlesnake. My pulse had quickened, and I was suddenly very hot in my graduation gown. After a moment, I slowly opened the Bible and peeked inside to confirm what I'd read. I quickly shut it.

"Sam," Ernie said from his seat one row over. "You okay? You look like you saw a ghost."

I felt like I'd seen a ghost.

"I'm fine," I said.

I gave the gift to my mother after graduation but didn't have time to talk to her before the dance. I was apprehensive about that as well, certain I'd be eating cookies and drinking punch alone until it was time to leave, but Mickie Kennedy would have none of that. She grabbed my hand the moment I walked in the door and pulled me out onto the dance floor. As she writhed and bounced and danced I stood flat-footed to the Rolling Stones' "Brown Sugar."

"I don't know what to do!" I shouted over the music.

"Just move, Hill."

"How?"

"Any way you want."

And so I did. I'm sure I must have looked like a kid with his pants on fire, but I did my best to imitate and stay up with Mickie. In no time, the dance floor was so crowded you couldn't move much anyway. That's when the music changed to Rod Stewart's "Maggie May."

I turned to go sit down, but Mickie, once again, would have none of it. "I don't bite, Hill. Besides,

I heard the dance ladies are worse than the lunch Nazis. We must keep six inches between us to make room for the Holy Spirit. You think you can stand dancing six inches from me?"

I could. I hadn't realized it before, or maybe I had, but I knew then, as I danced with one arm around Mickie's waist and my other, sweaty hand holding hers, that I liked Mickie—"like" being the limits of an eighth grader's affection for someone of the opposite sex.

I liked her a lot.

At home that night, my mother had the Bible out on the kitchen counter. My father looked just as perplexed as I was when I'd first opened it. My mother simply smiled. "Wasn't that a lovely gesture on her part?" she said.

"But why did she do it?" I asked.

"To let you know that she's keeping you in her prayers."

"Why? The woman hates me."

"She doesn't hate you, Samuel."

"But isn't this kind of hypocritical?"

"Don't question her motives, Samuel. Just accept the gift and be grateful for it."

I stuck the Bible on my dresser, never intending to look at it again. I would have thrown it out, but I thought there was some rule against throwing out Bibles and rosaries, and I didn't want to be trapped in purgatory for having done so. Throughout high school and college, that Bible remained on my dresser. When my mother died and I sold the house, I found it still there, without even a layer of dust.

It is now on a shelf in my living room.

We all moved on to high school—me with my red eyes; Ernie, the only black kid; and Mickie, the third misfit. Her mother and father would enroll her at the Sisters of Providence, the all-girls Catholic school in Burlingame, but Mickie would not last her freshman year. Officially, she "transferred" to the local public school; that's what her prospective college applications would state. Unofficially, she'd been expelled for smoking at a school dance, but even that didn't tell the whole story. Tired of the nuns and what she considered her stifling Catholic education, Mickie orchestrated her expulsion just as she had orchestrated her detention in the sixth grade. She came on to a senior at a dance, one everyone in Burlingame knew to be a pothead. The nuns did catch her smoking, but it wasn't cigarettes and it wasn't at the dance. Mickie was in the back seat of the guy's car, sucking marijuana smoke from his mouth.

PART FOUR

Nightmares and Fantasies

1

1989
Burlingame, California

David Bateman pulled open my car door, businesslike and professional. "Step out of the car, please."

I remembered Bateman as being a good head taller than me as a boy, but when I got out of the car, the disparity in our sizes was more pronounced. The marines had trimmed the fat and sculpted Bateman's body. His biceps stretched the fabric of his blue uniform, and his forearms looked like woven ropes, complete with a tattoo of the Marine Corps symbol—an eagle atop a globe.

"David," I managed to say, trying to sound like an adult and not a scared little boy.

Bateman held a long metal flashlight and directed it to a gold badge clipped to his breast pocket. "It's Officer Bateman."

I didn't respond.

"Say it."

"Say what?"

"Say 'Officer Bateman.'"

I hesitated until I remembered the five beers I had consumed. I was in no position to piss him off. "Officer Bateman."

He considered my wallet in the beam of light. "So, the devil boy is now Dr. Devil Boy, huh? What kind of doctor are you? No, let me guess. You're an eye doctor."

"Ophthalmologist," I said.

He looked up from my wallet. "Are you suggesting that I'm stupid?"

"No, I was just—"

"I know what an eye doctor is; I don't need you to tell me."

I bit my tongue.

"Have you been drinking tonight, Doctor?"

"I had a couple of beers watching the game."

"I had a couple of beers watching the game, *Officer Bateman*," he corrected, then cupped his hand to his ear like a drill sergeant.

"I had a couple of beers watching the game, Officer Bateman."

He shone the light directly in my eyes, causing me to squint and look away. "That's funny. I could have sworn your eyes used to be red. Is that what happens when you're full of shit? Do your eyes turn brown?"

I'd had enough. "What do you want, David?"

"What do I want?" He seemed to consider this. Then he said, "I want you to turn around and put your hands on the roof of the car—that's what I want."

"What for?"

He grabbed me by the collar, spun me around,

and immediately kicked my legs apart. His steel-toed boot hit my anklebone, and the pain caused my leg to buckle, dropping me to my knees.

"Get up," he shouted, grabbing me and lifting me to my feet. "I didn't say give me a blow job; I said put your hands on the roof of the car and spread your legs."

Though my ankle felt as though it was on fire, I managed to get to my feet. Bateman grabbed my right wrist and wrenched it behind my back, snapping on a cuff and pinching the skin. My left arm followed. The billy club pressed my head against the roof.

"Now I want you to listen and I want you to listen real good. You ready?"

"Yes." He shoved my head against the roof of the car. "Yes, Officer Bateman," I managed.

"Let me give you a little piece of advice. You fix my daughter's eyes, and you leave it at that. I find you talking to my ex-wife or anyone else about what you think may or may not have happened and I'm going to come looking for you, and next time I'm not going to let you off with a warning. Do we understand one another?" He shoved my head against the roof again. "It's impolite not to respond."

"Yes," I said.

"I didn't hear you," he said in the voice of that drill sergeant.

"Yes, Officer Bateman."

"Good." After another moment, he began releasing the cuffs. "I'm in a good mood tonight and I know you only have a few blocks to go to get home, so I'm going to let you go without a field sobriety test." I heard him step back, thinking the worst over. Then the billy club whapped me hard across the back of my hamstrings, a pain that dropped me again to my knees. Had I not grabbed the door handle of the car, I would have collapsed onto the pavement. I stayed there, fighting back the pain and the humiliation, recalling how as a little boy I had lain on the ground at the Ray Park playground until I could no longer hear Bateman and his two goons. I pulled myself to my feet, the backs of my legs stinging. David Bateman sat behind the wheel of his patrol car. He smiled as he drove off.

2

By the time I got home, the pain in my ankle and the backs of both thighs was so excruciating I could barely limp upstairs. I made it to the bathroom and shimmied out of my pants. Using Eva's hand mirror, I examined the damage. The baton had left inflamed red lines—each six inches long and an inch wide—across the backs of my thighs. They looked like two massive tapeworms burrowing beneath the skin. The capillaries around the welts had burst, causing a spattering of bright-red blotches, but from what I could tell in the mirror, it was unlikely I would develop a hematoma, though the backs of both legs would eventually become ugly bruises.

I gingerly made my way downstairs to the kitchen and cracked ice cubes into two towels. Closing the refrigerator, I noticed the magnetized notepad on which Eva and I left each other messages. I took it with me as I made my way to the sofa, gently placing the towels with ice beneath each leg and slowly sitting. The fabric of the towels rubbed the welts, aggravating the pain, but I forced myself to stay seated, resting my head back against the cushion.

I felt like that seven-year-old boy again, the one forced to lie about my beating, calling it a bike accident. I had realized, even at that young age, that no one could protect me, no matter how much they said they could. And then another thought came to me, and it frightened me so much I sat up. I'd been right. David Bateman had hit his daughter in the head. He had seriously injured her, maybe blinded her in one eye. And that wasn't all. Bateman knew I was an ophthalmologist. He knew where I practiced and lived, and he knew that his ex-wife had come to see me. He was stalking her, and in so doing, he was stalking me. That was the reason for Trina Crouch's ardent denial. She had reached the same conclusion I had reached as that young, beaten boy. She and her daughter were on their own. She could not call the law; her ex-husband was the law. To whom was Trina Crouch going to run? To whom was she going to protest? It was why she had laughed at my suggestion that I could somehow help her. Help her? Help her how? What was I going to do, call the police?

I picked up the phone and dialed the number for the hotel in Boston, not even considering the three-hour time difference. I asked for Eva Pryor's room, and in the moments before it rang I fought to pull myself together and not sound like a child.

The phone rang twice before I heard the receiver lift.

"Hello?"

The voice was groggy, muffled, someone awakened from a dead sleep, face maybe still buried in a pillow, brain not quite aware.

But most definitely male.

"Hello?" he said, this time more forcefully.

And just as I was about to say, "Sorry, wrong room," I heard covers rustling and the faint whisper of Eva's panicked voice.

"Shit," she said.

3

1971
Saint Joe's High School
San Mateo, California

My transition to high school was not the same as my rude introduction to grammar school, but it was also not a smooth landing. I believe my high school teachers were forewarned about the kid with the red eyes. As for my classmates, there was an initial coolness; those first few days I caught them staring at me and whispering in the hallways, but my friendship with Ernie went a long way toward breaking the ice. At a school where sports were revered, Ernie became an instant rock star, and I was accepted like one of his roadies. No one dared to insult me with Ernie Cantwell at my side, and eventually, the larger environment allowed me to blend in—to the extent I was ever able to blend in.

At Saint Joe's, kids were lumped into groups. You had your jocks, the nerds, the dorks, and the stoners. I straddled the lines between the nerds, dorks, and jocks, with jock being the most tenuous. Though I was far from an impressive athlete either in build or ability, I did make the freshman basketball team on sheer determination and hustle. My coach told me, in a not so ringing endorsement, "How can I cut a kid who tries so hard with so little success?" I didn't care. Making the team gave me the chance to show my classmates that I was just a normal kid, except for my "condition."

I didn't get the chance to play in games very often, but when Coach did put me in—usually when we were way ahead or way behind on the scoreboard—I swarmed my opponent like a whirling dervish, and the combination of my red eyes and pest-like defense frequently rattled him into mistakes. My teammates, and the few fans that came to those games, loved it, and responded with cheers like, "Give him Hell! Give him Hell!" The nickname stuck. For the remainder of my four years at Saint Joe's I was "Hell." My mother didn't like it, but unlike "Devil Boy," I did not perceive the name as derogatory or negative. At an all-boys' school, it seemed everyone had a nickname, and mine was rather benign compared with others'.

4

I was six the first time my parents took me to the Sixteen Mile House restaurant to celebrate my birthday. My father had me convinced that at any moment Wyatt Earp and other gunslingers of the Wild West would push through the swinging doors and mosey up to the wood-and-copper bar in boots with spurs, or sit at one of the round tables to eat a flame-broiled New York steak. I loved the wood-plank floors strewn with saw-dust and the man in the top hat and striped shirt who played an upright piano. Every year I ordered the steak, baked potato, and salad. I thought it just about the best restaurant in the world. But this night, my sixteenth birthday, I was preoccupied.

"Sam, slow down," my mother said as I dug in to another piece of meat. "You'll choke if you don't chew your food."

That morning my father had kept his promise and taken me to the Department of Motor Vehicles to obtain my driver's license. I passed with a ninety-four. My test and score are right there in the scrapbook labeled *1973*. Ernie, a month older, had also passed on his birthday, and his parents had surprised him with a tomato-red Volkswagen Beetle. I had my hopes up that my parents would do the same, though I knew money continued to be tight for my father.

"I don't think he's chewing," my father said. "I think he's inhaling."

"Just hungry," I said.

"Well, even hungry people can have manners, Samuel," my mother said. "Don't talk with your mouth full."

Half an hour into the meal, I pushed my plate aside. "I'm stuffed."

"You haven't finished your baked potato," my father said. "That isn't like you."

It wasn't like me. My mother liked to tell everyone that I was eating her out of house and home. I wasn't big, like Ernie, who had shot up to six-three and more than two hundred pounds of lean muscle, but I had grown to nearly five-nine and 140 pounds with the metabolism of a jackrabbit.

"I'm saving room for cake," I said, which awaited us at the house, along with, I hoped, that car I wanted.

5

My heart sank when my father pulled the Falcon into the driveway. No car blocked our path. I told myself I had no one to blame but myself. I had allowed myself to get my hopes up, and I, of all people, should have known better. My father was working even longer hours at the store, and a new car was simply not realistic. I appreciated that, certainly I did, but I was sixteen with a new driver's license burning a hole in my wallet.

I pushed out of the back seat and slowly made my way up the walk.

"All night you've been giving us the bum's rush, and now we finally get home and you're as slow as molasses in the dead of winter," my mother said.

As my father opened the front door, he turned to my mom. "I think I left my reading glasses in the car," he said and stepped as if to get past me. Then he pivoted and gently pushed me into the house.

"Surprise!"

The light burst on. Ernie, Mickie, and about half a dozen of our high school classmates from Saint Joe's crowded into the hallway, along with Mr. and Mrs. Cantwell.

"Now do you see why I was eating so slowly?"

my mother asked. "You almost ruined your surprise."

The surprise party, I would learn, had been Mickie's idea, and she had leaned heavily on Ernie to get some of my classmates to attend.

At the dining room table, my mother and Mickie embarrassed me by insisting that I wear a pointed party hat, something my friends also encouraged. The photographs are also in the scrapbook and, ironically, everyone in them has red eyes from the flash of the bulb. After I blew out the candles, my mother cut and served the cake while I opened presents.

Ernie handed me a card. "This is from all of us."

"Seven guys, one card. That sounds about right," I said. Glued to the inside of the card was a brown paper bag with six five-dollar bills.

"Jensen still needs to pony up," Ernie said. Rich Jensen, the center on our basketball team, was a notorious cheapskate; I didn't expect I would see his five dollars.

The Cantwells handed me a wrapped box, which my mother said was unnecessary but thoughtful. I unwrapped it and found a baseball autographed by none other than the great Willie Mays encased in a clear plastic, like a priceless jewel. "No way," I said, turning the case and considering the signature from every angle. "How did you get it?"

Mr. Cantwell shrugged. I knew his business was doing well, because he had moved out of the garage to a high-rise office building, and, of course, he'd bought Ernie the car.

My mother sent us downstairs to the basement, which they had converted to a teen hangout. My father had put in a television, pool table, dartboard, and pinball machine, all of which he'd obtained from the owner of a bar on Broadway that went out of business. Mickie ran the pool table like a hustler. No one could beat her, though it didn't stop my friends from trying. They were clearly more interested in watching her, and with good reason. I had been shocked the prior summer when Mickie had accompanied my family to the Russian River and wore a bikini. She had a lean, athletic build with a tiny waist, rock-hard abs, and a butt my classmates joked could be used to snap off a bottle cap on a beer. They were enjoying watching her chalk the cue and bend over the table, something Mickie did dripping sexuality. Everything she did dripped sexuality. It was apparent to me she was enjoying the attention.

"Don't you think you should give someone else a chance?" I whispered.

"I would if someone could step up and beat me," she said. "I thought Saint Joe's was a jock school."

This only led to further challenges.

Shortly after midnight my classmates departed, though not before three offered to drive Mickie home. She declined and sat on the sofa between me and Ernie, her head on my shoulder as we watched a late-night movie.

"Mickie, I better get you home," my father said, descending the stairs. Then he stopped. "What am I saying? Sam, you have a license now. Why don't you drive Mickie home?"

We made our way upstairs to the kitchen, where my mother was finishing the dishes. I hugged her from behind. "Thanks for the great birthday, Mom." I felt guilty about wanting a car, knowing how hard my father was working to make ends meet.

"Did you get everything you wanted?" she asked.

"Even more," I said.

"Driving is a big responsibility. You be careful and come right home."

I promised I would.

"And do not sit parked in the car," she said, giving me a knowing look.

"Mom . . ."

Mickie had entered the kitchen. "Don't worry, Mrs. H. I won't let him try any funny business."

"I know you won't, Michaela, because you are a young lady." My mother was the only person who could get away with using Mickie's full name.

"Okay," I said, feeling my face flush. "We're out of here."

My dad handed me the keys to the Falcon. I opened the front door for Mickie, but when I followed her onto the porch I bumped into her. She'd stopped suddenly.

"No way," Mickie said, looking and sounding dumbfounded.

The Falcon remained parked in the driveway but was now wrapped in a big red bow. I turned to my parents.

"Surprise," my mother and father said in unison.

"No way! No way!" Mickie said, stepping from the porch to the driveway, circling the car. "You got the Falcon?"

"Damn," Ernie said under his breath.

I'd expected a junker, something slow and safe, if anything at all. The Falcon was cool in and of itself—forget that it was also a convertible and fast. "Really?" I asked.

My dad shrugged. "Your mother wants a new car."

But I knew my mother still loved that Falcon, even if it now had some miles on it and tended to leak a little oil.

"It's mine?" I asked, still not believing.

"If you pay for your own gas and upkeep," my father said.

I had grown up spending Sunday afternoons

changing the oil and doing the tune-ups on the cars with my dad. I don't know if he did it to avoid Fast Eddy's garage or to save money, or both, but I had learned a lot and knew I could keep the Falcon running in tip-top shape. Paying for gas, however, would not be easy. My friends' thirty dollars wouldn't go far with gas at thirty-six cents a gallon.

"You'll be a chick magnet driving that car, Hell," Ernie said. "Especially with me in the passenger seat."

"You got a car," Mickie said, not sounding at all happy at my second surprise of the night.

"I'm talking Friday and Saturday nights," Ernie said. "Cruising the El Camino Real!"

"We'll wait a bit for that," my mom said, arching her eyebrows at Ernie. "Samuel just got his license."

"I'll watch out for him," Mickie said. "And make sure no chicks stick to the car."

6

As we drove the El Camino, Mickie slid across the bench seat and pressed next to me. This would become her unwavering spot. "You are so spoiled," she said.

"I'm not spoiled," I said, but I was unable to hide the huge grin carved across my face.

"They gave you a freaking car."

"It's not exactly new, and I have to pay for my own gas and upkeep. You heard my dad."

"Poor baby."

"If anyone is spoiled, it's Ernie; he got a *new* car."

"Please, a convertible Falcon or a VW Bug? Kids would kill to have this car. You might even get laid, Hill."

I felt my face flush.

Mickie leaned away, smiling. "Don't tell me you're still a virgin, Hill?"

"No," I said, but I was never a good liar, especially not with Mickie.

"You are," she said, smiling. "You're still a virgin."

"Okay, so I am. So what? A lot of guys my age are."

"That's because you go to a school without

girls, and you're all homos," she said, teasing me. But I was in no mood to be teased.

"No, it's because girls don't exactly swoon for guys with red eyes."

We sat in silence. At high school dances, there was never a shortage of girls who wanted to dance with the great Ernie Cantwell, and Mickie was surrounded like Scarlett O'Hara in *Gone with the Wind*. I usually held up a wall for a while, then found an excuse to leave. While it might have been Mickie's newly developed figure that drew the boys like flies to raw meat, I suspected it was also the reputation Mickie had developed since her expulsion from the Catholic girls' school. Ernie and I had heard guys talking about her and wanted to tell her, but we both lacked the courage to do so. For some reason, perhaps because I was hurt, I mustered the courage that night.

Mickie said, "Sorry, Sam. I'm just teasing you."

"You know, you've got to be careful, Mickie."

She gave me a sidelong glance. "About what?"

"Guys talk a lot."

"What, that Catholic-girls-are-all-as-horny-as-goats crap?"

I'd heard the same thing, but in my limited experience, I certainly hadn't seen any evidence to support the proposition. "Guys talk about you," I said.

She turned her shoulder away from me. "I don't give a shit what they say."

"You should."

She turned her head to me, defiant. "Why?"

"Because they're saying things about you, that you put out . . . and stuff."

"Those assholes can say whatever they want. They don't know."

"Why didn't you let someone else play pool tonight?"

"What's that supposed to mean?"

"I don't know. Didn't you see them looking at you?"

"So what? Am I supposed to let them beat me because you don't like them checking out my ass?"

"I didn't say that."

"Then what?"

"Never mind. Let's just drop it."

"Why didn't you say something to them?"

"Because I'm not your boyfriend."

"You got that right."

We drove the El Camino in silence, both of us staring out the windshield. When I pulled up to her house and parked, Mickie turned to me. "Sorry," she said. "I didn't mean to make you feel bad about being a virgin. I was just teasing you. It's kind of cute, actually."

"It's okay," I said, feeling like a puppy. "And I'm sorry about saying you should have let someone else play."

She smiled, but it had a sad quality to it. "I'll

tell you what, if you're still a virgin when you turn eighteen, Hill, I'll sleep with you before you go off to college."

I tried to force a laugh, but it came out sounding like I was choking. Then I said, "What, and spoil this beautiful thing we have going on?"

"What do we have going on?"

I felt the temperature in the car drop again. "What do you mean? We're friends."

"Yeah," she said. "We're friends."

"What's wrong? What did I say?"

"Never mind." Mickie slid across the seat and pushed out of the car door.

I leaned across the red leather, speaking out the window when she closed the door. "Hey? What's the matter with you?"

The small box hit me in the face and fell to the seat. "Happy birthday," Mickie said, and she ran up the driveway.

Perplexed, I picked up the box and opened it. Inside, on a thin square of cotton, was a silver chain with a medal of Saint Christopher, the patron saint of travelers. I turned over the silver disc. Even without the dome light, I could read what Mickie had inscribed.

To keep you safe.
M

7

In the spring of my sophomore year, I made the junior varsity baseball team. Despite my initial incompetence at three flies up, my mother's willingness to spend her Saturdays hitting me ground balls and pitching to me had helped me develop into a decent singles hitter and fair defender. But by mid-season, I'd suddenly begun to strike out frequently.

"What do you think it could be?" my father asked over dinner one evening.

Frustrated, I said, "I don't know. It's like I'm not seeing the ball."

My mother had me in Dr. Pridemore's office the very next day.

After an eye exam, Dr. Pridemore delivered his clinical diagnosis. "You're *not* seeing the ball. Frankly, I can't figure out how you're seeing the chalkboard in class. Have you been experiencing headaches?"

I had, but I'd compensated by moving up a row in all my classes.

"Your vision is slipping," he said, which caused my mother to slip—into full panic.

"How bad is it?" she asked. "Could he go blind?"

Dr. Pridemore assured her I was not going blind. "But you do need glasses."

I picked out sturdy black frames, like Clark Kent. They didn't do any wonders to improve my looks, which were average at best. My hair had darkened to a deeper shade of brown, my jaw had become squarer, and my forehead was broader. People said I looked like my father, and I saw the resemblance in pictures of him as a young man. As I wore the glasses, however, I noticed something I had not expected. The glasses seemed to soften my most obvious feature. Mickie, who was waiting at my house after my eye appointment, was gentle in her assessment. She called my new specs "sexy in a nerdy way."

Ernie was more honest the next day at school. "You look like Jerry Lewis in *The Nutty Professor*," he said.

8

Junior year, I'd survived the first round of roster cuts for the varsity basketball team, a heartless practice in which Coach Moran pinned the names of players still on the team to a corkboard outside his office. My name was second from the bottom, but I suspected my time on that list was growing short. Thirteen players remained for twelve spots. Coach had said he'd tell the final cut personally. When a student entered my fourth-period precalculus class carrying a pink slip, and my teacher looked in my direction, I wasn't completely caught off guard.

"Hell," he said, using my nickname, which had become common even among the teachers. "Coach Moran wants to see you in his office after class."

Coach Moran didn't send pink slips to be chummy. I was about to become one of the nerds, and possibly one of the dorks. I would no longer be one of the jocks.

To say that the Saint Joseph's locker room badly needed renovating was like saying the Watergate scandal had been a minor breaking and entering. Untouched since the school opened in the 1940s, the room had cement walls, narrow, mesh-covered windows, and the lighting, ventilation, and ambience of a Turkish prison. The metal lockers smelled like rotting fruit. Coach Moran's cramped office was in the corner of this mess, and I wondered whether the sour atmosphere contributed to his seemingly perpetual sour demeanor.

I pushed my glasses onto the bridge of my nose and knocked. Coach Moran yelled, "Enter," and I pushed the door open.

"You wanted to see me, Coach?"

Coach put a hand over the telephone receiver, which he was holding to his ear. "Come in and sit down, Hell," he said in a hushed tone. I sat in a folding chair beside several desks, one of which doubled as the trainer's table. I assumed Coach Moran was talking to his wife, since he sounded politer than I'd ever heard him and didn't drop a single swear word during the two-minute conversation.

"He's the best athlete I've seen," I heard Coach say. "And he's just a junior." He paused. "That's because the *Times* didn't cover us much last year, but trust me—you'll want to see this kid play."

I knew the kid had to be Ernie, who'd made the varsity football and basketball teams as just a sophomore and was their best player.

"That's why I'm calling. I thought maybe you could get a foot in the door before the wolves descend, and believe me—they'll devour this kid. At the moment he's flying under the radar, but that's going to change soon."

After another minute, Coach replaced the receiver and leaned back in his chair. The most valuable player on his high school football, basketball, and baseball teams, Coach Moran had his name stitched in gold letters on three navy-blue blankets hanging from the Saint Joe's basketball gym rafters. Lean and muscular, Coach still looked like he could go out and dominate in any of those sports.

"What am I going to do with you, Sam Hell?" He had a habit of saying a player's first and last names when imparting instruction or criticism.

"We can't have that, Sam Hell. No, we can't. You have to set that screen right there, Sam Hell. You don't and we're fucked. You understand me, Sam Hell?"

"Yes, Coach."

"Then set the goddamn screen, Sam Hell."

I knew Coach's question was rhetorical, but I saw it as a chance to lobby for myself. "Put me on the team, Coach?"

He chuckled at my boldness. "Hell, you have the heart of a lion, I'll give you that. I've never had a more determined son of a bitch play for me. All you're lacking to be a good basketball player is height, quickness, and shooting ability. You're too short, too slow, and can't shoot."

"I can learn to shoot," I said.

His smile waned. He lowered the front legs of his chair to the ground. "I have a hard decision to make, Hell. I have to choose between you and Chuck Bennett, and I only have twelve uniforms. Let me be straight with you. You'd be the twelfth man, which means you'd practice but rarely play. I have no doubt you'd practice hard, work your ass off, but . . ." He paused, looking at his hands folded in his lap. "Here's the thing, Hell. Mr. Shubb says you're a hell of a writer, that you got real talent."

I failed to see the connection. Dick Shubb was the moderator of the *Saint Joe's Friar*, the school newspaper.

"He wants you on his staff, but the staff meetings are after school, as is most of the production time." Now I saw the connection. "You couldn't do both, Hell." Coach ran a hand over his chin as if considering whether to shave. "Bennett, on the other hand, is a first-class fuckup. I cut him, and he'll end up in the pit smoking pot with the stoners. So, you see the problem I have, Hell?"

I did, of course, but facing the prospect of losing one of my dreams, being benevolent wasn't my priority. Then Coach asked, "What do you want to be, Hell? You have any idea?"

"I was thinking maybe a doctor," I said. "Maybe an ophthalmologist." The idea had come to me one day while Dr. Pridemore examined my eyes. Dr. Pridemore had always taken the time to explain to me not only my condition but the inner workings of the eye. It seemed like a natural fit.

"What do you think will benefit you most in the future, on your résumé—the ability to write or to shoot a free throw?"

Coach was right. We both knew it. Looking back, it was the most candid advice from the most unlikely source, and it changed my life in many ways, but goddamn, I wanted to play basketball and still be a jock, even if it was in name only. Then another idea hit me, and I quickly realized I could make this a win-win situation for me and for Ernie. I did love to write, and the newspaper would be a way for me to pad my résumé. And if the plan I was formulating worked out, I could also make some money for my college tuition. As for Ernie, while he excelled on the athletic fields, he continued to struggle in the classroom, despite my tutelage. Ernie's grades could limit his choice of colleges, unless he could get an athletic scholarship. That required notoriety, and Coach Moran was right. The local paper did a poor job covering high school sports.

"Coach, if it's all the same to you, I think I'm going to join the newspaper staff," I said. "I appreciate the spot, but my dad also needs a delivery boy at his store after school, and I don't see how I could do it all."

We stood and we shook hands. "Your name will be on the list I post this afternoon, Hell. You can bet your ass it will. I'll leave it up to you what you want to tell everyone."

I reached the door.

"Hell."

"Yeah, Coach?"

"Life is about heart. Yours is as big as any kid's I've ever coached. Don't you ever forget that."

"No, Coach, I won't." I left his office with one less dream but somehow feeling like I was seven feet tall.

"What happened?" Ernie asked the question even before the swinging door to the locker room had shut behind me. He'd been waiting in the hall.

"I made the team," I said.

He pumped his fist as we walked through a hall crowded with students coming back from lunch and hurrying to get to class. "I knew he'd keep you. You work harder than anyone."

"I turned him down."

Ernie stopped. "You did what?"

"Mr. Shubb is looking for someone to write sports for the newspaper and take over as the editor in chief next year."

"So?"

The first bell clattered, echoing loudly. "I think I'll get more out of that than playing sports. It's a big commitment—I can't do both. Plus, my dad needs me at the store."

"You're giving up basketball?"

"It's better for my future," I said over the clatter of the bell and the banging of lockers.

"You can't quit, Sam."

"I'm not quitting," I said. "I'm just choosing something different. Besides, think about all the great stories I can write about *you* now." This caught Ernie's interest. His eyes widened. "I'm going to call up the *Times* and get a job covering high school games. Coach says they don't have a high school reporter. When I'm done, you'll be a legend."

The idea to contact the *Times* had come from my eavesdropping on Coach Moran's telephone conversation. If I was going to be writing articles for the school paper, I might as well see if I could get paid to do it.

I called the *Times* sports editor when I got home and asked if he wanted a high school reporter. He asked me to see him the following day and to bring examples of my writing, which were essays I'd written in my English classes, since I hadn't yet written for the paper. Given that saying about beggars not being choosy, the *Times* hired me. They agreed to pay me thirty-five cents a column inch, plus my mileage to and from the games. They also gave me a press pass.

My coverage of Ernie's exploits appeared in the *Times* at least once a week during the next year and a half. By our senior year, I hadn't just made Ernie a legend at Saint Joe's; I'd made him a household name throughout the county. College recruiters showed up in hordes at Ernie's games and practices. The recruiting letters, which started as a trickle, became a deluge of envelopes stuffing his parents' mailbox and bore the insignias for USC, UCLA, California, Syracuse, North Carolina, Georgia, Florida, and Arizona.

Coaches offered him scholarships in basketball, football, and track, but it became apparent that football was the sport that best utilized all of Ernie's athleticism and provided his best chance at a professional career.

Giving up basketball for the journalism staff had two other unintended consequences. After a feature article I wrote about Ernie won first place in a journalism contest and I received a $500 scholarship, Mr. Shubb entered my writing in other competitions. By the end of my senior year, I had won close to $2,500 in scholarship money, which, as my mother liked to say, was no small potatoes. But I'm getting ahead of myself. Not playing sports also gave me the time to work at my father's store, and that led to the second unintended consequence.

I wouldn't need to take Mickie up on her offer when I turned eighteen.

10

My father's disappointment that I would no longer be playing competitive sports was tempered when I told him that night at the dinner table that I wanted to earn money working at his store and could save for college. I knew my parents were concerned about the expense. More than once my mother had intimated that the community college would be a great way to get my general-education requirements out of the way. She was right, I knew, and I didn't want to tax their budget any more than I already was, but I also really wanted to go to college.

"As of tomorrow, you are Broadway Pharmacy's part-time delivery and stock boy. And when Alex leaves for college next year, you can take on the extra days."

"Only if he keeps his grades up," my mother said. She expressed no disappointment at the end of my competitive athletic career. As she spooned mashed potatoes onto my plate, she said, "Maybe you'll become the next Woodward and Bernstein. Or Walter Cronkite. Wouldn't that be something, Sam?"

I agreed it would be, but I doubted anyone would want to hire a newscaster with red eyes. Much as I had come to accept my appearance,

I was not so naive as to believe people would readily accept me, someone who looked so different, and there was never a shortage of people to remind me of this when I grew too comfortable.

11

The Saint Joe's newspaper was produced every other week, with production taking place right after class. I could work the schedule so I could be at my dad's store in time to dust mop the floor, stock the shelves, and get out the door to make the deliveries. Shortly after the Easter holiday, I entered the pharmacy to find a new girl being trained at the front register by my dad's long-time assistant, Betty. Some months earlier my father told us at dinner that Betty had asked to cut back her hours. Her husband had taken sick. My mom suggested my dad hire girls from the local high school to work part-time for minimum wage.

The girl behind the counter looked up from Betty's tutelage and smiled without hesitation. "You must be Sam." She stuck her hand across the counter. "I'm Donna."

My mother would have called Donna "husky." The blue smock did not hang on her the way it did on Betty. It protruded over her chest. I suspected Donna was stacked.

"Hi," was all I could manage.

I set about my business but found mopping the floor more difficult than usual. It seemed no matter the aisle I moved to, Donna would appear to dust the merchandise and talk to me in between waiting on customers.

"Your father says you go to Saint Joe's." She flipped her hair from her shoulder and folded it behind her ear, revealing a silver hoop earring. Blue eye shadow painted her upper eyelids.

"I'm a junior," I said.

"I'm a senior at Burlingame. What's it like going to a school without any girls?"

"It's okay," I said. "You get used to it."

"I'd think an all-girls' school would be boring," she said. "I can't imagine going to one. It seems like my best friends are always guys. Your dad says you play baseball. I play first base on the softball team."

"I had to give it up to write for the newspaper," I said, which was an outright lie, since I hadn't gone out for the team.

"I know," she said. "I saw your stories in the window." My father displayed all my articles from the *Friar* and the *Times* in the store windows with great pride. "I liked the one you did about Ernie Cantwell hitting the last-second shot. You really made it sound exciting."

"You read my articles?"

"Not all of them, but the ones I've read are really good."

She was being kind. The *Times* edited my sports stories so much it was like that line on the TV show *Dragnet*—"Just the facts." Still, it felt cool to have a senior girl tell me she liked my stories.

"Maybe I'll come watch you play softball some time," I said. "Maybe I could write an article for the *Times*." I was hoping to impress her. The *Times* would never cover girls' softball.

"That would be great," she said. "Though I don't think you'd have much to write about."

I had never felt comfortable talking to girls, except for Mickie, of course, who was at my house even more than in grammar school. She and my mother continued to spend time together even when I wasn't home. They would shop together and occasionally go to the movies. Every so often I'd catch them alone at the kitchen table, and Mickie would look like she'd been crying, but when I asked about it, my mother's response remained consistent. "Girl stuff. It wouldn't interest you." Mickie gave me the same mantra.

Talking with Donna was easy. I felt no pressure and no reason to be self-conscious. She was eighteen and a senior, after all; she had no interest in someone barely seventeen years old.

I seemed to have an inordinate number of deliveries that afternoon and didn't make it back to the store until five minutes before closing. After ringing up the cash purchases, I hurried to the back room to grab my coat. Donna was standing on her toes reaching to hang up her smock. My assessment had been correct. A white

281

knit sweater did nothing to camouflage the size of her breasts. She turned her head, catching me looking.

Trying to cover, I stepped toward her. "You need any help?"

"I'm short but not that short. Thanks. Wow, polite and cute."

I felt my face flush and turned to grab my jacket from the hook behind the door. "Well, I'll see you tomorrow," I said.

"Wednesday," she said. "My parents don't want me working every day. I have to keep my grades up. I've got a full load this semester, and I partied a bit too much last semester."

"Okay, Wednesday," I said.

I knew Donna was just being courteous when she called me cute; I was, after all, the boss's son. Besides, it had sounded like something a big sister would tell her little brother. Still, I found myself thinking of her that night as I studied in my room, and during the next two days.

12

I arrived late to the store Wednesday after a journalism meeting went longer than expected, and I had just enough time to get out a quick hello to Donna as I raced past the front counter and pushed through the swinging door to the elevated pharmacy. My father stood at the counter hunting and pecking at the typewriter with two fingers.

"Sorry I'm late, Dad."

"School comes first." He ripped off a label and handed it to his tech.

"I'll catch up." I grabbed the dust mop and started down the aisles. Donna remained behind the counter talking with Leo Tomaro. Tomaro had been a football player of some repute at the local high school, but I'd heard he was also dumb as a post. Tomaro liked to come in to the store to talk sports with my dad, and I'd recently heard him say he'd "taken some time off" from college.

Tomaro talked with Donna the entire time it took me to dust mop, and he remained at the counter when I went to empty the garbage beneath the front register.

"Hey, sport," he said, making me feel like I was ten. "Your dad says you're a big-time sports reporter now, huh? You know what they say. 'Those who can, do. Those who can't, write about those who can.' " He gave Donna a toothy grin.

"I think the saying is, 'Those who can, do. Those who can't, don't,' " I said.

"Yeah, whatever."

"How's community college?" I asked.

"I'm taking a break," he said. "I had a business opportunity come up, and I didn't want to pass it up." He turned and pointed out the window to an older-model red Camaro parked at the curb. "Check out the new wheels. Cost me nearly a grand."

"Nice," I said and then, because I just couldn't help myself. "Tomaro's Camaro."

Donna snorted, then tried to cover it up as a sneeze.

Tomaro said, "Yeah. I'm thinking about getting one of those personalized license plates."

Donna's lips were pursed tight, as if she was holding her breath. I indicated I needed to get the garbage box below the cash register, and she took a step back to give me room. I knelt, biting my tongue to keep from laughing, and pulled out the box of garbage, which was filled with Kleenex— Betty had a perpetual cold—along with candy wrappers and receipts. When I reached behind the box to gather all Betty's frequent misses, Donna bent down behind the register. The blue smock, which she left mostly unzipped, fell open, revealing a silver chain with a locket and a considerable line of freckled cleavage. I tried to keep my eyes focused on the garbage, but then she said, "Here you go, Sam."

She handed me a balled-up scrap of paper and mimed sticking her finger down her throat. I laughed out loud. At that point, I think even Tomaro realized he'd been the butt of my joke. When I popped back up, he said, "So, are you in high school yet, sport?"

"I'm a junior," I said.

"At Saint Mo's?" He said this in a feminine voice and bent his wrist. "I couldn't do a school without the ladies. I guess you don't have that problem. Or maybe you do?" He bent his wrist again. My father called from the back of the store, indicating Tomaro's prescription had been filled. "Get that for me, will you, sport? You're the delivery boy, after all, aren't you?" He winked at Donna.

"No problem," I said.

I hurried like an obedient retriever, grabbed the white bag from the counter, and brought it back, handing Donna the paperwork to ring up the sale on the cash register. Tomaro pulled out a credit card and slapped it on the counter. "You keep working hard, and someday you might get some plastic."

"Oh yeah," I said, as if I'd forgotten. "My dad said to just rub that cream in twice a day, and it should take care of that rash in no time." My

285

father had said no such thing and would never have broken a customer's confidence, but having been at the store, I'd picked up a bit about certain medications. Before Tomaro could respond, I nodded to the window. A parking-meter cop stood on the sidewalk, flipping open her ticket book. "I guess the parking meters don't take plastic."

Tomaro grabbed his package and hurried out, but not before Donna burst out laughing.

13

I returned from my deliveries just before my dad locked the front door and flipped the sign in the window to **CLOSED**. Donna had stayed to help ring up the cash deliveries. Half an hour later we all departed together.

"See you at home," my father said, walking to his car.

"Could you believe that guy today?" Donna asked as we walked down the sidewalk.

"He hits on all the girls who work for my dad," I said, though Donna was the first girl to work at the store.

"Trust me, I know. He hit on all the girls at school, too. Everyone knows he's after one thing."

"Stimulating conversation?" I asked.

Donna laughed. "You're funny." I stopped next to the Falcon, and she said, "Now, that is a sweet ride."

I mimicked the sound of Tomaro's voice. "So where are your 'wheels,' sport?"

"No wheels for me, sport. My dad grounded me. Long story."

"Is someone picking you up?"

"Fat chance. When I'm grounded, I'm walking. It's my dad's way of punishing me. He says that maybe the exercise will clear my brain."

"Where do you live?"

"It's not far. I live in Hillsborough, just a couple miles."

Without thinking I said, "I'll give you a ride."

"You sure it's not out of your way?"

It was the opposite direction. "No problem at all."

Donna touched my arm, and it sent an electric pulse across my skin. "Like I said, polite and cute."

Inside the Falcon, Donna asked, "Can we put the top down?"

Though it was a bit chilly, I happily obliged. Other than Mickie and my mom, I'd never been alone in the Falcon with a girl. I hoped someone I knew would drive up and see me, the devil boy, with a high school senior riding in my car.

Hillsborough was a wealthy neighborhood with large homes, sweeping driveways, and expansive lawns. We made several turns, and I knew I would be hopelessly lost trying to get back home.

"Turn here," Donna said. I drove between two brick pillars leading to a driveway that curved past a manicured garden with English hedges, rosebushes, and other plants I couldn't name. I stopped the car beneath an impressive colonnade for a two-story stucco home. "What does your father do?"

"You mean when he's not on my case or grounding me? He's a big-shot lawyer."

"What about your mom?"

"She pretty much plays golf and cards at the country club all day. At night she drinks."

The statement hit me like a slap. I didn't know what to say.

Donna flipped her hair. "Do you party, Sam?"

I hadn't even had a beer up to that point. "When I can," was all I could muster.

"It's such a double standard. My mom is shit-faced half the time, and if I party, my father grounds me. How is that fair?" I recognized her question to be rhetorical. "Well, thanks for the ride," she said and exited the car, but rather than run up the steps, Donna walked around to the driver's side and rested her forearms on the door. Her shirt fell open, and her cleavage swallowed the silver chain and medal.

"Do you know how to get out of here?" I raised my eyes. Donna grinned. "You just take a right out of the driveway, turn left at the first stop sign, go one block, take another left, and follow the road back to the El Camino."

I nodded, but I doubted I would remember a single word. Then Donna leaned forward and kissed me hard on the mouth, her tongue forcing my lips apart, probing. Before I could even decide how to respond, she pulled back, smiling. Then she winked. "See you, sport."

Struck dumb, I watched her bound up the steps and disappear through the front door.

When I got home, my mother was finishing setting the table for dinner. She'd started to wait for me and my dad to get home so we could all eat together.

"What took you?" she asked.

"I gave Donna a ride home." I quickly added, "She didn't have a car and was going to have to walk, and it was getting dark."

"That's nice." She pulled open the fridge and retrieved the milk. "Wash your hands."

As I washed my hands at the bathroom sink, my mind drifted back to Donna's cleavage and her warm, moist lips pressed against mine, her tongue exploring.

"Sam, food's on the table."

Feeling flush, I lowered my head and splashed water on my face.

"Sam?"

"I'll be out in a minute," I said, using the hand towel to dry my face. I hoped it was a minute. I had my doubts. It had taken nearly the entire car ride home to lose my erection.

14

Donna did not work Thursday or Friday. I contemplated making some excuse to ask my father for her phone number, like she left something in my car, but the longer I chickened out, the less plausible that excuse became. Besides, I wasn't sure I'd be able to muster the courage to call her, or to hold a conversation for very long.

When Saturday finally arrived, I lay on the couch in the family room trying to act interested in a baseball game as I waited until Donna's shift began at noon. At eleven forty-five, I was about to leave when I answered a knock at the front door. Mickie stepped past me into the family room.

"Hey, where you been? I called you last night."

"I had an assignment for the *Times*," I said. "I got home too late to call you back."

"Since when?"

Mickie and I often talked well into the night and early morning, though I had to initiate anything after eleven to keep my mother from answering the phone.

"I was tired."

She sat in the chair and put her feet up on the ottoman. "*Westworld* is playing," she said. Mickie liked movies that scared the shit out of her.

She looked to the television. "Why are you watching UCLA? Isn't Stanford playing?"

"No. They're not televised, and I don't think I can go to the movies."

"Why not?"

"I got stuff to do," I said.

She picked up the newspaper, flipping to the movie section. "Like what?"

"I have to study."

"Come on, Hill. It's Saturday. You can't get any higher than an A-plus in every class."

I was about to protest further when my mother walked in and brightened at the sight of Mickie. My mother's love for Mickie puzzled me; I was certain she knew Mickie wasn't exactly chaste, if not the full extent of Mickie's sexual exploits, and I couldn't think of anything short of a major crime, like murder, that would have made my mother more disappointed than to find out that her son was not a virgin, though I still very much remained one.

"Hi, Mrs. H, I'm kidnapping Sam to the movies."

"Good. He's been moping around here the past two days. Get him outside."

"I haven't been—"

"Have we been grumpy?" Mickie pinched my cheek.

"Stop."

"Someone *is* grumpy. Don't worry, Mrs. H. If

I can't cheer him up, I'll slap the grumpy out of him. Let's go, Hill. You heard your mother. Get your jacket and car keys. You can buy the tickets since you're employed."

15

As we drove the El Camino with the top down, Mickie slid across the seat to her customary position next to me. I turned down Broadway.

"It's at the Century Cinema," she said.

"I want to take the freeway. And I need to stop and see my dad."

Broadway bustled on Saturdays. People ran errands they couldn't get to during the week or ate leisurely breakfasts at one of the diners. I lucked out and found a parking space in front of my dad's store and searched the ashtray for change to pay the meter. When I looked up, I saw Donna at the counter, staring through the window at the tableau of Mickie sitting pressed beside me. I quickly opened the door and got out. "I'll be back in a minute."

I nearly closed the door on Mickie's leg. "Hold on." She slid out. "What the hell, Hill? I want to get some candy for the movie and say hi to your dad."

Donna smiled when we entered.

My father left the prescription room and walked down the aisle to greet us. Mickie gave him a hug. "Hey, Mr. H."

"What are you two up to now? Do I dare ask?"

"We're going to the movies," she said. "We're smuggling in candy."

"I don't blame you," my dad said. "Not with the prices they charge. Sam, did you introduce Mickie to Donna?"

I turned, but before I could say anything Donna had walked out from behind the counter. "What movie are you going to see?"

"*Westworld*," Mickie said.

"I heard that's *really* scary."

"That's why I take Sam. He doesn't mind if I jump in his lap."

"You don't jump in my—"

"When we saw *The Poseidon Adventure*, I practically shared his seat the whole movie."

"That was like freshman year or something," I said. "We're just friends." That went over like a lead balloon. My father and Mickie both looked puzzled. Donna just smiled.

After the moment of silence, my dad said, "Donna, Mickie gets the family discount, ten percent off." He said goodbye and started back up the aisle. "Have fun at the movies."

Donna rang up Mickie's candy. "Anything else?"

"Don't look at me," Mickie said. "My *friend* here is the one with the money."

I paid for the candy, and Donna put it in a brown bag. "I want a full report on the movie later," she called out as we were leaving and for a moment I felt that everything was okay. Then she added, "Sport."

When I opened the car door, Mickie stood waiting to slide in ahead of me. "You better go around," I said. "There's not much room."

She looked at me like I'd gone crazy. "What are you talking about? There's plenty of room." She squeezed past and slid onto the seat. I looked to the store window. Donna was waiting on a customer. When I slid in, Mickie was closer than ever. "Can you move over a bit?" I said.

She looked annoyed. "What's wrong with you?"

"There's nothing wrong with me. I don't want to get in an accident."

"Your mother's right; you are grumpy."

"Why, because I don't want to get in an accident? You're practically driving the car."

"Fine." She slid all the way to the passenger door. "Happy now?"

As I backed out, I looked again to the store windows, but Donna was not at the counter.

"*Oh,*" Mickie said with a grin. "Now I get it. You got a thing for the girl with the big tits."

"What? Who? Donna? Please. She's eighteen."

"You do. That comment—'We're just friends.' You have a crush on Betty Boobs."

"I don't have a crush on Betty . . . her." I stepped down on the gas pedal too hard, causing the Falcon to shoot backward from the space. A car horn blared. Tires squealed. I hit the brakes, causing us to jerk to a stop. The bag of candy slid off the seat onto the floorboard.

Mickie was laughing. "Why so nervous?"

"I'm not . . ." I swore and waved an apology to the driver of the car I'd nearly hit. When he passed, I backed out more carefully.

"Maybe your mind is on other things?"

"Will you just stop," I said, feeling myself getting more and more upset as we drove down Broadway toward the freeway.

Mickie said, "I didn't take you for a guy that liked fat chicks."

"I don't . . . She's not . . ."

"You're a tit man."

"Can we just drop it, please?"

"What, are you afraid she'll think I'm your *girlfriend?*"

"I'm not afraid of anything. You're not my girlfriend."

"You can bet your ass I'm not; I expect my boyfriends to treat me a hell of a lot better than you're treating me."

I'd lost it by this point. "What, do you want me to unbutton your shirt and grab *your* tits, then not call you?" I regretted the words as they were leaving my mouth, and if I could have I would have snatched them back.

"Stop the car."

"Mickie, I didn't mean it."

She punched me on the arm. "Stop the fucking

car or I swear to God I'll jump out." She started to stand on the seat.

"Okay. Okay." I turned the corner and pulled over. Mickie got out of the car and slammed the door shut behind her, storming down the sidewalk. I got out of the driver's seat and chased her down. When I caught up to her, I grabbed her arm, but she spun from my grasp and punched me in the chest.

"Don't fucking touch me." She hurried away from me. People now stood on the sidewalk, watching the two of us.

I ran to catch up and lowered my voice. "Will you just stop? I'm sorry, okay? I'm sorry."

Mickie brooded and continued walking.

"I'm sorry," I said for at least the fifth time.

She whirled on me. "How am I supposed to know you're having a wet dream over some fat girl?"

A couple with a baby stroller slowed their approach, looking wary.

"Will you stop yelling and just let me say something?"

She crossed her arms. "Fine. What?"

I waited for the couple to walk on. "I'm sorry."

"You said that." Mickie started up the street, and I gave chase.

"Wait. What I mean is I'm sorry that I didn't tell you . . ." She stopped, hands on her hips. "Okay. Maybe I have a crush on her."

"Then why didn't you just admit it?"

"Because she's eighteen! She's a senior. I'd look . . . you'd laugh at me."

She shook her head. "I'm not one of your stupid guy friends, Sam. I wouldn't laugh at you. But what you said really hurt me. I don't expect that from you."

"I know and I'm sorry. I'm an idiot."

"You're not an idiot. Sometimes you just act like one. Is that what you think of me?"

"What?" I asked.

"That I let every guy grab me? You don't believe those morons, do you?"

"No, Mickie. I don't think anything. That's my problem—I don't think."

She wiped her eyes, and I realized she was fighting back tears. "Because I don't, okay? I know what people say about me, but I'm not like that. Look, sometimes I just like to feel like . . ." She turned her head, but I saw a tear escape, rolling down her cheek. "My house . . . it's not great, Sam. My dad is working all the time, and he and my mother fight a lot when he's home. I usually have to take Joanna away," she said, meaning her little sister, who was eight years younger than Mickie. "And then I can't get my homework done." Her chest heaved. "I'm failing two classes. It's a real mess."

"I didn't know."

"Of course you didn't know. You live with

Ward and June Cleaver, for Christ's sake. Why do you think I'm always at your house? It's nice being someplace where people aren't yelling and screaming at each other all the time."

"How long has it been like this?"

"Forever, but apparently not for much longer; they sat us down the other night. My dad is moving out. They're getting a divorce."

"I'm sorry." I opened my arms, and Mickie stepped into them, sobbing. It was one of the few times I can recall Mickie crying.

"Hey," I said. "We're going to miss the previews." I wrapped my arm around her shoulder as we walked back to the Falcon.

Mickie wiped her tears from her cheeks, and I opened the passenger door for her and closed it after she slid in, making my way around to the driver's side.

"She likes you, Sam," Mickie said when I climbed behind the wheel.

"You hardly talked to her."

"I can tell," she said. "Be careful."

"About what?"

"Just be careful."

In hindsight, I know that Mickie's concern wasn't that Donna liked me. She couldn't say it then, but what she was contemplating was something I knew intuitively but refused to consider—why someone like Donna would like someone like me. I had never even been on a

300

date, and now this eighteen-year-old was sticking her tongue down my throat. Odd as it sounds for a guy who should have been sensitive to such things, I was blinded by the raw hope that maybe, just maybe, Donna did like me, despite the color of my eyes. She had, after all, kissed me, hadn't she? That had to have meant something, didn't it? And why couldn't she like me? I wasn't bad to look at, putting aside the whole eye thing for the moment. I was smart, and I could be funny, at times.

But I was being naive. I didn't know it then, but I soon would.

Mickie remained pressed against the passenger door. "Slide over, will you. It feels strange having you way over there."

Mickie picked up the bag of candy and slid over, pressing up against me so hard the armrest on the door dug into my side. She did spend much of the movie nearly in my lap, but rather than being annoyed, I savored it. Mickie was like Ernie; she had always been there for me when I needed her, and it felt good to be there for her when she needed me. We were misfits, the three of us. I didn't think of us that way back then, but looking back, I know now it was why we gravitated to one another.

After the movie I drove Mickie home, parking the Falcon beneath the outstretched limbs and full leaves of a gnarled hundred-year-old oak tree in her front yard. She didn't immediately get out. She sat staring at the front door of her family's two-story stucco home. "Are you going to be all right?" I asked.

"Yeah," she said. "I'll be fine."

"I'll be home after I run deliveries if you want to talk."

"I have a date," she said.

"Call me later?"

She nodded. Then she did something she'd never done. She leaned over and kissed me on the cheek. "I love you, Hill."

But, as always, Mickie was out the door and up her driveway before I had the chance to respond. I watched her until she disappeared into her home. "I love you, too," I said.

16

Donna sounded as friendly as ever when I entered the store after dropping Mickie at home. "How was the movie?" she asked.

"Good," I said, still preoccupied by Mickie's deteriorating family situation.

"Was Mickie scared?"

"She's tougher than she lets on."

I dust mopped and stocked the shelves while my dad got the deliveries ready. I contemplated telling him what Mickie had told me about her parents getting a divorce, then thought it would break a confidence and decided not to. I wondered if that was what Mickie and my mother talked about in their hushed whispers when I wasn't around. I felt sad for Mickie and for her sister, Joanna, who was still just a kid. Mickie's brothers were older, and from what I could tell, didn't have a lot on the ball. I was naive, I know. My parents weren't perfect. They argued on occasion, and there were times I'd get home and the chill in the house would be palpable. My mother also thought my father was "a little too wed" to his Manhattan each night and said that it set a "bad example" for me, and I'd heard him tell her she was a bit too zealous when it came to religion. Still, I never even contemplated my parents divorcing, and I couldn't imagine what it would be like to enter our home and not have them both living there.

When I went to empty the garbage, Donna handed me the box beneath the counter so I didn't have to bend down and retrieve it. "Thanks," I said.

"How long have you been friends?"

"Who? Me and Mickie? Since the sixth or seventh grade. She's like my sister."

Donna grinned. "Uh-huh."

"No, she is. She's always at my house; she likes talking to my mom."

"I'm sure she does."

This was all becoming too complicated. My head hurt. "I better get the deliveries done." I walked to the back of the store, loaded up the box with the deliveries, and walked back to the front. "See you," I said, passing the front register.

"I'm still grounded," Donna said. She smiled. "Can I get a ride home?"

17

I played out the scenario of dropping Donna at her home a hundred times as I made my deliveries. In some I initiated the kiss. In others she led, but this time I eagerly responded. I breathed into my cupped hands to check my breath. If I had the chance, I'd get a pack of gum from my father's store.

Just after closing, we all left the store together, but this time when she got into the Falcon, Donna said, "I'm cold. Can you put the top up?"

"Sure," I said, though the temperature was warmer than the last time I'd driven her home.

As we drove the El Camino Real, Donna said, "I need to go to school; I left my math book in my locker, and I have a test on Monday. I don't dare tell my father. He'll just say I'm irresponsible. Would you mind?"

"No, I don't mind, but will you be able to get in the building on a Saturday? They lock down Saint Joe's like a prison on the weekends."

Donna smiled across the car at me. "I don't think it will be a problem."

Burlingame High School looked like an East Coast college campus, with an expansive front lawn and a grove of evergreen and redwood trees. The three-story white building reminded me of the stately southern mansions I'd seen in *Gone with the Wind*, with wide staircases leading to a colonnade entrance and tall doors. I had played youth baseball at the field next to the school for years, which was accessed through a driveway on the edge of the campus. Donna directed me through the parking lot but had me turn toward the baseball grandstands.

"The school is the other way," I said.

"Park behind the backstop," she said.

Confused, I pulled behind the backstop, and before I had shifted the car into park or could ask any questions, Donna had slid across the seat and smothered my mouth with hers. I didn't have to worry about turning off the engine. Donna did that for me, all the while continuing to kiss me, her tongue exploring, tiny moans coming from her throat. I felt horribly ill prepared, clumsy, and unsure what the hell I was supposed to do. Donna took my left hand and placed it firmly on her right breast. "Rub them," she said. "Like this."

She moved my hand over her breast, and I felt the padding and wires of her bra beneath her sweater. I was just trying to keep up when she took my hand again and lowered it beneath her sweater. I felt the warmth of her skin and didn't think anything had ever felt so good.

I was wrong. She stopped kissing me and sat back. "Wait." With a quick move, the sweater was over her head and on the car seat. She tousled her hair, which fell in curls to her shoulders. Her pale-blue bra was much larger and seemingly more sturdily built than any I had ever seen my mother wear. Donna reached behind her back like a contortionist, and the two cups popped as if under pressure. She smiled down at me. "Do you want to see them?"

I couldn't swallow. I'm not sure I was breathing.

"I know you watch me, Sam."

Her fingers moved to the wires at the bottom of the two cups, but again she paused, the longest moment of my life. "You have to ask," she said.

But I had been struck dumb.

"Say, 'Show me your tits.' "

The words blurted from me, sounding like a foreign language and much louder than necessary. "Show me your tits!"

Donna's grin broadened into a huge smile. "Please . . ."

"Please," I said.

"See? Polite and cute." She lifted the cups, and her breasts fell forward, two mounds of flesh with nipples the size of pancakes, and the same rich brown color.

"Do you want to touch them? You have to ask."

"Can I touch them?" I said.

"Please . . ."

"Please."

She took my hand, instructing until instinct and

desire took over, and I rubbed and squeezed. Her nipples hardened.

"You're turning me on," she moaned, and I thought those the best four words any girl would ever utter to me. She fell forward and pressed my face in the canyon of her cleavage. I was lost in warmth and darkness and didn't want to ever surface. Then I felt her hand at my belt, tugging, undoing the clasp, the button of my jeans. She took a moment to unzip my fly. I felt her hand slide beneath the waistband of my briefs, and at the first sensation of the warmth of her fingers, I exploded.

18

As Donna pulled her sweater over her head, I sat looking out the window, feeling embarrassed. Donna's fingers touched my chin and turned my head. She was smiling.

"Sorry," I said.

"Don't be. I like knowing I turned you on so much."

"We could try again," I said, sounding a bit too eager.

She looked at her watch. "Your parents will get suspicious. But we can try again Monday."

Monday? That was an eternity.

"You can't tell them, Sam."

"I wouldn't."

"You can't tell anyone," she said, "especially not Mickie or your friend Ernie. If I find out you told anyone, that you're bragging, I won't. *We* won't do it again."

"I won't tell," I said, having little to brag about, since I didn't think we'd done it that evening.

She flipped her hair off her shoulders. "Good. Because the best is yet to come."

19

I lost my virginity the following Monday in the front seat of the Falcon while parked in the same location. Donna took her time. I think she wanted to be sure she did not cause a repeat of my prior performance. It was over before I knew it, and slightly anticlimactic, given that I'd had two full days to think it over in my mind. This time as she refastened her bra, Donna said, "You'll get better. I'll help you learn to last longer."

I didn't know what to make of her comment, but I suddenly felt like Adam in the Garden of Eden after biting the forbidden apple, suddenly very aware of my nakedness.

Over the course of the remaining school months, Donna did teach me, and I was an eager and willing student. We had sex in the Falcon so many times, sometimes climbing in the back seat, I was certain we would wear out the shocks. After one of these occasions, I mustered my courage and asked, "Do you want to go to a movie Saturday night?"

Donna was refastening her bra. She paused. Then she said, "I can't Saturday."

"How about Friday, or there's a matinee on Sunday?"

"I'm busy this weekend. I have to study."

"All weekend?"

"I told you, my father is a slave driver."

"Maybe you could take a break for dinner."

"We have a commitment. A relative is coming to town. Gag me," she said and stuck her fingers as if choking. "I'd invite you, but trust me, it will be so boring."

"What night?"

"I pretty much have to stick around the whole weekend. Come on—I better get home. It's getting late."

Other times that I'd asked Donna to go out she would say she had commitments to the graduation committee, which added to her already-heavy school workload, or she'd say she was grounded by her father and couldn't go out. I held out hope she would invite me to her school prom, but she told me she decided to go with some of her girlfriends who didn't have dates, and she didn't want to make them feel bad.

Confused, I finally broke my promise and confided in Mickie as we drove to watch one of Ernie's track meets. With Mickie you got brutal, blunt honesty.

"She's using you as her personal vibrator," she said.

"It's not like that."

"It's exactly like that. She's saving on batteries by humping you."

"She just said it would be awkward if we were seen in public."

"Of course it would be, for her. She just turned nineteen, and she's screwing a seventeen-year-old."

"I haven't done anything I didn't want to do. I mean, it isn't like she forced me."

Mickie shook her head. "You need to end it, Sam. You need to tell her either you're good enough to be seen with her in public, or you're ending it. If she says no, then you'll have your answer. I just hope to God you've been wearing a condom."

"I have," I said. "And she said she's on the pill."

"Screw that. I'm not worried about her getting pregnant—I'm worried about you catching a disease."

"A disease? No. She said I'm the only one."

Mickie rolled her eyes. "Please. If she's screwing you, she's screwing others."

"She said she wasn't." And practically I didn't see how she could. We spent so much time in the Falcon, there seemed little time for Donna to spend with anyone else. Then again, I knew, deep down, I was being naive, just as I knew that the reason Donna didn't want to go out with me in public was because she didn't want to be seen with a boy with red eyes. But I really liked those

312

moments in the Falcon, and what red-blooded boy wouldn't?

"This is not going to end well, Sam," Mickie said sadly. "Trust me on this one. End it."

20

I found any number of excuses not to end it. In a sense, I suppose, I was addicted to the sex. Even the occasional pangs of Catholic guilt were not enough for me to give up Donna cold turkey. Mickie eventually stopped asking if I had said anything to Donna, though she'd still occasionally make a face or a sound to convey her disgust. Then, as the end of the summer neared, Donna surprised me with an invitation to her house on a Saturday night for a belated birthday celebration.

"See," I said as Mickie helped me pick out a gift. "She was just waiting for the right moment."

"Yeah," Mickie said. "Sure."

"She was," I protested. "Come on, Mickie— think of it from her perspective."

"I've no doubt she's thinking of it exactly from her perspective."

I had thought through Donna's reticence to be seen with me in public and concluded it had nothing to do with the disparity in our ages. "What I meant was it's not like you just spring a guy with red eyes on your parents."

"No, much better to keep him hidden in his car where you can bone him at your convenience."

Seeing no point continuing the conversation, I

bought sterling-silver hoop earrings and picked up a bouquet of flowers. Donna had instructed me to park the Falcon around the back of the house beside her father's Porsche 911. She greeted me at the back door barefoot. She wore jeans and a low-cut orange mesh sweater over a halter top. The freckles were on full display. She took the flowers, kissed me passionately, and led me inside.

I was nervous about meeting her family, especially her father, who sounded like an ogre. I hoped she had eased the transition by telling everyone about my "condition." But as I entered a kitchen with more marble than a mausoleum, I began to get the sense we were the only ones in the house.

"My parents are gone," Donna said, putting the flowers in a vase and filling it with water. "They've left for Tahoe for the weekend. Surprise!"

Bewildered and no doubt hearing Mickie's warnings in the back of my mind, I couldn't match Donna's enthusiasm. "I thought we were going to celebrate your birthday."

"We are. Won't it be romantic? We don't have to do it in a car." I set Donna's gift on the marble counter. "Well, won't that be great?" she asked when I hadn't responded.

"You said your parents were having a belated birthday for you."

Her smile faded. "I know. I wanted to surprise you. What's the matter?"

"I don't know. It's just—I've never met your parents."

"I've spared you, trust me. I want to do it in their bed."

"I don't know . . ."

"And we can do it in the Jacuzzi."

I thought of what Mickie had said, and this time I didn't talk myself out of asking the question. "How come I've never met your parents or your friends? How come we never go out?"

"What are you talking about? I see you more than my friends."

"We're always in my car."

She stepped forward and played with the collar of my shirt. "Are you complaining? I thought you liked it."

"I do like it, but . . ."

She grabbed my hand and pulled me from the kitchen into a living room with a vaulted ceiling, dark wood molding, bookshelves filled with the spines of old-looking books, and expensive-looking furniture. "And this is so much better, Sam. Trust me. We'll have room to do all kinds of things, things I haven't even showed you yet."

"But why don't we ever go to a movie or dinner—"

She wheeled around. "Fuck, Sam. I knew you'd fuck this up."

"What? No, I'm not—"

"I told you at the very beginning; I told you that you can't tell anyone. How would it look if we went out to a movie? Huh? How would it look?"

"I don't know, like we were going to a movie?"

"I'm nineteen. You're sixteen."

"Seventeen."

"I'm not one of your *little* friends. People would know right away you were fucking me."

"Because we went to a movie?"

"Come on, Sam—why else would I be with you?"

I took a step back, feeling the blow of her words. Goddamn Mickie. She was always right.

I left the gift on the counter and backed the Falcon down the driveway. Despite what Donna had just said, I still half hoped she would come running out the door, chasing after me like in the movies, telling me it was her anger talking and she was sorry. But this wasn't the movies. And I was no movie star worth chasing after. The back door never opened.

"Goddamn Mickie," I said, repeatedly slapping the steering wheel.

I drove down the El Camino past the entrance to Burlingame High School, where I would normally turn to reach the place behind the backstop, and it dawned on me that during all our encounters Donna and I rarely ever spoke. It was always the same, Donna discarding clothes quickly, then hurrying to get dressed so that I could drive her home. I thought maybe I'd found a girl who liked me despite my eyes, but it turned out Mickie was right. I was Donna's personal vibrator. And as I continued driving, I had another realization.

I couldn't go home.

I'd told my parents I was going to a movie with friends. I contemplated calling Mickie, but I was mad at her for being right, again. So I went to the movies by myself and sat through something called *The Longest Yard* with Burt Reynolds, but my heart wasn't into it. Halfway through I began to have second thoughts. Donna had been honest about things from the start, and I *had* promised not to say anything to anyone. Telling Mickie had broken that promise, and it had been a mistake. Things had been going fine with Donna. Besides, she was right—it wouldn't have looked appropriate for the two of us to be seen together, not under the circumstances, not with our age differences, not to mention her working for my dad. And my parents never would have approved. And I liked doing it. And what was so wrong with that? Mickie was a hypocrite. Why was it fine for her but not for me? Amazing what we can talk ourselves into when we want to, and I talked myself into believing Donna hadn't meant what she said, and Mickie didn't always have to be right.

I hurried from the theater, doing everything in my power not to press the gas pedal to the floor as I drove back to Donna's house. When I turned up her street, I was apprehensive about what to say and what she might say. I decided that I would apologize right away and tell her I was sorry and that I hoped I hadn't hurt her. I knew she cared about me. Mickie wasn't always right. She should have just kept her big mouth shut.

As I turned in Donna's driveway, I shut off the headlights, deciding I'd surprise her. The windows in the house were dark. I feared Donna had left and gone out with friends. I drove past the house, turned toward the garage, and braked hard, nearly rear-ending the car parked beside the Porsche 911.

A red Camaro.

21

I spent the rest of the weekend moping around the house and dreading the thought of having to face Donna Monday afternoon. She had one more week of work before she left for college, but barring an illness, my father depended on me to stock the shelves and run the deliveries. The chain pharmacies didn't offer free deliveries, another perk he was using to try to keep his customers loyal, despite the chain stores' persistent price squeeze.

"I broke up with her," I told Mickie when she came over Sunday. "She's leaving for college anyway, so there's no point."

"How'd she take it?" Mickie asked.

I shrugged. "I don't doubt she'll rebound quickly."

"I'm sorry, Sam." Mickie stepped forward to give me a consoling hug, but I wasn't in the mood to be consoled.

"I have homework," I said, turning and trudging up the stairs to my room.

Late the next afternoon, as I approached the store, I'd steeled myself to not act like a little kid, which I now knew to be Donna's perception of me. I had thought of dozens of retorts, things I could say to let her know I knew about Tomaro, that I wasn't as young and naive as she thought, but in the end I realized: I hadn't known about Tomaro, and I *was* as young and naive as she believed—which was why she had chosen me in the first place. I'm sure my eyes had played into her decision as well. Donna had figured out that my "condition" certainly limited my options—to zero. I had been a dolt. What was the point of acting like I hadn't been? Who was I fooling? What would I accomplish except to further embarrass myself?

I was also angry—angry at God for giving me red eyes, angry at Mickie for being right, and angry at my mother for perpetuating the nonsense that my eyes were extraordinary and a precursor of the extraordinary life I was destined to live. There would be no extraordinary life. There would just be life, with all its trials and tribulations.

I took a deep breath and walked into the store, prepared to be courteous and act like I really didn't care. I'd rehearsed what I'd say if Donna said anything. But Donna was not behind the cash register. Betty was training a young woman I'd never met but who I assumed would be Donna's replacement. As I walked the center aisle, Betty introduced me. The woman did a double take.

"She's starting today," Betty said.

I scurried to the back. "Dad?"

My father's fingers pecked the typewriter

keys—he typed faster with two fingers than anyone with ten, then he zipped off a label, peeled the backing, and slapped it on the prescription bottle. When busy, my father was a prescription-filling machine, cranking out as many as 140 a day by himself. "Hey, Sam." He counted tiny capsules in a tray with what looked like a butter knife, then scooped them into the orange plastic vial. "Did you meet Sandra?"

"What happened to Donna?"

"Friday was her last day." He snapped the top on the bottle and set it on the counter, moving on to the next task.

"I thought she had another week."

"She's leaving for school early." Something in his tone indicated something more unsaid. Something he wasn't telling me.

"What happened, Dad?"

His fingers tapped and the typewriter clattered, his eyes focused on the task. "Her parents thought it best if she left a week early for school."

"Why?"

My dad's fingers stopped. I felt a lump in my throat. He nodded to the storage area behind the prescription room. I followed him in, wishing I'd never asked.

"I'm sorry to tell you this, Sam. I know you and Donna have become friends." I felt the floor start to fall from beneath my feet. "Mr. and Mrs. Ashby have suspected for a while now that Donna was seeing a boy on a regular basis, but that she was keeping it from them . . . that she'd been promiscuous." My dad paused, as if I might not know what this word meant, and he was debating whether to explain it to me. Then he said, "Mr. Ashby found a package of condoms in Donna's purse."

"Oh," I said.

"I think we all know where she got them," which was the source of my father's anger. I'd never felt so ashamed, and I realized the depth of my own betrayal. It wasn't Catholic guilt. The church had nothing to do with my guilt-ridden conscience this time. My parents had trusted me to behave as they had raised me, so much so that they apparently didn't even suspect that the boy could be me. Then again, it might not have been trust at all that cloaked their eyes to that possibility. It might have been disregard, which hurt even more. My parents never even considered that a girl like Donna would have wanted me, the kid with the red eyes.

"Rather than confront her and risk having her lie, they told her they were going to Tahoe for the weekend when they were going to a friend's house," my father said. "They snuck back home and caught her in their bed with Leo Tomaro."

My tongue felt glued to the roof of my mouth.

"I'm sorry, Sam. I know you two developed a

nice friendship, but . . . well, you never really know about people."

I dust mopped the floor in a daze, thinking about how close I had come to being Leo Tomaro. My mother said I had been blessed with a vivid imagination, and I could only imagine the scene that had played out in the master bedroom of the Ashby home Saturday night. But even my vivid imagination could not conjure up the scene that would have played out in my own house had it not been for Mickie's warning that things would end badly if I didn't end my relationship with Donna.

Things ended badly, but it could have ended a whole lot worse.

Damn, Mickie.

PART FIVE

NONE OF US ARE GETTING OUT OF HERE ALIVE

1

1989
Burlingame, California

The light was blinding in its intensity, and for one horrified moment I thought David Bateman had invaded my home and was shining the flashlight in my eyes. Then I felt a cold, wet tongue licking me vigorously across the face, and I heard the rattle and jingle of Bandit's dog tags against his chain collar. I was home in bed. Mickie was in the room, though I couldn't see her, and she'd brought Bandit. The big dog had pinned me on my bed, his black-and-white body wagging with such joy and excitement it felt like someone had stuck a quarter in a cheap vibrating hotel bed.

"No, Bandit," I mumbled. "Down, down."

He ignored me.

"Somebody had one hell of a party." Mickie stepped into the stream of light piercing my bedroom window and my eyes. It backlit her like an angel with a full-body halo. She held the empty bottle of Dewar's that I had drunk straight—all available ice cubes having been wrapped in towels and pressed against the backs of my thighs.

"Down," Mickie said, and Bandit dutifully

leaped to the floor with a thud and a jingle. "I often wonder why he likes you so much, especially finding you like this. Is this something I need to worry about, you drinking yourself into a coma alone? Or did the lucky lady leave without even a note on your pillow? I'm not judging, mind you."

"What time is it?" I said.

"Well past morning and rounding on noon."

I had no recollection of how I'd made it up the stairs to my bed or even what time that occurred, but I was glad I'd had the sense to do so. My body would thank me for not having passed out on the sofa. I also did not remember finishing the bottle, though thankfully it had been only a quarter full. I chose it because it was Eva's favorite; she liked to save it for special occasions. Well, it didn't get any more special than when a man learns the woman he nearly sterilized himself for is cheating on him.

"Why are you here?" I asked.

"You mean, 'Hey, Mickie, thanks for coming and checking up on me when I didn't show up in the office this morning. I could have choked on my own vomit and died like some loser rock star. Oh, and thanks for covering my patients'?"

"I don't have any patients. I took the day off."

"Yes, but that was before your aborted trip to Dr. Snip It and your unexpected attendance at the office yesterday afternoon."

I managed to sit up. Mickie was dressed in office attire—beige slacks, a blouse, flat shoes. My T-shirt stuck to my chest, and I could feel sweat dripping down my neck. The room had already begun to swelter, despite the shade of the maple tree in my front yard. There would be no respite from the heat this day and, I sensed, no respite from Mickie. "How did you know about that?"

"It was on your calendar." She walked across the room and slid open the window, bringing the sound of birds chirping but not much of a breeze. "And I wasn't snooping. I was looking to see if maybe you had an appointment. What the hell, Sam?"

"No pun intended, right?"

She didn't laugh. Though my schoolmates had called me Hell, Mickie never had. "Was that Eva's idea?"

I waved her off. "My head hurts too much to argue. Besides, I hate it when you're always right."

"What then? Don't you want kids?"

"So we agree. End of argument."

"There is no argument. That was just plain, dumb-ass stupid."

"Yes, dear."

"I hope to God you're not going to go through with it."

"Can't say that I am."

She exhaled. "At least now I won't have to have you committed for *totally* losing your mind."

"You know your problem, Mick? You're too subtle. You need to learn to express your opinions."

She sat on the edge of the bed. "Really, Sam. Why?"

I let out a breath. "Eva doesn't think she wants to have kids."

"Doesn't want kids or doesn't want your kids?"

"I don't know," I said, though I suspected I did, just as I'd suspected that Donna had been using me as her personal vibrator.

Mickie shook her head. "Can I ask you something?" This made me laugh, Mickie asking permission. "Why do you put up with it?"

"With what?"

"With her bullshit; why would you let her convince you to do that?"

"I love her. At least I thought I did. I don't know. Maybe I don't. Maybe I just felt lucky to have someone like her . . . like me."

Mickie looked like she'd sucked a lemon. Whatever she wanted to say, she held it in with great effort. She held up the bottle. "What is this all about?"

"I had a bad dream that turned out to be real." I didn't know where to begin, and I had to pee like a racehorse. "Hang on." I managed to stand and immediately grimaced. The backs of my thighs burned. I made it halfway to the bathroom before Mickie spoke.

"Jesus, what the hell happened to your legs?"

"Nightmare," I mumbled, not bothering to turn around. "I need a shower."

2

After my shower, I provided Mickie with an abbreviated version of David Bateman administering a whack with his billy club across the backs of my thighs, and Mickie helped me smear Vaseline on my welts and wrap them in gauze.

"What are you going to do?" she asked.

"I don't know."

"You have to report it, Sam."

"To who?"

"He has to have superiors. This is assault and battery."

"It's more than that. It's psychotic. That's what I'm worried about."

"Exactly why you have to report it."

"I'm afraid it would only make things worse for his wife and daughter."

"So you're not going to do anything?"

"At the moment, I'm just trying not to throw up. Listen, this isn't like when I was a kid. I'm not afraid of David Bateman"—though in a sense I guess I was more afraid of him as an adult than as a child—"but reporting it would only help my ego. It wouldn't solve the problem. This isn't about some welt on the back of my leg. That will heal."

"No, but it might get him kicked off the force

and prevent him from doing it to someone else."

"But not to his ex-wife or his daughter," I said.

Mickie sat again.

"As much as I'd like to hurt that asshole, this isn't about me," I said. "It would be the selfish thing to do. You know how this goes. She's too afraid to do anything, so she'll deny it. If she did, by some miracle, agree to back a complaint, Bateman would deny it. I need to outsmart him. I need to find a way to end the abuse for them, not for me."

"I don't want you to get hurt, Sam."

"You mean more hurt, I presume? First thing we need to do is correct that little girl's eyesight. Then we need to figure out a way to get them away from that psychopath for good."

"Any idea how to do that?"

"Not yet."

Mickie left me to dress. I found a pair of shorts baggy enough that the material didn't grip my thighs but long enough to cover the gauze. I slipped my feet into sandals and pulled a gray Stanford T-shirt over my head. As I dressed I smelled spices wafting up from the kitchen— the pungent odor of garlic and the sweet smell of pepper and onions sautéing made my mouth water.

When I made my way downstairs, Mickie stood at the counter, adding ingredients to what looked to be scrambled eggs and everything else edible in my fridge. I saw bits of potatoes, tomatoes, zucchini, onions, and hamburger patty. Bandit sat beside her, licking his chops.

"I can't eat anything," I said. In response, she handed me a bright-red concoction in a sixteen-ounce glass. "What's this?"

"The best hangover medication you will find anywhere. Drink it."

"What's in it?"

"I'm a freaking doctor. Trust me."

"Where have I heard that before?"

"Drink."

The first sip tasted awful. I groaned and put the glass down.

"You really are a baby. It's supposed to taste terrible. It's punishment for abusing your body." Mickie had become a health freak. She didn't drink, smoke, or do drugs. "Now finish it before I hit you across the backs of your thighs with this spatula."

I downed the rest of the concoction, though not without further complaint. At first I thought I would throw it all right back up, but to my surprise, my stomach started to feel better. My head still hurt, but I hoped the Tylenol would kick in and at least dull the beating drums. "You should bottle that stuff," I said. "We'd make a killing."

"Old family recipe," she said without humor.

She put a huge plate of food on the counter in front of me and found a fork. It dawned on me that Mickie had probably cooked more meals in my kitchen than Eva. As I sat at the counter eating, Mickie cleaned the pots and pans. "This is good," I said. "Better than good."

She poured herself a tall glass of water, grabbed a fork, and joined me, systematically swallowing a handful of pills and eating eggs. "So, you want to tell me the rest of what happened?"

"I told you what happened."

"You told me about Bateman. You didn't tell me why you tried to drink yourself into a coma."

I proceeded to give Mickie the blow-by-blow of my evening. Bandit sat at our feet, his head alternately swiveling back and forth, watching us like he was watching a tennis match. When I got to the part about calling Eva's hotel room in Boston, Mickie asked, "Could they have connected you to the wrong room?"

"I heard her. She was there."

Mickie nodded but did not offer further comment. Silence was not like her. Discreet silence was really not like her. Then the reason began to crystallize through my considerable cobwebs. "You knew."

She arched her eyebrows.

"How long have you known?"

She shrugged. "How long have you been dating?"

"What? You think she's been cheating on me the entire time? I don't believe it."

"You'd have to ask her that question, but yes, I think she has been."

"Why would you think that?"

"The way she interacts with you, the way she treats you."

"What's wrong with the way she treats me?" I asked and, under the circumstances, immediately felt like an idiot. Thankfully Mickie did not take the opportunity to beat me senseless with logic.

"She treats you more like a brother than a lover, Sam. You two are more like roommates than soul mates."

"That's an exaggeration."

"Really? Why did she move in?"

"I asked her to."

"Yes, but why? Did you not say it would save on rent and utilities?"

"It does."

"And she said it made *sense,* didn't she?"

"It did make sense."

"Yes, if you were business partners, but last I checked that's not so good a reason for committing to a lifelong relationship together."

"It doesn't mean she's cheating on me."

Mickie looked exasperated. "She keeps a separate room."

"She has to get up at four in the morning a lot, and she doesn't want to wake me."

"Very considerate of her."

"It doesn't mean she's been cheating on me, either."

"No, but the guy I saw rubbing up against her on the dance floor at a club a month after she moved in here was a pretty good indication."

I nearly choked on my eggs. "And you didn't tell me? You didn't say anything?"

Mickie got up and retrieved her purse. "I have to go."

"Wait a minute." I stood. "You can't say that and then just walk out."

She dropped her purse on the couch. "Fine. What was I supposed to say?"

"Oh, I don't know. How about, 'Hey Sam, you know that woman you're about to have your testicles cut off for? She's cheating on you. She's *been* cheating on you'?"

"Don't drop that in my lap; I had no idea you were stupid enough to contemplate having a vasectomy until I saw it on your calendar."

"So tell me she's cheating on me, and maybe I never go down that path."

"Okay, I tell you. Then what? You just said, 'I don't believe it.' You tell me I'm wrong. You tell me it's bullshit, that Eva loves you, that you love her. You ask her and she denies it, or she says it was an old friend and maybe I should just mind my own business. She tells you she doesn't want to be around me. Then what happens to our friendship, Sam? You come to work every day, and we both pretend that nothing has changed? It's none of my business what she does, Sam; my business is being your partner and your friend."

"Is that why you've never liked her?"

"I've never liked her because she's not good enough for you. You've sold yourself short, again. You always have, since high school and that fat chick with the big tits."

"Donna Ashby." Mickie and I had had this discussion about me selling myself short when it came to relationships more than once. Okay, maybe fifty times. I had a modest history of failed relationships with women who could look past my eyes, but only far enough to see a successful doctor who made a decent living. None of them could see far enough to see a life with me.

"You pick women who aren't good enough, and then you rationalize how they treat you rather than just telling them they aren't good enough for you."

"Thanks. That improved my self-esteem immeasurably. Do you have Kim Basinger's phone number? I'm feeling much more confident."

"Would you rather I lie?"

"Sometimes."

"Fine. Next time I'll lie, and you can continue making the same mistake."

"Wait a minute. How is this any different from the guys you date?"

Mickie's eyes blazed, and I regretted my question. "How? I'll tell you how. Because I'm not living with any of them or thinking of marrying any of them." Mickie checked her wristwatch and retrieved her purse, moving across the room toward the front door. "You don't want my advice? I don't give a shit. But don't compare my relationships to your relationship with your roommate. And I don't have to apologize to you or anyone else for who I date or who I sleep with, though I don't sleep with nearly the number you apparently seem to think I do, like those idiots in high school used to speculate."

"I didn't—" I started, but Mickie was on a roll.

"And yes, I like getting laid. I like the feeling when I watch their faces contort in sheer, unadulterated joy, when they gasp with pleasure and look at me completely and totally disarmed. And do you know why?"

I didn't dare answer.

"Because at that moment, they would do anything, anything that I asked of them to experience that feeling again. But I don't ask anything of them. Not one goddamned thing. I'm not in a committed relationship, Sam. I haven't moved in with anyone. I also haven't told anyone I love them and they're the person I want to spend the rest of my life with, because when I do, that will be the last person I ever sleep with." She opened the door and wheeled on me. "You deserve better. You use your eyes as an excuse for not believing you could do better and for not standing up for yourself and telling women they're not good enough for you. You want to settle for someone like Eva, someone who cheats on you, who mistreats you, go right ahead. But for God's sake, at least get a prenup, because I am not ever giving her any part of our damn business just because you're blind."

As the door closed, I was uncertain what had just happened or what exactly had set Mickie off, at least to that level of intensity. Then I thought of what she'd just said to me and I realized something else, something I had never really considered before.

Eva had never told me she loved me.

3

Just before three in the afternoon, Eva had still not called. She had a built-in excuse; her flight from Boston left at six in the morning East Coast time, which was three in the morning my time. Maybe she'd say, "I didn't want to wake you," and I could reply, "I didn't want to wake you two, either."

She had a six-hour flight to concoct a story. Maybe she'd play dumb, deny receiving the phone call at all and make me think that I had called the wrong room . . . and what type of person did I think she was, anyway? Or maybe she wouldn't even bother with the charade; maybe she'd do us both a favor and just admit she'd been cheating on me from the start. Maybe she'd get it over with and say she didn't love me, we had no future together, and she'd move out. I'm a coward, I know, but it would have been so much easier that way. Easier because, as angry and hurt and bitter as I was, there was still a part of me, the part that had been willing to go back to Donna Ashby in high school even though I knew she had used me, the part so afraid that I could never find anyone else and that I would spend my life lonely and alone.

I made the decision not to tell Ernie about

my encounter with David Bateman or Eva's infidelity. I knew how much he was looking forward to attending a World Series, and I didn't want to be a downer. Even the weather was cooperating—still unseasonably warm, high eighties. The rest of the nation would tune in to see Giants fans clad in black-and-orange T-shirts instead of the parkas and ski hats we traditionally donned to attend games at the wind tunnel known as Candlestick Park.

Ernie arrived in full Giants attire, shirt and hat. Mickie once threatened to shoot me if she ever saw me wearing a professional team's jersey unless it said "Loser" across the shoulders, but I slipped on my Giants jersey for that day. When I got in his Mercedes, Ernie handed me a hat just like the first time I'd gone to his house to play three flies up. This one was new, black with an orange *SF* stitched on the front. "My father bought it for the client. I see no reason for it to go to waste."

"Neither do I." I adjusted the size, slipped it on my head, and pulled down the visor. "We look like a couple of really big Little Leaguers," I said.

4

Candlestick Park was draped in red, white, and blue bunting that made even the concrete mausoleum look festive. The grass was a rich green, and the cloudless sky radiated a pale blue. I could smell steamed hot dogs, popcorn, and roasted peanuts.

"Let's get a beer," Ernie said as we walked through the ticket gate. "I want to be in our seats for the opening festivities."

We bounded up the concrete steps and found the shortest beer line. It didn't take long for the first admirer to say, "Hey, aren't you Ernie Cantwell?"

"Not today," Ernie said. "Today I'm a Giants fan, just like you."

"I used to love to watch you play," the man said. "What the hell happened to you?"

Ernie got these kinds of questions all the time, and though he did a good job hiding it, I know it bothered him when people thought of him as some washed-up former athlete who walked off the field and disappeared. "I retired," he said. "Now I work for him." Ernie pointed to me.

"Yeah, what do you do?" the man asked.

"I rehabilitate washed-up ex-jocks," I said, which ended the conversation.

I looked out and watched the last stream of cars inching into the parking lot just as the stadium began to shake. Ernie and I looked at each other and would later recall we had the same initial thought—that we were missing something inside the stadium, something so incredible as to cause sixty thousand fans to stamp their feet in unison. Then we both stumbled off balance. It felt like waves were rolling beneath the stadium. Out in the parking lot, car alarms blared in unison.

"Earthquake!" someone yelled.

My instinct was to run; we were not far from an exit, and all I could think about was the tons of concrete hanging over our heads, ready to fall and crush us in an instant, but Ernie grabbed my arm and looked me in the eye. "Don't run!"

People looked as if they were standing on the deck of a moving ship, their legs unsteady, listing back and forth, fear etched on their faces. When the earthquake had passed, there was a moment of eerie, stunned silence, fear that the earthquake could start up again. People looked up at the cement overhang, then at one another, and the crowd let out a collective, spontaneous roar—as much a sigh of relief as an acknowledgment that we all had just experienced something beyond a normal tremor and had lived to tell about it. Strangers just seconds before the shake, they all now talked animatedly and high-fived one another. The televisions behind the concession stand, which had gone black, flickered back on. Announcers stood on the grass field fitting in earpieces and looking confused. Players milled about behind them, some looking up into the stands for family members. The TV station cut away to a familiar newscaster sitting behind a desk in a San Francisco news studio, but I couldn't hear what he was reporting over the buzz of the crowd. The guy in front of us, however, was wearing earphones and holding a transistor radio.

"Holy shit," he said, spinning around and pulling off his earphones. "The Bay Bridge collapsed."

Someone farther up the line confirmed it. "The Bay Bridge collapsed."

That's when it got serious. The crowd became quiet, and I'm sure most were thinking what I was thinking: there would be no game this night and what was the fastest way out of the concrete mausoleum threatening to squash us? The newscaster on the TV continued to mime. Pictures of the bridge appeared over his right shoulder. The bridge had not completely collapsed, but a section of the upper span had collapsed, and a car dangled precariously close to the edge.

The guy with the earphones issued another report. "There are fires in the Marina District. They're saying a lot of homes have collapsed, and there are gas leaks. They're evacuating."

Looking north, I saw plumes of black smoke rising and hovering in the stale, stagnant air. The guy with the radio began to voice reports of more damage throughout the stadium and the city. The vendors behind the concession stands closed the rolling metal screens. Beer sales had been suspended.

Ernie looked at me and said what we both knew. "I have to get home."

With the electricity out, the escalators were not working. We took the stadium stairs two at a time, twisting and weaving, trying to beat the logjam that would surely ensue on the lone exit road from the ballpark. Others in the stadium had made the same decision, and now it was a footrace to the parking lot. I was no match for Ernie under normal circumstances, but with the gauze on the backs of my legs tugging and pulling with each step, rubbing the welts raw, I was even slower. I could feel Ernie's urgency, his primal instinct to protect his wife and kids, and so I pushed through the pain.

Inside Ernie's Mercedes I tuned the radio dial in search of news as Ernie wove between cars. The mayor had ordered bars throughout the city closed. Police officers had been called to service, and the governor was calling for the National Guard. Many parts of the city were without electricity. Phone service had either also been severed or the system was so overwhelmed you could not place calls. The black clouds to the north had grown and darkened in color. They looked like mushroom clouds from a dropped bomb. The City by the Bay was burning.

An hour later, when Ernie finally pulled into his driveway, Michelle raced out the front door with tears of worry streaming down her cheeks. Ernie barely got out of the car before she wrapped her arms around him in a bear hug. The boys followed, each grabbing one of their father's legs, holding him tight, looking scared.

I stood alone.

5

1975
San Mateo, California

My senior year in high school, Mr. Shubb named me editor of the *Friar* newspaper. I'd like to tell you this was a great honor, but in truth no one else wanted the job. Being editor in chief was a lot of work, and it necessitated that I give up the sports beat, which allowed me to go to Ernie's games as a spectator and sit in a raucous student section where most of my classmates were so drunk a lit match would have caused an explosion. On one of those Friday nights, as I was leaving the journalism trailer, I ran into Michael Lark, the middle linebacker of the football team.

"Where are you going, Hell?"

I don't think Lark had ever spoken ten words to me when I didn't have a notepad and pen in hand, but that was true of many of the jocks. "I was going to get a sandwich and go to the game," I said.

"Fuck that," Lark said. "You're going to Vista Point with me."

Vista Point was a stop along the freeway with views overlooking Crystal Springs Reservoir and secluded enough that many in the cheering section went there to drink before just about every school function. Ernie refused to put a drop of alcohol into his well-sculpted and smooth-running body, and for three years I had followed his lead when he dragged me to parties, dances, and sporting events. I'd never been to Vista Point, though I was curious as hell to see it for myself. I didn't even care about Lark's motive, though that soon crystallized. Lark explained that he'd lost his driving privileges and had been serving detention, what Saint Joe's called "jug," and he had missed his ride to Vista Point. Okay, so I was his chauffeur, and at least for one night I was his best friend. I couldn't go anywhere without him handing me a beer, or a shot from some bottle, and he wouldn't take no for an answer. The first beer made it easier to say yes to a second, and next thing I knew he and I were in a beer-chugging contest, and Lark was shouting to anyone who would listen that I was "all right for a red-eyed little bastard."

I don't know how Ernie did that night on the court. I never made it to the game. It was the only high school game of Ernie's I missed. I spent much of the night leaning against my Falcon, struggling to remain upright. Then the car tilted as if struck by a rogue wave, and I landed on the pavement. Luckily, I used my face to break my fall. Beyond that, I don't remember anything. I later came to learn that I was thrown into the

Falcon, and after much debate about what to do with me, one of my less inebriated classmates drove the Falcon with a second car following. I assume they obtained my address from my driver's license. The problem, of course, was how to deliver me. I remained passed out, with bloodstains down the front of my shirt and a welt on my forehead the size of an egg. With limited options, my new drinking buddies did what any eighteen-year-olds would have done. They propped me up against the front door, rang the bell, and ran.

Like I said, I don't remember any of this, mind you, and there isn't any account of it in any of my mother's scrapbooks comprising my high school years, but my companions provided a detailed accounting the following Monday at school. My father didn't wait that long. He rousted me at seven Saturday morning by throwing a glass of cold water in my face. Then he sat in a lawn chair reading the newspaper while I pushed the lawn mower around the yard in a cold sweat, throwing up just about every three feet. With my head pounding, he sat me down to talk. My mother came out to join us, but my father suggested she get breakfast ready. She departed without a word, which was really unlike her.

"You made quite an entrance," he said. My father explained how, when he opened the door, I entered the house face-first, just missing the staircase banister, my fall broken only by my mother's potted fern. "Your mother loved that fern."

"I'll pay for a new one," I said, though I knew this wasn't about flora.

"Your mother wanted to rush you to the emergency room to have your stomach pumped. I wanted to leave you on the floor." My father handed me a glass of iced tea. "I went to high school, Sam, and I went to college. I have no desire to do it again. I can't be in the car with you or live in your dorm next year. You've reached an age to make your own decisions. I hope you make those decisions because you feel they are the right thing to do, not because of peer pressure or because you're trying to fit in. Do you understand what I'm saying?"

I nodded.

"Don't ever think of yourself as being something less than the person you are because of your eyes, Sam. If you do, people will take advantage of it, and you'll find yourself doing things you don't want to do."

"I understand. But why did you make me mow the lawn?"

"Being a man means having to live with the consequences of our decisions, like getting up and going to work with a hangover. That was your lesson today."

I waited for my punishment, hoping it wasn't

something severe. My father would certainly suspend my driving privileges and likely ground me.

"Take a shower and try to get something into your stomach," he said. Then he stood and left me sitting alone in the backyard.

My mother had not agreed with my father's decision to appeal to my sense of responsibility. Had it been left to her, I would have been enrolled in the local chapter of AA and never allowed to leave the house again. But that moment in the backyard, when my father called me a man, had been my rite of passage. He was telling me that I needed to make my own decisions in life, and I needed to decide for myself what type of person I intended to become, independent of what others thought of me.

6

My father didn't ground me, but, feeling guilty, I decided to lie low and spend Saturday night at home. Ernie had a date, so going out wasn't really an issue. Mickie, surprisingly, didn't have a date and joined me downstairs to play pool. I heard the doorbell ring and voices upstairs.

"Sounds like Ernie," Mickie said.

"Can't be. He's got a date."

Moments later, the door at the top of the stairs opened, and Ernie came down dressed in jeans, boots, and a button-down shirt.

"What are you doing here?" I asked.

"You want to hang out?"

I checked my watch. "Don't you have a date?" Ernie had met a girl at a party the prior weekend and had been talking about how hot she was the entire week.

Ernie glared at me. "Do you want to hang out or not?"

"Yeah, sure," I said and risked a glance at Mickie. She arched her eyebrows and shrugged.

"Then just rack the balls. Is that too much to ask?"

I'd never seen Ernie this upset. His eyes blazed. For a moment, I thought he might hit me. I racked the balls in silence. Mickie handed me her cue stick and backed away from the table, sitting on a bar stool near the paneled wall.

"I'll break," Ernie said. He hit the cue ball so hard it soared off the table and left a dent in the paneling less than a foot from where Mickie had retreated. Ernie snapped the pool cue over his knee and turned his back to us.

After a beat I said, "I've seen worse breaks."

Mickie let out a snort and covered her mouth. Ernie didn't immediately turn around, but I saw his shoulders begin to shake. When he turned he, too, was trying not to laugh. "You're an idiot, you know that?"

"That seems to be the consensus this weekend."

He put down the broken cue. "Sorry," he said. "I'll buy a new one."

"I do it all the time," I said, then pretended to be unable to break a cue over my knee.

Ernie laughed more and sat on a bar stool.

I set my stick down on the table. "What happened?" I asked.

He took another moment to compose himself. "I went to pick her up, and her dad met me at the door. I put out my hand to greet him, and he stared at it like it had shit on it. Then he said, 'My daughter does not date jungle bunnies.'"

"He didn't," Mickie said, getting off her bar stool. "That cocksucker."

"Then he told me to get my black ass off his

porch before he called the police and had me arrested for trespassing."

"Son of a bitch," Mickie said. "Let's go egg his fucking house."

Don't get me wrong. Burlingame wasn't Mississippi in the 1960s. People weren't wearing hooded robes and burning crosses on lawns, but that was not to say racism didn't exist. Ernie had been taunted with the N-word on the football field and during basketball games. Once as a child he was accused of stealing in a store because the store owner believed that's what colored people did.

As we got older, Ernie and I both realized one of the reasons we spent so much time together was because we were the two kids in class most frequently discriminated against. The racism was hidden in high school because of Ernie's athletic exploits, but only to an extent. At dances and parties, there was never a shortage of girls who wanted to dance and flirt with the great Ernie Cantwell, but I'd also started noticing a pattern, perhaps because I was all too familiar with it myself. If the girls were white—and most in Burlingame were—Ernie's flirtations rarely progressed beyond the flirting. It was one thing to be friendly to a black kid; it was quite another to have him show up at your house to meet your parents and take you on a date. Girls made excuses not to give Ernie their phone numbers.

Those who did usually met him someplace rather than have him come to their home, and those who did go out on a date with him usually had excuses why they couldn't go out with him a second time.

"Let it go," I said to Ernie, though it was Mickie who responded. Mickie never let anything go.

"What? How can you say let it go? The guy is a racist asshole, and his daughter is a stupid bitch for not knowing better."

"He's ignorant," I said. "He's an ignorant, racist, asshole cocksucker just like you said, which means he would be too stupid to understand why we egged his house even if we did. In his mind, it would only justify his belief system."

"Fuck that—"

"You can't change people's irrational beliefs, Mickie. Trust me—I know." I looked at Ernie. "So does Ernie." Ernie glanced at me and nodded. "And that guy, he's not the guy you have to worry about. The ones to worry about are the ones who cloak their discrimination behind some other excuse so you can't call them out."

Unfortunately, as our senior year in high school was coming to an end, Ernie and I would have to experience those people yet again.

7

Each year the Saint Joe's trustees, a group composed of parents, alumni, and prominent community members, chose the class valedictorian from a field of the top ten candidates. As far back as anyone could remember, the honor always went to the student who finished number one in his class, and that student, in the graduating class of 1975, was me. So, while Ernie—the greatest athlete the school had ever produced—was on the short list, he had already conceded defeat and had spent much of the week leading up to the announcement pumping me up.

I'd tried not to get my hopes up, but I had to admit that I'd also considered the announcement, scheduled for a Friday afternoon, a formality. In fact, I'd already begun to draft my speech, intending it to be the best valedictorian speech ever given. It had to be. This was another opportunity to prove myself, much the same way I saw my chance to be lector at OLM as a chance to show that I was just a normal kid. I could only hope being valedictorian had a better ending.

I found the draft of my speech inside my mother's scrapbook labeled *1975*.

I never did write a final version.

Friday afternoon during my free period, I was

laying out the last edition of the *Friar* in the journalism room, a portable trailer located at the back of the junior-class parking lot with no hookup to the school PA system. When the bell rang, I hurried across the parking lot into the main school for my physics class, but found the main hall crowded with students hooting and hollering and quickly realized I'd missed something important. "What's going on?" I asked the first student I saw.

"They announced class valedictorian," he confirmed. "Didn't you hear?"

Obviously I hadn't, and I was wondering why the kid hadn't congratulated me. Everybody in school knew, at the very least, who I was. In fact, no one passing in the hallway stopped to congratulate me.

At that moment a group of students spilled out of one of the classrooms into the hall, Ernie in the middle of the pack receiving pats on the back and congratulations. In a novel, this would be the place where I told you that Ernie and I made eye contact, or that I graciously marched up and congratulated him. But I didn't do either of those things. I slunk back into the crowd and quietly slipped into my fifty-five-minute physics class, which seemed to pass like an eternity. When the final bell of the day rang, I hurried to the Falcon without going to my locker and quickly departed. I didn't want to talk to anyone. I especially didn't want to talk to Ernie. For three years I had been building up Ernie on the athletic fields to the point that he was a demigod at Saint Joe's and a household name throughout the county. Even national newspapers had been writing stories on him and speculating which of the three dozen scholarships being dangled by some of the best schools in the country he would take. And he wouldn't have even gotten that far had I not dragged his ass through grammar school.

Did he also have to be class valedictorian—the only accolade I had a chance to win?

I did not immediately tell my mother of my latest slight when I got home from school. Not that she bothered to approach me. My mother had remained cool in the aftermath of my drinking incident. She had not reached the level of acceptance my father had, unwilling to admit I was a man capable of making decisions for myself. My mother had spent her life advocating for me, ensuring that I received the same opportunities as any other child, and her maternal instinct, finely honed from those years, would always be to protect me. But at this moment I knew she was worried as to whether she could protect me from myself. I understood her worry, but I also couldn't help but be a little bitter. Once again, her steadfast faith in "God's will" and my destiny to live an extraordinary life had rung hollow.

I waited until we were all seated at the dinner table, deliberately breaking my mother's rule forbidding conversation that could be disruptive to our digestion. As my mother served fried chicken, I said, "I have some news."

My father placed a chicken breast on his plate and looked to me. My mother tossed the salad. "Oil and vinegar okay?" She proceeded to pour the mixture without our input or acknowledging me.

"Maddy," my father said. "Sam said he has news."

My mother stopped tossing the salad and looked at me, but before I could utter a word, her eyes went wide in anticipation. "Is it the class valedictorian? Oh, Sam, I knew you would get it. I knew it. I'm so proud of you."

"I didn't get it," I said.

My mother slowly set down the wooden utensils and slumped into her seat in silence. "What do you mean?"

"I mean they chose Ernie," I said.

We listened to the hum of the refrigerator and the tick of the clock in an awkward silence my father finally broke. "Well, that's quite an honor for Ernie, isn't it? We'll have to call the Cantwells and congratulate them. Won't we, Maddy?"

But my mother did not answer. Her mouth was pinched tight, and her brow furrowed. She turned her head to avoid crying in front of me.

I stood and walked to her, placing my hand on her shoulder. "It's okay, Mom," I said.

"No," my mother said, crying tears of anger. "It's not okay, Samuel." Then she did something I had not heard up to that day or since. She swore. "Damn it! It is not okay! Those members of the board of trustees are cowards. All of them are nothing but a bunch of cowards."

"Maddy," my dad said. "Let's not be ungracious."

"Why not?" she seethed. "Everybody else is."

"Ernie's had it rough, too," I said, trying to be sympathetic to the racism Ernie had endured. Inside, however, the pain was excruciating, and I wondered if I'd be able to face Ernie again without bitterness.

"You earned this, Samuel," my mother said. "You earned this, and they are not going to take this away from you. Tomorrow morning I am going to make some calls and let them know they can't—"

"No," I said, interrupting her. "No calls, Mom."

"This is not right. It is not right."

"No calls," I repeated, with a firmness that gave both my parents pause. "Maybe it isn't right. But it's the way it is. Okay? It's the way it is, and the sooner we all realize this, the better it will be. We won't be getting our hopes up for things that are unreachable." I sat back down. "Do you remember the time you said that the sooner I

361

learned to accept the fact that I was different, the sooner I could learn to deal with it?"

"I never said any such thing to you."

"To Dad," I said. "When I didn't get accepted to OLM and you went to that reporter friend of yours and it was all over the news. Dad said it would have been better to just let me blend in, and you said that could never happen because I can't blend in and the sooner I learned to accept it, the better."

"Samuel, that is not what—"

"I've accepted it, Mom. I've accepted who I am. Okay? I'm not a kid who's going to get picked to play kickball, or to be the lead in the school play. I'm not going to be invited to parties or be chosen class valedictorian. I'm not. And I'm okay with that." It sounded convincing, though I wasn't okay with it. It hurt like hell, rejection. And the pain lingered like an open wound that, just as it started healing, was ripped open again.

"Well, I'm not," my mother said quietly.

"Well, it's not your life," I said, and again everything came to a sudden halt. "It's mine. And I'm the one who has to live it. I'm the one who has to deal with it."

Tears welled in my mother's eyes. I knew it hurt. Reality could be painful to acknowledge, but there came a point when we all realized we weren't going to walk on the moon, star in a

Hollywood movie, or be president of the United States. We'd be who we were, and we could either come to grips with this fact and like the person we'd become, or live with regret and disappointment. My reality was that I was not going to live some extraordinary life, as my mother so fervently believed, and prayed for.

Life's a bitch, kid. And then you die.

My mother turned as if to grab something from the counter, wiping at her eyes with a dish towel. My father gave me a subtle nod, not of approval but of understanding. This was another of those rite-of-passage moments. "Then we'll respect your wishes, Sam. Maddy," he said, calling her back to the table. "Why don't we eat, and after dinner we can call the Cantwells to congratulate Ernie."

But that also wouldn't be necessary. As we washed and dried the dishes, the front doorbell rang, and when I went to answer it, I discovered Ernie and his parents standing on the porch. His mother carried a box with her, but none of them looked happy.

"Hey, Sam," Ernie said, sheepish.

"Hey, Ernie."

My parents walked into the entry, and after an awkward greeting, the silence was palpable. My mother finally invited us all into the living room. She offered to make coffee or tea, but everyone declined.

"Ernie has something he'd like to say," Mr. Cantwell said.

Ernie looked to me. "I'm going to turn it down."

"What?"

"The class valedictorian. I'm going to turn it down."

"Ernie, you can't do that," my father said. "This is a great honor."

"It isn't right," Mrs. Cantwell said. "Sam finished first in his class. This is his honor. He deserves it."

I shook my head. "They're not going to let me do it," I said. "Let's face it. They don't want a kid with red eyes representing the whole school in front of the archbishop and all the parents. If I can't do it, I'd just as soon it be Ernie."

"Well I'm not doing it, either, then," Ernie said.

"Ernie, you should do it," my mother said, though I still detected the disappointment in her voice.

"They chose me because I'm black."

"What?" I asked.

"They've never had a black valedictorian. I'd be the first. They think it would look good for the school, for recruiting people of color."

"People who can play sports," Mr. Cantwell said.

In my self-pity, I had been too busy thinking of the reason why the school had not chosen me. I hadn't stopped to consider why they would have chosen Ernie over the other eight candidates. Ernie was certainly the best known among us, in large part thanks to my coverage of his exploits on the athletic fields, but his grade point average was nowhere near the top of the class.

"They told you that?" I said.

"Of course not," he said. "They can't come right out and say it, just like they can't come right out and say why they didn't choose you." I heard anger in his voice.

"They didn't have to tell us," Mr. Cantwell said. "They roll Ernie out to talk to every black athlete who visits the school. And I have a friend who's a trustee on the board. He told me it wasn't expressed verbally, but the intimation was loud and clear. Discrimination is difficult, because in its worst form, it is not overt. It is subtle. We feel the same as Ernie. The honor belongs to Samuel. If they won't honor him, Ernie will not stand in his place."

After another prolonged silence, I said, "Who will they choose, then?"

Ernie shrugged. "I don't care who, because it won't matter. Once I turn it down, everyone is going to know what they tried to do. Kids were already talking about it at school, about the fact that you have the highest grades and they didn't choose you."

"They were?"

"Of course they were. If you don't get it, nobody is going to want to do it."

"Are you sure you want to do this?" I said. "I mean, you could look at it like you'd be opening the door for other kids of color."

"Those kids will open that door on their own, in the classroom," Mr. Cantwell said. "Just as you have done."

8

Ernie's declination did cause a stir, but not enough of one, apparently, for anyone to ever apologize or ask me to be the valedictorian. In hindsight, the trustees couldn't very well have done that, not after passing me over. It would have been a tacit admission that they'd had ulterior motives for not choosing me in the first place and, perhaps, an admission that their motives for choosing Ernie had also not been honorable.

Despite this latest snub, my mother was far from finished pushing me to lead an extraordinary life. If anything, those moments only motivated her to push harder.

Later that month, as I sat at my desk studying for finals, my mother entered my room with a load of folded laundry. I detected, however, that she had an ulterior motive and had timed this delivery for that reason.

"Mrs. Cantwell called," she said, putting folded T-shirts in the third dresser drawer from the top. "Ernie's excited about the senior prom this Saturday."

"Do you think I should start my English essay with a parable?" I asked.

"You do know the prom is this Saturday?"

"It would make Father Peter happy, but it might make me look like a brownnoser."

"Don't be disgusting, and stop avoiding the subject. Have you considered going?" my mother asked.

"I think Ernie already has a date."

"Samuel—"

"People would talk, Mom. It's already an all-boys school."

Humor did not pacify my mom when she got upset. "Fine, be that way," she said, though she didn't leave, and that was far from the end of the conversation.

I put down my pen and took off my glasses, resting them on my homework. "I'm not avoiding it, Mom. Yes, I've considered going. In fact, I've asked three girls, and each has turned me down. Ernie also tried to set me up with one of Alicia's friends, but she chose to stay home rather than go with me." I had visions of me showing up at my date's house and having her father greet me at the door with some remark like, "My daughter does not date red-eyed sons of the devil!"

My mother used a rag to wipe at invisible dust motes atop my dresser and rearranged the knick-knacks, including my priceless Willie Mays–autographed baseball. "I think Mickie might be available Saturday night," she said.

Good old Mickie, she was always there for me, but I couldn't do that to her. I couldn't ask her to be my senior prom date. She'd know I'd struck out with other girls, and she was the good reliable replacement, like that second pair of glasses stuffed in a drawer to serve as a backup if you lost the first pair. "Maybe I'll hang out with her in the basement," I said.

My mother tossed her dust rag at me. "Samuel, you get one senior prom in your life; you are not going to spend it in the basement playing pinball."

"You're right. I'll go to a movie."

"You're going to the prom, and you're doubling with Ernie and his date, young man."

"Why do you always do this?" I asked.

"What, try to create memories for my son?"

"Fit a square peg in a round hole, Mom."

"You're only a square peg if you allow yourself to be treated as one. Now you're going to the prom, and you're going with Mickie, or so help me I'll get out one of my old prom dresses, and you'll be taking me."

If there was one thing I had learned about my mother, it was that she did not make idle threats. The image of me walking into a hotel ballroom with my mother was enough to get me out of my seat and moving to the telephone. "Fine," I said snatching the phone from the cradle.

My mother followed and took the receiver from my hand. "No way, young man. You do not call a young lady on the phone to ask her to the prom. You drive to her house and ask her proper."

At that moment, I just wanted to get away, so I hurried down the stairs with my mother yelling something about flowers on the kitchen counter, which I ignored. I grabbed the keys off the hook and slammed the front door.

9

Mickie's mother invited me in with what I thought to be a wry smile, further convincing me this was a conspiracy. A moment later Mickie bounded down the stairs dressed in jeans and a powder-blue UCLA hooded sweatshirt. "Hey, Hill, what's up?"

Joanna, her younger sister and often her shadow, shuffled down the steps behind her. "Hey, Hill, what's up?" she mimicked.

My paranoia now led me to suspect from their poorly disguised grins that Mickie and Joanna knew exactly what was up and were also a part of the conspiracy. "You want to go get a yogurt?" I asked. Frozen yogurt was new and all the rage at that moment, and a new shop had just opened on Broadway.

"Are you buying?"

"Are you buying?" Joanna asked.

"Yes, I'm buying."

"Then I'm eating."

"Then I'm eating."

Mickie slipped on sandals and convinced Joanna she could not go with us, as Joanna sometimes did, sitting in the back seat with her head between the two of us like a dog just excited to be out for a ride. We promised to bring her home a yogurt. I stormed out the door and down the front walk ahead of Mickie, not even bothering to open her car door for her. Inside the Falcon she slid across the front seat, closer than normal, which only increased my irritation.

"Everything okay?"

"Fine."

"Are we grumpy?"

"Just tired."

At the yogurt store, Mickie waited at one of the tables while I stood in a considerable line, growing more and more irritated by everyone and everything. After twenty minutes, I delivered Mickie a strawberry yogurt.

"Where's yours?"

"I'm not hungry. Do you want to go to the prom with me or not?"

Mickie spiked the tiny plastic spoon in her yogurt. "Is that the best you can ask me?"

"I assume my mother has already asked you the 'proper way,' " I said, putting the last two words in quotes.

"As a matter of fact, she didn't."

"Come on—like you didn't know."

"I didn't know, and you know what, if I had, I would have told you not to bother and saved you the drive. Jerk." Mickie stood and left the table, then came back to retrieve her yogurt. "Thanks for the yogurt, asshole," she said and stormed off again.

The two workers behind the counter, and everyone standing in line, were now staring at me, and not because of my red eyes. I'm not certain they could have distinguished them from my red face. But I was still irritated and in no mood for gawkers. "What, haven't you people seen anyone with red eyes before?" I said, causing them to quickly turn away. With that I stood and went outside.

Mickie was leaning against the passenger door of the Falcon, eating her yogurt.

"I'm sorry," I said. "I'm mad at my mother, and I'm taking it out on you."

"Why are you mad at your mother?"

"Because she always does this."

"Does what?"

"I was content to stay home."

"So was I."

"Well, say no, and we can both stay home."

"You haven't asked me yet."

"I asked in there."

"Doesn't count."

"Fine. Do you want to go to the prom with me?"

"Yes."

"What? You just said—"

"I said I *was* content to stay home. Now I want to go."

"You're just doing it to spite me and appease my mother."

She put the yogurt on the roof of the Falcon and folded her arms. "Have you ever known me to do anything to appease anyone?"

I hadn't. Mickie stood her ground, I'd give her that.

"Then why are you?"

"Because I think it could be a lot of fun, that's why. Because it means I get to spend the night with my two best friends. It means I get to spend time with you."

I felt about two feet tall. "I'll pay for everything," I said. "If you need a dress . . ."

"You're not paying for my dress, Hill." She'd resumed eating her yogurt.

"I just don't want . . . I know this is . . ."

"Do you want to shut up now?"

"I'm sorry about the way I asked you."

"You should be."

"I know. You're doing me a favor—"

She groaned. "Stop saying that. It's not a favor, Hill. Why can't you get that through your thick head?"

"You don't have to say that."

"Hello! Have you ever known me to say anything I didn't want to say?"

Again, I hadn't. "No. Usually you say things I don't want you to say." She smiled and put the spoon in her mouth, being playful, and at that moment—I've heard people say things like being struck dumb—but it was as if I had never really seen Mickie before, seen how truly beautiful she was. Her head was tilted, and her hair, caressing her neck, had streaks of gold that glistened and made her eyes stand out, a vivid blue.

"What?" she asked wiping at her chin with the napkin. "Do I have yogurt dripping down my face?"

"No," I said.

"You okay?"

I nodded and briefly contemplated telling her what I had been thinking, but I knew Mickie would not take me seriously. She'd blow it off and say something sarcastic like I should get my eyes checked again.

"Okay," I said. "Saturday night then."

I walked to the driver's side, opened the door, and slid in. Mickie had walked to the passenger door. I put the key in the ignition, but Mickie remained standing outside the car. I checked the door lock to make sure the knob was up. It was. I looked up at her. "What's the matter?"

"I'm waiting for you to open my door for me like a gentleman. It will be good practice for Saturday night."

10

The following Saturday, I stood in the marble foyer of Mickie's house in a burgundy tux with a ruffled shirt and burgundy bow tie. A photograph, much to my chagrin, remains in my mother's scrapbook for 1975.

"Did you take a job as a waiter?" one of Mickie's brothers asked. My luck they were home from college.

"A job as a waiter," Joanna laughed, holding on to the banister and swinging back and forth.

"Is that velvet, Hill? I think we have drapes made of the same material," Mickie's other brother said.

"We have drapes made of the same material," Joanna repeated, laughing.

Thankfully Mickie's father had moved out of the house by this point.

Joanna stopped swinging and yelled, "Hey, Mickie! Sam's here, and he has flowers!" She started up the stairs. "I'll get Mickie, Sam. My mom is putting tape on her boobs."

I had no idea what that meant and flushed a color to match my tuxedo.

Mickie's brothers and I sat in the den with the television blaring. After the initial ribbing, we made small talk about the Giants and the Forty-

Niners. I felt like the room was a thousand degrees. Finally, I heard the click of high heels on marble, stood, and almost dropped the corsage. I'd seen pictures of my friends at their proms. The girls wore long dresses that made brides-maid dresses look good. Not Mickie. She wore a burgundy dress that seemed to defy gravity, held up by nothing more than two thin shoulder straps. It sank low enough to reveal a hint of cleavage, hugged her hips, and ended just above her knees. Her legs were free of nylons, her calves toned above white high heels. I couldn't tell you the fabric of the dress, but it looked like silk. I really didn't care. As eye-catching as I found the dress, Mickie's face stole my attention. She looked like something created by a great artist, with her hair curled and diamond earrings protruding from her lobes.

"Close your mouth," she said. "You'll catch a fly."

"Oh, Michaela," her mother said.

"You'll catch a fly." Joanna rolled on the ground in hysterics. "You'll catch a fly."

"This is for you," I said, holding out the corsage.

"Aren't you going to pin it on?" Mickie asked.

I studied the thin straps.

"Here, Sam, I'll do it," Mickie's mother said, coming to my rescue and giving Mickie a reproachful look.

The corsage in place, Mrs. Kennedy instructed us to stand this way and that as she took pictures and promised to make an extra set, which my mother would date, label, and slide into the photo album right next to the photograph of me in my tuxedo.

Mickie rested her hand on my arm to keep her balance on her high heels as we walked down the front steps to the Falcon. I opened the passenger door and waited until she'd gathered a matching shawl and slid across the seat. When I got in the driver's side, Mickie sat in her customary spot.

"Everything okay?" she asked. "You were kind of quiet in there."

This time I did not hesitate to say it. "You look beautiful." I did not feel the least bit self-conscious saying it. I was stating a fact, like looking at a waterfall and calling it breathtaking. "Really. Really beautiful."

Mickie blushed, beaming. Then she leaned over and kissed me on the cheek.

My mother's suggestion that I invite Mickie turned out to be a stroke of genius. We met Ernie and his date, Alicia, at a local restaurant, and dinner was not the awkward first date so many of my friends experienced on prom nights. The conversation flowed, and the four of us laughed as much that night as any other. I didn't think the night could get any better. Then it did. When Mickie and I walked into the hotel ballroom holding hands, a lot of heads turned, and while other couples stood or sat at tables looking bored, Mickie dragged me straight to the dance floor. She sparkled beneath the strobe lights and spinning silver ball. Her years of dance and gymnastics classes had given her the ability to move in a manner that was part burlesque, part Ginger Rogers. I did my best to keep up, but I was grateful for the slow songs, which allowed me to catch my breath and to feel Mickie close against me. This time we didn't need to leave six inches for the Holy Spirit, as we did in grammar school. She rested her head on my chest, and I felt her breath on my neck and smelled the scent of her perfume. It sent shivers up my spine.

Late in the evening, when the band took a break, Mickie and Alicia went to the bathroom, and Ernie and I ventured to the bar to get soft drinks.

"Mickie's a good sport, huh?" Ernie said.

"The best," I said.

"You two look like you've been together for-ever."

"I've known her forever."

"So have I," Ernie said, "but we don't interact like that."

I looked at Ernie and suddenly wondered if this had been a mistake. Mickie and I were as close as Ernie and me, though in a different way. There were things I would discuss only with each of them. If I screwed up, I'd lose Mickie. "Do you think it could be a mistake?" I asked.

Before Ernie could respond, I saw Alicia hurrying toward us with a look of alarm. "I think you better get out there," she said.

I ran from the ballroom. Mickie stood before Michael Lark, the linebacker I had beaten in the drinking contest the night I'd ended up passed out in my mother's fern. One of the spaghetti straps of Mickie's dress dangled loose, and she had a finger pointed in Lark's face, the other hand balled in a fist. A group of my classmates surrounded Lark, some trying to pull him away.

"Don't you ever touch me," Mickie was saying.

"What's going on?" I asked.

"I was just playing around," Lark slurred. I could tell Mickie had slapped him. His right cheek was cherry red.

"Did you touch her?" I asked.

Another classmate stepped forward, looking anxious. "He's drunk, man; we're getting him out of here before he gets busted."

Lark smiled at me. "Like, who hasn't touched her," he said, and in that moment I no longer saw Lark. I saw David Bateman. "We all know it isn't the first time. Come on, Hell, you've gotten some of that, right?"

"Knock it off, Lark," I said.

"Hey, man, you and I are drinking buddies."

"Not tonight."

"Come on, Hell. Everyone knows that girl has had more dicks between her legs than in a football huddle."

I lunged at Lark, but Ernie quickly stepped in to hold me back, which was a good thing, because Lark would have likely killed me. I turned and focused on Mickie, hearing Ernie behind me saying things to Lark like, "uncool." Mickie's mascara had run, and her eyes were red from crying. That's all it took. I turned for Lark. "It's cool," Ernie said, putting a hand on my chest. "He's drunk. They're getting him out."

"It's not cool." I said it loud enough that everyone came to a standstill. I slapped Ernie's hand away and walked past him. "Lark."

Lark turned, looking at me through glassy eyes and giving me the drunkard's grin. Even though he was stooped over, I still looked up at him, and he outweighed me by a good forty pounds. But I also knew he had a full ride to play football at Brown and that I was forty times smarter than him. "You need to apologize," I said.

He stumbled. "We're cool, man. I didn't mean nothing."

"Not to me. To Mickie."

Lark's brow furrowed.

"Sam," Ernie started again.

I cut him off, keeping my focus on Lark. "Stay out of it, Ernie."

Lark looked to Ernie then to me, his eyes

registering confusion. "I apologized already."

"Not to her you didn't."

He leaned forward, close enough that I could smell the acidic odor of alcohol on his breath. It reminded me of Sister Beatrice, and I had the same revulsion. I'd never been in a fight except for my jaunt around the schoolyard on David Bateman's back. "Last chance," I said.

"Or what?"

"Or we're going to go at it right here."

Lark smiled. "I'll fucking kill you, Hell." He said it without animosity, with a chuckle in his voice.

"You'll have to kill me," I replied in the same even tone. "Because once we get started, I'm not stopping. Then we'll both get expelled and throw away our futures, and next year the senior class can come by the McDonald's where you and I will be flipping burgers together instead of you playing football at Brown. Explain that to your mother and father."

For a moment Lark's face looked like he was attempting to solve a complex mathematical equation and failing miserably. Then he grinned, and I felt everyone in the room breathe a collective sigh of relief. "You're a red-eyed crazy motherfucker, Hell, but I like you." He stepped past me to where Mickie stood with Alicia and Ernie. "Hey, Mickie." She considered him with scorn. "I'm sorry. I shouldn't have done that, or said those things. If Hell likes you, you must be okay."

Mickie wiped her cheeks but did not respond. Lark looked at me and nodded. Then he left.

11

I retrieved Mickie's shawl and escorted her through the hotel lobby to the parking lot. She kept her head down, her shawl draped over her shoulders. I opened the passenger car door and helped her in, gathering her shawl for her so it wouldn't get caught in the door. As I walked to the driver's side, I took a moment to catch my breath. We were misfits, Mickie, me, and Ernie. For all his exploits, Ernie remained the black kid. For all my achievements in the classroom and on the newspaper staff, I was still the devil boy—or at least the kid with the red eyes—and Mickie was the girl with the reputation. We were something for other people to talk about and make fun of. I thought of all the times Mickie had stood up for me, all the times she'd been there for me. She had been having so much fun that night, happier than I might have ever seen her. I wasn't about to let Lark ruin her evening. When I slid in, Mickie remained pressed against the passenger door.

"We have a problem," I said. Mickie raised her head to look at me, her makeup still smeared. "I can't drive with you sitting way over there."

"I'm sorry," she said.

"You're sorry because Lark is a drunken moron?"

"I'm sorry you had to go with me, if I embarrassed you."

"I *had* to go with you? Are you kidding me? I wouldn't be here if it wasn't for *you* going with *me*."

"Maybe that would have been better."

I had never seen or heard Mickie defeated like this, never truly realized the depth of her pain. Her home life had not improved with her parents' divorce. Her mother drank most nights and either passed out or became belligerent, belittling Mickie. Her father had moved on, found himself a hot young girlfriend, and expressed little interest in being a father. It was a loveless home, and I wondered if that was why Mickie was promiscuous, if it wasn't about the sex at all, but about feeling loved, if only for a little while.

"Did you see the heads turn when we walked in?" I asked.

"I know why the heads turned."

"Really, was it because I look so great in this frilly shirt and burgundy tux? I look like a frigging red-eyed waiter in a Las Vegas Denny's."

Mickie grinned.

"They turned because you look beautiful, Mickie, because you are beautiful. And Lark just did what every guy in that room wanted to do. I felt like I was escorting a movie star, and I'll tell you something else—"

But I didn't, because I didn't get the chance. Mickie had leaped across the seat and pressed her lips against mine. Unlike Donna Ashby's kiss, no tongue probed my mouth, just the warmth of Mickie's lips. She pulled back and curled beside me. "I love you, Sam Hill," she said.

And this time I got the chance to reply. "I love you, too, Michaela Kennedy," I said, and she did not even protest that I'd used her real name.

12

As our senior year wound down, Ernie was mulling scholarship offers from all over the United States. I was debating between a few colleges, trying to determine what my parents could afford. I had received a $2,000 journalism scholarship for a feature article I'd written about Ernie, and the organization that gave me the award held a luncheon to honor me. My mother and I drove to Monterey and sat at a table with the president of the association, a man named Howard Rice. My father couldn't attend because of work. Rice was a 1944 Stanford University graduate and prominent booster, and he seemed intrigued by what I had accomplished, probably because I'd done so despite my "condition." At the luncheon, Rice was seated beside my mother and said, "I hope your son is considering Stanford."

Stanford was $14,000 per year in tuition and room and board, more than I felt fair to ask of my parents even with my scholarship money and what I'd saved working at the store.

"He's considering several different choices," my mother said diplomatically.

"Sam," Mr. Rice said, turning to me, "I want you to apply. I'll have an application sent to you tomorrow, and I want you to put me down as a reference. I will write you a letter of recommendation."

Mr. Rice was a man of his word. A week after the luncheon, an admissions packet arrived in the mail. I wasn't going to fill it out, but my mother insisted, saying, "We don't know God's will, Samuel. Have faith. Besides, it would be rude to Mr. Rice not to fill it out. He went to the trouble to send it, after all."

More to appease my mother, and because Mr. Rice had gone to the effort, I filled out the application. I prepared my essay the night before the application deadline, writing about my life with ocular albinism. I mailed off the packet the following morning and promptly dismissed it.

About that same time, I wrote an article on Ernie Cantwell's college recruiting experience for the final issue of the school paper. The *Times* liked the article so much they ran it on the front page of the sports section. I was thrilled. As I sat reading my article in the journalism trailer, my editor from the *Times* called.

"You're famous, Hill. The Associated Press picked up your article and ran it on their wire service. Your name is atop the article in hundreds of newspapers in dozens of cities."

The following day, as Ernie toweled off after track practice and I waited in the locker room to drive him home, Coach Moran—who had become the athletic director, in addition to the varsity basketball coach—burst into the locker room looking like he might have a heart attack. "Cantwell! My office."

"Okay, Coach, let me get dressed—"

"Now!"

"Coach, let me put on my—"

"Stanford is on the phone, Cantwell. Coach Christiansen wants to talk to you about playing football at Stanford University next fall. Or do you want me to tell him you're too busy toweling off your ass?" As Ernie sprinted past him, tucking a towel around his waist, Coach Moran spied me. "You come, too, Hell."

"Me? Why me?"

"Because you started this—he read that article you wrote, and he might have questions I can't answer."

Coach Christiansen only had one question, and it wasn't for me. He asked Ernie how he'd like to play football at Stanford University. Ernie committed on the phone. When he hung up, Coach Moran was wide-eyed and aghast. "You committed? What about all those other schools waiting for an answer? What am I supposed to tell them?"

"Tell them I'm going to Stanford, Coach. It's close to home. My mother and father can watch me play, and my father wants me to major in business and computer science."

The Cantwells threw an impromptu barbecue that night in their backyard. I attended in a dual capacity—as Ernie's friend and as a journalist. The *Times* wanted the scoop on Ernie's commitment to Stanford, a local-boy-stays-local kind of story. I interviewed Ernie's mother and father and his maternal grandparents. I also interviewed his coaches at Saint Joe's. I spent much of the party calling in my story to an editor at the sports desk. By the time I had finished, everyone had eaten, but Mrs. Cantwell had saved me a plate with two hamburgers and potato salad.

I took my plate outside to sit by the fire pit while everyone else went inside to eat cake and drink coffee. Ernie had to make phone calls to give the bad news to the other recruiters. As I sat by the fire, I sensed someone's approach. Mickie sat down beside me, the flames flickering shadows across her face. "Great news about Ernie, huh?"

"Yeah, great," I said and blew at the smoke threatening to engulf me.

We stared as the flames spit an assortment of colors. Mickie had decided to attend UC Davis near Sacramento. Her grades weren't great, but she had obtained a near-perfect score on the SAT. It also hadn't hurt her chances that I had helped her write her application essay. We chose the difficulties of growing up in an alcoholic household as her topic.

"Don't judge him, Sam," Mickie said. "He didn't make up the rules."

"I know," I said.

My mother would have called it "God's will" for Ernie to go to Stanford, but I couldn't help wondering why I had spent so many hours studying to achieve perfect grades. I'd made the same fatal mistake as when I was nominated for class valedictorian—I'd allowed myself to get my hopes up. Stanford hadn't responded to my application, but I wasn't going to make that mistake again. I'd applied to the University of California schools, which had negligible tuition for California residents and were a better fit for my family's budget. I had been accepted at UC Davis, as well as at Cal Berkeley and UCLA. They were all good schools, and if I went to Davis, I'd have Mickie to hang out with and I could get home occasionally to visit my parents.

I drove Mickie home after the Cantwells' barbecue and stayed to watch a late-night movie with her and Joanna. They both fell asleep on the couch. I carried Joanna up the stairs and put her to bed. When I pulled the covers up tight under her chin, Joanna awoke briefly, threw her arms around my neck, and pulled me close to kiss my cheek.

"I love you, Sam."

It was the sweetest thing anyone had ever said to me, because I knew it was unconditional. Joanna was not my mother or even my friend; she had no obligation to say those words to me, and she didn't want anything, except maybe a stable house and someone to love. I smiled down at her. "I love you, too, Jo-Jo."

When I started from the room, I found Mickie leaning against the doorjamb, staring at me with an impish grin. We shut the door and stepped into the hall. "You don't have to walk me to the front door," I whispered. "Go to bed before you fall asleep on your feet."

"Aren't you going to tuck me in, too?" she asked, also keeping her voice soft.

I smiled. I'd thought about it, ever since the night of our senior prom, but I also didn't want to screw up our friendship, especially with Mickie leaving in the fall. If we both went to UC Davis, things might be different, and maybe I'd have the chance to be Mickie's boyfriend. But if I chose to go elsewhere, I didn't want to try to get through college and think about the boys she was dating.

"You're going to be a great dad someday, Sam."

"I don't know about that."

"Don't know that you'll be great?"

"Don't know about being a dad," I said.

"Why not? You had a great role model, and you have so much love to share."

"Maybe. Maybe someday I'll adopt."

Mickie stepped back, squinting at me. "Why would you say that?"

"You know why. I'd be worried my children would be like me, you know. Have my eyes."

"They should be so lucky," she said.

"Lucky?"

"Yes. They made you the person you are, and I happen to believe you're a very good person, Sam Hill. And I know Joanna feels the same."

Then Mickie pushed away from the jamb and gave me a warm hug that felt as sweet as Joanna's and made me think that maybe I could be a dad someday, and Mickie a mother. Maybe they'd be our kids.

14

By the time I arrived at home, my parents had long since gone up to bed. My mother had left the kitchen light on for me, as was her habit. I heard the television in their room filtering down the darkened stairs, opened the fridge, and poured myself a glass of milk. As I did, I saw a white envelope on the tile counter addressed to me. The return address was in red ink.

OFFICE OF UNDERGRADUATE ADMISSIONS STANFORD UNIVERSITY

Twenty-four hours earlier, I would have torn that envelope open like a presenter at the Academy Awards, but now I just held it, thinking the envelope was too thin to contain an admissions packet, and I was in no mood to be rejected once again. That envelope reminded me of the bright, sunny morning when my mother and I walked to the mailbox on our street and found the envelope from OLM. She'd been so excited, but I recall even then that I'd held back my enthusiasm. Maybe it was just a young kid fearful of attending school, or maybe I was thinking of the cruelty and the mistreatment of which my father had spoken. Whatever the reason, I'd had my doubts. I held the Stanford envelope up to the light but could not see through it. Finally, I turned off the kitchen light and carried the envelope upstairs with me.

"Sam?" my mother called out to me when I reached the top step. I could have taken off my shoes and crept up those stairs quiet as a burglar—I knew the location of every squeak in every board, and where to step to avoid it, yet my mother would still call out the moment my foot touched the landing.

I walked into their bedroom. The blue-gray glow of the television cast shadows across their bedspread and flickered on the wall behind it. My father lay propped on two pillows, watching a show. He had been feeling under the weather, more tired than normal, and had been going to bed early. My mother was sitting up, rosary beads in hand.

"You got an envelope from Stanford," she said with practiced calm.

I held it up.

My father turned his head. "What did it say?"

I shrugged. "I haven't opened it yet."

My father pushed himself to a seated position and clicked on the lamp mounted to the wall on his side of the bed. The light accentuated his gaunt features and the dark circles beneath his eyes. "You know, son, it's not the school that makes the student."

I didn't want to hear it, but I refrained from saying anything.

"Open it, Sam," my mother said. "Whatever it says, it's God's will."

And I really didn't want to hear that.

I opened the envelope and pulled out a single sheet of paper.

THIS IS TO ADVISE THAT YOUR APPLICATION HAS BEEN ACCEPTED.

I shrugged. It was like the buildup to a movie climax, then being let down. "They got my application. I guess they don't decide on the non-football players for a while."

I left the letter on the bed and headed for my room. I got as far as the doorway when my mother started yelling my name. "Sam! Sam!"

I rushed back in. "What is it?"

My mother sat crying. "You got in, Sam."

"I what?"

"It says your application has been accepted. Accepted! Sam, you got in."

15

The morning of my graduation, my elation at having been accepted to Stanford and the realization that I would be rooming with Ernie had not subsided. I'd been walking on air ever since that night. The news had even tempered my disappointment at having been passed over for valedictorian. My mother, of course, was convinced that it was all a part of God's will for me, that it was all part of the extraordinary life God intended me to live.

I stood at my dresser futilely trying to use the mirror to knot a tie when my mother's high heels clicked outside my bedroom door. My father wore a Windsor knot as tight and perfect as any tied by the king of England himself. My attempts had produced a lump that looked to be strangling me and had caused the collars of my shirt to stick up like airplane wings.

"Let me," my mother said, walking in and slapping at my hands.

I tilted my chin so my mother could undo my abomination and deftly craft the knot. At six feet, I had surpassed her in height, but standing there on the day of my high school graduation, it seemed that mirror revealed much more than our discrepancy in height. My mother had aged.

We had celebrated her forty-third birthday that year, and now, standing so close to her, I could see the depth of the crow's-feet at the corners of her eyes, what she called her "worry lines," and how her once-unblemished skin now displayed the inevitable markings that only time delivers.

I had never wanted to turn back the clock. Despite my friendships with Ernie and Mickie, my grade school years had not brought fond memories. I had been happy to leave David Bateman and Sister Beatrice behind. High school had been better, but for all my achievements, I could not ignore the fact that, but for Ernie, I was rarely invited to parties, no girl had invited me to her school prom, and, but for Mickie, I would have missed mine. Yes, I'd achieved straight As, but that was a little easier when you spent most nights, including weekends, studying. Still, I had not considered that my mother would someday grow old. Grandma O'Malley, who had come down for my graduation and waited downstairs in the living room, had once proclaimed, "Time is wicked. It comes and goes like a thief in the night, stealing our youth, our beauty, and our bodies." I had watched Grandma O'Malley, a proud and simple woman, shrink and wrinkle and turn white over the years. But we expect that of our grandparents. Not our parents. For some reason, we think our parents will never grow old, perhaps because when they do, we are forced to acknowledge that we will one day grow old, and we face our own mortality.

The barber who cut my father's hair and now cuts mine said it more simply than Grandma O'Malley. "None of us is getting out of here alive."

My mother pinched the knot and slid it up to my neck. As she raised her eyes, I saw that she had accomplished the task through tears.

"There," she said, turning her head.

I reached out and hugged her. The tears we shed that morning were our silent acknowledgment that while the years might not have been extraordinary, as she had so diligently prayed, they had been ours. Come the fall, I would be leaving for college and my mother would lose her little boy, and I would lose the person who had always been there for me, my fiercest advocate since the day I'd been born.

"I love you, Mom."

"I love you, too," she said. Then she stepped back, gathering herself. "Enough. I'm going to get makeup all over your white shirt."

"You don't need makeup, Mom."

"I agree." My father stepped in from the hallway. He'd been feeling better but still looked thin and tired. However, I knew nothing short of wild horses could keep him from attending my graduation. I don't know how long he'd been standing in the hall, or how much he'd observed and heard. My father knew the depth of my relationship to my mother, and he didn't begrudge us a moment of it. My relationship with him was different. He'd raised me to be a man, and he was proud of me. But to my mother—I suspect to all mothers—their little boys will always be their little boys, no matter how old those boys become.

I retrieved my royal-blue cap with the gold tassel and grabbed the hanger with my matching graduation gown. My mother had ironed the fabric until the pleats could cut paper. When I turned back, I watched my parents depart my room, my mother wiping at tears, my father's arm around her shoulders, consoling her. I remember being glad they would have each other for support when I left the following fall, and I realized how much I would miss them.

16

After the ceremony, we celebrated at a restaurant with the Cantwells. Mickie joined us. Her graduation from the public school would not be for another two weeks. After the restaurant and all the toasts to our futures, Ernie and I dropped off our parents and grandparents to head to one of several graduation parties.

"Are you going with them, Mickie?" my mother asked as she stepped from the car.

Mickie begged out. "Not me, Mrs. H. I don't want to be the only girl in a testosterone-fueled room full of glory-days jocks reminiscing about their high school sports careers. I'll stay here and watch TV with you, if that's okay."

When Mickie put it that way, I couldn't blame her. But I also knew that was not her motivation for staying with my mom. My mom had done her very best to put on a happy face. That's not to say she wasn't sincerely happy for me, but with every new beginning, there is an inevitable end we must first accept, and my mother was struggling to accept that her boy had finished high school and would be leaving home in just a few short months. Mickie had begged out of the parties to be with my mom and to cheer her up. In many ways, Mickie had become the daughter my mother never had, and, I suspected, my mother had become the mother Mickie wished she'd had.

That night Ernie and I hit four parties. There was a bit of the glory-days reminiscing, as Mickie had predicted, but not by Ernie or me. We weren't viewing graduation as an end, as were some of our classmates who had chosen not to go on to college or who had enlisted in the military. Despite my reticence when it came to new adventures and meeting new people, I was looking forward to attending Stanford and living with Ernie. I'd already looked up the school paper, the *Stanford Daily*, and was hoping I could write for it.

I drove Ernie home at just after one in the morning. When I pulled up to his driveway, he gave me his customary handshake, grabbing my thumb. He pulled me close and put his other hand around the back of my head. "You've been like a brother to me, Sam. I never would have made it this far without you."

"You're not going to kiss me, are you?" I said.

"I'm serious, man. I've ridden your coattail for twelve years. I hope you don't mind if I ride it for four more."

"You keep getting me sideline passes, and we'll work out some arrangement," I said. Ernie stepped from the Falcon. "Ernie?" I said. He turned back, but when I couldn't find the words, Ernie said them for me.

"I know," he said.

17

My mother had left the light on in the kitchen. I shut it off and started up the stairs, but I didn't make it halfway before I heard someone call my name.

"Sam?" Mickie stepped from the shadows of the living room, startling me.

After catching my breath, I went down the steps to where she stood, her arms wrapped around her body, though it wasn't particularly cold. All kinds of thoughts were flashing through my mind—her mother or father had died, or something had happened to Joanna—but then I realized that Mickie had not been to her home. She'd been with my mother.

"What are you doing here so late?" I could see that she'd been crying, and my concern became fear. "Mickie? What happened?"

She shook her head, sobbing. "It's your father, Sam."

"What?"

She couldn't speak.

I looked to the staircase and raced up two stairs at a time. "Dad? Dad!" The rumpled blankets and sheets hung catawampus off the side of my parents' empty bed, and my fear multiplied and nearly overcame me.

18

As Mickie and I entered the waiting room of Our Lady of Mercy Hospital, my mother looked up from a chair. Her eyes were bloodshot and puffy. Tears streaked her cheek. She held her rosary beads, as she always did. I was certain my father had died.

"Where is he, Mom?" I asked. I recall this moment as the moment I became a man. It had not been my first beer or hangover, or the first time I'd gotten laid, as I had thought. It had not even been earlier that day, when I'd tossed my blue graduation cap into the air. It was the moment my mother needed me, and I was there for her.

My mother pointed to a door at the end of the hall that read **INTENSIVE CARE**. Then her fingers moved to the next bead, and she continued to pray silently.

I asked Mickie to stay at her side and went to the nurses' station. A young woman had her head down but looked up as I approached. "I'm Max Hill's son," I said. "Can you tell me what happened?"

The nurse did the all too familiar double take when she saw my eyes. "The doctor is with him now. They're running a series of tests."

"He's alive?"

"Yes, he's alive."

"What kind of tests? What for?"

"That's what the tests will determine. The doctor will explain everything once we have the test results back."

"A heart attack? Was it a heart attack?"

"The doctor will talk to you," she said. "I'll let him know you're here."

When I returned to the waiting room, Mickie was seated with her arm draped around my mother's shoulders. "They're running tests," I said. "The nurse said it shouldn't be too much longer."

I sat on the other side of my mother and watched her fingers manipulate her rosary beads as never before. An hour after we'd arrived, the doctor entered the waiting room wearing blue hospital scrubs and introduced himself as Dr. Thomas Laurence.

"How is he?" I asked.

Dr. Laurence looked too young to be a doctor. His curly, sandy-brown hair showed no signs of gray, but I suspected from his practiced demeanor that he was older than he looked. "Your husband is alive," he said to my mother. "He's suffered a cerebrovascular accident—a stroke."

Dr. Laurence took great care to explain that a blood clot no bigger than a pebble had dislodged itself from inside my father's heart. Riding the pulsing wave of blood, it had traveled swiftly through the arteries in his neck to the right side of his brain before becoming lodged in a branch too narrow for it to pass. "The brain tissue beyond the occlusion becomes starved for oxygen," he said. "It will begin to die in less than ten minutes."

"Meaning what?" I asked.

Dr. Laurence grimaced. "Practically, it means the right side of your father's face is flaccid, and he is incapable of moving his left extremities."

"Can't you take the clot out?" I asked.

Dr. Laurence shook his head. "The MRI shows some blood has already accumulated around the affected area. If we give him thrombolytics—the clot-busters—we could cause a massive hemorrhage in the brain and make things worse."

"What can you do?" I asked.

Dr. Laurence shrugged. "Watch and wait."

"Will he get better?" my mother asked, her voice a whisper.

Dr. Laurence furrowed his brow. He had intense blue eyes, but now they seemed to soften. "It's too early to make predictions," he said, though I could tell he already had. "Your husband will be in the hospital about a week. I would recommend we get him to an acute rehab unit as quickly as he is able. We've had some success treating stroke patients by beginning a regimen of intense physical therapy. I'll have the rehab specialist come by in a day or two." Before leaving Dr.

Laurence turned to me. "May I talk to you?"

Dr. Laurence and I stepped outside the room. I noticed the slight pause when we made direct eye contact. "I didn't want to say anything in front of your mother."

"I know," I said. "How bad is it?"

"The acute rehab unit will give you and your mother some time to consider a long-term care facility."

"What do you mean, long-term? Are you saying he's *never* going to come home?"

I could tell from Dr. Laurence's expression he was trying to be honest without being an alarmist. "It will depend on how he progresses," he said. "That doesn't need to be determined tonight."

I decided not to press him further. "When can we see him?"

"You can go in now. He's in the recovery room. We've given him some drugs to sedate him. He'll be in and out, but you can be with him."

"Can he talk?" I asked.

"Not at the moment. But he'll recognize you, and he'll know you're there. I think it would be a great comfort to him. Your father did manage to ask for you."

"For me? Are you sure?"

"What's your mother's name?"

"It's Madeline, but he calls her Maddy."

"Then I'm certain he said 'Sam.' " With that Dr. Laurence turned and walked away.

I watched Dr. Laurence depart, staring at his back as he went. I turned but did not immediately go back to the waiting room. The realization of what had happened hit me hard at that moment, as manhood often does. I imagined it was not unlike all those young men who join the military, go to boot camp, and then get deployed in a military zone, with no one there to wipe their noses or console them. My father had called my name for a reason. He needed me, and not the other way around. He needed me to be the man of the house. I was just eighteen, but then, so were some of those men taken from the jungles of Vietnam on a stretcher.

When I got back to the waiting room, Mickie said she'd go down the hall to call Ernie and the Cantwells, and I sensed she wanted to give my mother and me a moment of privacy with my father.

When we entered my father's room, I almost did not recognize the man in the bed. Though he had just a single tube snaking from his right arm, my father looked so much older than he had that morning, his hair seemingly grayer and his face thin, his skin a sickly yellow. The nurse removed the mask covering his mouth and nose, and the side of his face had sagged like wax melted in a hot sun. I hung back as my mother bent and kissed his lips, whispering to him words I could not hear while gently smoothing his hair. After a minute or two, she motioned me forward, but I could not get my legs to move. My father was my hero, the strongest-willed man I had ever known. Nothing had ever defeated him—not the chain-store pharmacies, and not the monthly struggle to make his business succeed. I wondered if that was why he lay here now in this unforgiving hospital bed, if his unwillingness to ever give in, the incredibly long hours he worked at the store, had led to the stress and anxiety that caused his stroke.

My mother took my hand and brought me forward so my father could see me.

"Hey, Dad." His face did not move, but his eyes acknowledged me. I touched his arm, which felt cold and soft, and bent and kissed his cheek. For better or for worse—and too often it is for worse for so many of us—adulthood had arrived, whether I wanted it to or not.

"I'm here, Dad," I whispered in his ear. "And I'm going to make sure everything is okay. I'm going to take care of things. I'm going to take care of Mom. You just concentrate on getting strong again."

19

The nurses brought in a hospital bed for my mother. "I've slept with that man for twenty years," she said, weeping. "I'm not going to stop now."

Mickie and I left the hospital together at close to morning. I passed the turn for our house and continued south on the El Camino. "I'm not going home, Sam," Mickie said. "I'm going to stay at your house."

"Okay," I said without any further comment. "But I have someplace I need to go before we go home."

I parked on Hillside Drive directly in front of the OLM church.

"Sam?" Mickie said.

"You can wait here," I said. Mickie had stopped going to church years earlier. She said she believed in a higher being but not in religion. I had continued going to Sunday Mass to appease my mother. Anytime I suggested I would not go caused friction between us. It had been easier on all of us if I just bit the bullet, though I'd long ago begun to question my faith, or perhaps my mother's faith. After all, I could not recall any occasion when God had stepped in and helped me, despite smashing my prayer bank repeatedly.

I figured if there was ever a time for God to show himself, this was it.

"I'll go with you," Mickie said.

The front doors to the church were locked, but the side door remained open.

Inside, the stained-glass windows were dark. The overhead fixtures offered only a dull light. Shadows from the flames in the bloodred candles flickered and danced across the walls and the statues of the various saints as Mickie and I walked down the center aisle. She took a seat in the first pew. I continued to the railing, genuflected, and made the sign of the cross, but I did not kneel. This was not between me and the man on that cross. I turned to my right, walking to the alcove with the white statue of the barefoot Blessed Mother crushing the snake beneath her feet. I knelt and looked up at her brown porcelain eyes as I had done as a child on that aborted first day of school at OLM. I had the same strange sense I had felt back then, that the Blessed Mother was looking down at me, using the eyes of the statue to see me. I wasn't sure where to begin or what to say. I was angry and upset. If God knows everything, then he knew that much.

"Why?" I finally asked. "All she's ever done is pray to you. All she has ever done is ask for your help. Is this what she gets for her devotion? I'm done asking for things for myself. I'm done asking to be normal, for my eyes to change

411

color, but she deserves better. My father deserves better. If this is God's will, then I'm asking you to intervene and for once show me why I am supposed to believe that all of this is for a reason. I want to believe," I said, struggling to hold back tears. "I *want* to believe, okay? But you have to give me some *reason* to believe. Please. Please give me a reason to believe that everything she's taught me is real and that your son has not abandoned her. Don't do it for me. Do it for her. Heal her husband. Heal my father."

Then I thought again of my prayer piggy bank, and in my mind I smashed it open—this time, I knew, beyond repair. I laid every prayer at the bare feet of the Blessed Mother.

I don't know how long I knelt before her. At some point, I felt Mickie's hand on my shoulder. "Come on, Sam. Let's go home."

On our way out, I stopped before the flickering candles, fishing in my pockets for change. "I don't have any money," I said.

Mickie grabbed one of the long sticks and lit it, then handed it to me. "I don't think God cares about the money at this point," she said. I lit one of the candles, said a silent prayer for my father and my mother, and we left.

Mickie drove us home, guiding me upstairs to my room. I felt utterly exhausted, unable to perform even the simplest tasks. My graduation already seemed like months ago. I sat on the bed. Mickie disappeared into the bathroom and emerged wearing one of my T-shirts.

"What am I going to do?" I asked. "What are we going to do without him?"

Mickie untied my shoes and slipped them from my feet. I stood, and she helped unbuckle my belt and the button of my jeans. When I sat, she slipped them from my legs, and I fell back onto the pillow. She slid under the covers beside me, pulling my head to her chest.

"She'll be lost," I said.

"Shh," Mickie said, running her fingers through my hair. "Go to sleep, Sam."

20

Dr. Laurence's words would prove prophetic. My father remained in the hospital for four days before they moved him to the rehab facility to begin physical therapy. My mother attended every session, getting to the hospital after attending 6:00 a.m. daily Mass. She stayed until late at night, hoping, as I was, that my father would recover enough that she would be able to take him home. As the weeks passed, however, I began to suspect that my prayers would not be answered. Dr. Laurence confirmed it one day in the hospital.

"Your mother needs to begin considering a long-term care facility," he said.

"She wants to take him home and care for him," I said, though I could tell from my father's current condition that would never happen.

He shook his head. "Your father is going to need constant care, Sam. She couldn't even leave him home alone to go shopping or run an errand. Even if she brought in outside help, the insurance would run out before . . ."

"Before he dies," I said, the realization dawning. "So he isn't going to get better?"

"His condition will improve, but we're talking about minute increments, not leaps and bounds."

"Never as he was," I said.

"Never as he was," he agreed.

I'd had these conversations, or some semblance of them, at home with Mickie and with Ernie, when my mother was at the hospital, but those had just been esoteric speculation of what might happen and usually ended with Mickie telling me not to get ahead of myself, to wait until the doctors knew more. Dr. Laurence's words were not speculation. They were reality.

We had closed the pharmacy during my father's illness, but we couldn't keep it closed forever, not if my mother was going to survive. My mother, though, was in no condition to get the store reopened, to run the house, pay the bills, and take care of everything else. It dawned on me then that I wouldn't be leaving in the fall to attend Stanford. That couldn't happen. No matter how much my mother tried to convince me, and I knew she would, I could not leave. It was more than just the finances. My father needed me, as did my mother, even if she would never admit it. My acceptance had been nothing but a false hope, yet again.

That night I brought my mother home from the hospital, but I left again, telling her that I had an errand to run. I parked at the curb in front of OLM and climbed those wide concrete steps. This time the tall wooden doors were unlocked. I stepped through them and made my way down the aisle to where the candles burned, where I had lit a candle for my father. I couldn't recall the exact candle—not that it would have mattered, since that candle had certainly burned down. It didn't matter, I told myself. The prayers flickering here were not going to be answered. Licking my thumb and index finger, I reached inside one of the bloodred glass jars and pinched out the flame.

21

The following week, my mother and I drove a winding two-lane blacktop through the northern Santa Cruz Mountains. Though we were just half an hour from our home in Burlingame, the brown grass, scrub brush, and two-hundred-year-old oak trees that pockmarked the open hills made it feel as though we were far removed from the city.

"This one looked nice in the brochure," I said as we neared the care facility.

"They all look nice in the brochure." My mother stewed in the passenger seat, a red-and-white scarf tied in a knot beneath her chin to protect her hair from the wind and sunglasses covering much of her face. She looked the way she had always looked when I had been young and she had been driving the Falcon. But I no longer felt young, and she had not driven the Falcon for two years. "That's why they have brochures, to make them look nice."

As I had predicted, my mother resisted any talk of my father not coming home. The only way I could even get her to look at the care facilities was to tell her that this need not be permanent, that, in time, if he improved, Dad could come home. He still could not talk, though he was doing better making sounds like words, and he'd recovered some movement on the paralyzed left side of his body. My mother, however, had never failed at anything she'd set her mind to, and she'd set her mind to my father coming home. At this point I could have said something like, "Maybe it's God's will," but it only would have been hurtful. Besides, I no longer believed in God's will. I was not willing to accept that it was God's will for a good man like my father, a devoted man, to spend his final days in some care facility.

After an intervention with Dr. Laurence and my father's physical therapy team, my mother at least agreed to look at various long-term care options. We had visited five of the six facilities on the list, but my mother had deemed each too sterile or too clinical, and she thought the staff to be either too robotic or too cavalier. I hadn't liked them, either, for much the same reasons. "If your father has been sentenced to live out his life in a facility, it will not be a prison sentence," she'd said after leaving one of the facilities. "That place had all the warmth of a mortuary."

At the top of a hill we came to the Crystal Springs Long-Term Care Campus. Upon first sight, I sensed it to be different from the other facilities. The two-story stucco buildings were connected by covered walkways and painted the same beige color as the dried grass, blending in nicely with the rolling hills. With tiled roofs, arches, and a center fountain, Crystal Springs had the feel of a Spanish mission.

"This looks nice," I said, not bothering to add that it should, given that it was the most expensive facility on the list.

"You don't judge a book by its cover, Samuel," my mother said.

I parked in a space reserved for visitors. The temperature was pleasant, high seventies, with a cool breeze that rustled the leaves of palm trees and sent ripples of sparkling diamonds across the surface of the Crystal Springs Reservoir in the valley below.

We walked a red concrete path to the main entrance. Several patients sat on benches or in wheelchairs soaking up the sunshine with staff nearby dressed in maroon shirts. Inside the facility, I asked to speak with Shirley Farley, Crystal Springs' chief administrator. I'd made an appointment earlier in the week, and for some reason I had expected a midfifties, heavyset woman in a white nurse's uniform with a stern demeanor—Nurse Ratched from *One Flew over the Cuckoo's Nest*. The woman who greeted us wore navy-blue slacks and a white blouse and had a smile on her face. She looked and sounded too youthful to be running a care facility.

"Mrs. Hill," she said directly to my mother. "I'm glad you could come on such a glorious afternoon. Did you notice the views on the drive?"

"I noticed," my mother said without enthusiasm.

"They're spectacular," I said.

"I wish every day was like this," Farley said. "Unfortunately, we get fog in the fall, and it can be hot in the summer. We try to take advantage of days like this when we can."

"I don't want to be driving that road in the fog," my mother said to me. "And I hope those poor patients don't get sunburned."

Farley glanced at me, and I smiled. To my mother, she said, "May I show you around the campus?"

"Campus," my mother scoffed.

"Yes, please," I said, though it felt like a waste of time and effort given my mother's recalcitrant demeanor.

Shirley Farley walked us past the fountains and flower beds. "We try to get our clients outside as much as possible," she said. "Fresh air is so important."

"My husband needs constant supervision," my mother said. "I hope you don't leave patients alone."

"Dr. Laurence mentioned your husband's condition," Farley said. "He would have a member of the staff with him any time he is outdoors."

We proceeded to a communal dining hall. "Some of our clients prefer to eat in their rooms, and we accommodate that," Farley said, "but we have also found that communal activities, such

420

as dining, have therapeutic effects. We also have movie nights, a book club, chess club, and supervised athletic activities."

My mother looked away.

"What type of effects have you noticed?" I asked.

"Our clients exhibit lower rates of depression and increased energy, which promotes their rehabilitation."

"Do any of them ever leave?" my mother asked.

"Some have," Farley said. "But I'm going to be honest, Mrs. Hill. Most are here for the duration, which is why we do our best to make it as comfortable as possible. May I show you one of our rooms?"

The room Mrs. Farley showed us looked more like an apartment than a hospital room. The walls were a salmon color, the furniture beige and brown. A pony-wall partition separated the main room from a small kitchen with a two-burner stove top, an oven, a refrigerator, and cabinets. The bedroom and bathroom were off the living area.

"This is nice," I said, standing in the kitchen. "Mom?"

"Your father will not be doing any cooking," my mother said.

"I understood you liked to cook, Mrs. Hill," Farley said. I had mentioned it to her when we'd spoken on the phone.

"Me?" my mother asked. "Why would that matter? Don't you feed him here?"

Farley smiled. "Of course, but I assumed you would be spending much of your time with your husband, having meals together."

"She could do that?" I asked.

"Many of our clients' spouses eat with them."

That caught my mother's attention. "Could she spend the night?" I asked.

"I'm afraid not, but we have extended visiting hours." She looked to my mother, but my mother had moved to a sliding glass door that looked out on a small patio with a view of the mountains and the reservoir. When Farley looked to me, I shrugged. "Why don't I give you some time to think it over," she said. "I'll be in my office if you have any further questions. I've prepared a packet for you to take with you. It's at the front desk."

After Farley left, I walked to where my mother stood, and we stared out at the reservoir. No doubt she was wondering the same thing I was wondering—how had we gotten here? How had our lives changed so dramatically in an instant?

"What do you think, Mom?" I asked rhetorically. We both knew the facility was the best on the list. Neither of us wanted to feel as though we were dumping my father, but it didn't matter how we felt. This was reality, and sometimes reality sucked.

"I think this is the pits," she said.

"I know," I said. "But it's better than the others, and the staff seems friendly."

"I don't mean the facility," she said.

"I know," I said. But I didn't want to think of my father living in some facility, and I didn't want to worry about who was taking care of him and how well they were doing so. What was the point? We'd been told that this was our option, and this facility was the best we'd seen.

"I mean the whole situation," my mother said. "It's the pits, isn't it?"

"Yeah, it is, Mom. It really is."

"Your father worked so hard all his life, and for what? He's going to end up here? It makes you wonder, doesn't it?"

It truly did, and that was as close as I'd ever come to hearing my mother question her faith.

22

We didn't go home to think it over. My mother and I filled out the paperwork that afternoon in Shirley Farley's office. My mother chose a room with a western view. "Your father enjoys the sunsets," she said.

My parents' health insurance would cover most but not all of the costs. I saw no way that my mother could afford the difference, but when I mentioned this, she dismissed it. "Money will not dictate your father's comfort," she said.

We moved my father the next day, and after my mother and I got him physically situated, I told her I needed to run some errands and would pick up staples for his refrigerator. Ernie and Mickie were waiting for me at the house when I arrived with a small U-Haul trailer. Ernie and I loaded up my father's beloved recliner, side table, and lamp while Mickie boxed up framed photographs from the mantel. We also rolled up the throw rug in the living room and took a couple of paintings from the walls. I'd cleared this with Mrs. Farley but had not told my mother.

When I knocked on the door to my father's room, my mother opened it to find Ernie and me straining with the weight of the recliner.

"What are you doing?" she asked.

"If Dad can't come home, we're going to bring home to Dad."

Ernie and I set down the throw rug and recliner along with the side table and lamp. After my mother composed herself, she and Mickie arranged the photographs around the room, hung the paintings, and put away the kitchenware, pots and pans, and cutlery. By the time Mickie was finished, the refrigerator and shelves were stocked. It wasn't home, but it was the next best thing.

"There's only one thing missing," I said.

My mother looked at me inquisitively.

"I think tonight would be a good night for your lasagna," I said, and I pulled out one my mother had frozen.

Despite my mother's insistence, Mickie and Ernie did not join us for dinner, wanting to give us time alone. The three of us sat together at the table, my father listing in his wheelchair. My mother reached and took his hand as we created our traditional circle. "Dear Lord," she said. "Though we do not know your ways, we accept that everything that happens is your will. Help us to accept that which we cannot change, give us the courage to change what we can, and the wisdom to know the difference."

I humored her and said, "Amen."

My mother served me a wedge of lasagna and said, "We shared our first moments together, the three of us, in a hospital," and she told me again about the day I was born. I listened and asked the same questions, sensing that telling the story was cathartic for her. After dinner, we helped my father into his recliner, and my mother read the newspaper to him. Then we turned on the television for him, and my mother sat on the couch to say her rosary. Her continued devotion in the face of all that had happened amazed me, but at this point I had concluded that I no longer shared her faith in a God who controlled the universe like a puppet master pulling and tugging strings and making us all dance. Our lives, I believed, were more like billiard balls on a pool table, ricocheting randomly with the impact of the cue ball. To believe otherwise was to believe that a God to whom my mother had devoted her life had responded by striking down her husband and causing her so much pain. I couldn't accept that.

Shortly after nine there was a knock on the door. Two hospital staff members entered to assist in putting my father to bed. It was time to leave, and I had dreaded this moment more than any other. My mother leaned over my father's bed, her cheek pressed to his, her hands rubbing his face and combing his hair. It would be the first time since they were married they would not sleep in the same bed. She clung to him, tears flowing. Though the stroke had left my father's face an expressionless mask, I watched his eyes pool until a lone tear rolled down his cheek. It was unbearable, and became even more so when I had to step in and separate them.

23

The next week I held a meeting in the back room of the pharmacy with my father's longtime pharmacy technician, Betty, as well as a young girl my father had hired to work the front counter. They were understandably concerned not only about my father but for their jobs. It had been nearly three weeks since his stroke.

"The store will remain open," I assured them.

"How?" they asked in near unison.

"We're going to hire a pharmacist," I said. "All of us. The first one will be coming for an interview this afternoon." I hoped that including them in decisions concerning the store's future would ease their concerns and make them feel invested.

"There was a man here from Longs," Betty said, meaning the chain drugstore. "He wants to buy your father's files. He said he'd make a fair offer, and he'd hire all of us."

"I can't stop you from taking the job," I said. "But I'm not selling my father's files to a chain drugstore. I can't do that. Give me a month. That's all I'm asking."

Betty looked skeptical but agreed. "Your father worked too hard for us to give up. But, Sam, do you know what you're in for?"

Maybe I was being naive. Maybe I didn't know

what I was in for, but I also knew there was only one way to find out. "With your help I can do it," I said. "Just give me the chance."

We interviewed four pharmacists in two days and met again in the back of the store.

"I like Frank," Barb said, making our choice unanimous. "He most resembles your father's personality, and that will help to keep our customers from defecting."

"I have a plan for that also," I said. I handed Barb and Betty the flyer Mickie and I had created, an invitation to a Saturday reception to "Meet Your Neighborhood Pharmacist." "We're going to slip them under the windshields of every car parked on Broadway and mail them to every customer. Then we'll follow up with a personal phone call."

My mother was not involved in any of this. She arrived at the Crystal Springs campus at seven each morning, often bringing the staff doughnuts or bagels and fresh fruit, though our finances were tight. She spoon-fed my father his breakfast and helped him get dressed, then spent the day participating in his rehab. At night she kept to their routine, reading him the newspaper and saying her rosary while my father watched television until visiting hours were over.

I went to bed that Friday night and dreamed that I threw a party and no one came except David Bateman.

24

We scheduled the reception at the pharmacy to begin Saturday at 10:00 a.m. Mickie, Ernie, and I arrived at nine to set up a few tables, which looked pathetically bare until Mr. and Mrs. Cantwell backed up their Mercedes and started unloading trays of finger sandwiches, vegetables and dip, cheese and crackers, homemade cookies and brownies, and bottles of wine and cans of soft drinks. I didn't know what to say.

"You want a crowd? Serve them food," Mrs. Cantwell said.

Mickie tied helium-filled balloons to the parking meters in front of the store and to the ends of the aisles inside, giving the store a festive look. There was nothing left to do but wait.

I paced the floor like an expectant father. "What if nobody comes?" I said to Mickie. I knew Barb and Betty were pleased with Frank, but if we didn't have customers, we didn't have a store.

"They'll come," Mickie said. "Have faith."

"Oh, God, don't say that. You sound like my mother."

"Not faith in God," she said. Mickie professed to be agnostic. "Faith in your father—his customers loved him."

And it showed.

When we opened the door at ten, his most loyal customers were waiting. Some brought food to supplement our spread and for me to take home for my mother's freezer. Every one of them shook my hand and told me how sorry they were to hear about my father. Most important, they told me they weren't moving their files. They were staying put.

Betty and Barb poured mimosas, and Mickie and Ernie circulated the hors d'oeuvres while Frank and I greeted each guest. Frank was better than I'd expected, personable and professional. In between filling prescriptions and answering questions, he worked the crowd like a politician stumping for votes. I don't know if it was a testament to my father, or our efforts, but just about every client on my father's Rolodex came that day.

Afterward, as Mickie, Ernie, and I cleaned up, Mickie said, "You did it, Hill. You saved your father's store."

But I knew better. "This was just the first step. The most important day is Monday."

"What happens Monday?" Ernie asked.

"Monday, I go to work."

"What are you talking about?" Ernie said.

"My mother can't afford the care facility, but she also won't admit it. The insurance doesn't cover all the expenses, and their savings won't last more than a year. I hired myself to run the store. Betty said she'd train me to order merchandise and pay vendor bills."

"What about Stanford?"

"I'm going to defer for a year, until my mother gets back on her feet."

Ernie turned away, upset.

"She'll never go for that, not in a million years," Mickie said.

"She won't know," I said.

"How will she not know? Hello, you live in the same house."

But we didn't, not anymore. My mother stayed with my father until closing and, as a result, rarely arrived home until well after nine. By that time, she was too tired to do anything except kiss me atop the head and go upstairs to bed.

25

Every morning that summer, I awoke at six and went to the store to ready it to open. I stayed until it closed, ran the deliveries, then went to visit my father for an hour before covering whatever sporting event I could pick up from the *Times* to make extra cash. As the fall approached, I began to see Ernie and Mickie less and less as they prepared to leave for college. The night before their departures, I planned what I sacrilegiously referred to as our last supper.

I cooked a meal fit for three kings—barbecued steaks, mashed potatoes, green peas, and a squash soup. I even baked and frosted a cake, decorating it with candles and frosting and writing, "Good Luck, Mickie and Ernie."

"You keep this up and I might marry you," Ernie said as I put the spread on the table.

"Get in line," Mickie said.

As the three of us dug in, Ernie asked, "Have you told her yet?"

"No."

"You're going to have to soon."

"Maybe not," I said. "I hardly ever see her anymore, and when we're home, I might as well be invisible. Maybe she won't figure out that I never left."

"She'll figure it out," Mickie said. "And she isn't going to be happy about it."

"She has no choice in the matter," I said. "She can't get by without me. She can't do it all by herself."

"Neither can you," Mickie said. "You're exhausted, Sam."

"It won't be forever."

"No? How long will it be for?" Mickie asked.

"I told you, just until I get the store settled and running smoothly."

Ernie laughed.

"What's so funny?" I asked.

"You," he said. "I talked to Betty today. She raved about what you've done. She says the store never ran this smoothly."

I knew from the numbers that income was up 15 percent, and Frank was filling more than a hundred prescriptions a day. We were so busy, we were discussing bringing in a second pharmacist on our busiest days. And I was making an annual salary that would help make ends meet for my mother and pay all four years' tuition at Stanford.

"You have a knack for business," Ernie said.

"I'm meeting with a tax attorney in the morning to create a corporation. Frank wants to buy into it after his six-month probationary period ends," I said.

Mickie dropped her fork. "Probationary period?

Holy shit, Hill, you've become a hard-ass."

"I had to be certain he was the right fit," I said. "If it works out, his monthly payment will bring in extra money every month, which will help my mother get by when I'm no longer pulling a salary. I'm going to suggest she take over my position, but I'm not sure she'll do it if it takes her away from my father."

Ernie wolfed down a slice of cake and pushed back from his chair. "I have to go see Alicia," he said.

"Jesus, can't you give it a rest for one night?" Mickie said.

"I wish. She calls me all the time now. She's afraid I'm going to find someone else and forget about her."

"You will," Mickie said.

"Thanks, Mick." Ernie stood and slipped on his coat. "Maybe I should have you talk to her for me and provide that comforting reassurance."

After Ernie left we cleared the dishes. Mickie said, "They won't last three months."

"Probably not, but did you have to say it?"

"He said it before I said it."

"He didn't say that."

"He didn't have to *say* it. It was in his tone and body language. He doesn't love her."

"How do you know?" I asked.

"Because I practically grew up here, and I saw

what your mother and father have," she said. "What they have—that's love."

I didn't disagree, and their kind of love seemed more and more rare. I wiped down the table with a rag. "They deserved a lot better than what they got."

"Yeah, well, life isn't fair, Sam."

I threw the rag in the sink. "Thanks. That really cheered me up. Why don't you just tell me it's God's will, like my mother?"

"Because I'm not your mother."

"No kidding. My mother's a lot more compassionate than you."

"What are you looking for, sympathy?"

"Would it be too much to ask? I'm sure not getting any answers from him," I said, pointing at the ceiling. I was tired of Mickie discounting everyone's feelings. I knew she had it tough at home, and she seemed to be dealing with it by hardening her heart. "Maybe for once he could show me that he really does have some plan for me, because I'm damn tired of trying to figure it out on my own. My father's in a god-damn rehabilitation center, where everyone gets excited when he can mumble an understandable word, and my mother doesn't even know I exist anymore. I went from—"

"You went from being a kid whose parents did everything for him to being an adult. Welcome to the real world, Sam. Life is the shits, but the alternative is worse. Get over it."

"Why do you always do that?" I said, exasperated.

"Do what?"

"Minimize everything. Make it like it's no big deal. Say things like what you said about Alicia."

"Because this is the real world, and life isn't for pussies."

"Yeah, well, I'm tired of it, and what do you know about the real world?"

"A lot more than you. I've been on my own since I was fourteen."

"What are you talking about? I don't remember you running a business, cleaning the toilets, paying the bills, shopping."

"That's because you weren't there," she fired back. "And I didn't complain about it. My mother was sauced so often she couldn't get off the couch. Who do you think did all those things, the fairies? My lazy, good-for-nothing older brothers? I've been doing the laundry since I was twelve, shopping and making the school lunches while my mother slept off her hangovers. When I got my driver's license, Joanna cried because we wouldn't have to get in the car with my mother drunk anymore. Then my father moves out, gets himself a bimbo, and thinks he's a father because he sees us two nights a week. Or did you forget all of that? Don't give me your sob story. You talk about your mother not knowing you're alive for a couple of months? Big deal, Hill. My mother has never known I was alive."

We stared each other down, silently brooding, unwilling to concede. I had my arms crossed over my chest and my back against the kitchen counter. The urge came over me, and I couldn't resist. I picked up one of the peas from a plate on the counter and flicked it at Mickie. Under normal circumstances I would have missed by a wide margin, but these were not normal circumstances, and I did not miss. In a game of darts, I threw a bull's-eye. The pea hit Mickie between the eyes and, because I had overcooked them, stuck for an instant before falling.

Her jaw dropped. "Did you just really hit me in the face with a pea?"

"Yeah, well, life isn't fair, *Michaela*."

She squinted. "What have I told you about calling me Michaela?"

"I don't remember, *Michaela*."

Mickie sprang like a cat. She had her hand in the pea bowl, and the next thing I knew pea juice dribbled down my face. The war had begun. The peas flew. After we emptied the bowl, we found those squished on the counter and cabinets and continued flinging and mashing. I spun, felt my foot slip, and reached out and grabbed the first thing my hand touched—Mickie's pea-stained blouse. It nearly tore off as I pulled her to the ground on top of me. The rip revealed a black lace bra. I started to laugh, and after a moment, she did, too. We continued until my stomach began to hurt.

"Okay, get up," I said as our laughter subsided.

But Mickie did not roll off. She looked down at me as if she were seeing a thousand different things in my red eyes. Then she said, "Screw it," and pressed her lips to mine.

Unlike the night of my prom, Mickie did not pull back, and she did not stop at the first kiss. A part of me screamed to apply the brakes, knowing that what was about to transpire could not be a good thing, that it could ruin the best friendship I'd ever had, but that part of me quickly lost the battle to the part that longed to feel loved again, and to act on the deep, burning desire I'd always had to touch Mickie. I also knew that debate raged only in my mind. Mickie wasn't about to stop. Discretion and self-control were not hallmarks of her personality. She smothered me with kisses, her hands rubbing my hair and finding their way beneath my shirt to the buckle of my belt. I emptied my head of all doubt and allowed my body the freedom to become lost in the warmth and beauty of Michaela Kennedy.

26

Afterward, I wanted nothing more than to lie on the floor, covered in peas, and to hold Mickie close while we let the world of vendor invoices, dirty laundry, and drunk parents pass us by. I realized that I had wanted this, despite my own misgivings, for years. I loved Mickie, and not just as a friend. I saw in her the chance to have what my parents shared, what we both knew my parents shared. Love. Real love. But my fear, the one that had first entered my thoughts before my desire for Mickie shoved it aside, wiped away those thoughts and dreams the way my father's stroke had wiped away our bucolic existence.

Mickie got up quickly and gathered her clothes, slipping them on.

"Don't you want to take a shower?" I said.

"I have to go."

I got to my feet. "No. You don't. You don't have to leave."

"I have to pack."

"We were going to watch a movie."

But Mickie had already gathered her shoes and purse and pulled out her car keys. Her blouse hung open, beyond repair.

"Your shirt. Let me—"

She kissed me, not the passionate embrace we

had just shared but a peck on the cheek. "See you, Hill," she said.

And just like that, Mickie the tornado was gone.

27

I stood listening to the sound of the car engine grow faint as Mickie drove off, and I was soon lost in thought and regret. I should have stopped it. I should have told Mickie it was a bad idea, but damn it, I didn't want to. I knew that our friendship was complicated. No, we were not dating, but yes, we did spend a lot of time together hanging out, going to dinner, and watching movies. No, we'd never slept together until that moment, but yes, I'd thought about what that would be like and maybe, just maybe we could be more than best friends. Maybe we could be boyfriend and girlfriend. I was lost in that debate when I heard the garage door opening. For a moment, I thought Mickie had come back. Then I wondered why Mickie would be opening the garage door. She wouldn't be. She didn't have a remote. I looked up at the clock. My mother had come home early.

I barely had time to gather my clothes and rush upstairs into the bathroom before I heard the door leading from the garage into the kitchen close with a thud. I could only imagine my mother's chagrin at the sight of her normally immaculate kitchen covered in peas. I turned on the shower, half expecting her to open the bathroom door and yell something like, "What in tarnation happened around here?"

But the door did not open. I scrubbed quickly, but I had peas everywhere. Finally clean, I changed into sweatpants and a T-shirt. My mother was not in her room getting ready for bed. When I walked downstairs, I was prepared to act surprised that she was home, then take over the chore of cleaning up, but I also did not find her cleaning the kitchen.

"Mom?"

"In here."

She sat in the dark, in her customary spot on the living room sofa. I thought she might be saying her novena, but she did not have her rosary beads in hand.

"Why are you sitting in the dark?"

"I was with your father." Her gaze remained unfocused. "I was feeding him and I was thinking about all of the things I had to do for him, now that he isn't capable." I sat on the ottoman facing her. She was talking to herself as much as to me. She raised her eyes to mine. "And that's when it dawned on me."

"What?" I asked.

"That I hadn't done the wash or the shopping or cleaned a plate or cooked a meal. I haven't done any of those things. You've been doing it all, haven't you, Sam?"

"It isn't a big deal, Mom."

"And the store? Who's been running the store?"

"I hired a pharmacist. His name is Frank."

"You hired . . ."

"You'll like him, Mom. He's a lot like Dad."

"But what about the ordering, paying the bills, stocking the shelves, deliveries?"

I didn't answer.

She sighed. "Oh, Sam. I'm so sorry."

"You have nothing to be sorry about."

"This was supposed to be your summer. Your graduation. You've missed it all, haven't you?"

"Nothing to miss, really. Ernie said most of the parties were lame. He and Mickie spent most nights here with me."

"Mickie," she said. "She needs you, Sam."

I was no longer so certain. "I learned how to cook and do the laundry, so that's a good thing, right?"

She closed her eyes and took maybe the first deep breath she had taken since my father's stroke. Then she said, "We're going to get back on track now, Sam, now that you're leaving for college."

I looked away.

"Sam?"

"I'm not going, Mom."

She put up a hand. "Yes, you are."

"Not this year."

"Sam, I realize you've felt the need to take care of everything for your father and me, but I can handle this now. Your father has good care, and that will give me some time during the day."

"I already asked for a year deferral from the admissions office."

"Well, un-ask."

I shook my head. "It's done. They've reallocated my financial aid and assigned Ernie a new roommate."

She pressed the palms of her hands against her eyes, sobbing. I knelt at the foot of her chair and touched her forearms. "Mom, it's okay. This was my decision, and I'm fine with it. I'll take the year to learn to run the business. It will be the best education I could ever receive. And the money I earn, along with my scholarships and the financial aid package, will pay my tuition. When you have Dad set, you can take over for me. You'll need the income, and it will keep you busy during the day."

She lowered her hands and gripped mine. "Promise me, Sam. Promise me next fall you'll go—no matter what."

"I promise," I said. "Absolutely."

She took another deep breath and exhaled.

After a bit I said, "I better go clean up the peas."

"No. You've done enough." She stood. "I saw a movie on the table."

"Mickie and I were going to watch it, but she had to go home."

"If you wouldn't mind the company, I could use a distraction."

"I'll clean up the peas and make popcorn," I said.

"Forget the damn peas," my mother said.

28

The next morning, I awoke early, but my mother had already cleaned up the mess in the kitchen and left to be with my father. I picked up flowers and drove the El Camino. I would tell Mickie that I hoped she didn't regret what we had done, because I didn't. I would tell her that it wasn't going to ruin our friendship, because I wanted to be more than friends. I loved Mickie. I knew it then, and I was convinced it could be the same kind of love my mother and father shared. What was better, after all, than being in love with your best friend?

Walking up the driveway, I felt butterflies and had to tell myself this was the same person with whom, twelve hours earlier, I would have shared my darkest secrets. Joanna answered, looking up at me with her big brown eyes from beneath wisps of bangs and smiling brightly. "Hi, Sam."

"Hi, Jo-Jo." She leaned back, swinging on the door handle, smiling. "Is Mickie here?"

She shook her head. "Uh-uh. She's not home."

"Do you know where she went?"

"She went to college," Jo-Jo said, still smiling.

My heart sank. "She left already?"

"Who are the flowers for?"

I looked at the bouquet, and for a moment

I didn't say or do anything. Then I plucked the card from the plastic stem and handed the flowers to Joanna.

"They're for you," I said.

She took them, either too startled to speak or worried I might be joking. I turned and walked down the steps.

"Sam!"

When I turned back, Joanna stood on the top step, holding the flowers just beneath her chin. She looked like an angel. "Thanks for the flowers, Sam."

29

I didn't hear from Mickie, but I thought of her every day and occasionally contemplated calling her mother to get her dorm number, or driving to Davis and surprising her, but each time I found a reason not to go. I was grateful to be so busy. Each morning my mother and I ate breakfast together; then I drove to the store, and she drove off to be with my dad and participate in his continued rehabilitation. Eventually she would go with me to the store so I could begin training her to take my job. I'm not sure she would have done it for anything less important than getting me to college.

In November we decorated the store in anticipation of Thanksgiving. The holiday would mean several days off school for Ernie and for Mickie, and I wondered if either would come home. Ernie had a football game that weekend, and he and his parents had traveled back to Indiana for a game against Notre Dame, followed by Thanksgiving with the rest of the team.

The day before Thanksgiving, I answered a knock at the door, and there Mickie stood. She looked thinner than when she'd left, and her hair was longer, nearly touching her shoulders.

"Hey, Hill. How's it going?" She walked past me and plopped down on the sofa.

"It's going good," I said. "How's college?"

"The dorm food sucks, most of the kids are neurotic, and my chemistry teacher is a lecher I'm about to kick in the nuts. Can I get a glass of water?"

She made her way into the kitchen and pulled a glass from the cabinet, filling it at the sink, not far from where we'd had the war of peas and fallen to the floor to make love.

"I have soda," I said.

"Throw it out. We did this experiment where you put a piece of meat in the soda, and it eats the flesh."

"So you gave up soda?"

"And red meat. My roommate's a vegan, but I'm not going there. She doesn't shave her legs or her armpits, either."

"Please don't go there," I said.

"Your mom home?"

"She's at the store."

"She's working?"

"One afternoon a week to give me a break. How long are you home?"

"Sunday. You get me for four days, Hill. Let's catch a matinee. You're buying. I'm a poor college kid now, and you're a rich business mogul."

"Hardly."

She stepped forward and gave me a hug, and for an instant I thought she might kiss me. Then she pulled back and was again on the move. "All right, Hill, daylight's burning, and I want to stop at the store and say hello to your mother and use my discount to get some candy. I'm still family, right?"

"I don't know," I said. "The store is under new management, you know, and I hear the new boss is a real hard-ass."

She laughed and pulled me by the hand out the door.

We did not talk about what happened the night of the last supper. But I did not feel like a notch on Mickie's bedpost, as I had with Donna. Over the course of the fall months, I'd had a lot of time to think about Mickie and to consider what had happened that night. I knew Mickie loved me, or at least that's what I told myself. And I told myself that she'd fled that night because she had felt something with me that she had never felt with any of the others, and it had scared her. Mickie didn't want to be in love, burdened by the terrible lessons her parents had taught her. She didn't want the pain. Her knocking on our door that Thanksgiving was Mickie's way of telling me she loved me. It wasn't enough, not for me, but I was certain it was also all I would ever get out of Mickie.

30

The following fall, just before the start of my freshman year at Stanford, I drove to the Palo Alto Eye Clinic to see Dr. Pridemore. "What can I do for you?" he asked. My annual visit was not for several more months.

I had given God so many chances to show me his way. I felt betrayed, and never as much as when he failed to answer my prayers that he spare my father the debilitating effects of his stroke. If he would not do that, I knew he would not change the color of my eyes, as I had so fervently prayed when I was just a young boy. I knew now that only science could do that.

"God's will is not our way," my mother used to say. And I agreed. I had decided it was not my way. "I'm ready," I said. "I'd like to try those brown contact lenses."

PART SIX

Hello Darkness, My Old Friend

1

1989
Burlingame, California

With more and more damage caused by the earthquake being revealed by newscasters on Ernie's television, I finally got through to my mother's telephone. She was relieved to hear my voice and to know I was okay.

"I'm fine," she said. "The house is fine. Some of Grandma O'Malley's Spode china tumbled off the display shelf and broke. Nothing that can't be replaced."

I rattled off a series of questions. "Do you smell any gas? Did you check the pilot light on the water heater? Do you have bottled water?"

"I'm fine, Sam," she reassured me. "Stop worrying."

"Have you reached the rehabilitation facility?" I asked. "How's Dad?"

My father never recovered from his stroke, which the doctors said had also triggered the early onset of dementia. He became confused easily, especially if there was a break in his daily routine. "He's fine," she said. "The facility didn't suffer any damage."

"Do you want me to come by and help you clean up?" I asked.

"Don't think about it. It isn't much. Besides, I'm heading up to see your father. I want to be with him." My father couldn't do much in a wheelchair, but my mother had told me before that she didn't care. They sat together holding hands. Sometimes she would place a rosary in his fingers and help him move from bead to bead while she prayed aloud. "There's no place else I'd rather be," she'd say.

"I'll call you later. Probably tomorrow," I said.

I hung up, thinking of that night when I'd learned of my father's stroke, and the recollection made me realize again how precious life is, and how fragile. One minute you're celebrating graduation, and the next your father is near death. One minute you're getting ready to experience a World Series, the next you could be dead under a pile of concrete. Too short. Life was too short to settle for anything less than the love I had witnessed when Ernie pulled into his driveway, the love I had witnessed my entire life, the love Mickie said I deserved.

Damn her. She was always right.

Life was too short to settle for Eva. A part of me had always known that I'd stayed in the relationship longer than I should have because I lacked the confidence to believe I'd find someone else who would accept me and my condition. I was also smart enough to know that would never happen until I fully accepted me. When I started to wear contact lenses, I put up a bland, brown veil of normalcy not only to the rest of the world but to the person on the other side of the mirror. I no longer had to concern myself with the lingering stares or questions. I no longer had to deal with my condition. I no longer had to come to terms with who I was, as my mother had said would be so important when I was just a boy heading off to grade school. I hadn't dealt with the issue. I'd simply covered it up, literally and figuratively. Mickie's wanting me to tell Eva that I deserved to be treated better, that she was not good enough for me, had nothing to do with Eva. It had to do with me. Mickie recognized it as an opportunity for me to begin not just the process of accepting who I was, but liking that person.

As I sat with the Cantwells watching the television, the news became more and more sobering with each passing minute. Initial reports indicated cars had plummeted from the bridge into the San Francisco Bay. Others hung over the abyss. Reports from the East Bay were just as disturbing. The 880 Interchange, a double-decker concrete freeway, had collapsed. It could not have come at a worse time, filled with afternoon commuters. Dozens were said to be trapped beneath the rubble. People had died. The Embarcadero Freeway along the San Francisco waterfront had also suffered major structural damage. People had pitched tents on the lawn in the Marina District, afraid to go back to their homes and apartments because of a series of aftershocks.

Michelle made pasta and a salad, but none of us ate much. I called home. Eva did not answer. Her flight had been scheduled to land at the Oakland airport just after 4:00 p.m., which would have put her right in the heart of all the traffic. I would likely go home and find a message on the answering machine telling me she'd decided to stay in a hotel in the East Bay to avoid the mess. Terrific. She and Mr. Sleepy could hold each other through the trauma.

At nine o'clock I made another call and again got my answering machine. I hung up and told Ernie, "I'm going to head home."

"Did you reach her?" Ernie asked.

I shook my head. "She's probably staying at a hotel in Oakland rather than fight the traffic."

2

When I pulled up to my two-story house with the cedar-shake siding, I noticed the porch light was on, as well as another light in the front living room, and was certain Eva was home. I'd given this moment some thought, about what I would say. I'd decided to wait and let Eva speak, give her the chance to at least be honest with me. If she was, I'd tell her thanks, but it was time she moved out. If she wasn't, well, then, at least I knew who she truly was, and again, I'd ask her to move out.

When I looked to the upstairs windows I did not see a light on in the bedroom. Eva's car was not parked in the driveway. Strange. When I climbed the front steps to the covered porch, I heard a familiar bark. When I tried to open the door, Bandit pushed his bony head between the door and the jamb, whining and whimpering with excitement. "Okay, okay, Bandit. Back up, buddy. Back up." I stepped in and looked about the room while squatting to pet Bandit and scratch his sides. I didn't see any suitcases. Bandit's tail whipped the air. "Mickie?" I called out. "Eva?"

No one answered. I saw a slip of paper on the tile counter beside the answering machine.

Thought you might need some company.
M

Mickie, checking up on me.

The blinking red light on the answering machine drew my finger toward the button, but I changed my direction to the pantry. "You hungry, Bandit?" His tail whipped vigorously. When Mickie traveled, I watched her boys, which was what she called her dogs. I kept a bag of dog food in the pantry. Eva did not like pets. She reacted to any piece of dog hair on her clothing as if it was radioactive. I wondered if she'd come home but left when she encountered Bandit, but there was no sign she'd been in the house.

Bandit's whimpering became more pronounced at the sight of the food bag. I filled his metal bowl and barely got it to the floor before he dunked his huge jowls and began crunching. I filled a second bowl with water and set it out of harm's way; Bandit tended to slide his bowl all over my tile floor seeking every nugget. As I watched the big dog eat, I sensed the red light blinking behind me. When he'd finished, Bandit looked up at me with his dark, expectant eyes. "Sorry, buddy. Mickie says one bowl. You're getting too fat."

The skin above his eyes wrinkled in disappointment.

"I know. Women, right?" I opened the back

door to the yard. "Okay, time for both of us to take care of our business."

Bandit bounded out. I left the door open so he could get back in and made my way to the answering machine. When I hit the button, a computerized voice indicated there had been a power failure. Then the machine retrieved the stored messages. The first message was left at 4:12 p.m., before the earthquake. Eva.

"Hey, Sam, just wanted to let you know that my flight landed, and I'm on my way home. Looking forward to seeing you."

I didn't have a lot of time to react or analyze the message, because the machine beeped and the second message began playing. Mickie.

"Hey, it's me. I know you went to the game with Ernie, but I saw that it got canceled, and I'm checking up on you. I left Bandit at the house to keep you company. I hope you're all right. I'm fine. A couple cracks in my plaster in the living room, but otherwise no damage. Okay, I'm rambling. Call me and let me know you're okay. Love you."

The machine beeped a third time. I awaited the next message, the one from Eva calling to tell me that traffic was a bitch, and she'd decided to spend the night at a hotel in the East Bay, but there was no voice, just a hang up. The stilted, computerized voice indicated no further messages. I was about to walk off when the

461

phone rang. Isn't it always like that? *Your ears must have been burning.* Or *I was just thinking of you.* I took a deep breath, cleared my throat, and answered. "Hello?"

"Sam?"

"Eva?"

"No, Sam, I'm sorry, this is Meredith."

Eva's mother. "Meredith?" It dawned on me that she would be worried. They lived in Southern California and had obviously heard the news about the earthquake. "I'm sorry, I wasn't . . . Listen, Eva called and left a message that her flight landed. I'm sure she's in a hotel somewhere because the roads are a mess here, as you can imagine. The phone lines have been down."

"Eva's not in a hotel, Sam."

"Did she call you?"

Meredith was weeping. She could not continue. I heard someone take the phone.

"Sam?" Eva's father, Gary Pryor. "We got a call, Sam." He paused. He, too, was fighting tears. "They found Eva's car, Sam. They found it underneath the freeway."

3

Gary Pryor told me he would catch a plane to San Francisco in the morning and asked that I pick him up at the airport. He said someone needed to identify Eva's body. I wrote his flight information on the back of Mickie's note because I knew I would not remember any of our conversation. Then I hung up and stumbled to the couch. Bandit's paws clicked on the tile floor as he trotted in from the backyard, but he did not jump onto the couch or force his head into my hands to be petted. Sensing a mood change, he lowered his head and padded forward, his tail silent. When he got close, he stopped again, waiting for some sign. Did I want his comfort?

I opened my palm, and Bandit stepped forward and rested his head in my lap, looking up at me with a furrowed brow and sad eyes. I lowered my forehead to the bony knob atop his head. I wanted to cry, but I also could not stop a thought swirling in my head. I stood, startling Bandit, who jumped backward, wary. I paced the living room and tried to fill my head with any thought to avoid the one that kept circulating. Eva's father was coming. He was going to identify her body and fly her ashes back to Los Angeles for a funeral service. Her father was coming. *Her father.*

I stopped pacing. I remembered Ernie's two boys racing from their front door to embrace their daddy, gripping his legs.

This was Gary Pryor's baby girl.

This was something no father should have to do.

"No," I said aloud. "No."

I found the paper on which I had written the information and called the number. Gary answered on the first ring. "I'm going over to the morgue tonight," I said. "I'm going to identify Eva. I'll have her body transported to a funeral home here in Burlingame, and I'll ask that she be cremated. We'll fly her ashes home together."

Gary did not immediately answer. He sobbed, great gasps and moans that prevented words but that I understood. He'd been bearing up for his wife, for Eva's sisters, for the entire family. With the details of Eva's remains taken from him, he could mourn his daughter.

"Thank you," he said. "Thank you, Sam."

I hung up and called Mickie.

"Hey," she said. "I've been trying to reach you. Are you all right? I thought maybe you went to your mom's, but no one answered."

"I'm going to bring Bandit back tonight," I said.

"Keep him. Bandit loves it there. He gets a lot more attention, and you two bachelors deserve each other."

"Eva's dead, Mickie." I said the words because part of me needed to hear them to believe them.

"What?"

"I just got off the phone with her father. The freeway crushed her car. She's dead."

"I'm on my way," Mickie said.

4

We got back to my house at one in the morning. Mickie took the key from my hand and inserted it in the lock when I failed the task twice. I sat on the sofa petting Bandit while she opened the liquor cabinet.

"Going to have to be bourbon," she said. I had drunk all of Eva's scotch. "Do you have anything to mix it with?"

"Ice," I said. I heard her pull open the freezer and take the tray to the counter, the ice tumbling into a glass.

Identifying Eva's body was worse than I anticipated, and I had entered the makeshift morgue anticipating that nothing I would ever do in my life would be worse than this task. I was glad I did it, though, glad that her father would not have to do it, glad that the search-and-rescue team had been able to reach her car and her body. Further reports throughout the night indicated more cars remained trapped beneath the tons of concrete, people still inside, alive.

Eva's beautiful face had been spared damage, and that was all the attendee showed me. But as a doctor, I understood from the way the sheet draped her body that much of her torso had been crushed and disfigured, bones broken. She'd likely died instantly.

After the attendee had pulled the sheet back over Eva's face, she had moved to a second body lying beside Eva. "Are you here to identify the man in the car as well?"

It had felt like a stab to the heart.

Mickie had given me a look, but I did not tell her.

"No," I said. "I'm not."

Mickie walked from the kitchen into the family room and handed me my bourbon. She sat close, just as she used to sit when we drove the Falcon. For a long time, we did not speak. I drank my bourbon until only ice remained. Mickie took my glass and poured another drink. I could feel the effects of the alcohol on my already-tired body and weakened mental state. I took another sip. "Thanks for going with me tonight."

"Not something anyone should have to do alone," she said. She took a sip of water. "That's a brave thing you did, so her father wouldn't have to."

I blew out a breath. "I can't cry," I said. "Why can't I cry? What the hell is wrong with me?"

"There's nothing wrong with you."

"Do you know what my first thought was when I found out? When her father told me?"

"Don't—"

"Relief."

"Sam, don't."

"I felt *relief* that I wasn't going to have to confront her; that I didn't have to tell her it was over and that she needed to move out. What kind of a person thinks that way?"

"A good person."

"Nice try."

"I'm serious. A bad person wouldn't be that honest. They wouldn't feel any guilt at all. A bad person never would have done what you just did. A bad person would have punted the responsibility and told her family that he wanted nothing to do with any of it. But I know you. And I know that you'll go to your grave and never tell another living soul that she cheated on you, and neither will I. Her parents will bury the daughter they loved and get to keep all the memories."

The tears burst from me with a gasp, like a dam exploding. Now I could not control them, could not stop the flood. I felt Mickie pull me to her and place my head against her chest, stroking my hair, letting me sob. She removed the pillow from behind her and leaned back, holding me until I could hear my breathing slow and I drifted off.

5

Everyone at Eva's funeral seemed willing to play their part in a tragedy Shakespearean in its magnitude—the young couple about to embark on a life together ripped apart and forever separated by the forces of nature, leaving the future groom to pull together the pieces of his shattered existence.

Ernie and Michelle flew down with Mickie and my mother to be with me for Eva's funeral in Redondo Beach, and I was grateful they came. Their presence gave me back my identity and validated my existence beyond the role of the unknown grieving boyfriend.

At the end of the service, I followed Eva's casket out of the church with the rest of her family and watched the hearse depart. They had a town car for the family, but Ernie saved me. "You want a ride to the reception?"

I nearly hugged him.

The reception was held in the backyard of the Pryor home, a beautiful setting with a view of the Pacific Ocean and a light breeze that brought the smell of the salt air. I parked my mother beneath the shade of a table umbrella with a plate of catered food and a Diet Coke. Mickie and Michelle sat and talked with her while Ernie and I made our way to the bar. I noticed a few people from the church approaching and mentally steeled myself for their condolences.

"Excuse me," one of the men said, "but aren't you Ernie Cantwell?"

"Yes, I am," Ernie said.

"We thought so," the man said. "We saw you in church. Can we get your autograph?"

As Ernie signed the autographs, the men looked to me and introduced themselves. "How do you know Eva?" one of them asked.

"Just a friend," I said.

Ernie and I picked up our beers and found a corner of the yard.

"How are you holding up?" Ernie asked.

"Like an actor backstage in the green room waiting to go on again." I felt guilty saying it, but it was the truth. What seemed to be either lost on everyone, or at least unspoken, was the irony that we did not know one another. Except for a dinner at a restaurant in San Francisco that I had shared with Eva's parents when they came to visit, I had never eaten with them, never shared the holidays with the family, visited over a weekend, or attended family vacations. I had never even met Eva's sisters.

"We've gone through some crazy shit together, but this might be the craziest." Ernie sipped his beer, surveying the crowd, but I had already begun to realize that there was one more crazy thing I needed to do.

6

The following week Trina Crouch sat in my office. Mickie had taken Daniela down the street for an ice cream while I recounted my whole sordid confrontation with David Bateman the day I told everyone else that I had fallen off my bike. I told her of the meeting with Father Brogan at the OLM rectory that led to Father Brogan expelling David.

"You stood up to him," Crouch said. "You got him expelled."

Before our consult I had removed my brown contact lenses in a sign of good faith. "He got himself expelled."

"He said you told the priest, and the priest kicked him out. He said it humiliated his parents. He said his father . . . He was not a good man, either."

"I never told the priest, Trina."

"You didn't?" she asked, clearly puzzled.

"David's two friends ratted him out." I sat back, considering her. "I didn't have the courage to tell anyone, not the priest and not my parents," I said. "I didn't think anyone could help me or protect me. I was afraid. Had it not been for the other two boys' consciences bothering them, David would have continued to bully me."

"I don't have anyone like that," she said.

"You do," I said. "You have me. And you have Mickie."

She looked confused. She wiped her tears. "Why?"

"Because we all need someone."

"Can you help Daniela?"

"I can only repair Daniela's eye," I said.

Tears spilled down Trina's cheeks at my unspoken meaning. I rolled my chair to the sofa on which she sat and handed her the box of Kleenex.

"The retina is the neurosensory tissue that lines the back inside wall of the eye." I used a model of the eyeball and socket I pulled off the shelf. "It's sort of like wallpaper on Sheetrock or the film in a camera. The retina transfers the light coming into our eye into vision. The center of the retina is called the macula, and it is the only part capable of fine, detailed vision—the vision for reading. The remainder of the retina, the peripheral—"

"Daniela can't read books anymore. She says everything is blurry."

"When the retina detaches, it separates from the back wall. When it separates it is removed from its blood supply and source of nutrition. The retina will degenerate and lose its ability to function if it remains detached. Daniela will lose her central vision."

"She'll go blind."

I sat back. "Yes, for all intents and purposes she'll go blind in that eye. Fortunately, over ninety percent of retinal detachments can be repaired with a single procedure. There are three different surgical approaches that we can take—"

"I don't have any insurance," she said. "I lost my job three months ago."

I placed the model on the desk. "What about your ex-husband?"

"No," she said, shaking her head.

"He's a police officer. He must have benefits."

"No," she said more forcefully.

"Trina—"

"I can't have any interaction with him," she said, raising her voice like a frightened child. I gave her a second. She took a deep breath and said, "He took us off his benefits after the divorce, and I agreed to it because I had a job and I just wanted to be rid of him as much as I could."

I spoke softly, gently. "He has a responsibility to his daughter."

"He hates me so much for leaving him he'll do anything to hurt me, even hurt her."

"You could force him, in court."

She shook her head and smiled, though it had a sad quality to it. "It would only make him angry. He'd take it out on me and Daniela, and lawyers cost money, Dr. Hill. So do hospitals and funeral parlors. I don't want to bury my daughter or have her watch him bury me. I don't want to leave her to him. He's a monster."

7

I knew that once I set the wheels in motion, I could not stop or back out. But I wanted to give David Bateman a chance, and Trina ultimately gave me her blessing to talk to him. I still had a difficult time believing there did not exist some spark of decency in the man, that the boy who had terrorized me had done so because his father had terrorized him, that his bullying wasn't all his own doing.

The following week I chose Moon McShane's for a meeting because it felt like home turf, and I knew there would be people inside who knew me. Even still, sitting at a table near the plate-glass windows that looked out at peaceful downtown Burlingame, I couldn't dismiss my nerves, which I'm sure were Pavlovian.

Bateman parked his patrol car in a red zone, and those nerves intensified. I took several deep breaths as I watched him step out of his car and insert his billy club into his holster. He strode to the door in his uniform, the bulletproof vest beneath his shirt making him look even bigger. When he entered he nearly filled the door frame. He rested his hands on the black utility belt, gun prominently displayed. The night he'd assaulted me in the Presbyterian church parking lot, I had been too startled and intimidated to fully register the size of the man. With nub-short hair, he had become his father.

I stood from my seat as he approached the table, garnering looks from nearly everyone in the bar. He wore a shit-eating grin.

"Thanks for coming," I said over the sound of a football game. I offered my hand.

He ignored it and sat. "I see you're still wearing the contacts."

"Can I buy you a cup of coffee?" Bateman turned his head to the window, ignoring my offer. I got to the point. "Your daughter needs surgery."

He glanced at me. "So?"

"She has a detached retina. If she doesn't have it fixed soon, it will degenerate. She could go blind in that eye."

He shrugged. "How is this my problem?"

"She's your daughter," I said, somewhat disbelieving.

"She lives with my ex-wife. Take it up with her."

"I already have."

Bateman's eyes narrowed. "Yeah? What did she tell you?"

"She lost her job. She doesn't have health insurance." He smirked. "Your insurance would cover the cost of her surgery."

"She wants me to pay?"

"It would be the insurance company's money," I said.

"I earned the benefits. What if my rates or my deductible go up?"

I shook my head, not completely believing what I was hearing. It reminded me of when Father Brogan had confronted Bateman in the rectory, and Bateman had expressed no guilt. David Bateman was not just a man who'd suffered as a child. This was a sociopath, possibly a psychopath. "Are you for real?" I asked.

Bateman leaned across the table. "I'll tell you what I am."

"Grow up," I said, and the ferocity of my response momentarily startled him into silence. "You're not a nine-year-old boy anymore, and neither am I. So knock off the big bad wolf bullshit. Your daughter is going blind, and we both know it came at your hand. Your ex-wife didn't tell me. I figured it out on my own. So did the emergency room doctor. But I'm willing to let that go, David. I'm willing to cut you some slack and give you the chance to do the right thing, something decent."

Bateman stood, palms flat on the table. "You want me to do something decent? You tell her to do something decent. You tell her that when she comes home, I'll think about paying the bills. Otherwise, they're on their own, just as she wanted it."

8

I scheduled Daniela's surgery three weeks after my consult with Trina Crouch on a Thursday morning. When I entered the surgical room, I felt nervous. I usually had some nerves before surgery, but my nerves that morning were more pronounced. I knew in a way that I was Daniela's Pastor Brogan. I was the person fate had destined to protect her from the bully. The irony was she and I had shared the same bully. In some ways, I saw myself in Daniela, and this was my way of standing up to David Bateman.

"How's she doing?" I asked the anesthesiologist.

"She's doing great. Everything looks good."

"You ready?" I asked my erstwhile surgical assistant for that day.

"Let's save an eyeball," Mickie said.

We were lucky. We did not need to remove the lens, and there was minimal scar tissue. We finished the surgery in just over an hour. As we stripped from our surgical gear, Mickie gave me a wink. "Nice work, Dr. Hill."

I removed my surgical hat as I entered the waiting room, where Trina Crouch sat, looking worn and tired. "She did great," I said. "I'm very optimistic she'll recover full vision."

Crouch burst into tears. After a moment, she took my hand. "Thank you," she said. "I don't know what to say. I wish you would let me pay you something."

"That isn't necessary," I said. Mickie and I had donated our time, and the hospital administrator at Mercy cut the cost of the operating room and the instruments as much as she could.

Trina pulled an envelope from her purse. "It's a thank-you card, for the person who paid the hospital bill."

I'd told Trina that Daniela's benefactor wished to remain anonymous. "I'll be certain he gets it," I said.

Ernie had insisted on paying. He'd helped his father grow Cantwell Computers exponentially, and he had become a wealthy man in the process. He said there were new opportunities on the horizon, something about a new platform that would allow people to view pages on a computer like pages in a book, one hidden behind the other, as well as other technology that would someday allow us to send information from computers on our desks to other computers around the world. To me it continued to sound like a *Star Trek* fantasy, but then I'd never thought I'd be able to put a phone in my car, either.

"Would you like to see her?" I asked. "She's coming out of sedation, so she'll be groggy, but I think she'll feel better having her mommy in the room."

When Trina stepped into the recovery room, Daniela's head was swathed in bandages, and her eye was covered with a protective cup and gauze. It was heartless of me, I knew, but it was an image I wanted burned into Trina Crouch's own retina so that it would hopefully never again come to fruition. She held Daniela's hand and kissed the bandages around her forehead. There was not a dry eye in the room.

Later that afternoon, Trina sat in a chair in Daniela's room, sipping a Diet Coke, and we talked while Daniela slept. Trina looked at me and said the words I needed to hear. "I'm ready to end this. I don't ever want to see my daughter like this again."

90

Once seated, I began by expressing my suspicion. "The medical evidence, in my opinion, does not comport with a blow to the head from a bike accident," I said. "The incidence of detached retinas in children this young are rare."

"But it does happen?" Montoya asked.

"In rare incidents, but the emergency room injuries also do not substantiate that Daniela fell from her bike."

"Which were what?" Montoya asked.

LeBaron passed out her emergency room report. "Minor scratches. Some healed. I would have expected far more than a scrape on the knee if Daniela sustained a blow to the head of sufficient force to cause this type of injury."

"But you can't say definitively that he hit her," Montoya said.

"No," LeBaron and I said in unison.

Montoya's brow furrowed.

Trina, who had largely kept her gaze on the conference room table, raised her eyes. "Daniela can," she said.

This caught everyone's attention.

A tear trickled from the corner of Trina's eye, and I again became concerned she might back out, but the floodgates opened, and the words came in a rush. "She says her daddy hits her."

After a moment for Trina to compose herself, Montoya said, "But you've never reported any prior incidents of abuse—is that correct?"

"Would you have?" Mickie asked.

Montoya raised a hand. "I'm not judging. I'm just saying—"

"I know what you're saying and what you're not saying," Mickie said. "Everyone in the room knows it. Her husband's a psychopath, and he's a cop. Who was she going to report it to?"

"He'll deny it," Montoya said.

"Don't they all?" Mickie asked.

"It makes a more difficult case, and these cases can be difficult enough as it is. Without corroborating, contemporaneous evidence, it's her word against his," Montoya said, and I began to understand why child abuse cases were so difficult to prosecute.

"I kept a journal," Trina said.

Montoya sat up. "What type of journal?"

"A calendar. I wrote the days Daniela visited her father and the injuries she came home with. There was also an incident in which she broke her arm. He said she fell from a swing at the playground, but Daniela said he never took her to the playground. I took her to the hospital."

"There's a report," LeBaron said. "I saw it in the file."

"Where's this calendar?" Montoya asked.

Trina pulled two black day planners from a bag at the side of her chair. The pages appeared to be well worn.

"How far do these date back?" Montoya asked, flipping through the pages.

"Fourteen months," Trina said, crying again. "Since I divorced him. He started becoming more unstable. He'd always been volatile, but he got worse. He started drinking, and things deteriorated from there."

Montoya lifted her head from reading one of the entries. "Why didn't you say anything earlier?"

Trina dabbed at her eyes with Kleenex. "It's like Dr. Kennedy said. Who was I going to tell? David constantly threatened us, and Daniela wouldn't talk about what happened when she stayed with him. I don't know what he said to her, but whatever he'd said frightened her. I brought it up with him once when Daniela came home with a bruise on her arm. David said he'd already filed a report that Daniela came to his house with the injury, and that if I opened my mouth he'd take her from me. He said who did I think the police would believe? I was afraid for my daughter, afraid to make him angry."

"Can we go through some of these?" Montoya said, indicating the calendar entries. "I'd like to hear what the doctors have to say."

Trina went through her calendar. Dr. LeBaron did most of the commenting on the nature of the injuries and whether they were consistent with the reported manner in which they had occurred. As Trina revealed months of abuse at the hands of her husband, Mickie and I sat silent.

"He's been stalking you," Montoya said at one point.

"No doubt," I said and told of my nighttime confrontation with Bateman in the parking lot of the Presbyterian church.

"What's his attitude now? Is he asking to see Daniela?" Montoya asked.

"No," Trina said.

"I told Trina to tell David that I recommended Daniela remain in a familiar environment, that any fall of any kind could cause the retina to detach," I said.

"And he hasn't fought you on it?" Montoya asked.

Trina shook her head. "Not yet. But it's a matter of time. He uses Daniela to try to hurt me."

"I called him on the abuse at my meeting with him," I said. "It might have scared him enough to back off, but it won't keep him at bay forever. Trina says he has a real bulldog for an attorney."

"Alexander Cherkov," Montoya said. I knew the name from billboards and radio commercials. She addressed Trina. "Your husband has a court order giving him visiting rights. He'll move to enforce it. We'll need to file a temporary restraining order and seek a permanent injunction to keep him away from you and your daughter until we can get you full custody." Montoya looked to me and LeBaron. "I'll need declarations."

The conversation turned to how to best keep Trina and Daniela safe while the court process played out. "Is there someplace you can go?" Montoya asked.

"I have a sister who lives in Tucson."

"How much time do you need?" I asked Montoya.

"No way to know for certain."

"What if I write up a report recommending that Daniela go someplace warm to facilitate her recovery? I can say that the dry weather would be better for her recuperation. Trina's attorney could give it to David's attorney, if he makes a stink."

"It would buy us some time," Montoya agreed. "Give you a chance to get out of town before we serve him with the papers."

Trina nodded.

"What about you?" Montoya asked, looking at me.

"What about me?"

"He's come after you once. He could come again."

"If he does, he does," I said. I was done being afraid of David Bateman.

As the meeting concluded, I felt better with a plan in place, but I also couldn't help but think of something I'd heard a young heavyweight boxer named Mike Tyson once say. Tyson had risen to sudden stardom with his ferocious boxing style. When asked why he never deviated from his attack, no matter the opponent, Tyson replied, "Everyone has a plan, until they get punched in the mouth."

10

Two weeks passed without incident, though I felt as though I was walking barefoot over broken glass. Trina Crouch brought Daniela in for visits, and Montoya used those opportunities to come in to the office and get the legal papers prepared to secure a TRO, which would accuse David Bateman of child abuse. We were waiting until Daniela was capable of travel. When I deemed her fit, Trina loaded up the car in the middle of the night and drove to Tucson. She did not want a paper trail with an airline ticket. During that time David's attorney had never called, nor did David.

Montoya called me at the office late on a Wednesday afternoon a few days after Trina left town. "Okay," she said. "The papers are filed, and he's been served. Keep alert."

"When's the hearing?"

"Six days, though I expect his attorney will ask for a continuance to get competing declarations."

"Will it work?"

"Not unless he can find a doctor to counter your declaration and Dr. LeBaron's. The evidence is strong."

I stayed late to finish paperwork and left my office as the sun was beginning to set and dusk descended over Burlingame. Mickie had left three hours earlier for her yoga class—paper-work had never been her thing. As I walked down the sidewalk to the parking lot at the back of the building, a patrol car drove alongside of me. David Bateman sat in the passenger seat with the window down. I stopped, as did the patrol car. For a second I thought Bateman would get out and confront me. He looked as angry as the kid who had become a raging bull the day he had pummeled me at the park, nostrils flaring, eyes blazing. He made a gun with his thumb and index finger and mimed pulling the trigger.

I drove home conscious of the speed limit. Three blocks from my house, the police car reappeared behind me. I made a right turn. The car followed. I made another left, careful to stay on heavily trafficked roads and to drive the speed limit. The car stayed with me. Not wanting to drive home, I drove down Cabrillo and saw many cars parked in the OLM parking lot and others still arriving. Bingo night. I pulled in.

The patrol car drove past and continued down the street. I had to take a few deep breaths before I pulled from the lot and drove home.

When I arrived, I poured myself a drink and took a sip. The phone rang. "Hello?"

No one answered.

"Hello," I said again.

"You're going to lose," Bateman said. "And so is she."

"Who is this?" I said, though I knew exactly who it was.

"You know who it is. Be careful out driving late. You wouldn't want to get pulled over again."

"I'm recording this conversation," I said. "Go ahead, David. Just keep talking."

Bateman hung up.

The phone immediately rang again. I contemplated not answering; then I had a thought and picked it up. "Time to grow up, David. You touch me again, and I'll have you arrested. Then I'll sue you and take everything you own."

"Sam?" Mickie.

"Sorry."

"What was . . . Shit, he called you, didn't he?"

I told her about the drive-by.

"I'm coming over."

"You don't need—"

But Mickie had already hung up. She arrived at my house ten minutes later, still dressed in her yoga outfit. She'd brought Bandit with her.

"I'm leaving him here with you."

"You're making too big a deal out of this. If Bateman had wanted to do something, he could have tried. He's just a bully." In truth, I was beginning to realize how unstable David Bateman was, and I was grateful to have Bandit.

"He already did do something, or don't you remember?"

She reached into her purse and pulled out a

handgun. I knew Mickie had owned a gun since her midtwenties, when she'd been attacked on the UC Davis campus while attending medical school. She'd managed to get away, but the attack had unnerved her, and she told me that she never wanted to feel that helpless again. She took self-defense classes and shooting lessons and obtained a concealed-weapon permit.

"Mickie, I'm not going to use a gun," I said, conscious of those articles about people who owned a gun to protect themselves having the same gun turned on them.

She placed it on the counter, along with a box of bullets. "Most people who own a gun never have to use it. It's the threat of the gun that deters the need. Just keep it with you in the house. It will make me feel better."

"Fine. I'll keep it here, but I'm not going to use it."

"I hope you don't," she said.

11

Over the next five days, the practice kept me busy during the day, and I brought paperwork home with me so I wasn't at the office late. Mickie made a point of coming over for dinner a couple of nights, and she'd called Ernie and asked that he check in with me daily by phone.

"You're not doing wonders for my manhood," I said one night over dinner.

"I don't care," she said.

"Besides," I said. "I got the big boy here to watch over me." Bandit had become my most faithful companion, never leaving my side and sleeping in his dog basket in my bedroom.

"He's never going to leave you now," Mickie said. "You spoil him."

"Then I guess you'll just have to move in," I said.

She didn't respond.

On the sixth day, Montoya called with the news she'd predicted. Bateman's lawyer had obtained a continuance of the TRO hearing. In return, David had to agree to stay away from his daughter and his ex-wife until the matter was heard the following week. But that didn't happen, either. The court again delayed the hearing when the judge got reassigned to handle a murder trial.

All of this was incredibly frustrating and nerve-racking for Trina, and for me. Trina would get mentally geared up to fly back for the hearing, only to be told that it had been put off, and she had to wait and worry for another week. I didn't have to make those kinds of arrangements, but I had to keep my schedule open. Bateman's lawyer had subpoenaed both me and Dr. LeBaron to the hearing. Apparently, he intended to cross-examine us. There was little doubt in my mind that Bateman and his attorney were delaying the proceedings on purpose, just to screw with his ex-wife, and maybe with me.

When the hearing was set a third time, Montoya told me she'd call only if the hearing was put over.

Another week passed. The night before the rescheduled hearing, Trina Crouch called me to advise that she'd flown home and was staying in a hotel. She was nervous, her voice quavering, and seeking reassurance.

"I'll be there," I said. "So will Dr. LeBaron. And Montoya is confident the TRO will be granted and the judge will make it permanent. They didn't file any doctor's affidavits to counter our opinions. David's attorney can cross-examine us all he wants. He can't win. David can't win this time, Trina. He can't." A part of me was saying this just to calm her, but a part of me truly believed David Bateman could not win, not without some competing doctor's declaration.

I awoke at six the following morning after a fitful night tossing and turning. I gathered the newspaper from the driveway, my gaze drifting up and down the block, looking for a patrol car or a suspicious car I did not recognize. The hearing was set for 10:00 a.m. I spent the next two hours reading the paper, drinking coffee, and generally trying to keep myself occupied. At 8:00 a.m. I jumped in the shower. As I turned off the water, I heard my phone ringing, wrapped a towel around my waist, and answered the extension in the bedroom.

"Dr. Hill, it's Merilee Montoya."

My heart sank. "Please tell me they are not continuing the hearing again. What is wrong with our legal system? He's manipulating everyone just to cause his ex-wife emotional distress. She's a wreck. How can this keep happening?"

"The hearing isn't continued," Montoya said.

I didn't sense the same strength and confidence I usually heard in her voice. I sensed something different, something unnerving. Montoya sounded defeated.

"What do you mean?"

"She's dead," Montoya said softly.

I felt the floor fall out from under my feet, and my legs buckled. I stumbled to the bed so I didn't fall.

"We had a meeting scheduled at seven thirty to

go over everything. When Trina didn't show up and I couldn't raise her on her telephone, I sent a patrol by the hotel where she was staying." Montoya paused to gather herself. She was, or had been, crying. "He shot her. Then he shot himself."

12

David Bateman's murder of his ex-wife and subsequent suicide made headlines in San Mateo
County. I did not sleep that night, nor much that
week. I feared going to bed and closing my eyes.
David Bateman came every night, haunting me,
taunting me. Trina and Daniela called out to me,
pleaded with me, telling me that I had assured
them no harm would come to them.

My insomnia stretched to months.

When I did sleep, it was with the aid of a
pill, but even that did not prevent the nightmares, David Bateman shooting Trina Crouch,
silver flashes blinding me, the thunder of the
gun causing a ringing white noise in my ears
that did not abate after I awoke. The persistent
ringing prevented me from concentrating at
work. I missed appointments. Mickie covered
for me. I lost my train of thought in the middle
of sentences. Large chunks of my day seemed
to vanish, unaccounted for. My inability to sleep
brought fatigue, which brought lethargy and a
darkness I had never known.

At Mickie's suggestion, I consulted Dr. Pridemore, who put me in contact with one of his
colleagues at the Stanford medical school. The
diagnosis was post-traumatic stress disorder, the

illness so many young men brought home from the jungles of Vietnam. The doctor recommended therapy, which only confirmed what I had already concluded—I blamed myself for Trina Crouch's death. I had been the one pushing her to stand up to her husband, and I couldn't dismiss the thought that I had used her to do what I had been unable to do—to fight the bully. My counselor explained to me why that wasn't the case. He told me that I, too, had been willing to stand up to David Bateman in court. He reasoned that even if I hadn't, Trina still might very well be dead. He explained that David Bateman was psychopathic, so damaged as a child as to be beyond repair. It was all very rational and pragmatic, but it did not change the fact that Trina Crouch was dead and Daniela would be raised by an aunt in Tucson, without her mother or her father. It did nothing to cure my insomnia or my nightmares or to make me feel any less guilty. Now more than ever, David Bateman's face and voice haunted me. It was as it had been in grammar school, his specter ever present.

Mickie suggested more counseling, but I had grown tired of people asking me how I felt and what I wanted. What did I want? I wanted to understand. I wanted to believe what every person on the planet wants to believe—that God had a plan for me, and that "God's will" was not just a parent's answer to silence a child who asked too many questions. I also knew I would not find that answer in Burlingame.

I cannot say I left Burlingame in search of answers. That would be a lie. At that moment, I was not searching for anything. I was running. I was running from Trina's death, running from the memory of David Bateman, and running from a faith that seemed to solve every problem not with a solution but with an excuse.

"It's God's will."

PART SEVEN

Saying Goodbyes

1

April 1999
Costa Rica

Nine in the morning and I was already perspiring beneath a loose-fitting blue cotton shirt when my team of ophthalmologists arrived at an eye clinic set up in a concrete masonry building with a metal roof and no air-conditioning. Our visit, part of Orbis's rural-outreach program, had been advertised on the national radio for a week, and more than five hundred people waited in line for basic eye examinations.

The Orbis communications director walked my team down musty, faded-blue corridors, explaining that two staff ophthalmologists from the Hospital Nacional de Niños in San José, Costa Rica, would test each patient's sight. If the doctor decided the patient needed further treatment, he would direct the person to one of three examination rooms assigned to me and two of my Orbis colleagues.

It had been nearly ten years since I'd turned my private practice over to Mickie and climbed aboard the refurbished DC-10 owned by Orbis, an organization dedicated to saving sight throughout the world. I intended to take one trip. Then

I took another, and another, and just kept getting on the plane. Mickie had refused to buy me out of the practice, or to buy my home, though she agreed to move in and care for it. "Both will be here when you come back from wherever the hell it is you're going," she'd said, which was pretty much around the world. I worked in villages in Africa where at night you could hear lions moaning in the tall grass. I conducted eye exams in overpopulated slums in India and in Asia where people lived beneath sheets of metal and cardboard. I sent Mickie a postcard and a letter from every city I visited. She refused to write back. "I'll talk to you in person, when you come home," she'd say.

Over the years, with the advent of cell phones, desktop computers, e-mail, and the Internet Mr. Cantwell had predicted, Mickie relented. In fact, we communicated more than when we had worked together. At night, I wrote her long letters about my day. I also called Ernie, who had assumed the mantle as CEO of Cantwell Computers, once a week on average, and we also stayed in touch via e-mail.

My work and travels also gave my mother and me something to talk about when I returned to Burlingame, other than her persistent question, "When are you moving back home?" I'd taken up photography as a hobby, and we would dissect each photograph in detail. My mother's son,

I put them all in scrapbooks and labeled each one.

"Africa looks incredible," she'd said. "Your father always wanted to take a safari."

"There are some beautiful areas," I said, "but also so much poverty. We should go to Africa. And you would love China."

My mother would not leave my father. "You're treating God's children," she said, tears filling her eyes, hope filling her soul. In my mother's way of thinking, if not for the "incident"—which was how she referred to the murder-suicide of David Bateman and Trina Crouch—I never would have joined Orbis, and I would not have been helping so many less fortunate. In my mother's way of thinking, I had become God's missionary, down to my beard—which showed traces of gray— shoulder-length hair, round tortoiseshell glasses, and baggy clothes. She said it made me look like a disciple.

Mickie was not as kind. "You look like one of the freaking brothers, Hill," was her frequent greeting, referring to the Franciscans of our youth.

"That's Brother Hill to you," I'd say.

I didn't consider my work as "God's work," largely because I didn't believe in my mother's God. If anything, I'd classify myself as a Buddhist. I believed that every living thing came from the earth and was to be respected.

I meditated and I chanted and I found that it helped me sleep—as did the exhausting schedule I purposefully kept. Intellectually, I recognized that, in some way, this was not my way of helping others as much as it was my penance for the death of Trina Crouch. This was my purgatory, to atone for my sins.

Being a visitor to Burlingame also allowed me unencumbered time to spend with my father, who had learned to speak again, though in a halting, ghostly rasp. We spent many hours together under the shade of that gnarled oak tree at the rehabilitation center. When I took him and my mother on excursions, Mickie would join us. We pushed his wheelchair across the Golden Gate Bridge, around Sausalito, and over to Alcatraz Island. When we had exhausted San Francisco, we went north to the Napa Valley and Mendocino, east to Yosemite, and south to Monterey. My mother took great joy in planning these trips to coincide with my visits. These were the cruises and vacations she and my father thought they would take in the twilight of their lives but never got the chance.

Ten hours after my day had started at the makeshift clinic, I was nearing the finish line and dreaming of a cold shower, colder beer, and something more substantial than the light snack I had rushed to eat. Alejandra, one of the clinic assistants, knocked and opened my door.

"That bus has arrived," she said. "Do you have it in you?"

The bus contained thirty orphans from a rural village outside Atenas, an hour's drive west of the capital. We'd been getting updates throughout the day of its progress. The bus had been scheduled to arrive first thing in the morning, but heavy spring rains washed out a road and caused them to take a long detour. Then their bus broke down.

"I can hold out," I said, "if you can find me some sugar."

Over the next two hours, I examined eight children and three adults while sipping a warm soft drink and chewing almond cookies. I was examining a young girl whose name I do not recall but whose beautiful face would forever be etched in my memory when Alejandra interrupted again.

"Dr. Hill? Sorry to disturb," she said, sticking her head into my room. "There's a child here Dr. Rodriguez would like you to see."

I was tired, with several more patients of my own still waiting. "Is it something in particular?"

"Dr. Rodriguez thinks so."

I sighed. "Give me a minute." I had become the most experienced doctor on staff.

I finished my consult and walked down the short hallway, mentally bracing myself for what was likely a complex medical condition. Lynn Rodriguez stood outside the door.

"I know you're tired," she said.

"We're all tired."

She pushed open the door. The young boy sat on the rolling stool with his back to the door. I guessed from his size that he was six or seven. An older woman, one of the caretakers from the orphanage, sat in a chair along the wall. She spoke to the boy in Spanish, and though I had picked up much of the language, I was not fluent and did not understand everything she said. From what I could surmise, she was trying to get the child to turn around and face me, but the boy would not do so.

"What's his name?" I asked Lynn.

"Fernando," she said.

At the sound of his name, the boy spun on the stool. When Fernando looked up at me, it took my breath away.

2

Just as quickly as he had looked at me, Fernando lowered his chin and turned his head. It was a self-defense mechanism to avoid my stare and stunned reaction. His mop of curly brown hair flipped across his forehead, seemingly too thick for his thin, small frame of caramel-colored skin, but long enough to cover his eyes.

Lynn whispered, "The children call him *el hijo del Diablo*."

The son of the devil.

As I approached, Fernando glanced sideways with distrust and trepidation, a child who had been rejected and bullied and grown wary of the world and everyone in it.

"*Hola*, Fernando," I said, trying to sound cheerful. He did not answer. I sat in the patient chair and allowed him to swivel atop the doctor's stool, swinging his legs. "*¿Cuántos años tienes?*"

My question was again met with silence. I looked to Lynn Rodriguez. "*Supongo veintitrés*," I said. *I am guessing twenty-three.* I noticed the corners of Fernando's mouth twitch, but he kept them from inching into a grin.

The woman seated with her back to the wall answered for him. "*Seis*."

"*¿Seis?*" I said. "*No es posible.*"

"*Sí*," the woman said.

"But I understand he is as smart as a twenty-three-year-old," Alejandra said, continuing to speak Spanish.

"I can tell," I said, considering a blank sheet in my file. "It says here that this boy is extremely bright and . . . that he is also very strong." Fernando wore a T-shirt with the green image of the Incredible Hulk on the front. "It says that I do not want to shake his hand because he is as strong as the Incredible Hulk—so strong that he might crush my fingers."

Now I had Fernando's attention. He could not hide his grin, which was electric. It lit up his face and the room. I tentatively stuck out my hand. He eyed it with suspicion. Then, willing to play the game, he placed his hand in mine, but so lightly it barely touched my skin. When I squeezed, he also squeezed. I grimaced and flinched. "It is true, Alejandra. It is true," I said in Spanish. "He is crushing my hand."

Fernando giggled, a sound as pure and true as the chimes of the bells that rang from the steeple of Our Lady of Mercy.

"Please, do not crush my hand," I begged. "I have patients I must treat."

He released his grip.

I sighed and flexed my fingers. "Thank you, Fernando. Thank you. I'm Dr. Sam," I said. "Alejandra, I'll bet you that Fernando likes

Popsicles; do you think you could find one for him while we talk?"

Alejandra left to find Popsicles. I said, "Fernando, can I share a secret with you?"

His brow furrowed, and his eyes narrowed.

"It is a secret that no one else knows. *Tus ojos son extraordinarios*," I said. He lowered his chin. "*Muy especial*," I continued. When Fernando retreated into his shell, I said, "You don't believe me?"

He shook his head. "*Ellos son los ojos del Diablo*."

"No," I said. "They are not the devil's eyes. You are one of God's children."

Again, he shook his head.

"But I can prove it," I said. Fernando looked skeptical; so did the woman seated in the corner. A gold crucifix dangled from a chain around her neck. "I have been all over the world, Fernando, and I have searched for someone with eyes so extraordinary, but you are the first person I have found to be so blessed. Now, are you ready for my secret?" I asked.

He nodded, becoming curious. The woman, too, leaned forward.

I walked to the sink, washed my hands with soap and water, and slowly removed my brown contact lenses. Fernando watched with fascination, perhaps never having seen anyone do such a thing. I did not bother to put them

509

in a contact case. For the first time since I had started wearing contact lenses at eighteen years of age, I was ashamed of myself. I turned on the tap and allowed the water to wash them down the drain. When I returned to my chair, with my sight slightly blurred, Fernando's eyes widened. The woman made the sign of the cross, lifted the crucifix to her lips, and kissed it.

"They used to call me the devil boy," I said. "But you see, I am not the son of the devil, and neither are you. God gave me extraordinary eyes so that I would live an extraordinary life. And I have, Fernando. If God had not given me these eyes, I would never have met you." Fernando's lower lip quivered. "God did not make you different, Fernando. He made you special." I put the tip of my finger to his chest. "But what is most important is not the color of your eyes. What is most important is what is inside." All my mother's lessons came pouring out of me, along with the need to console someone who had likely never been consoled. "Now you know that you are not alone. Now you know there is someone like you. And I am going to make you a deal, Fernando. I am never again going to hide the color of my eyes or be ashamed of them. And I want you to promise me that you will also never be ashamed." I put out my hand. "Is it a deal?"

Fernando jumped from the stool and shot past

my hand, wrapping his arms around my neck, hugging me. *"Todo va a estar bien,* Fernando," I said. *"Ten fe. Todo sucede por una razón." Everything is going to be okay.*

3

There are moments, I believe, when we are capable of communicating with those we love without using our voices, moments when we think of someone and the phone rings, or we speak the person's name and suddenly they are standing beside us. I had often felt this connection to Mickie. When I returned to my room late that night after meeting Fernando, I was filled with a strong urge to talk to her. And just like that, my phone rang.

"I have something amazing to tell you," I said. I rambled on about Fernando for several minutes until I detected a subdued quality in the tone of Mickie's voice that was unlike her.

"You need to come home, Sam," she said. "You need to see your mother."

4

Mickie filled me in as we drove from the airport to Our Lady of Mercy Hospital. Two months earlier, as I had been traveling in India, my mother had been diagnosed with an aggressive form of breast cancer, but she had chosen not to tell me or Mickie. Knowing my mother, she saw no point in burdening or alarming us for what she believed to be God's will. The cancer had already infiltrated her lymph nodes, and the doctors subsequently found tumors in other organs, including her liver, kidneys, and lungs. They gave her three months to live without treatment, perhaps six months with an aggressive regimen of radiation and chemotherapy that would leave her sick and weak. My mother, always the tough Irish lady, chose not to have the treatment. She was in the hospital because her kidneys had begun to fail.

When I entered her hospital room, she had her eyes closed. I hardly recognized her. Her collarbones protruded from beneath her thin gown, as did the bones in her hands, which even now clutched her rosary. Her skin, always pampered with lotion and creams, was wrinkled and sallow and appeared translucent. The worst part of being a doctor is that other doctors cannot lie to you. They cannot give you false hope of a miracle. I had known cardiologists who diagnosed their own heart attacks, and dermatologists who diagnosed their own malignant moles. No one needed to tell me what I already knew. My mother was dying.

I took her hand and leaned close. "Mom?"

She opened her eyes and smiled. Then she placed her hand on my cheek, and her eyes widened. "My boy," she whispered, looking into my eyes. She started to cry. "My baby boy with the extraordinary eyes."

"Why didn't you tell me, Mom?"

"What's to tell?" she said. "It's my time, Sam. It's God's will."

"You're too young, Mom."

"I've led a wonderful life, Sam, more wonderful than I had a right to ever expect. God gave me the kindest, gentlest man to be my husband, and he gave me the most precious baby boy."

I fought back tears of guilt. I should not have left her. Maybe I would have noticed something—fatigue or jaundice, something. "I'm sorry, Mom. I'm sorry I haven't been around more."

"Sorry for helping the poor and the sick? Sorry for helping God's children?" She shook her head. "Don't you think of it," she said. "You've made me so proud. You've been everything to me and more. I had no right to keep you to myself. It was God's will for you to do his work."

Initially, it did not feel this way. Initially, my

work felt as I had intended it, an escape and a penance, but in Fernando I saw the truth in my mother's words, and I hoped they would help to relieve the tremendous guilt I knew I would feel for having been gone.

"You don't owe me anything. You took care of me when I needed you most, when your father became ill. You saved me, Sam. You saved the store. You saved it all."

I shook my head.

"Your father," she said, worry creeping into her voice.

"I'll take care of him," I said. "I won't leave again. I'm staying home, Mom." I sat on the edge of her bed. "Are you in pain?"

"I'm hoping to free a lot of those poor souls in purgatory before I go," she said.

"Is there anything you want?" I asked. "Anything I can do?"

"There is," she said. "There's an old friend down the hall. She's dying, Sam, poor thing. She's in a lot of pain. She asked to see you if you came."

"Of course I'd come, Mom." I was struggling to breathe, holding on. "She asked to see me? Who is it?"

"She's just down the hall. Two doors. Go see her, Sam. She needs to see you now." My mother closed her eyes.

5

I entered the room two doors down the hall to the sound of the television. The woman in the bed, propped up on pillows, had thinning white hair and the same sallow skin as my mother, but she was unfamiliar to me. I thought for a moment that my mother, in her drug-induced state, was mistaken, that she had hallucinated this friend. But as I turned to leave, the woman stirred and opened her eyes. I recognized her only when she put on the thick, black-framed glasses.

"Who are you?" she asked. The cancer had stolen her voice. What came out was harsh and raw.

"I'm Sam, Sister Beatrice," I said. "I'm Sam Hill, Maddy and Max's son."

She smiled, and it looked odd, because I could not recall ever seeing her smile. "Your mother said you would come. I wasn't so sure."

I didn't bother to tell Sister Beatrice that my mother had avoided telling me the identity of the "old friend" in the room down the hall, and that if she had, I might not have obliged her.

"She visits me every day," Sister Beatrice said. "Even though she's sick, she still comes, your mother."

"She's a good person," I said.

"I'm sorry I wasn't, Sam." I started to wave off the apology, but she wouldn't have it. "I had a problem. You knew that. But you never said anything to anyone, did you?"

"I never did, Sister."

"I was teased as a child, made fun of for my lisp and my buck teeth. I found comfort in the bottle when I got older. It isn't an excuse for the way I treated you, Sam. It isn't an excuse for my acts of unkindness."

A part of me wanted to not accept her apology. A part of me wanted her to know the pain she'd caused, but I was beyond that. The ordeal with David Bateman and Trina Crouch had made me realize that holding grudges only caused more pain. "We all do our best in life, Sister. We all do our best with what we're given. You had a disease. I don't blame you for that."

She reached out her hand. I hesitated. Even though the woman I had likened to the Wicked Witch of the West had become a frail, little old lady, a part of me still feared her. I allowed her to take my hand. Like my mother's, hers was cold to the touch, and I felt every bone and knuckle.

"I'm an alcoholic," she said, "since I was sixteen. I stopped drinking when they sent me for treatment. Do you remember?"

"I still have the Bible," I said.

She seemed amazed. Tears pooled in her eyes. "I'm so glad you have something decent to remember me by. It's been a lifelong struggle, Sam. I stopped drinking, but I've never stopped being an alcoholic. I came to your mother's home looking for you. I wanted to tell you that I was sorry, Sam. I wanted to tell you that not a day goes by that I don't think of how I mistreated you, how wrong it was, how un-Christian. I'm hoping you'll forgive me, Sam. I'm hoping that you'll find it in your heart."

"There's nothing to forgive, Sister. I know it was the alcohol."

She smiled and squeezed my hand. "You are your mother's son," she said.

And of that I have no doubt.

6

When Mickie and I left the hospital and returned to my house, Mickie's new pit bulls greeted us with enthusiasm. Bandit had died years earlier. Mickie buried him in my backyard and planted a rosebush to mark his grave. I told Mickie of Sister Beatrice, and in true Mickie fashion, she said, "You're a better person than me. I might have punched her."

"It's time to let go of the past," I said.

Mickie made dinner, meat loaf with potatoes and peas, and I opened a bottle of Syrah and put on a John Coltrane CD. Though we were both now in our forties, Mickie still looked the same—thin, with hair the color of gold and not an ounce of fat on her body. We sat at the kitchen table discussing my mother and my father and the guilt I felt for having traveled so much. Then I broached a different subject.

"You asked me long ago if I wanted to be a father," I said. "Do you remember?"

"You were about to get snipped," she said.

"I know the answer now." Her brow furrowed. "I want to adopt Fernando."

She sat back. "Do you think the guilt you're feeling now could be coloring your judgment?"

"Of course it is. But so what? It would be the

right thing to do, to raise that boy as my son, to teach him all the things my parents taught me, to give him a home where he's loved and can feel safe."

"It could be a long process, Sam. And you really don't know the depths of the emotional torment that child has been through."

"I have time," I said. "And I've already considered the process."

"You have?"

"The application is being sent to me. I looked at what I would need as far as recommendations and that sort of thing. There are companies that can help."

"What about traveling?"

"I'm not leaving again."

She smiled. "I'm glad."

"I have a better chance of adopting if I'm married," I said, throwing it out there like a fisherman throwing out a line. I could get lucky and get a bite, maybe just a nibble, and if I pulled the line in without so much as nibble, I was in no worse shape.

"Maybe we should start by getting to know one another again."

"I've known you my whole life, and I remember every day of it."

"Really. Do you remember this?" She picked up a pea and flicked it at me. We both burst out laughing.

"You realize, of course, this means war," I said.

She leaned forward, wineglass in hand, mischief in her eyes. "And what are you going to do about it?"

Truth was, I didn't know. I held another secret not even Mickie knew. I had remained celibate since Eva's death. I'd had opportunities, but this was by choice. I recalled Mickie once telling me that emotionally the act of having sex meant nothing to her. She just liked the pleasure it brought, a respite from the pain in her world. Though I had taken it to the opposite extreme, I understood what she meant. Without an emotional connection to the person, I was simply not interested in the physical act. Now, however, I longed for an emotional connection, to feel another person's body next to mine—Mickie's body.

I sat back and shrugged. "I've been gone so long," I said. "And I haven't . . . There hasn't been anyone, Mickie. I spent most of my days thinking of what I would write you when I got back to my room."

Mickie never took her eyes from mine. "No one?"

I shook my head.

She stood slowly, swaying to Coltrane's saxophone as she made her way around the table. The jeans hugged the contours of her body, which remained lithe and sexy. Her T-shirt drifted just above her waistline, revealing her still-toned stomach. She tilted her head, her hair falling just off her shoulder, and ran her fingers along the surface of the table, across the back of my hand, up my arm, across my shoulder. It sent a lightning bolt through me, and I felt my body shudder. She leaned close, her breath warm on my neck. When she kissed me, the moisture of her lips reminded me of my senior prom, a kiss I wished had lasted longer and that we could have repeated many times. Her teeth nibbled the lobe of my ear, and I felt as though I had burst into flames and was melting right there at the table in my home.

"I've never forgotten *our* night," she whispered.

I pushed back my chair and she slid into my lap and wrapped her arms around my neck. She kissed me gently, her lips barely touching mine. "Do you remember the prom?"

I nodded, eyes closed. I felt like I was floating.

"You told me you loved me," she said.

Another kiss.

"I've always loved you," I said. "Since the moment I laid eyes on you in the sixth grade."

"That was lust," she said, kissing me harder.

"It still is."

Another kiss. "Dance with me, Sam."

She pulled me from my chair and pressed her face to my chest, swaying to "The Night Has a Thousand Eyes." I felt every curve of her body against me, and I couldn't help but think we were one. My hands found her back beneath her shirt and the warmth of her skin. She moaned gently. Then she tilted up her chin and kissed me again. "Make love to me, Sam."

She led me by the hand upstairs to the bedroom, where she slowly undressed me.

"Is it still lust?" she whispered.

"Desire," I said.

Mickie pulled her shirt over her head and undid her bra, letting it fall to the floor. She sashayed her hips and slid off her jeans, then her panties, standing naked before me. I ran my fingers along her shoulders and down her arms and came up along the toned ridges of her stomach, cupping her breasts. She pulled me to her, and I took her nipple in my mouth as she caressed my head. I kissed her shoulders and neck, then kissed her hard on the mouth. I wanted to kiss every inch of her, to tell her I loved her. She took me in her hand, gently stroking me. Slowly, she lay back on the bed. This time there were no voices in my head telling me to stop or warning me that this would be a mistake. Nothing in my life ever felt more right. There was only my unbridled love, and lust—oh yes, my never-wavering lust for Mickie Kennedy.

This time, after we made love, Mickie did not flee. She slept with her head on my chest, breathing heavily. I had never watched Mickie sleep, never heard the rhythm of her breathing or considered the way her body flinched and twitched. I pushed aside sleep, refusing to close my eyes, not wanting to miss a single moment with her.

In the morning, I awoke to find Mickie's side of the bed empty, but before I could become melancholy, I smelled bacon cooking downstairs.

Mickie stood at the stove, the coffee percolating. She handed me the newspaper and a mug. I set both on the counter, then wrapped my arms around Mickie, kissing her. "The world can wait. How about round two?"

She smiled. "Breakfast first. You'll need your stamina. Besides, there's an interesting story on the inside page I think you might like." She retrieved the paper and handed it to me with an impish grin. "I think this is your week to clear your closet of its skeletons."

"Sister Beatrice?"

Mickie nodded to the paper, then went back to the bacon, though I knew she was keeping an eye on me. I flipped through the paper, scanning the headlines, but it was a name in a caption beneath a photograph that first grabbed my attention.

Judge Donna Ashby Gage.

The Associated Press article was two columns to the right of the photograph beneath a bold-type headline.

Boston Judge Resigns amid Allegations of Sex with Minor

Though the headline said it all, I read the article. Superior Court Judge Donna Ashby, a graduate of Burlingame High School, had been caught by a court bailiff having sex in her office with a twenty-year-old law school clerk. The clerk admitted to a three-month tryst of sexual acts in Judge Ashby's office and car. Further investigation revealed several other relationships with her judicial clerks. Married and a mother of three, Donna had resigned from her position. The article quoted her attorney as saying she was seeking counseling for an addictive personality.

"And she still has the big tits," Mickie said.

I considered the photograph and saw enough in Donna's face to peel away the years to reveal the heavyset nineteen-year-old girl who had stolen my virginity and used me as her personal vibrator, as Mickie had so aptly put it.

I set down the paper. "At times, I used to think my time with her was the best sex I'd ever have."

Mickie's eyebrows arched. "Oh, thank you very much."

I came around the counter and held her. "That's not what I meant. What I meant was that, at seventeen, the sex came without strings, without baggage, without expectations. It was just sex."

"And at other times?" Mickie asked.

"I resent her."

Mickie pulled back from me and gave me a curious stare.

"She intended to steal my virginity from the moment I walked into my father's store, and she did. She saw me as easy pickings, and she relished the thought that she would be my first."

"Well, whatever it is that makes that *titillating* for her, it's apparently never gone away," Mickie said.

"No pun intended?"

Donna had taken something I could never get back, something my monastic years helped me admire about my parents' relationship, the knowledge that they had loved only each other. Donna was part of the reason I chose to be celibate. She did not come to my dreams and memories as a sweet recollection; she brought back the shame and humiliation I'd felt when I realized, standing in her kitchen, that love can be faked and, therefore, never fully trusted.

"You know, my desire for you has never gone away," I said.

Mickie put down her coffee cup. "Oh no, you're not getting off that easily."

"For what?"

"For saying she was the best sex of your life. We'll just see about that." And she pulled open my bathrobe.

8

Late that morning, after a shower, Mickie and I stood in the bathroom, brushing our teeth and combing our hair. We were going to retrieve my father from the rehabilitation center and bring him to the hospital to visit my mother. I broached an idea that came to me while sitting in my mother's hospital room.

"I want to take my mother to Lourdes," I said.

Mickie spit toothpaste in the sink and considered me in the mirror. She stood in her underwear. She was wider in the hips but otherwise not much different from the young woman with the hard body in the bikini I first set eyes on at the Russian River. "France?"

"Yes. It's said that the Blessed Mother appeared to Saint Bernadette back in the eighteen hundreds and it's since become a Catholic pilgrimage. My mother has been devoted to the Blessed Mother her entire life," I said. "She deserves to go."

Mickie rinsed with mouthwash, spit again, then walked closer and put a hand on my shoulder. "No doubt. But you do realize there won't be any miracles, Sam."

"Last night and this morning were miracle enough for me," I said.

Mickie smiled, closed lips. "Typical guy. You get laid, and the world becomes a Disneyland ride."

I took Mickie's hand. "I'm long past believing in miracles," I said. "I just want to see her happy."

"Do you think she could physically withstand the travel?"

"A commercial flight? No. No way."

"Then how—"

"I'm going to make a call to David Patton," I said, meaning the founder of Orbis. "I'm going to see if he'll let me rent one of the planes."

I could afford it. In 1997 I had been in Santiago de Cuba when Ernie called. "Do you remember that thirty thousand I *forced* you to invest in Cantwell Computers?"

I remembered, and I was familiar with the growth Ernie had predicted for Cantwell Computers since he used my money to purchase my initial shares of stock for pennies on the dollar. After repeated splits of the stock, I had no idea how many shares I owned in the company or their value. At the time, given my monastic lifestyle, I didn't care.

"We just closed a deal with a software company," Ernie had said. "Our stock has hit an all-time high. I hope you don't mind, but I authorized your broker to sell. You did give me durable power of attorney when you left on your mission. Anyway, the bottom line is, you're rich, Hill. You won the freaking lottery."

And I had won the lottery, though it had changed my life very little. This was a chance to use the money to do some good.

"It's a flying hospital," I said to Mickie that morning. "If anything were to happen, she'd be well taken care of. There would, after all, be at least two doctors on board." Mickie straightened. "I'm done traveling without you, Mickie." A tear rolled down her cheek. I wiped it away with my thumb, lifting her chin. It was the most vulnerable I had ever seen Mickie Kennedy since the night of my senior prom. "Besides," I said, "I'll need help with my father."

And she punched me on the arm.

9

The doctors at Our Lady of Mercy advised against the trip; they said my mother would never withstand the travel, that it would be too arduous, too difficult. They pointed out that, after the plane landed, we would still need to take ground transportation to and from the airport into Lourdes. In the end, I left the decision to my mother.

She looked at her doctors as if they were all nuts. "It's a pilgrimage," she said. "It's not supposed to be easy."

We put two hospital beds in the plane's audio-visual room just behind the classroom and pushed them together. My mother and my father held hands, giggled, and talked like schoolchildren on a field trip. My father looked and acted healthier than I had seen him in years. Though the stroke had taken the twinkle from his cobalt-blue eyes and dulled his facial expressions, he hung on every word my mother spoke, savoring each as if it might be her last, and I was certain I saw him smiling behind the mask.

Somewhere over the Atlantic, they drifted off to sleep. The two nurses I'd hired to accompany us suggested Mickie and I also get some rest, and we lay down in the recovery room at the back of the plane, waking when the wheels touched down at the airport outside Lourdes.

One of the nurses knocked on the door. "The van has arrived," she said.

My mother was already awake. She asked Mickie to help with her makeup and the special dress she'd brought to wear, one I knew she would ask me to bury her in.

"Why are you putting on makeup?" I said as Mickie held a mirror. "It's impolite to be the most beautiful woman in a foreign country, and makeup will only make the contrast between you and every other woman more noticeable."

That comment brought a crooked grin from my father.

My mother swatted at me with a towel. "Go away, you. I can't have the Blessed Mother see me looking like a ragamuffin."

The morning weather in the Pyrenees was forty-three degrees with a light mist. We bundled my mother and father in knit hats, heavy coats, and gloves, loaded them into their wheelchairs, and wheeled them out of the plane. After passing through customs, we boarded a van I had hired to accommodate wheelchairs and set out for Lourdes. I had done research before our trip. Lourdes was a small town in the mountains not far from the Spanish border. It had been a quiet and unassuming city until February 1858, when a fourteen-year-old Bernadette Soubirous went into the local garbage dump to find firewood and instead encountered a beautiful woman dressed in blue-and-white robes. The woman would identify herself as the Immaculate Conception. For six months the woman appeared to Bernadette and eventually instructed her to tell the bishop to build a church above the escarpment. The bishop balked until the Blessed Mother instructed Bernadette to dig in the ground. As the story went, when Bernadette complied, she uncovered a freshwater spring that has flowed continuously for 140 years, though no one has ever found its source. Millions of sick and infirm pilgrims venture to the small town each year to be dipped in the waters of that spring, which are said to have healing powers and to have produced enough miracles for Pope Pius XI to canonize Bernadette a saint.

The drive to the Massabielle grotto, what had been the garbage dump before the Blessed Mother appeared to Bernadette, would take just under thirty minutes. We drove through rolling green fields with French cottages at the foot of the snowcapped Pyrenees. My mother was not interested in sightseeing. The drive was just enough time for her to lead us all in praying the glorious mysteries of the rosary. I sat on the seat beside my father, helping him move the beads through his hands and largely humoring my mother. I had not recovered my faith, but I had mellowed with age. I knew what the rosary meant to her. Mickie was also a good sport, and I was surprised she still remembered all the prayers.

"You never forget what's beaten into you in Catholic grade school," she whispered.

We drove through Lourdes, a beautiful mountain village of narrow streets, compact cars, and two-story stone buildings pressed side by side as tightly as impacted teeth. The road was free of traffic, but for an occasional scooter, and the sidewalks were virtually deserted, the shops not yet open. I rolled down my window and breathed in cool, crisp, pollution-free air.

The driver stopped just outside the gate to the grotto; cars were not allowed to proceed farther. We loaded my mother and father into their wheelchairs. I made sure I had a way of reaching our driver in case we needed him earlier than we had agreed upon, which, translated, meant if there was a problem. We wheeled my parents down the sloped road, past statues of the Blessed Mother and walls lined with cut flowers. The three gold-and-white steeples of the Basilica of Our Lady of the Rosary loomed just beyond a huge square to welcome the pilgrims. Though there were already a substantial number of people in the square, it remained peaceful and quiet and had the feel of a college campus at spring break.

Father Pat Cavanaugh, the chaplain at Saint

Joe's High School when Ernie and I attended, was in Lourdes on a pilgrimage with a group from the Knights of Malta. In fact, it had been a conversation with Father Cavanaugh in the hallway outside my father's hospital room after he'd suffered his stroke that led me to the idea of taking my mother to Lourdes. Father Cavanaugh had told me that he made an annual pilgrimage with the Knights of Malta. I had sought his advice planning my parents' trip. He had suggested I coordinate the trip to coincide with the Knights of Malta's visit, which would circumvent the substantial lines that would otherwise threaten to keep me from attaining my goals—having my mother go to confession, receive the Eucharist at Mass, and be dipped in the healing waters, all in a single day.

My worries were unnecessary. To my and Mickie's astonishment, each time we wheeled my mother and father to a line, whether to light a candle or to attend Mass in the huge underground cathedral called the Basilica of Saint Pius X, the line of people parted and allowed us to proceed.

"Why are they doing that?" Mickie whispered.

"It's in the Bible, Michaela," my mother said. "In heaven, the last shall be first and the first shall be last. This is heaven, Mickie. You're in the presence of God."

I could not refute my mother's assertion. In a world in which people would trample you to get a seat on a bus, it was miraculous to watch them spontaneously give way to the sick and suffering.

After attending Mass in the basilica, Father Cavanaugh's group had arranged for a significant number of priests to hear confessions. Since the sun had broken through the cloud layer and the temperature had warmed, the priests set up chairs outside.

"A forgive-your-sins assembly line. They should just have a drive-through window," I said, which generated a frown from my mother but a grin from my dad.

We wheeled my parents to the next available priest, and Mickie and I looked for a place to catch a short nap. My mother, never one to miss an opportunity to save my soul, grabbed my arm. "Go for me," she said.

"Where?" I asked.

"Don't be insolent. You know what I mean. Go to confession."

"You're pushing it, lady," I told her, but ever the dutiful son, I agreed.

In a mild protest, I avoided an American priest and found a Spanish-speaking priest from Mexico. Just my luck, he spoke better English than I did. I probably could have talked to him for several hours, but I gave him the abbreviated version and, my sins absolved, I returned to find Mickie waiting with both my parents.

"Had a long list?" she asked.

"Couldn't remember the bloody Act of Contrition," I said.

Mickie and I wheeled my parents into the grotto of Massabielle, a place of incredible beauty. Atop a hundred-foot escarpment, where once stood a fortified castle, was the Basilica of the Immaculate Conception, a white-and-gold Gothic cathedral with multiple spires and elaborate carvings. At its base, on the banks of the river Gave's flowing bluish-green waters, dozens of candles flickered beside a natural cave perhaps fifty feet in length, ten feet high at its tallest, and five feet in depth. Just above and to the right of the spot where the spring emerged was a cleft in the stone. In it was a statue of the Blessed Mother to mark the location where Bernadette saw her apparition. It struck me that I had seen this statue before, though I could not place where.

We pushed the wheelchairs closer to the escarpment. The ground on which Bernadette had knelt had been paved with asphalt and the hole she had dug covered by a thick sheet of Plexiglas. The water flowing beneath that glass was illuminated by light. As we passed, my mother made a sign of the cross with her rosary. Water also trickled down the stone escarpment, and my mother asked that I stop just below the statue of the Blessed Mother.

"Give me your arm," she said, and she used it to stand and touch the rock, wiping the water over her face, then over my father's face. As she leaned forward and kissed the stone, Mickie gave me a look, but I had no answer for how my mother was accomplishing these feats. I knew it wasn't a drug that had relieved her considerable pain and allowed her to do this, because she had refused to take any. "One does not see the Blessed Mother on drugs," she'd said.

"I'll bet some people have," I'd joked.

"Don't be sacrilegious, Samuel," my mother had replied.

She set her hand on the wet stone and rubbed the water over my face.

"You'd at least think the Blessed Mother could have used warm water," I said.

"The warmth comes later," my mother said. I had no idea what she meant.

The baths were our last stop, and despite the collapse of my own faith, I could not deny that a part of me had brought my mother to Lourdes hoping for exactly what Mickie had warned against—a miracle. The lines were long, but again the faithful willingly stepped aside to allow the sick to proceed first. Mickie took my mother to the side of the grotto with small underground pools reserved for women. I took my father to the pools reserved for men. We entered a small, dimly lit, cave-like room, where an elderly Italian volunteer assisted me with the task of removing my father's clothing. Then I removed mine. We both wrapped cold, damp towels around our waists, and then the Italian volunteer and I helped my father stand from his wheelchair and step down into a sunken stone bath, which was perhaps seven feet long, three feet wide, and a couple of feet deep. We held my father while he prayed to a tiny statue of the Blessed Mother at the foot of the bath. When he had finished, the volunteers instructed him to sit. My father complied. Having never lost his sense of humor, he looked at me and spoke the clearest words I had heard him speak since his stroke.

"You'd think the Holy Spirit could have at least heated the water," he said, mimicking me.

Then he fell back and was submerged. My father surfaced with an expression like a child who had just walked in on his own surprise party. After a moment, he began to laugh, giddy, looked at me and said, "Warm."

I thought he was making another joke, because when I entered the bath, the water made my ankles and calves go numb. I faced the tiny statue uncertain what exactly to say. So I said what I had said throughout the trip. "For myself I seek nothing. Grant my mother and father peace. May all my mother's novenas not have been in vain. Give her a sign that her prayers have not gone unheard. And bless Mickie."

No sooner did I sit, however, when I heard a voice. I know how that sounds, but trust me, that voice was as clear as the bells ringing in the steeple of OLM church.

Have faith, Samuel.

The words were spoken so clearly that I looked to the Italian volunteer, who was waiting for me to give a signal that I was ready to be submerged, but he showed no sign of having heard them. I held up my hand for a second and looked again to the tiny statue. "Help me to understand," I said. "I want to believe. Help me to believe. Help me to have faith."

And I was submerged. Surfacing, I felt the strange warmth my father had spoken of. It radiated from the center of my chest down each limb. The Italian volunteer, who had undoubtedly witnessed thousands of similar expressions, smiled knowingly at me, then he bent close to my ear and, speaking quietly, as if sharing a secret, he said, "*Spirito Santo. Spirito Santo.*"

10

I pushed my father's wheelchair from the baths back into the stone portico to look for Mickie and my mother among the crowd. I remember that, at that moment, I felt light, as if a great weight had been lifted from my heart, and I had been liberated to see the world through a new pair of eyes and with a clarity that until that moment had eluded me. I felt sympathy and compassion for David Bateman and Sister Beatrice, and for every other person who had bullied, ignored, stared at, or made fun of me.

And I forgave them.

But that wasn't even the strangest part. The strangest part was that I realized that by forgiving them all, I had forgiven myself.

My father spotted my mother and pointed the direction through the crowd. When my mother saw us, she gave a short wave. Then she stood. Mickie held her arm as my mother walked toward us, looking as radiant as I felt. I was dumbstruck, and, yet, at the same time, I felt as though we were tethered together, my mother and I, bound by some invisible force drawing her to me. As she neared, her eyes widened and her gaze shifted above my head and slightly to the left, a gaze so intense that I turned to see what she was considering, but I only saw the stone ceiling. When I turned back, Mickie gave me a slight "I don't know" shrug, confirming that she, too, noticed my mother's gaze.

After another moment, my mother lowered her eyes, a huge smile emblazoned on her face as she continued forward. Reaching me, she held out a closed fist and handed me her rosary.

Then she collapsed in my arms.

11

My mother's vital signs stabilized when we got her back on the plane, but she continued to drift in and out of consciousness. One of the oncology nurses told me my mother was exhausted, and her body was without resources to recuperate. She also told me that her liver and kidney functions were declining. She did not tell me what I already knew. This was the end.

As my mother slept, my father lay in his hospital bed, holding her hand. The mask that had become his face continued to imprison his emotions. Only the tears that streamed down his face revealed his agony.

At two in the morning, somewhere over the Atlantic, I suggested Mickie get a couple of hours' sleep. No sooner had she left, but my mother softly said my name. I checked the machines monitoring her vital signs. Her liver functions had worsened; her pulse had slowed. Her breathing was labored. I kissed her forehead and caressed her hair. Even then it remained soft as silk.

"It's okay, Mom," I whispered. "You don't have to fight so hard. If you want to go see the Blessed Mother, you can go. I'll take care of Dad. I promise. I'll take good care of him."

And she opened her eyes.

"Were you playing possum with me?" I asked.

She smiled. "Don't cry."

But I couldn't help it. In so many ways, I remained a child, in need of someone to care for me. That person had been my mother all my life. I feared losing her. I feared not having her near me, not having her around, a part of my life, a part of Fernando's life, if I was so lucky as to be approved. Mostly, though, I knew that I would miss her something fierce.

"I'm going to miss you, Mom."

She pointed to my chest. "I'll be right here. You felt it, didn't you?"

I had. "It won't be the same."

"She's so beautiful, isn't she?"

I thought she was speaking of Mickie, but then, uncertain, I asked, "Who, Mom?"

"The Blessed Mother," she said. "You saw her, too, outside the baths." And I realized why my mother's gaze had shifted when she approached me in the grotto. Had she actually seen the Blessed Mother of Jesus Christ? I don't know. What I know is her gaze was so intense and so focused at that moment that I am convinced she saw something. And if she says she saw the Blessed Mother, I'll go to my own grave supporting her belief, as she had so ardently believed in me.

My mother took a deep breath, and I was certain it would be her last.

"Mom—"

She exhaled, took another shallow breath. "Do you know what I prayed for in the baths?"

I shook my head.

"For a miracle."

"I wish it was so," I said, taking her hand in mine. "I wish it was so."

"For you," she said.

"For me?"

"The miracle of Lourdes is acceptance, Sam. I asked God to help you to understand and to accept yourself." And I thought again of that moment at the baths when I had forgiven so many who had bullied me and, in so doing, I had forgiven myself. Could it have been my mother's prayer? Could it have been her final act as my mother to once again take care of me?

"Come close," she said. "I want to see the eyes that looked up at me the moment you were born." She touched my cheek. "My baby," she whispered. "When you were born, I thanked the Blessed Mother for making you extraordinary."

"You were always there to take care of me," I said.

"Everything happens for a reason, Samuel. Never forget that. Have faith in God's will."

Then she closed her eyes.

They would be the last words she ever spoke to me.

12

My mother did not regain consciousness, but she also did not die on the plane or during the transport back to her house. She was too stubborn. She once told me she wanted to die in her own bed, with the man she loved beside her. She got her wish.

Her wake and funeral were held at Our Lady of Mercy. The pews were filled with so many people from our past that the pastor had to open the choir loft, something usually done only during the holidays for the attendees my father had called Christmas Catholics.

I buried her at the Catholic cemetery. Six weeks later, I buried my father beside her. He simply could not live without her.

13

Several months after my parents' deaths, at the end of January, I walked in the door with two six-packs of Corona and margarita mix. Sunday nights, Mickie and I either cooked or went out for Mexican food. Tonight, Ernie and Michelle were joining us. They had taken their youngest son off to college the prior weekend after a few semesters at the local community college, and we were celebrating their freedom as empty nesters. I recalled Dr. Fukomara's statement to me during my vasectomy consult that he and his wife were empty nesters and could have sex in any room in the house. When I said the same thing to Ernie on the phone, he'd responded, "Yeah, but do you?"

Mickie stood at the kitchen counter, sprinkling cheese over the top of a neatly arranged tray of tacos. Douglas and Blue, the two pit bull puppies Mickie had rescued from the Burlingame pound, sat at her feet, hoping for spillage.

Mickie and I had settled into a regular routine. We traded off cooking dinner and doing the chores around the house. To keep busy after my parents' deaths, I spent my free time working on bringing Fernando to live with us. Mickie loved to garden, something she got from those after-noons she'd spent with my mother. In no time, she had transformed my bleak and neglected front yard into something worthy of a picture in a magazine.

A part of me, the insecure part, still had moments of anxiety, moments when I would drive down the block, certain Mickie's blue Honda with the white racing stripe would be gone. But the car was always there, and so was she. I should have been happy with the situation; I should have accepted this was all Mickie had ever been capable of giving. Marriage was just not something she wanted to consider. When I brought it up, she had brushed it aside, asked why we needed a piece of paper to tell us what we already knew, that we loved each other and would never leave the other.

But that was not my nature. I was my mother's son, and it was our way to rock the boat.

"Do you want to marry me?" I asked, putting the Corona on the counter.

The cheese stopped falling.

When Mickie did not answer, did not look at me, I made a joke, which was also my nature. "This would make it official," I said. "Then we wouldn't have to worry what name Douglas and Blue should use at school or if they should hyphenate it. And there's Fernando," I said. "I'm still optimistic, despite the red tape. I'm optimistic we can have what my parents had. A family."

Mickie finally looked up at me. "I love you, Sam."

"I love you, too."

"But you know how I feel about marriage."

I tried to smile. "Is it against your religion or something, because I'm willing to convert."

"Don't joke."

"Help me to understand. I want to have what my parents had. I thought we both wanted that."

"We can't, Sam."

"I think we can."

"No."

"Why not?"

She picked up the tray of tacos as if to move past me. "You deserve someone better."

"I don't want someone better. I want you."

"Thanks a lot."

We laughed. I took the tray and placed it on the counter and put my hands around her waist. "So, is that a yes?"

She put her arms around my neck. "You're sweet, Sam. I regret a lot of the things I did in my life. I can't take them back."

"Is that what this is about? I don't care about your past, or who you've been with or what you've done. Do you love me?"

"I've always loved you, Sam, even when you didn't know it."

"Then why isn't that enough?"

"I gave away a part of me in my youth, Sam. I

don't expect you to understand, but it's a part I can't get back. It's a part that you deserve."

"What?" I was dumbfounded, but then again, maybe I wasn't. Maybe this was one of those things that Mickie had spent so much time talking about and crying about with my mother for all those years. At that moment, I felt fear, certain Mickie would tell me that I was going to lose her, too.

But before Mickie could answer, I heard Ernie's BMW in the driveway. "For such a great athlete, his timing has always sucked," I said.

"Can we table this for the night? Maybe talk about it when I get back from my conference?"

In the morning, Mickie was to leave for a College of Optometry conference in Puerto Vallarta, Mexico, on advances in the treatment of keratoconus, a degenerative disorder of the eye. I had intended on going with her, but we had turned our practice into a free eye clinic for the disadvantaged, and I needed to be there.

"Okay," I said, knowing it best not to push her. "We'll just enjoy Mexican Night."

"*Gracias, señor.*"

"*De nada, señorita.*"

We ate our tacos and drank margaritas while listening to the guitar riffs of Carlos Santana. "A toast," Ernie said. "To good friends."

We raised our glasses. "Is that the best you can

do?" I asked. "Thank God you didn't give the valedictorian speech."

"Don't start with me, you red-eyed son of the devil."

"Here's to life," I said. "And the three people in mine who helped to make it extraordinary. I love you all."

"You're not going to kiss me, are you?" Ernie asked.

Michelle hit him with a piece of tomato.

At just after ten, Michelle nodded to Ernie, who was falling asleep on my couch. "Well, I better get Romeo here home before he passes out on me. Our first weekend without kids, and he'll be snoring before his head hits the pillow."

Ernie perked up suddenly. "Did someone mention sex?"

Michelle looked at Mickie. "Ah, the romance," she said.

After Ernie and Michelle left, Mickie and I snuggled on the couch under a blanket to watch Tom Hanks in *The Green Mile*. Douglas and Blue curled up beside us. I didn't regret asking Mickie to marry me, but it troubled me when she put herself down and discounted who she was as a person. I knew it had to be an old and deep scar, one I was sure was inflicted in childhood, too deep, perhaps, for me to reach. I resigned myself to our arrangement and promised I would not ask the question again.

That night we made love with a passion ferocious even for Mickie, and afterward she clung to
me as never before, as if she might lose me if she
let go.

14

Wednesday afternoon I took Blue and Douglas for an afternoon walk, and I realized that I had not heard from Mickie in nearly twenty-four hours, though I was uncertain of the time change, if any, in Puerto Vallarta. I was consciously trying to give her some space, mindful of my mistake of asking her to marry me, but I couldn't get out of my mind the way Mickie had clung to me that night, or the memories of the other times in my life when Mickie had spooked and left.

When I returned home, I got the dogs water. Then I called her. The call went straight to voice mail. I took to the task of making dinner, listening to jazz with the doors open, enjoying a gentle, cool cross breeze, and waiting anxiously for my phone to buzz or ring. Three hours later there had been no call from Mickie.

I tried calling her again but got no answer. I started to worry that something could be wrong and went to the fridge and retrieved the piece of paper detailing the conference and the hotel. I dialed the number. "Mickie Kennedy's room, please."

I heard the desk clerk's fingers striking keys. "I'm sorry, sir—we do not have a registration for anyone under that name."

My heart started to sink. "Could you check Michaela Kennedy?"

After another beat, this one shorter, the clerk said, "I'm sorry, sir. There is no Kennedy registered."

"Could she have checked out early?"

"I can't give out that information, sir."

"Please. This is her husband. I'm worried about her. She was to check in Monday night, and I haven't heard from her, which is unlike her. I haven't been able to contact her on her cell phone."

I heard a pause, the desk clerk debating with himself. "Hold on," he said. My mind was racing, and I could not still my thoughts. Then the clerk came back and said, "We had a guest here by that name, sir, but she canceled her reservation after one night. She checked out Tuesday morning."

I closed my eyes, a stabbing pain in my chest.

"Is there anything else I can help you with, sir?"

"No," I said, disconnecting, my heart continuing to sink.

In my mind, I replayed our conversation when I'd asked Mickie to marry me. She'd said she couldn't, that she had given away a part of her she couldn't get back, that I deserved someone better. And then she had clung to me as if she would never see me again. I wondered if Mickie had already made plans to leave but couldn't bring herself to tell me, if that had been the reason she'd clung to me. She'd stayed to help me get through the heartache and pain of my mother's and father's deaths, but Mickie was still Mickie, at times rash and unpredictable. Marriage frightened her, which meant I had frightened her, and Mickie no doubt rationalized that she could never make me completely happy, and therefore she was doing us both a favor by leaving.

I shut the doors and turned off the lights. I contemplated calling Ernie, but he and his family were in Europe to celebrate Mr. Cantwell's seventieth birthday. My mother and father were dead. There was no one. I was alone.

I slumped on the couch, grief stricken and anxious. Douglas and Blue, sensing my anguish, curled up beside me.

And then I heard her—my mother.

Have faith, Samuel.

I raised my head, almost expecting to see her standing in my living room. "Have faith in what?" I asked. "Have faith in what, Mom?"

But the voice in my head would not be silenced.

Have faith, Samuel. We don't always know God's will.

"Is his will to make me miserable?" I asked.

But this time there was no answer.

I went upstairs and sat on the bed, uncertain what to do, feeling my anxiety starting to spread. My eyes were drawn to the top drawer of my dresser, but I fought the urge to open it. I had contemplated putting my mother's rosary in her casket, but at the last moment I held on to it, remembering how she had walked across the courtyard at the baths in Lourdes to hand it to me, her dying act.

I lay my head back against the pillows. Blue and Douglas entered and immediately jumped onto the bed, tails wagging. My eyes were again drawn to that top drawer. This time I stood and crossed the room. On the dresser was the Bible Sister Beatrice had given me as an eighth-grade graduation present, and wedged in the mirror was the card of Saint Christopher and the Irish blessing that our pastor, Father Brogan, gave me the night he expelled David Bateman.

I opened the top drawer. The beads were well-worn and misshapen; the gold crucifix and the links between the beads had lost their luster. I held my mother's rosary in the palm of my hand, staring at it, debating with myself, realizing I'd never won a debate with my mother in my entire life, and I knew I wouldn't now, either.

I pinched the cross between my thumb and index finger and began as she had taught me when I had been just a little boy. "I believe in God, the Father almighty, maker of heaven and earth . . ."

In between each prayer, I asked God not to take Mickie from me. I asked my mother to intercede, to ask the Blessed Mother to bring Mickie home to me.

Have faith, Samuel.

I started the second decade, then the third. I was having trouble breathing, getting the words out, but I would not give in. I plunged from one bead to the next, thinking again of my mother and begging her to intercede, bargaining with her.

"I won't question God's will again," I said. "Mickie is all I'll ever want or need. I'll take up your mantle, your devotion. I'll offer my pain up for some poor soul in purgatory. I'll return to church. Just please, Mom, please don't let him take Mickie from me. Whatever second thoughts she might be having, whatever it is she thinks makes her not good enough, please let her see how much I love her."

I don't know how many stanzas I completed before fatigue became so great I could not keep my eyes open.

I awoke, fully dressed, to the bells in the tower of Our Lady of Mercy ringing out and sun streaming through my bedroom window. Blue and Douglas, curled on the bed, sat up. I could not immediately recall the last time I'd heard the bells. And then that moment came to me. I had been in Dr. Fukomara's office, about to have a vasectomy. But I had imagined those bells, hadn't I?

I wondered if I could be imagining them again and quickly went downstairs, pulled open the front door, and stepped out onto the porch. Blue and Douglas remained at my feet. It was not my imagination. The bells rang as loud and true as Ernie had rung those bells in the sixth grade at the all-school Mass. Standing on the porch, I realized something else. I no longer felt anxious about Mickie. I felt the same comforting warmth and peace come over me as I had felt in Lourdes when it seemed to be radiating from my chest. I had been unable to define the feeling until that moment, and then it became very clear to me. It felt like my mother's loving embrace. It felt like it felt when she wrapped her arms around me when I was a boy in need of comfort.

Spirito Santo, the Italian man had knowingly whispered. *Spirito Santo.*

Douglas and Blue began to bark. Mickie had trained them not to leave the porch, and so they remained on the top step, barking, tails whipping the air, collars rattling. I looked down the street but did not see anyone out walking their dog or an approaching car. "What is it?" I said.

Blue looked up at me, but Douglas's gaze remained on the street. When I looked again, the taxi appeared over the slight rise in the road, slowing as it neared and then turning in to the driveway. Blue and Douglas were ecstatic, whimpering and whining, tails whipping at high speed. The back door of the cab opened.

And Mickie Kennedy stepped out.

15

Mickie looked up at me and smiled, but it had a sad, "I'm sorry" look to it. The dogs leaped and jumped all around me but did not leave the porch until I stepped down. They bolted to her. She'd started to cry, apologizing even before I reached her. "I got your messages. I'm sorry, Sam. I know I worried you."

"Why didn't you call?"

"I didn't have any service."

"I spoke to you Tuesday."

"I left."

"Where? Where did you go?"

"I wanted it to be a surprise, the best surprise. I'm sorry, Sam. I didn't see all your calls until we landed. I know what you were thinking, Sam. I know you'd thought I'd left."

I didn't care. I didn't care about anything except that Mickie was there in my arms. I kissed her and hugged her tight.

After a while she said, "Let's go inside."

I paid the cab driver and carried Mickie's bag inside, dropping it in the entry at the foot of the staircase. Mickie sat at the kitchen table. After we caught our breath, she said, "We never did finish the conversation the night before I left."

"It's okay," I said.

"No, it's not. Not if we're going to marry."

I stared at her, dumbfounded.

"I can't have children, Sam. It happened when I was younger. I had to have a hysterectomy. I didn't want to marry you and not be able to give you children. You deserve children. You're a good man and will make a wonderful father."

"I don't care about that," I said. "Why didn't you ever tell me?"

"I told your mother. I should have told you. But you know how hard it can be when years go by and you don't say anything? For so many years, when you were away, I rationalized that we would never be together and so it didn't matter. But now . . . I should have, Sam. I should have told you."

I felt a sense of relief that it was not something else, that it wasn't some fatal disease. "You're all I've ever wanted."

"But you do want children. I know you do, because you didn't go through with the vasectomy. You want to be a father, Sam. I've known since that day that you wanted to be a father. I just didn't have an answer—not until you came back and you spoke of Fernando. I wanted to wait to give you an answer until we knew for certain."

"Fernando?"

"I knew that he was meant for you, for both of us."

"I'm still hopeful—"

Mickie raised a hand. "I've been working on accelerating the process ever since you told me. Your mother helped."

"My mother?"

Mickie nodded. "I was hoping she'd live long enough to see her grandson. She was so happy for you, Sam. Happy for us."

"I don't understand."

"You said you wanted to adopt him but that it would help if we were married. Your mother and I filled out additional paperwork. You and I are married, Sam. It's the only fib I ever heard your mother tell in her entire life."

"My mother lied?" I said.

"White lie," Mickie said. "Anyway, I got the call from the orphanage as soon as I landed in Mexico. I checked out and flew to Costa Rica. All our paperwork is being processed, Sam. All they need is to personally interview you, but it's a formality. A woman at the orphanage said she already knew you, that she'd been in the room when you met Fernando."

"I remember her."

"She vouched for you, Sam." Mickie stood and took my hand. "She wrote a beautiful letter of reference for you. So did your colleagues at Orbis. Fernando will be our son, Sam."

"Our son?"

Mickie nodded and smiled. "We'll be a family, Sam. If you'll still have me."

I was speechless. I felt numb, and for a moment I could not move. I thought of my mother. "Don't move," I said. Then I started up the stairs.

"Where are you going?"

"Not a step. Not a single step," I said.

I ran into the bedroom and opened the dresser, grabbing the black box beside my mother's rosary. I hurried back downstairs. Mickie was in the same spot. For once in her life, she'd stayed put.

I dropped to a knee, my heart beating fast. I wanted to get the words out before she could say another thing.

"Mickie Kennedy," I said. "Will you marry me?"

I opened the black box and produced the diamond that had adorned my mother's wedding finger for more than forty years. I'd had it reset and surrounded it with tiny red rubies.

EPILOGUE

The first Sunday after we brought Fernando home, we took him to Our Lady of Mercy church. We arrived early, and I instinctively turned to the pew that had become my mother and father's pew during their years of devotion. Mickie had not rekindled her faith, but she wanted one for Fernando. When he was older, he could choose for himself. As Mickie sat in the pew, I took Fernando by the hand and walked him to the alcove to the right of the altar, where we knelt before the Blessed Mother.

"*Este es la madre bendita,*" I said. *This is the Blessed Mother.* "Ask her to help you, and she will. Prayers are like coins you put into a piggy bank. You store them for when you most need them."

Fernando looked at me and shook his head. "*¿Qué es una alcancía?*" he asked. *What is a piggy bank?*

I tussled his hair and started to laugh.

We intended to enroll Fernando at the local public school, which had an English as a second language program, but early that summer I received a phone call from the principal at OLM asking to meet with Mickie and me. She also asked that we bring Fernando.

Patricia Branick sat in the same office in which my mother and I had first encountered Sister Beatrice, though the pictures on the wall were now of Pope John Paul II and a priest I presumed to be OLM's pastor, but whom I had not yet met. The room was softer, a yellow color. Plants and vines grew in pots in the corners.

"I did not receive an enrollment application for Fernando," Mrs. Branick said.

Mickie and I explained our decision to enroll Fernando at the public school.

Patricia Branick listened politely; then she said, "Don't be silly. You'll enroll him here and we'll work through this together."

I smiled. "It's not just the language, Mrs. Branick. I'm concerned about a young boy with red eyes attending a Catholic school."

Her brow furrowed. "Of course you are. That's why I've asked you here, to alleviate those concerns. I assure you, Fernando's presence will be a blessing," she said. "What better way to teach these children Christian ideals?" Then she smiled. "You can argue with me all you want, Mr. Hill, but I will tell you now that no grandchild of Madeline Hill is going to attend a public school. She saw to that."

"I'm sorry," I asked, confused, and glanced at Mickie, thinking perhaps this was another of her and my mother's plans, but Mickie shook her head and shrugged.

"Your mother came to visit me before she went into the hospital. She told me that you would be adopting a boy from South America with ocular albinism and that you would be reluctant to send him to OLM because of your past experiences. I knew your mother from attending six o'clock Mass."

"And she told you she wanted me to enroll Fernando at OLM?"

"She did more than that, Mr. Hill. She paid Fernando's tuition. All eight years at today's prices. Your mother was no dummy."

I laughed. Never one to sit quietly in the boat, my mother had spent her life taking care of me, and now she was taking care of her grandson.

"No, she certainly wasn't, Mrs. Branick," I said. "My mother was extraordinary."

"Then it is settled." Mrs. Branick pushed back her chair and offered her hand across the desk. "I will greet you atop the red-tile steps off Cortez Avenue on the first day of school. Do you know the steps I'm talking about?"

"All too well," I said. "All too well."

The weekend before his first day of school, Mickie and I took Fernando on a drive in the Falcon, a rare treat. I did not drive it often. The Falcon was leaking oil and the transmission slipped, but like my mother's rosary beads, I would never get rid of it. I'd already decided to have it completely restored. After all, Fernando would need a car when he turned sixteen.

Mickie and I sensed Fernando was nervous about attending school and decided to take him to OLM for a trial run that we hoped would help ease his nerves. We parked on Cortez Avenue at the foot of the red-tile steps leading to the wrought iron–gated entrance. I contemplated the countless times my mother had walked me up those steps and the countless times I had run down them to find her waiting for me.

"I'll be right here," she'd say. And she always had been. It was her promise to me, her reassurance that I had nothing to fear, that I was never far from her love. Some afternoons I could not move my feet quickly enough to shuffle down those steps, lunch box clattering, hurrying to reach her. And when I slid across the seat, I would willingly allow her to embrace me, to feel her unconditional love. It was that same embrace, that same warmth I had felt comforting me the morning I prayed her rosary beads and asked for her to bring Mickie home to me.

Have faith, Samuel.

She'd never let me down.

"*Papá, venga, venga quiero ir,*" Fernando said, shaking me from my reverie. He wanted to keep driving with the top down.

"*Quiero mostrarte algo,*" I said. *I want to show you something.* "*Esto solo tardará un minuto. Ven conmigo.*" *It will only take a minute. Come with me.*

I pushed open the car door. Fernando retrieved the bouquet of flowers we'd bought earlier and together we all climbed the steps. They appeared more narrow, and not as steep as I recalled from my childhood, and because I was taller, she came into view much sooner than when I'd been a young boy. I saw her veil, then her face, then the beauty of her blue-and-white robes. I stopped my ascent.

"Everything okay?" Mickie asked.

It dawned on me where I'd seen the same statue, and I recalled my mother telling me on more than one occasion that the Blessed Mother was always watching over me.

"*La Virgen de Lourdes,*" I said to Fernando.

That evening, as Mickie prepared dinner and Fernando lay on the carpet watching television, I sat down on the couch to read the newspaper and heard the bells in the steeple of OLM ringing out the six o'clock hour. I'd started to notice the bells more frequently, and each time I did I closed my eyes and allowed the sound to transport me back to that sunny afternoon outside the rehabilitation center when my father looked up at me from his wheelchair, his body streaked with shadows from the branches of the oak tree, and spoke in his ethereal whisper.

There comes a day in every man's life when he stops looking forward and starts looking back.

Because of my father's circumstances, I had thought it a sad commentary on life, but I now understood that he was offering me his own gift, one that only time can provide. He was offering me the gift of perspective. My father was telling me that while we tend to remember the dramatic incidents that change history—Armstrong's walk on the moon, Nixon's resignation, and the Loma Prieta earthquake—we live for the quiet, intimate moments that mark not our calendars but our hearts: The day we marry. The days our children are born. Their first step. Their first word. Their first day of school. And when our children grow, we remember those moments with a touch of melancholy: the day they get their driver's license, the day we drive them to college, the day they marry, and the day they have their children.

And the cycle begins anew.

We realize it is in those quiet moments that each of us has the ability to make our lives extraordinary.

I reached into the bowl I kept on the end table, feeling the worn spots where her fingers kneaded each bead, and I started as she taught me.

For I am my mother's son.

ACKNOWLEDGMENTS

I'm not really certain what the genesis for this novel was. It was, I suppose, a number of different things rattling around inside me and looking for a way to escape, the way water will always weep through concrete, not matter how many times the concrete is patched, as Sam Hell observes. I'm one of ten kids, so the genesis of this novel couldn't very well have been my own childhood, and yet, in a way, I suppose it was.

On June 24, 1973, my mother gave birth to her tenth child, Michael Sean Dugoni. I was twelve years old and can also remember the births of my two brothers prior to Michael. This was like Christmas mornings for us. I'd awake and my older sisters Aileen and Susie would be in charge, telling me that "Mom is in the hospital having a baby." We would all wait with great anticipation for her and my father to return home. On this particular occasion, however, things were different. It was not the joyous occasions of the prior experiences. Two things stood out to me. I remember when my father came home from the hospital it was without my mother, and he had been crying. His eyes were red and his demeanor subdued. Over the course of the next day or so, I was to learn that my brother Michael had Down syndrome.

I didn't fully understand the diagnosis, but I recall asking my older brother Bill, "Is he retarded?"

My brother looked at me crossly and said, "You better not use that word around Mom."

My mother has always been deeply religious and has a special relationship with the Blessed Mother. I recall her saying novenas on many occasions, and especially after the birth of my brother, but God never did "fix" my brother. In the hospital, doctors told my parents to put my brother in an institution, that he would be a detriment to our family, disruptive and difficult. My mother threw them out of her room. As with Sam Hell's doctors, her doctors didn't know what they were talking about, and they weren't going to prevent her from bringing my brother home.

My mother was one to rock the boat, and she rocked the boat mightily when it came to my brother. She was instrumental in getting laws passed that mandated the state educate the mentally disabled. Soon, young mothers with children like my brother would knock on our door to speak with her. My father was not one to rock the boat. He accepted my brother as he was, never expecting that he'd be anything more or less than who he is, just as he accepted each of us.

As all these thoughts rattled in my head, I was

sitting in my room at my computer one afternoon, and I found an article in the local newspaper. It was no more than an inch in length. It said that a young boy in Australia had been denied admittance to Catholic school because he had been born with ocular albinism, and the nuns thought he'd be disruptive to the other students. It turned out that the other students had nicknamed this poor child the devil boy.

That was all that I needed. The first draft of the story poured out of me in five weeks. I would find myself writing one scene and jotting down notes for four scenes to follow. I would awake at three in the morning flooded with dialogue, descriptions, and ideas for future scenes. Writing in first person made the novel personal to me, and I tried to balance that fine line between personal and professional.

When I completed that first draft, I made the fatal mistake of letting my agent read it. I've since come to learn that a first draft is written for the writer and should never be shared with anyone. She rightfully did not like the book and told me why. I took this as constructive criticism and, over the years, pulled the book out to work on it, making wholesale changes to the plot, cutting unnecessary scenes and molding it into a novel. I'm so grateful to Meg Ruley, Rebecca Scherer, and the team at the Jane Rotrosen Agency. One thing they said that really stuck with me was that the book was too episodic and needed a connecting thread to pull the reader through the story. I found that thread on a drive to, of all places, Mass. I asked myself what did Sam Hell really want throughout his life, and I found that what he wanted was no different than what I wanted—I think, what we all want.

Sam wanted to believe. He wanted to believe that God really did have a plan for him and for his life, that his hardships as a child would all help mold for him an extraordinary life. He wanted to believe that his prayers had a purpose, that God truly is benevolent, despite so many in the world so often being malevolent. He wanted to believe that God's will really meant something and was not just a mother's way of dismissing a curious son.

So, thanks as always to Meg and Rebecca and the Jane Rotrosen Agency for all of your patience, guidance, and perseverance. You push me to write the best novels I can, and it motivates me to do so. Thanks also to Gracie Doyle at Thomas & Mercer, who publishes my mystery and suspense novels and was kind enough to also read *Sam Hell*. Thanks to Danielle Marshall at Lake Union, my publisher, for her enthusiasm for this project, her guidance, and her steady hand. Thanks to Sarah Shaw, author relations, who always makes me feel special. Thanks to

Sean Baker, head of production, and to Nicole Pomeroy, production manager. I've said this before, but I love the covers and the titles of each of my novels, and I have them to thank. Thanks to Dennelle Catlett, Amazon Publishing PR, for her tireless efforts promoting me and my work. Thanks to publisher Mikyla Bruder, associate publisher Galen Maynard, and to Jeff Belle, vice president of Amazon Publishing.

Special thanks to Charlotte Herscher, my developmental editor. This is our seventh book together, and we have become quite a team. Charlotte's suggested edits also struck a chord with me and helped me get out of the way of the story so that the writer could edit, write, and rewrite the novel as never before, shaping and rounding it into a true journey. Thanks to Robin O'Dell, production editor, and Sara Brady, copy editor. When you recognize a weakness, it is a wonderful thing—because then you can ask for help. Grammar and punctuation were never my strengths, and it's nice to know I have the best looking out for me.

Thanks to Tami Taylor, who runs my website and creates my newsletters and some of my foreign-language book covers. I ask Tami for help, and she gets things done quickly and efficiently. Thanks to Pam Binder and the Pacific Northwest Writers Association for their support of my work. Thanks to Seattle 7 Writers, a nonprofit collective of Pacific Northwest authors who foster and support the written word.

Thanks to you, the readers, for finding my novels and for your incredible support of my work. Thanks for posting your reviews and for e-mailing me to let me know you've enjoyed them—always a writer's highlight.

Thank you to my mother, Patty, and to my father, Bill, who we lost a decade ago, but who I think about every day. Thanks to all nine of my brothers and sisters, especially Michael, who inspired so many of my siblings to become doctors, lawyers, a pharmacist like my father, a dental hygienist, an accountant, and a teacher, and to otherwise fulfill all of their potential. They are individuals I admire and respect. Thanks especially to my wife, Cristina, and my two children, Joe and Catherine. Thank you for teaching me that the true meaning of success can be found in the quiet moments of my life—the moments when you all fill my heart with love. Thank you for making my life extraordinary.

ABOUT THE AUTHOR

Robert Dugoni is the multimillion-copy best-selling author of the Tracy Crosswhite Series, including *My Sister's Grave*, *Her Final Breath*, *In the Clearing*, *The Trapped Girl*, and *Close to Home*. He has twice been a finalist for the International Thriller Award and was the winner of the 2015 Nancy Pearl Award for Fiction. A two-time finalist for the Harper Lee Award for Legal Fiction, Dugoni is also the *New York Times* bestselling author of the David Sloane Series, which includes *The Jury Master*, *Wrongful Death*, *Bodily Harm*, *Murder One*, and *The Conviction*. His stand-alone novel *The 7th Canon* was a finalist for the Mystery Writers of America Edgar Award and won the Spotted Owl award for the best novel in the Northwest, and his nonfiction exposé, *The Cyanide Canary* (with Joseph Hilldorfer), was a *Washington Post* Best Book of the Year selection.

Visit his website at www.robertdugoni.com, and follow him on Twitter @robertdugoni and on Facebook at www.facebook.com /AuthorRobertDugoni.

Center Point Large Print
600 Brooks Road / PO Box 1
Thorndike, ME 04986-0001 USA

(207) 568-3717

US & Canada:
1 800 929-9108
www.centerpointlargeprint.com